OF STONE AND SKY

CHARISSA STASTNY

Tangled Willow
Press

TITLES BY CHARISSA STASTNY

Ruled Out Romances

Game Changer

Package Deal

Collateral Hearts

Bending Willow Trilogy

Finding Light

Guarding Secrets

Embracing Mercy

Stand-Alone Novels

Between Hope & the Highway

A Wrinkle in Forever

Of Stone and Sky

*To those
who fought, and still fight,
for justice for ALL*

GLOSSARY

Albanian words
eja = come
vajze = girl
vajze e keqe = bad girl
bijë = daughter
policia = police
dreqin = hell
faleminderit = thank you
magjup = gypsy

Romani words
gadjo (male) *gadji* (female) = derogatory descriptor for an outsider; usually corresponds to not being an ethnic Romani, but can also be an ethnic Romani who doesn't live within Romani culture.

of
STONE
and *Sky*

PROLOGUE

*B*aba always said withholding facts was a form of lying.

I should've listened.

I should've done a lot of things, like telling Lincoln the truth when I had the chance.

About who I really was.

My true name, at least.

But it was too late. From the seat in the closet of my new husband's master suite, I looked out at rose petals on the white carpet leading to the king bed where we'd made love earlier. The vase of roses seemed to taunt me from the table. Lincoln had pulled one out to caress my bare body as we'd consummated our vows just a few hours ago. But now, lingering smoke from the burned-out north wing smothered their subtle fragrance.

Symbolic of the ruin of my life, maybe?

Baba had said no good could come from secrets. He'd been right, as always.

I glanced up at Lincoln and winced. Judging from the fury in every line of my husband's precious face, my revelation had torched all dreams of a loving family, leaving ashes. This man I adored, and who, up until a minute ago, I'd believed had loved me back, now seemed to loathe me.

Would he turn me over to the cops? Take Altin away from me?

Tears threatened but pity was the last thing I wanted, even if I was pitiful.

Time had run out.

I must disappear from Lincoln's life—even if that was the only place I wanted to be—because there were far worse outcomes than heartbreak or jail.

DREAMER

"You would have imagined her at one moment a maniac, at another a queen."

— *THE HUNCHBACK OF NOTRE DAME BY VICTOR HUGO*

LINCOLN

4 months earlier

The balding officer shut his notebook and assured me he'd check back in with my assistant when he found any leads in the investigation. I headed to the elevator, not holding my breath that the police would apprehend the perpetrators who'd upended my stable world.

"Any messages?" I asked my assistant as I passed his desk on the way to my office.

"No, Mr. McConnell."

I shut my door and slipped out of my suit jacket. Sleet outside mimicked the storm brewing inside me. I dropped my shirt and tie on a chair and pulled on well-used boxing gloves. Leather bags suspended from the corner ceiling had been placed there for days like today.

I flexed my muscles and struck. *Punch. Punch-punch-punch. Jab!*

I watched the mirrors, focusing on form and footwork as I moved around each bag, imagining an encounter with the gypsy thugs who'd shattered another car window in the parking garage this morning.

Punch-punch-punch!

I'd knock them out of this world, or at least out of my life. My gaze strayed to the court summons on the desk, and I missed the bag and boxed air.

I cursed and staggered forward. For a moment, the past assaulted me—leaving the office late, unaware of hundreds of protesters in a stand-off with the police just a block away—the mob busting out my rear window before I could back up and escape—racing home to find my pregnant wife intoxicated—our fight, and then...

No! I focused on the timing bag. *Jab-jab-jab-jab-jab.*

Why couldn't Angeline move on? Two years had passed, and it wasn't like she needed the money. Her new husband was loaded.

Punch-punch-punch.

I ground my teeth, recalling her knock-out blow that'd landed me in jail and had dissolved the remains of our pitiful marriage.

Jab-jab!

Last time, I hadn't fought. All I'd wanted was Angeline out of my life. Loss of assets, pride, and reputation had been paltry sacrifices to achieve that end.

Problem was, the greedy woman wasn't gone yet.

Punch-punch-punch!

I yanked off my gloves and towel-dried my body, then donned my shirt, jacket, and tie again.

Time to get back to work.

I propped open my office door to hear the soothing hum of phone chatter from the sales team. The sound of money being made, money EcoCore desperately needed now that my ex had decided to go for my jugular.

A giggle from one of the cubicles brought the lulling music to a screeching halt, like an old-time record pulled off against the needle.

I growled. Giggling signaled poor productivity and a lack of respect. And no intellect.

Finding the culprit in the maze of cubicles wasn't difficult since she giggled twice more. I caught the lazy airhead mid-giggle, feet on desk, leaning back in the ergonomic chair I'd purchased because research had shown that physical comfort in the workplace led to a fifteen percent increase in production.

Not so with the giggler.

I stopped, feet apart, arms crossed to keep from yanking the girl out of her chair. A nameplate proclaimed her to be Gemma Stone. A dumb name for a silly girl who wouldn't be working for me much longer.

Ms. Stone hadn't noticed me yet, judging by how she wiggled her exposed toes on the desk. Leather cording from her chunky pumps wrapped around shapely calves. I did a double take. Were those pompoms dangling off the straps? A few dozen braids coiled down her back, feathers and beads sticking out of them.

"Why thank you. That's so sweet." She giggled again.

I cleared my throat.

She flinched, and her feet swept off the desk and hit the carpet as she swiveled around to gawk at me with wide green eyes. Mesmerizing eyes.

I shook my head. Mesmerizing like a wildcat.

"Can you hold for a sec, Jerry?" She cupped the receiver. "May I help you?" She didn't even act guilty.

I longed to fire her on the spot but couldn't bypass procedures set in place to keep order at EcoCore. Doing so had bitten me in the past. I did an about-face and marched back to my office without a reply.

I had the information I needed.

I paused at Lionel's desk. "Get the head of HR up here."

"Yes, Mr. McConnell." His stiff British accent and hard-work ethic eased my surface stress. Too bad I couldn't clone him.

"And have legal send someone up as well. Tell them I need to terminate a Gemma Stone in sales."

"Yes, sir."

I shut the door, wondering if I should've told him to call Joe Carter in as well. He was the slacker's direct manager.

But no. Last year, Joe had been forced to let someone on his team go, and it'd almost destroyed him. My friend didn't have the balls for the ugly stuff.

No matter. I'd fire her for him. Joe had always had my back, and he'd put together a top-notch sales team. I wouldn't ask him to cut off a weak twig he'd agonize over. With all the dead branches in my own life, I itched to take a power saw to one of them.

2

SAEMIRA

Age 7 - Fushë-Krujë, Albania

COMPASSION: A desire to help.

*B*aba tugged his daughter's hand. "Keep up, Saemira. We can't dawdle."

Her fingers slid off the flower growing up through a crack in the cobble-stones. "But I want to study that flower with my magnifying glass." Where did it get water and dirt to grow?

"Not now, princess. A boy needs our help."

"Can I study it on the way home?"

"Maybe. Let's see how bad the boy's injuries are first."

She skipped to catch up to him and Mama. A gas line had exploded in a building in the Roma village. Zinzan had come to their house to beg for help.

"Why don't they take him to the hospital?" Baba wasn't a doctor. He was a teacher.

"The hospital won't admit Roma."

"What's wrong with Roma?"

"Nothing. Mama's Roma, which makes you half-Roma."

She twirled to make her dress fly up around her legs. She was also half-American since Baba came from Detroit, Michigan in the United States of America.

"Why don't we live in the village with Mama's people?"

8

"Because we're lucky," Mama said.

"Blessed." Baba took the jug from Mama, switching her for the medical kit. "Which is why we must show compassion to those less fortunate than us."

"Compassion," Saemira repeated. "What does that mean?"

He shifted the jug. "To have sympathy for someone in need and to do something about it."

She would write that in her English book later. "Why won't the hospital help Roma? That's not nice."

"No, it isn't. Some people fear those they don't understand."

She twirled her pretty skirt again. "Maybe I'll be a doctor when I grow up. I'll let Roma in."

Baba patted her head. "A worthy goal."

They rounded a bend, and she skipped ahead when she saw the river.

"Stay away, Saemira," Baba called after her. "It's polluted."

She kicked a rock and repeated the funny-sounding word. "Polluted?"

"The river will make you sick," Mama said.

Saemira wished to take her shoes off to wade in the shallows for a minute. But she returned to Mama.

"Such a good girl," Baba said, patting her head.

She grinned. Her name meant *So good.*

They rounded a bend and she saw naked children and scrawny dogs playing about a pile of garbage. She wrinkled her nose.

"Ew. This place stinks."

"Less talking, more walking," Baba said.

A man ran out of a house. Zinzan. The Roma king bowed to Baba, and they spoke in Romani. She only picked out a few words: boy, face, ear.

Baba thanked him and turned to take her hand.

"Is this the village?" she asked.

"Yes." He handed the water jug to Mama and took the medical kit.

"Why doesn't Zinzan live in a castle since he's king?" His place looked broken and black from smoke.

"He's a respected leader, not a king," Baba said. "Zinzan came here long before the dump polluted the river and air. Like your mama, he fled the troubles in Kosovo. These condemned buildings were a godsend back then."

They climbed a crumbling staircase and Saemira repeated the hard English word in her head. *Condemned.*

"Watch your step," Baba said.

She stepped to the side to avoid animal dung. People with skin the color of burnt wood nodded as they passed.

"*Eja,*" a woman said, motioning for Baba to come.

9

"Wait for Mama," he said, leaving her to jog ahead.

Saemira backed away from a missing piece of railing. This place was scary.

Mama caught up to her. "Do not be afraid, darling." She dripped water from her jug on the doorstep, for luck, before following Baba inside, where he waved for her to join him.

Saemira looked around the crowded, dirty room. People buzzed like bees and growled like dogs. A skull on the floor made her shiver. Chickens darted about. Flies landed on her face. She shooed them, but more took their place.

"Come, pretty girl." A dark man with a hoop earring patted his lap. She backed away, wondering how he knew English. *"Eja,"* he said in Albanian.

"Saemira," Baba called, and she ran to him. "Stay by Mama." He leaned over a groaning boy.

She cringed at the white patches of skin that oozed blood on the boy's dark face and arm. His ear was gone, and the red flesh around his eyes and nose sagged.

"Clean his arm, *bijë*." Mama handed her a damp rag. "Gently, to wash away impurities."

She focused on her task to avoid seeing the boy's awful face. They were indeed lucky and blessed not to live here. They'd never had an explosion at their house.

"Is the boy worth saving?" The man with the hoop earring spoke in English again, making her jump as he brushed her skirt.

"He's a child of God," Baba said in Albanian. "Of course, he's worth saving."

The man switched to Albanian. "Bengalo's a child of the devil, same as his whore mama. Nothing but trouble since she abandoned him."

The boy winced and closed his eyes.

"I have a room," Baba said. "He could stay with us."

The scary man spat on Baba's shoe. "He might be the son of the devil, but he's Roma. He will not be contaminated by American *gadjo*."

She wanted to ask what that word meant, but Baba turned his back to the mean man and kept working.

"Bah!" The man turned and left.

Saemira kept washing the boy's burns, but her tummy felt sick. She didn't like touching the ugly, burned boy. She tugged on Mama's sleeve and cupped her mouth.

Mama glanced at her and frowned. "Do you not feel well, *bijë*?"

She shook her head.

"Go outside for air. I'll check on you soon."

Saemira ran through animals and people to get outside to a spot where the railing wasn't missing. She leaned over and gagged, but nothing came out.

"*Vajze e keqe.*" The man with the earring grabbed her arm and dragged her backward. "You pretend to help but steal from me?" he said.

She cringed. He was hurting her arm. "I didn't steal."

His fingers dug deeper into her skin as he pulled her inside another apartment and shut the door.

"My gold amulet's missing. It was near the boy when you worked on him."

"I didn't—"

"Empty your pockets, thief." He shoved his hands in her skirt before she could obey and brought out her magnifying glass and a gold piece of jewelry.

"How?" Saemira started shaking. She'd never seen that before.

"*Gadji* thief! You robbed me. I should call the *policia*. Have you thrown into jail."

"No!" Saemira cried. "I'm a good girl. I don't know how it got there."

He shook her hard. "A little liar and a thief."

"No. I d-didn't take your amulet."

"Yet it was in your pocket." He shook her again. "The gods cursed Bengalo for his evil. Do you wish to lose half your pretty face by fire as well, Temptress?"

"N-no." She started crying.

The mean man crushed her against his hard body and squeezed her face. "Quiet, or I'll tell the *policia* and your baba what you've done."

Vomit burned her throat as he licked her face.

"Saemira!"

"Mama," she whimpered.

The mean man squeezed her all over and pinched her bottom through her skirt. "May the gods curse you, little whore. Burn the thief out of you."

She didn't want to burn like the boy, her skin melting like wax. "I didn't mean to—"

"Do not speak, Temptress. I should tell your baba and mama what you've done."

"No. Please. Take my magnifying glass." She held it out to him.

"What good is that? I'd rather have you." He licked her face again, making her gag from his foul breath.

"Saemira!" Mama called again, closer.

The man hissed like a snake. "If you speak of me, the *policia* will throw you in jail." He squeezed her cheeks hard. "Understand?"

"I-I w-won't s-s-say a word."

He shoved her away, making her stumble. "Go. Mend your ways, whore, or the gods will drag you down into the fiery pits of *dreqin*."

She ran out the door, squinting from the bright sunlight as she staggered to the railing to vomit. Mama found her there and wiped tears from her face.

"Ah, *bijë*. You must have eaten something that didn't agree with you."

Saemira's heart beat faster than hummingbird wings. What if the mean man came out and told Mama what she'd done? They had to get away.

"Can we leave?"

Mama wrapped an arm around her. "Soon. Baba's almost done."

She stayed by her side as they returned to help the boy but she couldn't stop looking at the door. What if the man came in? Would he tell her parents about the amulet she'd stolen? Would they call the *policia*?

The boy groaned. She peeked up at his scary face and feared the gods would burn her as they'd burned him. She had done a wicked thing by stealing.

Baba spoke to a large woman and handed her a few bills before they left the broken, stinky village.

Mama carried the empty water jug. Baba carried the medical kit. Saemira carried words in her head. Ugly ones.

"What does *gadjo* mean, Baba?"

He frowned. "Someone who's not Roma."

"So I'm half-*gadjo*?"

"That's a bad word. Do not use it."

Her stomach still churned. Would it ever stop? "Why did the man call you that when you helped the boy?"

"Helping does not make me one of them."

Not fair. "What will happen to the boy?" Would he die? Would she?

"He will heal," Mama said. "Compassion always heals, even if it doesn't take away pain."

Saemira wanted to ask what a whore was. She wanted to know if someone could steal and not know it. She wanted to ask about the bad feelings inside her still from the man touching and licking her. She wished it was bath night.

But she bit her tongue, not wanting her parents to discover her evil and throw her in jail.

Gemma

A BRISK BREEZE made the bare branches in the courtyard quiver. I tipped my water bottle to let a few drops fall to the cobblestone. An offering to the water gods for luck. In a few weeks, when spring began fighting winter for dominance, a flower might peek its hardy head out from between the stones, doubling mine.

One could never have too much luck.

Mama had said it was lucky for a man to meet a woman carrying a full jug. That's how she'd met Baba. But American women didn't carry jugs of water around, as in Albania. My thirty-two-ounce water bottle had to suffice. Baba had teased Mama about her superstitions, but maybe dismissing her gods had contributed to his tragic end. My life had been a chain of unlucky events until I'd reinstated Mama's rituals. Now, I worked in an urban high-rise castle with a bunch of high-class white people, in my very own cubicle. I even had a high-tech trashcan that opened with a wave of my hand.

I played with Mama's amulet on the ride up to the sales floor. The necklace was one of the few possessions I had left of hers. She'd given it to me at a dark point in my life, saying it would protect me. And it had.

The elevator dinged. I tipped the bottle to let a few drips fall to the floor and sent a prayer up to whichever god wanted to claim it.

I had sales calls to make and quotas to break.

In my cubicle, I propped my feet up on the desk and wiggled my toes. Pompoms had become my new best friend. Cheap, gorgeous, and cheery.

Someone cleared their throat behind me.

I whipped my feet down and swiveled in my fancy chair, worried it might be the intimidating CEO again. That guy had necessitated the trip down to the courtyard in the first place.

It wasn't him, thank the gods. A sour-faced, middle-aged guy with sandy-blond hair stood outside my cubicle.

"Miss Stone?"

"That's me." I tapped the name plate with Angel's dumb alias for me gorgeously displayed in white letters.

"Will you please follow me to my office?"

"Depends on what you want to do with me there."

He gave me a blank stare.

I giggled to put the poor stiff at ease. Angel had said I could get anything if I laughed. I'd experimented with giggling to clinch sales, and people seemed to relax and let down their guard when I made them laugh. At least, that's what my increasing sales stats seemed to suggest.

"Just joking, Mr...?" I raised a brow, signaling it was his turn to give up

13

info. It seemed off of him to show up at my cubicle and order me to follow him to his office without an introduction.

"Mr. Davidson, from HR."

"I'd be honored." I bowed, in case he was in charge of giving out the raise Mr. Carter had hinted at yesterday.

We passed the CEO's spacious office, and I glanced through the glass. My cubicle was cool, but king-man's office made my space look like chopped liver. Not that I'd ever tasted that to know. Americans had strange similes.

The CEO glared when he caught me staring. Crap! I focused on the back of Mr. Davidson's boring blazer and hurried to the elevator.

When we arrived at human resources, he ushered me into a room with two other people who appeared even grumpier than him.

Note to self: don't apply to work in HR.

Mr. Davidson pointed to the other man. "This is Mr. Jefferson, from security."

Nice. I wasn't the only person of color in the room. Mr. Jefferson was a few shades darker than my olive tone.

Mr. Davidson gestured to an angular woman with bright blond hair. "Ms. Hernandez, from Legal."

Wow. It must take lots of people to present a raise. EcoCore went above and beyond with everything, from garbage cans to pay raises.

"It's an honor to meet you." I gestured to the woman's feet. "Love your shoes." They weren't quite my style, but the pink pumps had potential.

"Thank you. They're Jimmy Choo."

I wiggled my painted toes to show off my cool wedges.

"Mr. McConnell, the CEO, has asked us to discuss your employment."

I rubbed my hands together, eager to learn how much more moolah I'd be making.

"He's upset with your work ethic, or lack of it, and has asked for your termination."

The bouncing energy inside me froze like a polar vortex of catastrophic proportions, the kind that must've buried the dinosaurs beneath miles of ice.

"Say what?"

Botox lady dangled a ballpoint pen in front of me. "Sign here. Mr. McConnell was gracious and paid you for the next two weeks so you won't be without income."

I blinked. "This uh, must be a mistake."

She raised an eyebrow. "Please sign."

What the freak was going on? I took the pen from her vampire fingers

14

and glanced at Mr. Jefferson, hoping for a sign of camaraderie. But he looked unmoved.

"You have the wrong person," I said. "Mr. Carter told me yesterday—"

"The CEO himself fired you for"—Mr. Davidson glanced at a paper—"giggling and wasting time on the clock. You have no recourse but to sign and be escorted from the premises."

Wasting time? Were they smoking something? I'd been doing my job. Quite well, in fact.

"We need your signature," Mr. Davidson repeated.

I scribbled my alias where Botox lady had X'd, hoping to wake up from this nightmare.

"My men will escort you out," Mr. Jefferson said.

"I need to collect my things." And talk to my manager. Mr. Carter would stop this madness.

Meeting him months ago had been a blessing from the gods. I'd been vacuuming and dusting offices in the wee morning hours, when I'd opened his door to find him already there. I'd almost wet myself. But he'd been cool and had struck up a conversation. In the end, he'd told me to visit human resources and to say Joe had sent me. I'd explained that I had no sales experience, but he'd said he had a feeling about me.

"Your desk and cubicle have been cleaned out. Your personal belongings are in a box outside." The gruff voice startled me back to reality. "My men will see you to your car."

Well, weren't they efficient.

I staggered to the door, my wedges heavy as concrete blocks. Two security guards waited for me out in the hall. One held a box with my sweater and satchel strap sticking out of it. Had they found the copies of *Popular Science* I'd taken from the lobby? Would they add theft to the reasons to fire me?

I struggled to breathe as we took the elevator to the bowels of the parking garage. How would I pay rent? Where would Altin and I go?

The guards stayed beside me as I approached old Fisnik. Gray, beat up. Like how I felt. I set the box on the backseat, noticing the magazines under my satchel. Guess I'd keep them.

"Hey Gemma."

I turned to see my boss, Mr. Carter, getting out of his car.

"You heading to lunch early?"

I slammed the door and huffed. "How could you get my hopes up for a raise then fire me?" Tears threatened, but I refused to lose it in front of these people. "I thought you valued my contributions."

"Are you kidding? You're my star team member. What's going on?" He glanced at my goon escort.

"Mr. Davidson fired me on the CEO's orders because I giggled on calls. Giggled!"

He made a face. "That's ridiculous." He gestured for me to follow him. "Come on. I'll get to the bottom of this."

My jailers blocked us. "Our orders are to see Ms. Stone off the premises."

"I don't care what your orders are." Mr. Carter tried to shove past them, but the oafs didn't budge.

"We can't allow Ms. Stone back inside the building. Mr. McConnell's orders."

My boss always smiled. But not now. "Wait in your car, Gemma." He glared at the guards. "Don't send her away or you'll answer to me." He pushed a button on the elevator. "I'll be back."

Though Mr. Carter was the least threatening man I knew, he seemed like the Terminator right then.

Hopefully, he would not fall back to being Mr. Rogers.

3
LINCOLN

The latest edition of the *Salt Lake Tribune* lay open on my desk. Angeline had released a statement claiming SmartGlass as her intellectual property, not mine. As if she knew the difference between an algebraic equation and the X's and O's slapped on a love letter. She was suing for half of EcoCore's current shares, claiming the company's growth was due to her brainchild. If she won, she'd be the majority shareholder since I'd split my shares with Joe when the company had teetered on the brink of bankruptcy.

I swept the paper onto the floor.

My attorney had denied her allegations, calling them meritless and frivolous, but I'd learned that truth didn't matter in court. The person who played dirtiest and threw the most money around usually won. And no way would I outdo my ex when it came to playing dirty.

I'd have to win another way.

A disturbance in the outer office made me glance up. Joe Carter yelled at Lionel in the other room and pointed my direction. Catching me watching him, he marched past my guard dog.

"Have you lost your freaking mind?" He slammed my office door.

Lionel raced in after him. "I'm sorry, Mr. McConnell, I'll—"

"It's fine." I waved him away and powered off the SmartGlass to give Joe and I the privacy we needed. My friend hadn't been this worked up since junior high when some jocks had dunked Tony Meyers's head in a toilet. I gestured to a couch. "Have a seat, Joey."

He pounded a fist into his palm. "Why did you fire my best team member without consulting me?"

I kicked a leg up on the coffee table. "I did you a favor. Ms. Stone was making personal calls on company time. I caught her myself."

Joe scowled. "You arrogant, bitter fool."

I clutched my heart. "Such language, Joey. You wound me."

Joe was a clean-cut, conservative, goody-goody church boy who didn't swear, didn't drink, and didn't miss a day praying to God. I was the opposite —an agnostic, die-hard liberal pessimist. Despite our differences, we'd been friends since junior high.

"You need to void her paperwork. Gemma's out in her car right now being treated as a criminal when she's done nothing but make you money. Lots of it. I had the paperwork ready to take to HR to give her a raise. She's freaking gold. And you fired her?"

"She kept giggling." I clenched my hands. "I caught her with her feet on the desk. I won't tolerate laziness, even if you will because you're too nice to do anything about it."

"Lazy?" Joe threw his hands up and stormed out of the room. Maybe I'd gotten through to him.

I returned to my desk, but Joe walked back in and slammed papers down in front of me. "I'll grant that she's unconventional but check out her stats."

I tossed the quarterly report aside. "I've read this. Your team did well."

He banged my desk. "Look at Gemma Stone's stats, you bloody idiot."

I clucked my tongue. "You can still go to hell for cussing in Brit, you know?"

"Read the damned report."

I stood and pointed. "Sit your ass down and remember your place. I'm still your boss."

He didn't move. "Not if Gemma leaves. If she goes, so do I."

I blinked. Joe had been with me from the beginning. We'd struggled together to build the company into what it was today.

"Don't be ridiculous." His heart belonged to EcoCore, like mine.

"I'm not joking, Link."

"Fine." I scanned the page for *Stone.* "These figures can't be right." I added up the numbers in her column again. "You must've entered the data wrong."

He set another paper on top. "I knew you'd be stubborn, so I brought Accounting's report." He tapped the column with her name. "Note the amount collected matches her stats on the sales report."

I compared both and scratched my chin. "This can't be."

Joe sighed. "You can be so damned infuriating."

"You're going to have to pray longer tonight, Joey. You've used more cuss words in the last five minutes than you have in your whole life."

"Because you...you make me so mad." He ran a hand through his hair, making it stick straight up. "How could you fire my top team member without consulting me?"

"I'll void it." Obviously, I'd screwed up.

"No." He stood and paced in front of my desk. "I'm sick of your unending grudge against life. I'm sorry Angeline hurt you, but you need to stop taking your bitterness out on the rest of us. You humiliated Gemma for no good reason. Now, you'll beg her to work for EcoCore again and give her a huge raise. Or I walk."

Did he really see me that way? As a bully?

"I'm serious, Link."

"Fine." I waved him away, done with this conversation. "I'll call HR and have them send her up." The things I did for him.

He left, and I shoved my nagging conscience aside. So I'd made a mistake. Big deal. It shouldn't be difficult to fix.

SAEMIRA

Age 8 - Fushë Krujë, Albania

SQUANDER: to waste an opportunity.

arbage blew in front of her as Saemira pulled the goat's rope. "What about Billy?" She petted her furry, new friend. "Or Gruff?"

"Maybe you should let Bardhana name him," Baba said. "It'll be her goat."

She tugged her new friend away from a crushed soda can. "She'll like the name Billy."

"Don't press her, princess. Her baby's sick, and she's worried. Be a big girl."

"I won't press."

Baba had gone to the Roma village for months to help the burned boy get better. She'd stayed home with Mama, not wanting to visit there ever again. But Mama had needed rest today so Baba had made her come with him.

The village was still stinky and broken, but Bardhana's place was swept, at least. She was one of Baba's students and needed milk for her baby. Hers had dried up.

Baba placed baby Frenk in Saemira's arms so he could show Bardhana how to milk Billy. Saemira put the bottle to the baby's mouth, but Frenk wouldn't move his lips. Milk streamed down his chin.

"He won't eat." She moved the nipple against his lips.

20

Baba took the baby and gave Bardhana a look that said something bad was happening and little girls wouldn't understand. But she would if they'd speak with words, not faces.

"Come outside, Saemira." He led her out the door. *"Eja,"* he called to someone in the courtyard.

Saemira shivered when the burned boy skipped up the stairs to join them. His face and arm didn't have bloody white patches anymore, but the skin on one side of his face still puckered. A ghastly hole where his ear should be made her gag. His eyeballs moved around in the whites of his eyes, not staying still.

"This is Saemira." Baba put a hand on her shoulder. "She helped tend your wounds. Do you remember?"

He nodded.

She wished she didn't remember that day. Thinking about the mean scary man she had stolen from made her want to hide. Were the gods still angry with her?

"Bardhana's baby needs my attention. Can you stay with my daughter until I'm done? Be her friend?"

Saemira clung to Baba's coat. "I want to stay with you." If the gods noticed her with the bad boy, they might explode this whole building.

"Play with your new friend, *bijë*." He patted her head and left.

She pressed against the wall as the boy moved closer. "Go away."

He stopped, then walked to where the railing was missing and dangled a foot over the ledge. On purpose!

"Don't!" If he fell, he'd be sorry.

He grinned, making her shiver.

"You're a stupid idiot," she said in English, not wanting him to tell Baba on her.

His creepy eyes widened. "You speak Een-glees?" He said *English* funny.

"Yes. Baba is American." Which made her special, according to Mama. "Do you know English?"

He frowned. "Little." He switched to Albanian. "Uncle knows it. He lived in Canada as a boy." He switched to English again. "Yerra soopid eedeeyah."

"No." She poked him. "You're a stupid idiot."

He touched his chest. "Bengalo es soopid eedee-it?"

Bengalo must be his name. "Yes."

He touched her shoulder. "Saemira?"

"Saemira is good and pretty."

His eyeballs crossed. "Saemira esgud en pritt-ee."

It wasn't quite right, but she nodded.

He patted his neck. "Bengalo es soopid eedee-it."

"Bengalo is also dirty and ugly."

He turned, and she shuddered at his ear hole. He begged for more English words. She taught him all the bad ones she knew. The good ones she kept.

When Baba came out, Bengalo ran to him and pointed. "Saemira essa gud, prit-tee preen-sess."

Baba laughed. "Very good English, son."

The boy tapped his chest. "Bengalo essa soopid, ee-diot, ugly, steenk-shit."

Baba's eyes narrowed, and Saemira ducked her head. Dumb boy.

Baba gave him coins, then took her hand and left. Not until the village was far behind did he speak.

"Saemira, I'm disappointed. You squandered an opportunity to make a friend today."

"What does squander mean?"

He lifted her in his arms so she could see the world up high. "It means to waste because you do something foolish, like teaching poor boys naughty English words."

"I didn't mean to squander."

"He definitely had a knack for English."

"So, I didn't squander?"

"You did. Bengalo is a good boy, not a stupid idiot, and definitely not a stink-shit."

She frowned. "He did stink."

Baba kissed her cheek. "His people don't have much. But even the stinkiest, dirtiest person has a piece of divinity in them."

"A piece of Sky God?" That's what Mama called his God.

"Yes."

"Will Sky God curse me for squandering?" She didn't want to worry about Him as well as Mama's gods.

"No, bijë. He's not petty. God lives to forgive, but He also has high expectations and wants us to love our brothers and sisters. You don't want to disappoint Him, do you?"

No. But Bengalo wasn't her brother.

Gemma

22

MAMA'S AMULET gave me courage to pull back my shoulders and walk off the elevator toward the intimidating CEO's office.

"Breathe, Gemma," Mr. Carter said beside me. "You're not in any danger of losing your job." He stopped outside a door. "You're in a unique position."

The only unique thing I felt was the urge to barf up the Cheetos I'd eaten earlier.

"Mr. McConnell screwed up and needs to apologize. My advice? Make him grovel."

Easy for him to say. Mr. Carter had a family. A cute wife. Twin boys. Probably grandparents and aunts and uncles. He was white, not brown like me. He was in no danger of becoming homeless.

"I don't care about an apology," I said. "I just want to get back to work."

"You can't squander this opportunity."

My mouth fell open when he threw Baba's words at me.

"You can get a much larger raise from him than I'm authorized to give you. No matter what, your job's secure. So make him grovel."

My hands fisted as I recalled the humiliating way I'd been escorted out of the building. "He fired me for giggling. Who does that?"

He laughed. "That's my girl. Hold onto that fire."

The snooty Brit stuck his nose in the air as we entered the outer office. "May I help you?"

"We're here to see the Big Cheese," my boss said.

Brit-guy scowled. "You mean Mr. McConnell?"

Mr. Carter's playful mood made me careless. "We mean Mr. Giggling-Intolerant."

My boss snickered, but someone else—not Brit-guy—growled.

I whipped my head up to find the CEO glaring at me from his open door. Damnation and jello.

"I've been waiting, Ms. Stone." He gestured for me to enter his inner sanctum.

"Give him hell," Mr. Carter said as I walked past him.

The CEO shut the door and pointed to a white chair on the other side of a massive desk the size of an airport runway. "Take a seat."

I looked around the gorgeous office space which had everything from gym equipment to a cozy fireplace with plush couches surrounding it. His chair dwarfed mine, probably on purpose. A blizzard blurred the view out of floor-to-ceiling windows. I'd need to leave early to get home on time.

The man raised an eyebrow.

I gulped. Beautiful bananas. How had I not realized how gorgeous he was? The pinstripe suit was boring but fit him to perfection. His dark brown hair was styled, not a hair out of place. A hint of facial hair emphasized a strong jaw and luscious lips. And steel-gray eyes were set off by thick lashes.

"Do you dress this way every day, Ms. Stone, or just on special occasions?"

I gripped my fringed satchel. "I could ask the same of you? Do you always wear a suit?"

"I do. You might want to consider dressing more professionally in the future as well. It would have improved my first impression of you and saved us this meeting." He steepled his fingertips. "HR messed up. Please accept my formal apology on their behalf. Mistakes happen."

Whoa. Mr. Davidson had read Mr. McConnell's exact words. This man had *meant* to fire me. Yet he now cast blame on HR and pretended to be magnanimous?

"You're right." I flipped a few braids over my shoulder. "I made a huge mistake working for a company run by a liar." I stood, slipping my satchel over my shoulder.

"You're calling me a liar?"

He should be glad I hadn't called him worse. "If the shoe fits." I held my head high but worried he would tell me to leave. To go without collecting two weeks' severance pay. Mr. Carter had promised I wouldn't lose my job, but did I dare beat this figurative lion with a stick to test that assumption?

His jaw twitched. "Fine. I did fire you, but Joe made me see my error. Seems you're a valuable asset to his team, so I'm asking you to stay."

"I *seem* to be valuable?" Could this man be any more condescending? "No, thanks. I won't stay where I'm not appreciated." I headed to the door, hoping he'd call my bluff.

He blocked my escape, making me yelp. I hadn't heard him get up from his desk. Was he a freaking vampire?

He took hold of my arm. "Mr. Carter needs you to stay."

I stared at his hand, which made me buzz like an electrical current. "Mr. Carter didn't fire me."

He released me and stepped back, still blocking the door. "Will you stay for a six percent raise?"

Whoa, Nelly. Was he joking? I'd hoped for five percent at most. Mr. Carter was right. I could get more out of this guy if I played him right.

"Ten percent."

He hissed. "Don't be greedy. Six point five."

"Please move out of my way."

"You can't leave."

I put hands on my hips. "Will you tie me to a chair to keep me here?"

He rolled his eyes. "Mr. Carter threatened to quit if you go."

Ah. That's why my boss had been confident Mr. McConnell wouldn't fire me. Good for him. He acted meek and mild, but the guy had backbone.

"Guess you'll lose two valuable employees today." I tried to nudge him out of the way, hoping I wasn't taking my bluff too far. The rich jerk pushed every button I possessed.

He took my hand, and the tingly sensation swept up my arm again. "No other company would understand Joe's worth. They'd make him claw his way up the corporate ladder for years, and he'd go along with it, stepping down to help a more aggressive chump climb past him."

I wriggled out of his grip. "And that's my problem because?"

"Because he has a wife and kids. And he just moved into a sweet house in the Avenues that I encouraged him to buy. He can't afford to downgrade careers."

"I'm sure Mr. Carter is bluffing." Like me.

"Any other man, I'd agree. But Joe is honest to a fault. When he says he'll quit if you go, he will. Integrity is more important to him than a paycheck."

"I like Mr. Carter." He gave me hope that not all men were evil.

"As do I. So will you take a seven percent raise and keep working for him?"

"No." I folded my arms in case he got any more ideas about touching me.

"Why not?" He threw his hands in the air.

"Because you're grumpy. I don't want to work for someone who tries to control who I am, even down to whether or not I laugh on a phone call."

"I thought you were making a personal call."

"Whatever. I don't want to work for someone who's so proud they can't apologize."

"I apologized."

"Oh, please. You read from a script. You're not sorry you fired me. You're only sorry you had to fess up to your mistake. You don't seem like a man who cares to admit he makes them."

"Because I don't!"

I laughed, and—shocker—so did he. And wow. The man became ten times sexier. I held onto Mama's amulet.

He sighed. "So you want a sincere apology?"

"That'd be a good start."

He gestured to the chair. "Sit, please."

I did so, and he returned to his desk.

"Let me dig deep to find my humility."

25

Had he just made a joke? Of course not. This was boring CEO-man. He wouldn't know a joke if it bit him in his tight butt.

"Don't pull a muscle," I said.

He didn't crack a smile.

"Are you—"

He waved, as if shooing a fly. "Be quiet."

"See? You're a total grump."

Most people found me amusing, but Mr. McConnell seemed made of stone, which worried me because he held my fate in his strong, manicured hands.

He let out a long sigh. "I've had a terrible morning. One piece of bad news after another. When you giggled, I assumed you were playing around. It didn't help when I saw your feet on the desk. And your unprofessional attire."

What?

"I made false assumptions. I should've gone to Joe, but I believed I was doing him a favor by not bringing him into the conflict. He has a stroke when he has to make someone else suffer. But I was wrong not to do a more thorough check. If I had, I would've seen that even if you had been talking to a boyfriend, you were still doubling every other sales associates' stats and could get away with it."

"I don't have a boyfriend."

He shook his head. "Whatever. I'm trying to say sorry. I made not one mistake but several and have no excuse for my behavior."

Huh. I hadn't thought he'd be able to step down from his high horse enough to apologize. But that hadn't been half bad. Baba would've said I was seeing the divine in him. A teensy tiny spark.

So I stood and started clapping, giving credit where credit was due. "There. That wasn't so hard, was it?"

He scowled, and I laughed. Poor guy didn't possess an ounce of humor, which made his reactions funnier.

"Now," I said, "put your money where your mouth is. Make me an offer I can't refuse."

AARON, my cubicle neighbor, waited for me when I returned from my heart-stopping ordeal with the CEO.

"Gemma-girl. I thought they fired your butt. Tommy saw you and Joe heading into the big man's office and said it looked serious. So spill. What happened?"

"I was fired and rehired." No putting off Aaron.

"No way! The CEO's wack, man."

"Preaching to the choir, dude." I pushed past him, noticing my box of belongings beneath the desk. One could never complain about HR's efficiency.

"Was it terrible?"

I moved my satchel into a drawer. "What do you think? I had to grovel to get my job back." It still irritated me that I'd been fired in the first place.

"McConnell's an ogre. Since things went down with his wife, everyone's terrified of him."

I set the pilfered magazines back on my desk. "What happened?"

"You don't know?" He stared at me as if I'd turned into a cotton-candy-eating lizard or something.

I swiveled to face him. "I've only been in sales for two months." I'd cleaned toilets before that. "Enlighten me." And let me get back to work. I was behind schedule.

Aaron rolled his chair into my cubicle and leaned closer. "The CEO's got skeletons in his closet."

In my experience, everyone had a few. "So what?"

He reared back as if I'd blown cotton-candy bubbles through my lizard nostrils. "You really have no idea, do you? The guy roughed up his wife and made her lose her baby."

Whoa.

"She divorced the bastard but dropped all charges in exchange for a huge settlement. Jerk should've gone to prison, but millionaires always escape justice."

"You're not messing with me?" Those were some serious allegations, and Aaron was a gossip.

"Google him. It was in the paper."

I did just that, pushing Aaron out of the way. A minor headline from two years ago popped up. Another hit from yesterday. I covered my mouth as I skimmed the first article.

Hell's bells. Aaron hadn't lied. I studied a picture of the CEO next to a gorgeous blonde with enormous *gjinjtë* revealed by a low-cut gown. Another photo showed the same woman with an arm in a cast and bruises covering her body. A closeup showed a hand-shaped bruise on her face.

I shuddered, thinking how close I'd been to that hand just a few minutes ago.

His wife had received millions in the divorce, but Aaron was right. The CEO had deserved prison. His poor wife had probably been too intimidated to press charges.

I clicked on the newest article, which stated that his ex was suing to obtain shares in EcoCore. Good for her. She'd finally found her backbone. Probably had to wait for it to heal after her monster husband beat her. He'd apparently stolen her intellectual property—SmartGlass.

"Bastard," I said, since Aaron wasn't offended by real swear words.

"Right? Guy's a double douchebag."

Ooo. I'd have to remember that one. "Thanks for the heads-up."

"Anytime." He rolled away. "I've got your back. When I thought they'd fired you, I was ready to grab a picket to protest."

Yeah, right. Only if donuts had been involved.

I leaned back in my cushy chair and propped my wedges on the desk, vowing to stay clear of the CEO. I already had one too many monsters in my life. No way would I add another into the mix.

5

LINCOLN

*C*louds blocked my view of the mountains, making me scowl. Soggy springs never helped my mental state.

"Another beautiful rainy day," Joe said, entering my office.

"Did you tell her?"

"Nah." He sank onto a couch and bit into a cookie. "I'll leave that to you. She's on her way."

"Do you ever not smile?"

He took another bite. "Admit it, Sausage Link. You need my eternal optimism to keep from slipping into despair. And I need your pessimism to ground me in reality."

I ignored his bantering. "Will your team be okay without her?"

He kicked a foot onto his knee. "I'll miss her, for sure. But with the lawsuit, we need another person on board. I've got Janey and the boys to think about now. I can't be working eighty hour weeks, even if I believe the cause is just." He raised an eyebrow. "But I'll need at least two more team members to replace her."

"Done. You have the green light."

"Wow. That was easy." He broke off a piece of cookie and handed it to me.

I shooed him away.

"Try to lighten up, Link." He popped the rest of the cookie into his mouth. "Smile when Gemma gets here. Don't scare her away."

"I'll smile when there's something to smile about."

"You have plenty to smile about. I offered you a cookie, and I let you steal my star team member." He grinned. "You'll enjoy working with Gemma. She has a quirky sense of humor, like yours before Angeline smothered the life out of you."

I pounded my desk. "Don't say her name." My ex was a forbidden topic. "I don't need Ms. Stone for anything but to entice investors. And don't talk with your mouth full."

"Aye-aye, sir!" He gave me a taunting salute.

I held up my middle finger, making him chuckle as he left.

Minutes later, Lionel informed me that Ms. Stone had arrived.

The girl entered, and I bit my tongue at her attire. Parachute pants and a kimono sweater that hung to her knees. A gaudy ensemble of necklaces like a damn flower child. Her hair was even worse. Two buns on top, with the rest in those awful braids. Elton John mashed ruthlessly into Princess Leia.

I motioned to a couch. "Would you like something to drink?"

"No, thank you."

"Then I'll get right to business. I have a proposition for you, Ms. Stone."

Her feline eyes narrowed. Did she have Middle-eastern roots? Some other exotic blood?

"I've watched you for the past month and am impressed with your stats." But not her garish outfits.

"Thank you."

She had a lovely voice, so at odds with her flamboyant style. Did I detect an accent? Her English was perfect, but her cadence sounded more pleasing to the ear than that of a normal loud-mouthed American.

"To reward you, I'm offering you a promotion. And a raise."

Her lips pressed together. "A promotion?"

"Senior Associate, Capital Development. You'll work with me to entice new investors to EcoCore." I'd spare her the legalese. My attorney would, in simple terms, funnel new investments she could drum up into a shell company my ex wouldn't be able to touch, if she by chance won her suit against EcoCore. I gestured to the adjoining office visible through the SmartGlass. "That'll be yours. You'll do much the same as now, except with much higher stakes."

"I'm not interested. I enjoy working for Mr. Carter."

"He's on board. Besides, I haven't told you the best part. I'll be doubling your salary."

Her eyes widened, and I knew I had her. Money moved everyone.

"That's uh, very generous, but my answer's still no." She stood. "I enjoy the sales team."

So this was her greedy game.

I blocked her retreat, making her flinch and take a step back. "Name your price." She seemed to have an intuitive sense when it came to negotiation.

"It's not about money. I just don't want to work for *you*."

I reared back at her figurative slap in the face.

"I won't leave Mr. Carter's team no matter what you offer."

My fists tightened and loosened. "Don't be ridiculous. Only a fool would turn down this opportunity."

"I'm a fool then." She pushed past me and walked out the door.

6

SAEMIRA

Age 8 - Fushë Krujë, Albania

MAGIC: supernatural power. Mama believes in magic from her gods.
Baba says Sky God does miracles, not magic.

*A*ruckus near the edge of the schoolyard made Saemira look up. Esad, one of the older boys, yelled and pointed at something. She left the jump rope game to see what was happening.

"Gypsy freak!" Esad shook his fist at the cursed, burned boy standing near the road.

She didn't know what *gypsy* meant, but Esad had gotten the freak part correct. Bengalo looked scary.

Esad threw a rock, and Bengalo ran off. "Don't come back! Horrid gypsies. Thieves, all of them." He looked at her. "They steal your soul."

She chewed her lips. "What happens if a gypsy takes your soul?"

"You become their slave, and they make you do bad things."

That must be what had happened to her. The cursed boy had stolen her soul when she'd cleaned his burned skin, making her steal his uncle's amulet.

"Gypsies target little girls like you."

She shuddered. "What should I do?"

Esad pulled a rock from his pocket. "See how the gypsy ran when I threw my magic stone at him?"

"Can I have it?"

He rubbed his chin. "What will you give me?"

She frowned. Baba didn't let her carry money around. Too dangerous. But gypsies and angry gods seemed scarier.

"What about these?" Esad rattled the bracelets on her arm. Her lucky ones. "These and your lunch for the next week."

Saemira handed her bracelets over.

He stuffed them in his pocket and gave her the rock. "Use it quick before the magic wears off. Have money for another, no?"

She stared at her new rock. Shouldn't a magic stone be pretty? This one looked like all the others in the schoolyard. But the gypsy had run off when Esad had thrown his stone. Maybe it didn't have to be pretty to be magic.

Gemma

I touched Mama's amulet as I peeked inside my boss's office. "You wanted to see me, Mr. Carter?"

He glanced up from his desk. "Come in, Gemma. Have a seat." He gestured to some chairs by the wall. "And call me Joe."

I liked how his chair didn't make me feel puny, as the CEO's had. Mr. Carter—Joe—pulled a chair around to face me. So personable. The nerve of Mr. McConnell to suppose I would betray such a kind man.

"Coffee?"

"No, thanks. I'm caffeined-up."

He fidgeted. "I heard you turned down Link's"—he made a face—"I mean Mr. McConnell's promotion."

"Yes." I sat up taller.

"Why? He offered to double your salary."

"Aren't you glad I chose to stay on your team? Don't you value my efforts?"

"I do. Which is why I can't hold you back."

What did he mean by that? "You're firing me?"

"Heavens, no." He laughed. "Besides a couple of engineers who've been with Link from the beginning, you're the most valuable employee in this company right now. I just don't want you to flat-line on the sales team when you have the opportunity to maximize your potential by working with Mr. McConnell. Think of what the sales team would've lost out on if you'd never moved up from the janitorial staff."

"But I don't want to work with him."

"Why? Lincoln's a good guy."

"No, he isn't." My hands fisted in my lap. "He beat his wife and made her lose their baby." I thought of my own mama's many losses, which made the CEO's actions especially repugnant.

"You read the old article?"

"Once I decided to stay, I researched Mr. McConnell to learn more about the man I indirectly work for."

"Did you research me?"

"I already know you're a good guy."

He cocked an eyebrow. "But I'm Lincoln's best friend."

"What?" I twirled a lock of hair.

"We've been friends since seventh grade when his family moved here from Baltimore. They lived a few doors down from me. Lincoln's little sister, Cora, had muscular dystrophy. First thing he said when we met was we couldn't be friends if I wouldn't let Cora hang out with us. I thought that was cool. We became the three stooges—until she died our senior year."

"That's why he's so...mean now?"

He snorted. "Heavens, no. Cora's death inspired him to make the world a better place for those with disabilities. Look at his products—the EcoWalker, the EcoLift, the EcoAssist." He ran a hand through his hair. "Please don't take what I'm saying outside this room. He isn't a man who likes to talk about his problems."

"Of course."

Ben held out a plate of cookies. "Want one? My wife made them."

I couldn't pass up a homemade treat. "Thanks."

"Link was doing great until Angeline came into the picture. His ex-wife." Joe grimaced. "I don't know all the details of his time with her—we kind of had a falling out—but she seriously messed with his head. I know in here," he hit his chest, "that she manipulated facts to make him appear to be a monster. I know my friend. He would never have touched her in anger, especially if she'd been pregnant. He wanted to be a father more than anything."

I swallowed a bite of cookie. "But I saw the photos. The poor woman was brutalized. She couldn't have made that up."

Joe growled. "The *poor woman* could and would. But you're right. The police believed her. So did the reporters. Lincoln spent a couple days in jail before he called me to bail him out. And then she dropped all charges like magic. If he'd beaten her, do you really think she would've let him off the hook? But it wasn't about what was right. It was about the money. It still is." Joe turned his chair around and dropped back down. "Will you do me a favor?"

I sighed. "You want me to work with him."

34

"It's your choice. But I'm hoping you'll give him a chance. Try the new position for a month, let's say. Put what you read out of your mind. Get to know the real man. Honestly, I want this for him as much as you. This is the first time in years he's been willing to let an outsider into his circle. Maybe you'll get his heart pumping again."

"Uh, that's not in my job description."

"No, but you have a zest for life that's contagious. Maybe it'll rub off on him. He's only had Lionel around for years. Those two zap the fun out of everything."

That was for sure.

"Will you do it?" Joe asked.

"I guess. One month, you say?"

"Yeah. But I hope you'll stay longer."

"Don't hold your breath." I wanted to believe Joe, that his friend was innocent. But I'd interacted enough with the CEO to know he wasn't a nice guy, even if he didn't pound on women. And the guy already seemed to despise me. Maybe for the color of my skin. Or for what I wore—he'd been vocal about his distaste for my outfits. No way would I work for him any longer than necessary.

That was as misguided as believing in magic stones.

Joe moved the last of my meager belongings into my new office and tapped the desk. "I believe that's everything."

Aaron had razzed me that I'd forget him and the other peons in sales now that I'd moved up in the world. Whatever. He didn't know I'd be back in my safe, cute cubicle in four short weeks.

I squirmed, not liking being so close to the CEO. Only SmartGlass separated our offices. Yet I trusted Joe, and he wanted me to do this.

Mr. McConnell joined us. "Thanks for accepting the promotion, Miss Stone."

"It's temporary. Mr. Carter said to give you a month."

He glared at Joe, and I chalked up a point against the rich snob.

"Relax, Data-Link," Joe said. "I'm sure your charming personality will win her over, and she won't give me and the sales team a second thought."

I snorted, drawing a scowl from my new boss. "Oh, wow." I picked up a fancy name plaque that read: *Gemma Stone: Senior Associate – Capital Development*. The golden letters glowed in the sunlight, shouting to the world, or at least to those who entered my office, that I was someone important. For a month, anyway.

"Well, I'm off. You two have fun, but not too much." Joe winked. "There's work to be done, you know?"

Mr. McConnell flipped him off, making me chalk up another point against him.

He gave me a quick perusal once we were alone, the twist of his lips revealing displeasure. Probably wanted me to dress all boring. Or show more skin.

Three points against Mr. M. This would be a quick month.

"The best way to prepare you for your new duties is to give you a tour of development, down a level. Come with me."

He led me to the elevator, telling me about different products in the planning stage. I studied my new boss as we descended. He was physical perfection, but what did his sexy face and body hide? Was he the monster the papers had exposed? Or the kind, wounded man Joe had depicted?

We exited, and Mr. McConnell led me up a hall and pressed a finger to a keypad.

"You know," I observed as metal doors opened, "you might want to add a second fail-safe to the keypad, such as a code. A bad guy who wanted to break in and do corporate espionage could cut off your finger and get into this lab quite easily." I'd watched a TV show where someone had done just that.

"Is that something you're planning to do, Ms. Stone?"

"Not today."

His lips twitched. Not exactly a smile, but I'd take it.

Mr. McConnell led me around the lab and had different engineers give me demos of the products in various stages of development. I'd assumed, after reading his ex's allegations, that Mr. M was an opportunist who'd stolen her ideas to pass them off as his own. But watching him banter back and forth with the engineers revealed he understood as much as, or more, than they did. This didn't necessarily prove his innocence, but it did give me pause.

The man was smart.

This lab was better than Disneyland. Not that I'd been there. I asked tons of questions, and surprisingly, my boss didn't get annoyed. In fact, he grew more animated with each question, totally falling into his element.

Still, I wasn't quite ready to let him off the hook. If he'd been innocent, he would've defended himself against his wife's accusations. And he hadn't.

My brain soaked in the science like a dried-out sponge. When we headed back upstairs, I pondered the new data. Before the tour, I'd have given my chances of working with Mr. M long-term a zero out of ten. Now, I'd raise it to a four. Besides my doubled salary, I'd have opportunities for bonuses. If I could keep Duke from finding out about my luck, I might get ahead and escape his tentacles.

Mr. M's phone rang. "Yes?" He listened, then smacked his leg. "Damn it. No. I'll be right there."

The elevator dinged, and the doors opened to the sales floor.

"Meddling gypsies," he muttered.

I flinched. Was he angry at me? Had I done something wrong?

"There's been an incident in the garage," he said. "Go ahead and get settled in your office. We'll talk more later."

I hurried off the elevator, and the doors shut behind me.

Whew. He hadn't been angry at me, but he obviously didn't like my kind either. And to think he'd almost convinced me he wasn't an ogre.

Lesson learned. I could not afford to let down my guard around the guy. Men like him could, and would, hurt me.

7

LINCOLN

*J*oe and I high-fived each other as Gemma clinched another deal —her third since she'd taken on her new role a week ago. My friend had been right. Ms. Stone was gold. She could get people to trust her and to invest in the dreams she made them picture. After picking up on my vision during the tour of development, she'd been stoked to get to work.

She spotted us through the glass and held up both thumbs.

We entered her office, which appeared as though a rainbow had vomited all over it. Pompoms hung from her desk. Beads and other colorful doodads decorated a potted tree. A garish blanket with tasseled edges draped the filing cabinet.

Gemma gave Joe a dazzling smile. That and her beguiling eyes gave me hope that if she dressed more conservatively, I could use her in face-to-face meetings.

"How was that, Mr. M?"

I frowned at her casual address.

"You were spectacular." Joe gave her a fist bump.

Gemma kicked her funky pumps onto the gleaming surface of the Macassar ebony.

I cleared my throat. "That desk cost me twenty grand. Please don't use it as a doormat."

Gemma jumped out of her chair. Quite gracefully. "Holy shiitake!"

Her words surprised a laugh out of me.

"I hate to say it, Mr. M, but you got ripped off. I paid a fifth of that for my car."

Joe snickered.

"Your car isn't half as nice."

Gemma shrugged. "Nope. Old Fiznik has car warts and hair growing out of his hood."

"You named your car?" I asked.

"Don't you name yours?"

"Absolutely not."

"You used to," Joe said.

I pointed at the door. "Don't you have a sales team to run?"

He winked at Gemma. "Ask him about his Jeep in high school." He waved. "See ya later, Linked-In."

Gemma turned to me when we were alone. "So?"

"I don't name my cars."

"I'm not surprised. People who dress as boring as you are too lame to think up names for their cars."

"And people who dress as atrociously as you and decorate their desks with pompoms can't help but give their cars frivolous names."

She stuck out her tongue.

I schooled my features. As much as I appreciated my new senior executive, she also exasperated me.

"Now that we have the daily insults out of the way, let's discuss the Wilder Foundation." This funder was huge. Alexander Wilder had deep pockets, but he was a tough-as-nails recluse who hated everyone. She'd have her work cut out for her, trying to soften up the old man.

Gemma pursed her lips. "I studied his file last night. His oldest daughter had a stroke three years ago which left her severely impaired. If I focus on the handicap line, I might hook him."

I cringed. "Disabled. Don't ever use the H word with Wilder. It's politically incorrect."

She nodded. "Got it."

"Maybe mention the motion-barrier sensor technology we're working on."

She twirled a horrendous braid around her finger.

"You know," I said, "this type of discussion tends to go over better face-to-face. If you dressed more professionally and did your hair in a more conservative style, you could go after Wilder in person." Which was what it'd take to secure his support.

"You mean dress like a robot?"

"I mean don't dress like a circus performer."

She scowled. "Has anyone ever told you that you're a jackasp?"

I counted to ten. "Just consider it. My publicist could set you up with a new wardrobe. He has an eye for these things. I'd pay, of course."

"Of course." She picked up her satchel and walked out, slamming the door behind her.

I shook my head. What was up with her?

I STEPPED off the elevator and scanned the garage. A habit since the vandalism had begun months ago. A first sweep showed all clear. A second search made me tense up. Someone crouched beside a car on the third row. Should I alert security?

Muscles clenched as I pulled out my phone and crept closer. I did a double take when I saw who sat against a flat tire of an old Ford Focus.

"Ms. Stone?" I stood and scratched my head. She'd marched out all huffy forty-five minutes ago. Why was she still here?

She glanced up and groaned. "Ugh. Go away."

I wanted to. The storm last night had dropped fresh powder, and I itched to try out my new fat tire bike. But she'd seen me, and I couldn't pretend not to have seen her.

"Have you been sitting here all this time? Why didn't you call security?"

"I don't like your security people. Besides, there's nothing they could do. My spare's flat, too."

I didn't want to take time to find a spare and change her tire. But I couldn't leave her stranded.

"Come on. I'll give you a lift home." That would take less time than messing with her tire.

She perked up. "Really?"

I clicked my key fob. "Can't leave you here to wallow."

She stood, and my eyes widened. Her tire wasn't flat. It'd been slashed.

"Damned gypsies," I muttered, snapping a picture of the damage with my phone to send to the detective. Why were these hoodlums targeting my business?

"Excuse me?" She placed hands on her hippie skirt. "Didn't 2020 teach you better than to bash other races?"

I wasn't bashing a race. These were criminals. I had video footage of two of the punks breaking a window of an employee's car last month. The cops had verified that they were part of a gypsy criminal ring. When I'd questioned him about gypsies in Salt Lake City, the officer had explained how an organized crime syndicate used undocumented gypsies to sell drugs, steal, and traffic people.

I opened the door of my Jag for her. Not until we were out of the parking garage and I asked for her address did I learn she lived clear out in ghetto West Valley City.

Twenty-five minutes later, I pulled up to a sketchy apartment complex. Mountain biking was out now, since by the time I made it back to the canyon, it'd be dark. Being a nice guy never paid off.

A quick sweep of the area made me shiver. I tried to avoid places like this.

"Thanks for the ride." Gemma opened her door and stepped out.

I locked my Jag and ran to catch up to her, though I wanted to drive away and never set foot in this neighborhood again. A dark man in the shadows watched her.

Gemma waved me away. "You don't need to walk me to my door, Mr. M. I'm a big girl."

I scoffed. "You're barely 5'4." I kept my eyes on the thug.

"Will you just leave?"

"Not until you're in your apartment." With the doors locked. I peeked back at the man, wishing he'd go away. "You're a target for guys like that," I whispered.

She huffed. "You're totally profiling."

"Can you frickin' blame me? This place is a crime scene waiting to happen."

"Then leave. You're obviously out of your element."

"Where's your apartment?"

"Third floor." She headed up the stairs.

I followed, trying to prove something to her. Or me. At her door, she turned to tell me to leave again, but I put up a hand.

"I'll see you inside your apartment. That's what gentlemen do."

She smirked. "You think you're a gentleman?"

"I try to be." Hell, didn't driving her all the way out here count for anything?

The door opened, and a wrinkled Hispanic woman marched out, poking Gemma in the chest.

"Lo dejo," she said. "You pay money."

A small kid ran out and wrapped his arms around Gemma's legs. "Mama."

Mama?

The older woman pointed at him. "Chico malo!"

41

"No." Gemma put a protective hand on her son's shoulder. "He's not bad. You just don't understand him."

The older woman must be his caretaker, though she didn't look very caring. I nudged her toward the stairwell, pulling out my wallet.

"How much do you owe her?"

Gemma frowned. "This isn't your concern."

"How much?"

She hung her head. "One hundred seventy dollars."

I paid the woman and shooed her away. "You're fired." She started to protest, but I glared at her, and she stomped down the stairs.

Gemma smacked my arm. "What is it with you and firing people?"

"You want someone like her watching your son?"

The boy buried his face in her skirt. My jaw clenched when I noticed a ring of bruises on his arm.

"No, I—" Gemma lifted him into a hug. "There's just no one else."

Ah, hell. She was right. This was none of my business. "We'll find somewhere better for him."

"I can't afford—" She choked up.

Wanting to leave so she could fall apart without an audience, I nudged her inside her apartment. "I'll pick you and your son up in the morning. We'll find somewhere safe for him, okay?" I looked down the darkened stairwell. "Lock the door. I'll be here at half past eight. Be ready. I don't like waiting."

SAEMIRA

Age 8 - Fushë Krujë, Albania

DUPED: to be tricked.

They passed the fig tree, and Saemira sensed eyes watching them. Cursed eyes. Soul-stealing eyes.

Esad's magic stone warmed her hand as she pressed closer to Baba and peeked over her shoulder at the dirty gypsy following them.

"What did you learn in school today?" Baba asked.

"Teacher made me read in my primer." Boring. She could read much more advanced texts, but Teacher had slapped her hand with a ruler when she'd asked for harder books. She kept quiet now.

"Who did you help today?"

He always asked that, but she couldn't answer because the gypsy was getting dangerously close. Not wanting him to steal her soul, or Baba's, she whipped around.

"Go away, gypsy!" She threw the magic stone, but it didn't go straight or true. It clattered harmlessly against a door.

"Saemira, shame!" Baba's sharp voice startled her almost as much as the swat on her bottom.

Tears filled her eyes. Baba had never spanked her before.

He turned to Bengalo, but she grabbed his arm. "Don't look at him, Baba. Gypsies steal your souls."

"Hush, *bijë! Eja.*" Baba waved to him. "My daughter owes you an apology."

"No Baba. Esad said—"

"You will not listen to the small minds of others. I've taught you better."

"But Esad's eleven."

He frowned. "Age does not bring wisdom. Kindness does."

Bengalo approached, chewing his puffy lips. She huddled into Baba's long coat and lowered her eyes so he couldn't make her do another bad thing.

"Let me get my magic stone so the gypsy won't hurt us," she whispered.

Baba smacked his leg. "Don't use that vile word again, Saemira. Your words have way more power than that rock."

"But Baba."

"I forbid you from using that word. Remember what I taught you? Words can lift or destroy. *Gypsy* is a very destructive word."

"But, Baba."

"No buts." He knelt in front of her. "I gather one of the older boys at school taught you misinformation. That's a fancy word for lies." He spoke in English so Bengalo wouldn't understand. "He's Roma, as is your mama. Small-minded people call them gypsies. Do you think Mama steals souls?"

"No!" How could he ask such a thing?

He stroked her hair. "Roma are no different from you or me. They can't steal souls. But they do have feelings. There are no such things as magic stones. Your classmate duped you."

She sniffled. "I gave him three of Mama's bracelets and my lunch for a week."

"Oh, princess." He hugged her. "By their fruits you shall know them. This Esad sounds like a rotten apple full of worms."

"Sorry."

"Tell him you're sorry, not me." He pulled Bengalo closer. The boy's lips pulled up on one side. Was he smiling?

"Sorry," she said in Albanian.

He smirked. "You throw like a girl."

Baba chuckled as she pouted. "Join us for dinner, son. My wife will feed you. Saemira will teach you English words." He raised an eyebrow. "Good ones."

She froze. The gods would curse her if they brought Bengalo home. Their house might explode, or he might make her steal again. But she could tell by the way Baba had his arm around the boy's shoulders that he wouldn't change his mind.

Mr. McConnell's car was fancy with a capital F. It stood out in my crummy neighborhood like a neon sign when it pulled up to the curb where Altin and I waited. I climbed into the back and buckled Altin into a toddler seat which appeared brand-spanking new. Had he bought this for Altin?

"You don't need to sit back there with your son," Mr. M said when I shut my door.

Ugh. Judgmental much? "I want to."

"So, I'm the damned chauffeur?"

"I didn't ask you to fire my sitter."

He grunted.

I moved my butt around in the heated seat and played with all the buttons on the door to see what they did. Mr. M rolled his eyes as my window went up and down, but he didn't tell me to stop. Dang. I'd hoped to elicit a reaction to discern his fruits. Speaking of fruit, I'd forgotten to grab a banana on my way out the door. My stomach grumbled.

This would be a long day.

"How can you live in that slum with your son?"

I sighed. "I wondered when you'd start interrogating me. Is your tongue bleeding from biting it?"

His jaw clenched. "Your car should be fixed by the end of the day. My mechanic said your tires were balder than Captain Picard, so he replaced them. He also fixed your transmission."

What? Who was Captain Pickart? "I don't have money for that."

"No charge. Call it a work perk. I'd prefer to never drive out to your ghetto apartment again."

Ugh. Jerk. "I'll pay you back."

"Not necessary."

"I think it is." I didn't like owing people. "Now tell me what you named your Jeep in high school."

"I don't name my cars," he said with a growl.

"Joe said—"

"Joe's an idiot."

I huffed. "He is not!"

"What's wrong with your son?" he said, changing the subject.

I tensed. "Nothing's wrong with Altin."

"Gemma," Altin said.

I tapped his nose. "Good job, sweetie." I'd been trying to get him to use my name for months.

"You let him call you by your first name?"

Grrr. I fiddled with the window controls.

"I can't find the right caregiver if you're not forthcoming about his issues. How old is he? He seems big to not be talking much."

"I don't need your help. I can take care of myself."

"By living in the hood? Your son deserves better." He tossed a notebook back. "I made a list of schools. I wasn't sure about Altin's setbacks, but I had Lionel make appointments to visit these places."

"I can't let you do that." No way could I afford a ritzy childcare center.

"It's not all about you. Don't you want better for your son?"

The veins in my hands popped out. "Stop judging me! You have no idea about my life so don't act like you do. We aren't all swimming in money like you. I have a ton of medical debt and don't have the best options available." A lump clogged my throat.

"Sorry. That came out wrong." He frowned. "I just want to help. Don't worry about tuition. We'll work something out with a bonus. Get Wilder on board, and I promise you can afford the best. And I'm adding a new place to your contract. I have a small rental sitting empty in the Avenues. You can move in ASAP. I'll have Lionel send movers to get your stuff out of that dive."

"That's not necessary."

"Your commute wastes precious time which could be spent winning Wilder to our side."

Was this a subtle form of control, taking over my life by pretending to be kind?

"What's your favorite food?" he asked.

What the fudge? One minute he offended me, the next he threw out a question as if we were friends?

"Mine's Asian."

"Albanian," I said, to shut him up. "Shish Kabab House."

"Albanian?"

I cracked my knuckles. "I'm into weird ethnic dishes. El Salvadoran, French pastries, Japanese sushi, African wildebeest. If it's weird food from a weird country, I'm all over it."

"That's not surprising. You seem the type to prefer weird."

I glared at the back of his head. Had he meant that as an insult?

THE SOUND of children playing sliced into me like a dagger as I sat with Mr. M on a bench in the shade of a playground. I recalled my school days, before I'd been shunned because of my heritage. Altin clung to my penguin pants, watching the other children with fear and longing.

"Play with them." I nudged him. "Don't those toys look fun?" They appeared like paradise to me. A paradise I couldn't afford, no matter what Mr. M said.

This was the third school we'd visited. The way the directors at each had fawned over us made me wonder if another force had been in play behind the scenes. A force of green bills. Or maybe all white people got fawned over like that. I wouldn't know.

I propped a foot on my knee as Altin took hesitant steps toward the sandbox. Had I done right in taking him away from his foster family? Seeing the perks at these schools, I realized he'd missed out on a ton. Maybe I should've left him with that family in Michigan, far from the gods who seemed to hate me.

Mr. M walked over and took Altin's hand. "Want to build a sand castle, bud?" My mouth fell open when my boss knelt in the sand—in his suit!—to show my brother how to fill a bucket with a toy shovel.

No man who acted so sweet with kids could've beaten his wife, could he? He'd spent the last three hours driving me and Altin around to different centers and asking thoughtful questions I never would've considered. He definitely wasn't perfect, but he wasn't a monster.

"Wow. That's...busy."

I flinched as he joined me again, staring at the cutwork design on the bottom of my sandal.

I twisted my foot. "Took me forever to carve this."

"You did it?"

"Well, duh. Have you seen store-bought shoes with such awesome detail on the bottoms?"

"I've never looked."

"Most people don't, but they should. Your shoes are your signature to the world. Most people's footprints are boring and not worth a second glance, but these"—I wiggled them—"say 'Follow me. I'm someone you want to know.'"

He smiled. "You're definitely one of a kind." His gaze turned thought-ful. "What do you think about this place?"

"It's great, but I can't afford it."

"What facility would you choose if cost wasn't an issue?"

"The second." Altin had warmed up fast to a Miss Tina there.

"He did come out of his shell there." He pulled out his phone. "I'll tell

Lionel to get Altin enrolled with Miss Tina as his teacher. The woman seemed open to extra nanny opportunities when I pulled her aside."

I laughed. Was he serious?

"What?" he said.

"I'm not the nanny-hiring type, in case you haven't noticed. There's no way in Helsinki I can afford that place."

He rested a hand on mine. "You can, Gemma. I just doubled your salary."

I squirmed, uncomfortable under his intense gaze. Sure, on paper I might seem to have scads of cash, but looks could be deceiving. "I've been paying extra on Altin's hospital bills."

"Please don't fight me on this. I want your son in an optimal environment. As for nannying, there may be occasions when I need you to work an evening, especially if Casey fixes you up and gives you new clothes to meet with funders in person."

"Who is Casey? And what in Helen Keller is wrong with my clothes?"

"Everything," he said. "They do what the bottom of your shoes do, except they scream, 'Notice me, but don't take me seriously.' And Casey's my publicist."

"Has anyone told you that you're a jerk?"

"Joe, often. And you've asked that before, except I think you used jackasp instead of jerk."

I huffed.

He motioned to Altin. "Your son's a good kid."

I refrained from rolling my eyes. "The best."

"But he's a challenge, too, I gather."

"All kids are."

"Don't you want the best for him?"

I refrained from shoving him off the bench. "Of course, I do. But it's not that easy."

"It doesn't have to be hard. His schooling will be part of your benefits, like health care."

I stared at him. "Why are you being so nice?" Did he have ulterior motives? Of course, he did. Men like him always had an agenda. But what was it?

"I'm not. I'm being business savvy. There's a difference." He watched Altin dump his bucket and start filling it again. "I live by the philosophy that if I take care of my team members, they'll take care of EcoCore." He stood. "I think we've seen enough to make a decision. Let's go."

Ugh. I slung my satchel over my shoulder and called to Altin.

Mr. M gave me whiplash.

9

LINCOLN

The daycare director was no-nonsense. Gemma answered her questions as I played the silent observer, along to provide clout to enable Altin to be accepted above a long waiting list of other children. Gemma had no idea I'd promised the woman a large endowment upon acceptance. I feared she'd never allow her son to attend if she did.

It was one of the reasons I'd come to trust her and why I'd driven all over town to interview potential schools. She'd surpassed my expectations at work and hadn't taken advantage of my kindness. In fact, she could be quite stubborn about accepting help.

"Altin's five, correct?" the director asked, pen poised above a notepad.

"Yes."

"He's small for his age, and developmentally behind by at least two years, from my observation."

"He's smart." Gemma fidgeted. "I'm hoping your program will help him catch up."

"What's his disability?"

Gemma frowned.

"To enable him to reach his potential, we must understand his background."

I perked up, curious about her answer. Gemma hadn't been forthcoming with me, either.

Gemma's brow furrowed. "His information will be kept private, right?"

"Of course."

Gemma squirmed in her seat. "He was born with Fetal Alcohol Syndrome."

"Ah," the director said. "That explains his facial features. And the lag in physical development. Does he have vision or hearing issues?"

The conversation continued as I chewed on the shocking news.

Fetal Alcohol Syndrome?

Why hadn't she been upfront with me about that? Had Joe known about her problem? What kind of woman had I hired?

I clenched my jaw, not liking the ramifications of this new information. From here on out, I'd need to be wary and watchful.

Gemma wasn't what she seemed.

No way would a woman manipulate me again.

I set my coffee down and switched the SmartGlass on to see into Gemma's office.

The weekend had passed in a blur. At first, I'd been livid that Gemma had deceived me about her issues. I'd considered starting the process to demote her back to sales. She was too much of a liability to keep working with such big stakes at play. But a story Gramps had told me about his sister Shirley, who'd struggled with alcoholism, had come to mind. Gramps hadn't hated his sister for her weakness. He'd reached out instead, giving her a job as his secretary, fixing things around her house, paying for her kids to be in sports, and just being there for her. That'd helped Shirl the most, he'd insisted.

I'd spent all Saturday and Sunday researching alcohol addiction and FAS—Fetal Alcohol Syndrome—so I'd recognize the warning signs and know how to intercede and help Gemma to recovery.

She straggled into her office, sliding her satchel onto the desk. She scowled when she looked up and caught me watching her.

"Good morning," I called.

"Can we switch the glass off?" she said. "I feel like I'm in a fishbowl."

Why did she want privacy?

"I like seeing out to the sales floor." No way would I give her an inch. Addicts ruined not only their own lives, but the lives of their families, friends, and employers as well.

Gemma grumbled something under her breath, and I returned my focus to the report development had sent up for me to approve.

Hours passed, and I noted that Gemma paced more than usual. Was she stressed? Suffering withdrawals? I'd overheard the call with Wilder, and it'd gone better than expected. The man hadn't committed, but his positive response to her had encouraged me.

That's why I couldn't let her fail.

One of the articles I'd read had suggested distraction as a helpful strategy for addicts. Get their minds off alcohol by playing games. Find new hobbies. Compete in sports or other events.

"Why are you pacing?" I asked as I entered her domain.

"Why are you being nosy?"

"You're going to wear a hole through the carpet."

"Did you pay too much for it, too, like my desk?"

She wouldn't be so mentally sharp if she was under the influence, would she? Lionel walked by, arms laden with take-out boxes.

"In here," I called.

My assistant backtracked and set containers on her desk. I flicked on the SmartGlass for privacy after he left.

"What's this?" Gemma took a seat.

"Lunch." Might as well use some distraction techniques now that I knew she had a problem.

"For me?"

"For us. To celebrate getting Wilder to laugh today."

She snorted, then sighed. "It smells divine." She opened a box and gasped. "Shish Kabab House? Are you kidding me?"

I smiled. She hadn't lied about liking Albanian food.

We spent the next half hour eating buffet-style as she explained what was in each dish and how to eat it. I'd definitely distracted her from whatever had been bugging her. Gemma was a serious foodie and relaxed the more she ate.

"How about a game before we get back to work?" I pulled a box of UNO cards from my suit pocket. Maybe that'd help her see I was on her side, that she could talk to me, if needed.

She laughed but caught herself. "Sorry. I know you hate my laugh."

"What? I don't hate your laugh. I actually love it." I'd missed hearing her giggle.

"Don't be ridiculous. You fired me for giggling."

"Not because I hated it. I thought you were playing around on the clock. Your giggle is actually...charming." I looked into her eyes to discern if she was clean. Her pupils weren't dilated. Or red. My gaze strayed to her lips, and my body temp skyrocketed.

I looked away.

Gemma was not only an addict but a struggling single mother with an atrocious sense of style and a bad case of snark. Maybe in a hippy commune she'd be considered beautiful, but not in my world. She was uncouth, unpolished, and unorthodox.

So why was my heart pounding in such an odd way?

SAEMIRA

Age 8 - Fushë Krujë, Albania

DIGNITY: feeling worthy, valued.

*B*engalo sat across from Saemira at the kitchen table. She shuddered, his face reminding her of what happened to those who offended the gods. Maybe he didn't steal souls, but he'd stolen Baba's attention...and maybe her pretty-smelling soap in the bathroom.

Bengalo ate three helpings of Mama's burek, thanking her with his mouth full. Baba waved away his thanks, saying God deserved all praise.

She would thank God when the cursed boy left.

Baba pulled out his sharkia. Mama closed her eyes and swayed, humming along as he played. Baba watched Mama, who watched something deep inside her head. Saemira watched Bengalo, who eyed Baba's watch on the table. Before he could steal it, she snatched it away from him.

"What a wonderful idea, Saemira." Baba stopped in the middle of his song and held out a hand. "A perfect gift for our guest."

"No," she started to say, but he took the watch from her.

"You are so good, princess." He presented the watch to Bengalo. "For you."

The boy gaped at him. She did, too. Had the boy somehow made him give it to him?

"As our honored guest, we will give you a new name as well. No longer will you be Bengalo to us. We will call you Engjell."

The boy repeated the name which meant *angel* in English.

"Do you like?" Baba asked.

He pounded his chest. "Engjell."

The boy left, holding his skinny wrist up to admire the new watch.

After the door closed, Saemira turned to her baba. "Why did you give him your watch? It was worth lots of money."

"People are worth more. That watch gave Engjell dignity."

"And the new name," Mama said from where she sewed coins around the sleeve of an old dress.

Baba growled. "How could his uncle call him Bengalo? So cruel."

"Why?" Saemira asked.

"It means devilish," Mama said.

"What does *dignity* mean?"

"Feeling valued," Baba said. "When a man, or a boy like Engjell, has dignity, he behaves as if he's worthwhile."

Mama smiled. "Your baba sees divinity in everyone, which is why I love him."

"I just see what is already there, love." He patted his lap. Saemira climbed up and snuggled against him. "Will you do an experiment with me, *bijë*?"

"Yes." She grinned. Experiments were her favorite.

"Let's study dignity. The problem, as I see it, is: What does Engjell lack that denies him dignity?"

"Clean clothes?" His were stinky.

"A good prediction." Baba smiled. "But dig deeper."

"An ear."

He winced. "Those are physical deficiencies. Think of opportunities that you and I take for granted."

"School?"

"Ah-hah. You nailed it. Our hypothesis will be: If we give a disadvantaged boy opportunities, he'll provide his own solutions to his problems."

"How will we test it?" That sounded different from their other experiments.

"I'll provide Engjell education and see that his basic needs are met. You provide him friendship."

"But the gods cursed him." No way did she want to be Engjell's friend.

"The Roma gods are nothing more than luck." He winked at Mama. "No offense, love."

She set down her dress and walked over to join them. "The gods would never curse such a sweet boy." She rubbed Saemira's head. "His hard life has been pure bad luck."

"God's given us two commandments," Baba said. "Love Him and love our neighbor. Engjell's our neighbor."

"No, he isn't. Mrs. Hoxha is." She lived next door.

"Our neighbors are anyone we meet. Engjell will be our subject. I see great potential in the boy."

Saemira only saw a hideous monster. But Baba had better eyes than she did. Maybe this experiment would help her see better so she wouldn't get exploded by bad luck.

Gemma

THE OPAQUE GLASS gave me a reprieve from my boss's prying eyes. Thank the gods. He always seemed to be watching me, waiting for me to screw up so he could judge me.

I crinkled Duke's note that'd been taped to Fisnik's window last night in the parking garage. The evil man had demanded five hundred more a month since I was, in his words, 'fraternizing with the CEO.'

I kicked the bottom of my desk. How did he always know what was going on in my life?

A sharp knock startled me. "Miss Stone, would you..." Mr. M paused as I slipped the note beneath my leg and swiped at my eyes.

"Are you okay?"

"Yes." Besides needing to get a grip on my emotions. I pointed at my name plaque. "Like what I did with my name do-hickey?"

He took a seat and grunted. "Very bedazzling."

"Was that a joke, Mr. M?"

He tilted his head and smiled. "It's been known to happen."

Be still my heart. That smile did things to my insides that were totally unprofessional. Good thing he didn't smile very often.

"Expect a call from Mr. Wilder soon," I said, hoping to spur him into leaving. "I totally lied about how awesome you are and how you were looking forward to speaking with him."

"Sweet." He propped a foot on his knee. "How's Altin liking his new school?"

Freak. Why wouldn't he go? "He doesn't hold onto my leg and cry when I leave him."

He grinned, and those unprofessional things happened inside me again. Grrr.

"What about the new place? How's it working out?"

I adored the house he'd rented to us in the fancy neighborhood just up the hill. "It's fine."

"Just fine?"

Dang him. He wasn't going to let me keep things light and fluffy. "It's incredible. Thanks for everything you've done." I owed him gratitude for pulling Altin and me out of the hood. My stress had nothing to do with him.

"Just part of what I'll owe you for bringing Wilder to the table."

"It's looking hopeful." I examined the bottom of his shoes. "Your footprint says, 'I have absolutely no creativity,' but your projects in development tell a different story." He had the coolest inventions ever.

He set his foot down. "You're not cutting into these."

"Please?" I put my hands together. "I'll have them back by morning."

"Do you have any idea how much these cost?"

I shrugged. "Probably way more than they should, especially with such boring bottoms. Don't you want some tread on them?"

"Don't tread on me."

I laughed. His dry sense of humor rarely surfaced, but he had one.

Still, the crumpled note beneath my leg reminded me why my boss was, and always would be, completely off-limits.

Joe's office door was open. I headed there to say a quick hello and to tell my old manager he'd been right. I wouldn't be returning to sales, though I'd miss him and my friends on the team.

Voices made me pause outside the door. Joe's voice. And Lincoln's. I should've done an about-face and returned to my office, but Joe said my name, and I leaned closer to eavesdrop.

"Admit it, Data-Link. You like Gemma. Why else would you care where she lives or where her son goes to school?"

They were talking about me? I pressed closer.

"She was living in freaking West Valley. I moved her strictly for business reasons. A dead Gemma is no good to EcoCore."

Joe chuckled. "Don't pretend you didn't order lunch in for the two of you the other day. Gemma said you even played UNO with her."

Duke's note had freaked me out. Lincoln had calmed me with the lunch and silly game. Probably why I thought of him by his first name now instead of Mr. M.

"She was stressed out from Wilder. I had to do something."

"Methinks thou dost protest too much."

"Oh, get real, Joey. I could never like a girl like her."

I reared back, holding onto Mama's amulet. A girl like me? Hadn't he had fun the other day? He'd laughed and said he liked the Albanian food.

Blood rushed to my cheeks. I was such a fool. He wasn't my friend. I was just an employee, and not one he even respected. Probably because of my skin color. Or low economic status.

I'd forgotten my place. He was right. A guy like him—white and rich—could never care for a girl like me, one who'd done terrible things that would shock him if he ever found out.

I vowed he never would.

LINCOLN

*T*he elevator doors opened, and I marched toward my office. The phone call with Wilder had gone far better than expected. Gemma had really softened the old guy up. Maybe too much. His last request still had me reeling.

Gemma was on the phone when I barged into her office and gestured for her to end the call. She gave me a dirty look and swiveled her seat so her back faced me.

I gritted my teeth. How would I pull this off? Gemma had made everything possible but she could also set everything to flames.

She didn't hurry to end her call. When she did hang up, she turned and gave me a flat look.

"You could knock, you know?"

"Why? You saw me through the glass." I flicked the SmartGlass to privacy mode and began to pace.

She opened a file folder. I reached over to close it. "I need your undivided attention."

She leaned back in her seat. "What is so mucking important?"

"I just talked to Wilder."

Her lips formed an O, and she straightened. This was what we'd been working toward.

"He wants to meet."

"Yea!" She clapped. "That's awesome."

She had a soothing voice. I could use that. But her flower-child pants and fringed-buckskin top that resembled a mashup of Pocahontas and Forrest Gump's Jenny had to go.

"Not exactly. He wants to meet with me...*and* you." Lord have mercy. "Tomorrow night. I guess there's a black-tie event he wants us both to attend."

"I can't go anywhere at night. Altin needs me."

"Miss Tina's already agreed to stay with him."

"Excuse me?" She bristled, feathers ruffled, ready to peck my eyes out. "You had no right to ask her to do that. I'm his guardian."

"I..." Her word choice made me pause. *Guardian?* Why hadn't she said *Mom?*

But she was right. I'd tried to decline Wilder's request, but he'd insinuated that if we didn't meet, EcoCore would be out of the running for future funding. And he'd been adamant that Gemma be present. That's why I'd called to secure Tina's services.

"I apologize. I only wanted to make things easier for you."

"Well, don't." She twirled her braids. "I'm not going to some fancy ball. I'd be a fish out of water."

More like a piranha in a bowl of goldfish. I ran a hand through my hair. "Wilder insists on meeting you." And what Wilder wanted, he got.

I stopped, noticing my office through the glass. I'd been so consumed with Wilder's request that I hadn't registered the mess when I'd entered.

"What in the hell?" I stalked through the connecting door. "My attorney will be here in fifteen minutes. Why would you do this?"

She winced. "I thought your office needed some flair."

"Lionel!" I yelled.

My assistant scrambled through the other door but stopped when he saw the toilet paper draping the entire space. "Mr.—"

"Clean this up. I have an appointment at 1:15."

"Yes, sir." He started running about, pulling TP down in fluttering trails.

I returned to Gemma's office and pounded her desk. "You *will* be my plus one tomorrow night."

"What? But I—"

"You owe me." How could she think toilet paper was funny? This was a professional office, not a teen-hangout. "My publicist will pick you up to make you presentable. Don't screw this up like you did my office."

SAEMIRA

Age 9 – Fushë Krujë, Albania

HOPE: to expect with confidence. Without hope, we despair.

⸻ ❖ ⸻

*M*ama washed dishes as Engjell and Saemira crowded around Baba. The boy still annoyed Saemira, but she liked getting out of chores and having someone else to practice English with when he came over, which was way too often.

"Is your uncle okay with you being out after dark?" Baba asked. The summer sun had just set.

"Duke don't care."

"Doesn't care," Baba corrected.

"He should care," Saemira said. With his melted skin and missing ear, Engjell got treated badly. Strangers turned away in horror when he walked down the street. Kids threw rocks at him. She'd once done the same. His mean uncle, who should've treated him best, treated him worst. He didn't care about him like her parents cared for her.

"Tell us a story, Mr. Nikolla." Engjell used Baba's formal title since Baba was his teacher.

"A new one." Saemira snuggled against Baba's chest, inhaling the smell of oil from sewing machines, the musty scent of paper, the clean of bleach. The scent of school.

"Have you heard the one about Hansel and Gretel?"

"Is it a love story?" She liked those best.

Engjell groaned, and his eyeballs rolled about in their sockets. His eyes didn't behave normal.

"No. This story came about during the Great Famine in Bavaria in the 1300s. That's up by Germany now."

"Germany that had the Third Reich and Hitler?" Saemira asked.

"Yes, but Germany is good now, remember?"

"I'm still mad at them for killing the Jews."

"Hush, Gem." Engjell had started calling her that since he thought her eyes resembled emerald gems.

"You hush."

Baba tapped her nose. "During this time, people couldn't grow enough food. Many, like the step-mama, became desperate. She convinced the baba to take his children into the forest and leave them so they would have fewer mouths to feed."

"That's what my mama did to me," Engjell said. "She was a whore and was going to drown me in the river. Uncle saved me."

"Desperate people do desperate things," Baba said.

He continued his tale, but Saemira couldn't stop thinking about Engjell's mean mama, trying to drown him. She was glad her mama didn't try to kill her.

"Hansel climbed out the window when everyone else slept to gather white pebbles by the light of the moon. The next day when his baba took them into the forest, clever Hansel dropped pebbles. When night fell and their baba didn't return from gathering firewood, Gretel cried, but Hansel led her home by following the white pebbles he'd dropped.

"The baba rejoiced. He'd felt terrible for leaving them. But the step-mama locked Hansel in his room and took them out herself the next day. Hansel had a piece of bread which he tore into small pieces to leave a trail of crumbs. When night fell, he led Gretel to his trail, but ravens had gobbled up the breadcrumbs."

"Oh, no!"

"Oh, no, indeed!" Baba said. "They couldn't find their way home. But they found a house made of burek and baklava."

"Yummy. I wish I could find a house made of those things."

"Hush." Engjell poked her side. "You talk too much."

She pouted.

"As they pulled off food to eat, an old woman invited them inside. She turned out to be a witch, and locked Hansel in a cage and forced Gretel to do all the chores."

"Mean witch!"

Engjell poked her again. "Let him tell the story."

"I am." She stuck her tongue out at him.

"The witch fed Hansel, to fatten him up to eat. Weeks passed, and the witch decided to eat him. She made Gretel light the fire in the oven and told her to climb inside to see if it was hot enough. But Gretel pretended not to understand. The witch climbed inside to demonstrate, and Gretel closed the door and locked her inside to burn to ashes."

"Yea!"

Engjell gave her a dirty look.

"Gretel freed Hansel, and they discovered treasure hidden in the witch's room. They took this to their baba, who'd missed them. The step-mama had died of starvation. Now, they were all together, with money for food, and they lived happily ever after."

"I'm glad the mean step-mama died," Saemira said.

"Only because you don't know her story." Baba winked. "If you did, you might feel compassion for her."

Engjell chewed his misshapen lips. "Will I ever know my mama's story? Duke said she was evil like me."

Baba patted his arm, making Saemira frown. Engjell was doing it again, stealing his attention.

"Your uncle doesn't know your mama's story. Or yours. You're definitely not evil. If you want hope in the future, you must forgive your past. Forgive your mama. And yourself."

"You can't forgive yourself," Saemira said, trying to get his attention back.

"You can, and you should. If we don't forgive ourselves, we can't forgive others, and we're stuck in a bad place." He tugged her braid. "Forgiveness frees us."

Engjell poked her. "We should make rock trails tomorrow."

"Two trails. One of rocks, another of bread for the birds."

"That's my clever girl." Baba clasped her hand. "What did you learn from that story?"

"To prepare in lots of different ways so if one way doesn't work, another way will."

Engjell moved his hand to mimic a flapping mouth, making Baba chuckle.

"What about you, Engjell? What did you learn?"

"To always hope."

Gemma

A LIMO PULLED up in front of my house. A limo! I turned to kiss Altin's cheek. "Be good for Miss Tina."

He jumped up and down. "Bye, Mommy."

The limo came with a chauffeur, who held the door open for me. So polite. Another man sat inside. He must be Lincoln's publicist.

I climbed in and held out a hand. "Hi. I'm Gemma."

"Wow." He ignored my outstretched hand as the door closed. "Lincoln wasn't kidding when he said I needed to pull a major fairy godmother on you."

Rude. I yanked my hand back. "You're a lame fairy godmother."

"Turning you into Angeline will be nigh on impossible."

"Who?"

"Lincoln's ex. The epitome of female perfection." He whistled. "Never understood why he gave that woman up."

I gripped mama's amulet. Lincoln hadn't warned me his guy would be so demeaning.

We drove to a day spa, where condescending Casey talked about me to the workers as if I didn't exist. After he left, a male stylist draped an apron around me and started taking out my braids. He wasn't like Casey, thank the gods. He was kind and funny as he oiled, combed, and shampooed my hair. While he worked, some ladies scrubbed and painted my toes and fingernails. Another woman gave me a facial.

I gasped as a huge clump of hair fell to the floor. "Leave me some hair, will you?"

"One must hack down bushes for them to thrive. Same with hair. Trust Pico." Another pile of my brown locks fell to the floor.

"You're going to make me bald." I pushed him away.

"Mia bella." He tipped my chin. "You are beautiful whether your hair reaches your waist or your shoulders."

"I haven't cut my hair since my dad died." It felt like a betrayal to snip it off.

"He'd want you to look your best, no?"

"Yes, but he loved long hair."

Pico kept cutting. "Not long damaged hair. I'm going to give you a Brazilian blowout after I chop off all your bad ends. To de-frizz."

He kept cutting, and my head felt ten pounds lighter without all the braids and beads. I probably resembled the pitiful sheep in Albania after shearing season. The Brazilian thingy-whatever took a long time. When Pico finally finished, he flipped my chair around so I could see the final result.

I inhaled sharply. "Holy Shih Tzu." That beautiful stranger couldn't be me. She looked nothing like those pink, shivering sheep.

Pico giggled. *"Gesundheit."*

I ran my hands through my hair. "It's so soft. And silky." My fingers didn't get tangled. I touched it again, loving how full it was, though it only reached a couple inches past my shoulders.

He winked. "I'm sending you home with lots of product and a sheet of instructions to follow like the Bible."

A woman entered and motioned for me to follow her. "Time to try on gowns."

Pico escorted me into an ornate room full of mirrors and a place to change in the corner. He made me laugh as he clapped and threw out more Italian endearments as I modeled each new dress the woman helped me put on. Pico and the girl settled on a gold sequined gown with straps. Gorgeous, but way too low in front for my liking.

"Don't slouch, *mia bella*." Pico tweaked my shoulders, pushing my chest out more. "Don't be ashamed of these curves. Every man will be drooling over you, and gay men, like me, will consider becoming straight." He blew me a kiss. "Now come. I must finish your hair."

He wasn't done?

I returned to his station, where he styled my hair into gorgeous waves that fell softly across my shoulders. The girl, Mia, put sparkling earrings in my earlobes.

Someone whistled.

I turned to see Lincoln's awful publicist checking me out. "Now, that's what I'm talking about." He strutted up to me and waggled his brows. "Lincoln owes me big time for doing the impossible."

Pico huffed. "As if you had anything to do with her transformation."

Casey tapped his hands together. "All right, people. McConnell will be here any minute. Make yourself scarce so I can unveil Cinderella."

I scowled, not liking how the creep talked about me.

Pico took my hand. "I'm not leaving you."

"Thanks," I whispered.

Lincoln entered, his presence filling the salon to bursting. I held my breath, waiting for his reaction. Waiting for a string of compliments.

He stopped when he spotted me. Silent. Uncomfortably so. "I guess that'll do," he finally said. "Come on. We're going to be late." He walked out without a second look.

"Bastard," Casey said.

Sadly, I agreed with him.

Inside the limo, Lincoln pulled out his phone. I sat there, dressed like a princess, but feeling like a silly impostor who'd been found out.

"When we meet up with Wilder, let me do the talking," he said, not looking up.

My hackles rose. I'd done everything he'd asked—or commanded, more like—and he hadn't even given me an appreciative glance. Or a thank you.

"Please don't embarrass me tonight," he said, nose down, eyes still on his screen. "This meeting could open up doors or close off all opportunities for EcoCore."

I clenched my teeth, counting to a million so I wouldn't go all cray-cray on the man. Though he deserved a good whacking.

13

LINCOLN

$\mathcal{T}$he limo pulled under the hotel *porte-cochère*, and a bellhop grabbed our door. I climbed out and turned to help Gemma. Lord have mercy. I couldn't help but stare as she placed her dainty hand in mine. What had Casey done? I'd asked him to make her fit in, not stand out as the sun on a stormy day. I hardly recognized her.

My hand burned where I touched skin at the small of her back. She looked every inch respectability, with an unhealthy dose of sexy mixed in to taunt me. Where in the hell had these curves come from? I had no idea she'd been hiding such hotness under layers of gaudy jewelry and circus clothes.

We entered the ballroom, and every gaze fixated on my companion. I searched for Wilder, reminding myself that this mirage holding onto my arm wasn't real. Though she smelled fantastic.

Wilder waved, and I guided Gemma to his table. Ms. Stone, I corrected myself. I needed to stop thinking of her by her first name, especially in that tantalizing gown.

Blast Casey!

Wilder stood. "So nice of you to come." He lifted Gemma's hand. "You must be Gemma. You're more beautiful than I imagined."

No joke. I'd known she had potential. But hell. The woman could be a model.

She gave him a glamorous smile. At least I'd known about her smile before tonight. Not that she'd given me any since I'd picked her up from the spa.

"And you must be Alexander."

The older man blushed. "Call me Alex, dear. Let me introduce you to the rest of the board."

There were four others—Wilder's VP, the CFO, the board president, and his personal secretary. Gemma quickly wrapped them each around her delicate finger.

I stiffened when I spotted Angeline and her new husband with the mayor several tables away.

Waiters brought out meals as Gemma dazzled our table companions, especially the CFO. The other men admired her, but Scaglione blatantly flirted and ogled her chest. Though I didn't blame him. The gown displayed her assets to perfection.

I kneaded my temple, not liking Gemma this way. She reminded me too much of my ex. Whenever I peeked over at Angeline, she, too, drew all the attention, toying with the mayor, though her husband sat beside her. I'd been a naïve fool during our marriage, believing her forwardness with other men hadn't meant anything.

I stabbed a crab cake. Was Gemma the same? Not that it mattered. She was my employee, not my date. We were only together because Wilder had demanded it. I signaled a waiter for more wine.

Scaglione stood. "Let's put business aside for a minute, shall we?" He held out a hand. "Would you care to dance, Gemma?"

I didn't like his use of her first name. Or the way he undressed her with his filthy gaze. Casey was too damned good at his job.

"Of course, Mr. Scaglione."

"Call me, Rick. Please."

I had some other names in mind for him.

They walked out to the dance floor. I gripped my silky napkin in a death grip as I noted the location of his hand on her backside. Way too low. Angeline and the mayor walked out to dance as well, and I couldn't concentrate on the conversation around me. Scaglione pulled Gemma close. Too close.

What was the man thinking?

Actually, I could tell all too well what was going through his mind. Without considering my actions, I marched across the dance floor and gripped the man by the shoulder.

"Mind if I steal my fiancée back?" I said.

Scaglione sputtered. "Uh, sure." He let go of Gemma and retreated with his tail between his legs.

I took Gemma in my arms, trying to ignore how my body reacted to holding her close. "Are you okay?" I asked, my gaze dipping to her cleavage.

"I had it handled."

"So do I." I focused on her face.

"By calling me your fiancée?"

I shrugged. "It worked, didn't it?" Somehow, she was closer. Had I pulled her against my chest, or had Gemma made the move? I didn't step back to put distance between us. Neither did she.

"Did I do something wrong?" Her breath caressed my neck.

"No. Wilder loves you. Just keep your distance from Scaglione. He's a perv."

"He seemed nice."

"You call his hand grabbing a handful of booty nice?"

She blushed. "I thought it was an accident."

I snorted. "Guys don't ever *accidentally* touch a woman's derriere. Switch me seats when we return to the table."

She didn't speak. Had I misread her?

"Do you want his attention?"

She flinched. "No! Ew. He's an old man."

"He's in his late forties." That wasn't old to most women. Angeline had gravitated to the older set. Her new husband was twenty years her senior.

She smacked my arm. "No, just no."

I grinned at this glimpse of the real Gemma. "Guess you're stuck with me."

"Ugh," she said, but snuggled closer.

I pretended not to notice, and we stayed that way until the song ended. When I led her back to the table, Wilder stood and clapped his hands together.

"Why didn't you mention you two were engaged? That's wonderful!"

I froze. Scaglione had squealed.

"When's the date?" Wilder asked.

"Oh, um, we're not—"

I interrupted Gemma before she could reveal that this was a huge mistake. The announcement of our *engagement* had infused Wilder with energy. We could use that to our advantage.

"Nothing's set in stone yet," I said, wrapping an arm around her waist, "but we've talked about next summer."

SAEMIRA

Age 13 – Fushë Krujë, Albania

ILLUMINATE: to brighten with light or to gain insight through knowledge.

The blue-green sea sparkled in the sunlight, making silhouettes of the boats out in the bay. Saemira leaned back on a towel, wondering if her handsome prince was out there on one of them. A fisherman, catching fish and dreaming about his future wife. Or a captain of a ship, longing for her as she longed for him.

An olive hit her. "Gem," Engjell said.

"What?"

He gestured to the waves. "Race you."

She shooed him away. "We've played in the waves already. I want to rest." Like Mama.

Another olive hit her cheek. Engjell was lucky she didn't throw him to the ground and pinch his neck. But ladies didn't allow dumb boys to bait them into behaving as heathens.

"Come on, Gem. You afraid I'll win?"

"Ha." Her legs were longer than his. He never won.

"Would you light the candle, Engjell?"

Bless Baba for distracting her determined tormentor. Engjell hopped away, leaving her to dream again. Green hills surrounded the bay. White stucco buildings stood as sentries behind them. Her handsome prince could be an actual prince, living in a tower with Persian carpets and tons of servants to wait on him. Clouds billowed in a sky dance. Maybe her true love flew airplanes. When he found her, he'd whisk her off to an exotic place like America or Tanzania.

The hiss of a match made her sit up. Baba and Engjell turned to reveal a cake with a large sparkler in it.

Saemira jumped up as the stick sizzled. "Where did you find the sparkler, Baba?" It was amazing.

"I found it." Engjell thumped his scrawny chest. He'd become fascinated with his body of late. Baba said his slight stature hid an unconquerable spirit and promised he'd put on muscle in another year or two. Her friend lifted his shirt at least once an hour to check if they had arrived yet.

"You don't have a *lek* to your name," she said.

"I didn't buy it. I told him where to get it."

"True." Baba's eyes crinkled at the corners as he handed Engjell the cake so he could kneel next to Mama.

Saemira bounced in front of the cake as they sang *Happy Birthday* to her. Baba and Engjell hammed it up at the end.

"And many more." Engjell bowed.

She watched the sparkler spit fire as it made its way toward what she hoped was lemon-cream frosting. "Do I blow it out?"

Engjell rolled his eyes. "You can't blow out a firecracker."

"How will I make a wish?"

"Say your wish out loud as the sparkler dies," Baba said. "Get ready. Five, four, three..."

She pressed her hands together.

"One!" Baba and Engjell yelled.

"I wish to find my true love," she said, as sparks turned into dying embers.

"You already have." Engjell thumped his chest. "Me."

She laughed. "You're my friend, not my true love."

He pouted. "Why? Because my eyes don't stay still? Or is it my missing ear?

"Don't be an idiot." She hardly noticed his defects now. He was just Engjell.

Baba wagged a finger. "You're both too young to be talking about love."

"I'm thirteen," she said. "A woman."

"And I'm a man." Engjell puffed out his beanpole chest, making her laugh again.

Mama handed them each a slice of cake. Saemira glanced at Mama's rounded belly, hoping she wouldn't lose the baby this time. She'd made an amulet to protect her new baby brother or sister.

Baba patted her head. "True love will come when you're both older. I've seen it in the stars."

"Really?" She set her cake aside.

"Yes, Saemira. *So good.*" He tapped her nose. "You'll find love, but the journey might be painful."

"How painful?"

He rubbed Mama's belly. "I had to lose both my parents and travel across an ocean of despair before I found your mama." He pecked her cheek. "Mama had to flee her home in Kosovo, leaving everything behind." He stroked her hair. "But in losing all, we both found the one thing we'd been missing. Each other."

Saemira pulled back her shoulders. "I'll suffer any pain or swim the deepest ocean to find my true love."

Engjell's eyes rolled about in their sockets. Baba called his eye condition nystagmus, but she liked the term 'dancing eyes.' That's what his eyeballs seemed to do.

"You don't know how to swim," he said.

"Neither do you. I'm talking figuratively, not literally." For being a genius, Engjell could be completely stupid.

"Open your gift," Baba said.

She'd received a new dress and shoes that morning, but her parents had made her save this gift for now. She pulled the paper off and squealed.

"A flashlight!"

"Not just any flashlight," Baba said. "A scientific one that uses ultraviolet rays which are invisible to the human eye. When you shine it, phosphors convert the UV radiation into visible light. It illuminates white clothes, teeth, even scorpions, making them glow in the dark. I thought it'd go well with your other lab equipment."

"Cool," Engjell said.

She held up the scientific light, already dreaming of experiments she could use this for. "Illuminates," she said, loving the new word. She hugged Mama, then Baba. "Thank you. I love it with all my heart."

Gemma

WHAT WAS HIS GAME? I studied Lincoln as he smiled at Mr. Wilder. My boss had treated me as an insignificant nothing all night, until he'd interrupted my dance with Mr. Scaglione with a lie. Then, for some odd reason, I'd experienced major tingles. Dancing with Lincoln had been wondrous, not icky like with Mr. Scaglione. I'd melted into him, wanting to be closer. And Lincoln hadn't pulled away.

But it hadn't meant anything. So why was he continuing the charade?

His hand fell to my knee and his lips touched my ear. "Play along," he whispered.

My body flushed with heat as I focused on the grandeur of the ballroom —the heavy golden drapes on the windows, the chandeliers, the fancy table linens. Everything proclaimed this to be the Prince's ball, and I was Cinderella. I didn't belong here, even in my fancy gown. I was Gemma. Saemira, actually. But no one could know that, especially my way-too-sexy boss who hadn't taken his hand from my knee.

"I'd love to have the two of you up to my cabin in Park City," Mr. Wilder said. "To get to know you better."

Oh, no, no, no. A fancy ball for a few hours was one thing. Having to pretend for a whole weekend would be ludicrous. Cinderella's magic had only lasted until midnight. I dared not push my own timetable.

"That's kind of you, Mr. Wilder, but—"

"We'd love to." Lincoln patted my knee, making me squeak as he smote me with another heart-stopping smile.

We bid Mr. Wilder and his crew goodnight and beat a hasty retreat out of the ballroom. Lincoln's hand burned the skin on my lower back as he led me through the glittering lobby. I gulped, trying to figure out why he'd lied about our relationship.

Someone called his name as we reached the exit. We turned to see a buxom blonde gliding toward us in the most stunning gown imaginable.

"Were you going to leave without saying goodbye, Linky?"

I grimaced. Linky?

My boss tensed beside me. "Angeline."

Holy cucumbers! This was his ex? Condescending Casey hadn't lied. She was perfect. Flawless, white skin. Luxurious blond hair. Sparkling blue eyes. A body built in all the ways men appreciated.

"I could feel you watching me on the dance floor, baby." She batted her fake eyelashes that must've cost a fortune.

Lincoln scowled. "I wasn't watching you."

She patted his cheek. "You keep telling yourself that, hun." She faced me. "I see you found a little plaything."

He pulled me closer, making the woman sneer.

"Be careful who you hook up with, girlfriend," she said. "You get burned when you play with fire."

No kidding. Lincoln's hand melted my dang skin. He'd never discussed his ex with me before, nor had he explained why he'd allowed her to destroy his reputation. But even not knowing, my gut screamed, *Snake!* This woman made my skin crawl.

"Guess Link and I are going to be a raging conflagration then." I put my hands on his chest and drew circles on his tuxedo. "Because sparks have been flying since he asked me to marry him."

Lincoln gulped.

"Where's your ring?" the snake in the expensive gown asked.

"Where's your leash?" I shot back.

She scowled at Lincoln. "I'll see you in court."

He whisked me out the door and into the waiting limo. I wondered if he was upset, but when the door shut, he started laughing.

Be still my heart. He had an amazing laugh, the kind that came from his belly and warmed me to my core.

"I can't believe you said that," he said, catching his breath. "Where's your leash?"

I elbowed him.

"Ow. What was that for?"

"For telling Mr. Wilder we were engaged. What were you thinking?" My traitorous body buzzed when he placed his hand on my knee again. Greedy kneecaps enjoyed his attention way too much.

"Did you see how excited he became? It won't hurt to play along."

"We can't spend a weekend at his cabin."

"Sure we can. It'll give you more time to charm the old guy. After we get his money, we'll go back to normal. Plenty of couples break off engagements."

"Wow. We barely got fake-engaged and you're already trying to end it?" I threw it out as a joke, but the truth stung. Running into his ex had revealed why he hadn't noticed me tonight. I was a dark-skinned Cinderella. "But seriously, this is a lie." My conscience rolled eyes at my hypocrisy.

"Life's about perception," Lincoln said. "Wilder never invites anyone to his place that I know of. This is a giant step forward."

"I don't know."

"How much is Altin's medical debt?"

Why was he changing the subject?

"How much?"

"A little over three hundred grand." Not that it was any of his business.

"Play along with this *business transaction*." He made air quotes with his fingers. "Pretend to be my fiancée, and I'll pay it off. I'll even throw in a new car. My fake fiancée can't keep driving that falling-apart Focus." He laughed as if he'd told a funny. "What do you say?"

I wanted to say, *Hell no!* And I wanted him to laugh again. Traitorous mind. I hated how he thought he had to buy my help. I'd help him without any reward. Between what Lincoln and Joe had said, I knew his slithery ex could harm EcoCore. Wilder's money was key to protecting the company from her greedy designs.

"Fine," I said. With my debt gone, I'd have more options.

"If we do this, the truth can't be leaked to anyone. Not Joe. Not your family. Not Casey. Especially not Wilder. The truth could cost us everything. Wilder isn't someone you mess with."

He didn't have to worry. I knew all about keeping secrets.

"Understood?"

I bristled. "Yes, boss."

He relaxed against the seat, his knee pressing into mine. His whole larger-than-life presence pressing me into a neat tidy box.

"I understand I just received the worst proposal in history and have the most callous, unfeeling, jerk of a fiancé ever. But long live EcoCore." I gave him a stiff salute.

Lincoln leaned forward to tap the window. "Pull over," he told the driver.

What was he doing?

The limo stopped. Lincoln opened the door and stepped out, turning to offer me a hand.

"Are you going to make me walk home?" Had I pushed him too far?

He rolled his eyes.

I wiggled across the seat, keeping my head held high. Consequences. If I upset my boss, I risked losing my job, getting demoted, or walking home in heels and a fancy gown.

He led me to a piece of green space, illuminated by a streetlamp, and knelt in the grass.

"What are you—"

"Shh." He pulled my hands into his. "Do you have a middle name?"

I did, but since he didn't know my first name, he didn't need my middle name of Elira. "Ann," I lied.

"Do you really think I'm callous and unfeeling?"

I gave him a *Duh* look. "You have been pig-headed tonight."

"Wow. Pig-headed, too? I have some fixing to do." We locked gazes and he squeezed my hands. "Gemma Ann Stone, I suck at romance, but will you be my fake fiancée and pretend to want to marry me?"

"Stop being ridiculous." I tried to pull my hands away, but he tightened his grip.

"Better ridiculous than callous and cold." He gave me a half-smile. My kryptonite. "I'm sorry for being pig-headed. I panicked when Scaglione told Wilder we were engaged. I didn't correct his assumption because I didn't want to look like a liar. But I shouldn't have been sharp with you."

"No, you shouldn't have. And why did you say we were engaged? You could've called me your girlfriend."

"I know. I'm an idiot. Will you forgive me?" He touched my cheek.

Oh, my. His touches were tender, not rough or possessive. Yet a naughty part of me wanted to be possessed by him.

"Will you pretend to tolerate me enough to pull off this ruse with Wilder?"

He didn't realize how easy that would be. And how dangerous. "It'll be tough," I said, words breathy.

"Don't I know it."

I scowled. Did he mean it'd be tough to tolerate me? I tried to shake off the blow to my ego as we returned to the limo.

"Now, you don't have to say you've received the worst proposal in history," he said, shutting the door. "Second worst, maybe. But not the worst."

I laughed. It was that or cry. But I could do this. For EcoCore. For the money. Money that would help Altin and I get settled on our feet...so we could run again.

NEGATIVE PEACE

"When one does wrong, one must do it thoroughly."

— *THE HUNCHBACK OF NOTRE DAME* BY VICTOR HUGO

15

LINCOLN

*L*ionel straightened as I entered. "Mr. McConnell, you're back." The man always stated the obvious. He handed me a silver box. "Your new name plate arrived."

I took the box. "Hold my calls."

"Of course, sir."

I shut my door and pulled out the new name plate to replace the last one Gemma had bedazzled. "Ms. Stone," I called, shrugging out of my jacket.

"What?" she yelled back.

I switched the glass to see-through. She grinned at me, feet defiantly on her desk.

A week had passed since the meeting with Wilder, the night she'd shocked me speechless with her beauty and elegance. The night I'd made a fool of myself by fake-proposing to her.

Gemma was herself again. Sort of. The classy lady in the gown had disappeared and she once more wore outlandish outfits with clashing colors, baggy fits which hid the luscious curves I now knew she possessed, and abominable accessories. Painted toes peeked out of bedazzled sandals. At least the awful braids were gone. Her hair looked soft, sensual.

Good grief. I blinked. Maybe I needed a girlfriend.

"Get in here."

She gave me a disgruntled look but pulled her feet off the desk and obeyed. I cringed at her tie-dyed skirt and the pompom necklace her son had probably made. Why wouldn't the stubborn woman conform?

"Take a seat."

"Yes, master."

I wasn't in a joking mood. "Wilder just called to inform me that he's throwing us an engagement party in May." My hands clenched. It had been more a command. "Said it's the least he can do since I've gypped you by not yet making our commitment public."

She plopped into a chair. "You say that as if it's my fault. If I remember correctly, I wasn't the one who announced we were engaged. And don't use the word gypped. It has racist connotations."

"I'm not blaming you. I'm simply saying we both need to up our game. Wilder reserved the Grand America ballroom and has invited everyone who's anyone to attend." Including my family. I shook my head, knowing that no matter what I did now, I'd end up looking bad. If I admitted the truth, I'd be a liar. If we went forward with this fake engagement and I broke things off with Gemma later, I'd be a playboy.

"Whose fault is that?" she asked.

"Mine. And yours."

"Beg your pardon. Did you say mine?"

I tapped a pen against the desk. "Wilder wouldn't have insisted on hosting this party if he hadn't assumed you wanted it. But you proved last time you can handle the heat of the elite."

"How poetic."

"It's on the third. Casey will pick you up to make you presentable again."

"Because I'm unpresentable as I am?"

"Your words, not mine." I gestured to the door. We were done.

She bristled. "You're the grumpiest boss ever."

I hit my desk. "This is no joking matter." With her pompom-loving blasé attitude, Gemma had to be the most unorthodox woman alive. She'd TP'd my office and bedazzled my name plaque and college diploma frames. She needed to take this seriously. "Once this ridiculous engagement goes public, we'll be walking a tightrope."

She pouted. "You did this. I didn't ask you to, and I didn't have to agree to go along with this ruse. Maybe stop talking like this is a problem I created for you." She picked up her fringed satchel and stormed out, slamming the door behind her.

I rubbed my aching head. Gemma definitely had a flair for the dramatic. But she was right. I *had* created this mess. The least I could do was be kind to her about it. I needed to stop acting like my dad. Be more like Gramps.

Was that even possible anymore?

16

SAEMIRA

Age 13 – Fushë Krujë, Albania

ETHICAL: courageous in doing what is right, no matter what.

*B*ells tinkled from a market stall. Saemira stopped to stroke a goat's spotted coat, wishing she could take him home. Goats had four stomachs and ate whatever you gave them. They were soft, playful. The perfect pet.

She spotted Engjell down the street and paused. What was he doing out of school? She'd stayed home to help Mama since she felt poor with the baby she carried. But Engjell didn't have a mama to help.

She almost called out to him but noticed his scary uncle and ducked into a doorway. Old voices she thought she had silenced taunted her.

She was a thief. A whore.

Hidden in the shadows, she observed Engjell's uncle point to certain people. Engjell left him and weaved through crowds until he followed the target, because that's what they were. He pilfered wallets and money from pockets and purses and slipped back to his uncle to drop the loot into a bag near his feet. Then he'd head off to prey on another victim his uncle picked.

His vile uncle eventually left with some other men, and Engjell spread a blanket on the crowded sidewalk and began begging.

A few kind people dropped coins in his hat. More kicked him or spat at his feet as they passed. She made her way over to where he begged and dropped a coin into his hat.

"Faleminderit," he said, without looking up. A scarf covered his missing ear and facial scars.

"You're welcome," she answered in English.

Engjell jerked his head up and cursed.

"Shame on you." She stomped her foot. "At least a beggar's better than a thief."

He stuffed his hat and blanket into a bag. "I wasn't doing anything those *gadje* didn't deserve." He pulled her onto a less crowded side street.

"What about the poor woman with the child? You took money from her purse while she wiped her child's nose."

"Shh." He glanced around. "She wasn't poor."

"Neither am I. Will you steal from me?"

He pouted. "I'd never steal from you or your family."

"You shouldn't steal from anyone. It's not right. I'm going to tell Baba."

"No. Please, Gem." He took hold of her arm.

She knew he wanted Baba to be proud of him. That's why he studied longer than her, why he stayed after school to help Baba clean and prepare for the next day, why he came over to hang on every word that left Baba's mouth.

"Promise not to steal ever again, and I won't tell him what I saw."

His shoulders sagged. "I promise, except when necessary."

She scowled. "Crime is never necessary. It's unethical."

He kicked a rock. "You're naïve. And spoiled. Roma don't have the luxury of abiding by ethics."

Tears filled her eyes.

He reached out to stroke her cheek. "Don't cry, Gem."

"I want you to be a good person." Not bad like his uncle.

"Fine. I won't steal any more." He took her hand. "You won't tell your baba?"

She squeezed his fingers. "I won't." Part of her was relieved to know her friend had faults. She wasn't the only one with secrets.

Gemma

ALTIN SAT AT THE TABLE, eating macaroni and cheese I'd warmed up for him. I paced the floor, still angry that I'd allowed Mr. M to get under my skin? I'd dealt with condescending men before and hadn't given them more than a silent middle finger. But Lincoln. Argh!

I jumped at a sharp knock on the door. Who was here? Angel didn't know about this place. My heart beat double time as I crept to the door.

"Who's there?"

"The big bad wolf," my boss answered.

I opened the door and put a hand on my hip. "Go away. I don't want to talk to you."

"Hello to you, too."

"Wink!" Altin climbed down from his chair and ran to him.

Lincoln picked him up and swung him around. "Hey, bud. Want to go for a walk?"

"He's not going anywhere with you." I started washing the table.

"You're coming, too." Lincoln glanced at my bare feet. "Throw on some shoes."

I turned my back to the irritating man but slipped into sandals. Maybe outside I could tell him off better than I'd done at the office. Or not done.

Spring had finally won the battle against winter. Tall maples and oaks looked lovely with bright green buds. Altin straddled Lincoln's shoulders, messing with his hair.

"Sorry for being the suckiest fake fiancé ever."

My lips twitched. "You should be."

"Will you forgive me for being abrupt so I can be the second-most-suckiest fake fiancé again?"

I rolled my eyes. "You'd better have a kick-butt apology."

He stopped. "I really am sorry for snapping at you. When we finish this walk, how about I treat you and Altin to ice cream? Will you forgive me then?"

"Hmm. That might work. The ice cream. Not your apology."

"Damn. I practiced the whole way here."

I knocked his elbow. "Don't try to be funny. I'm serious. You can't just apologize for the mess you've created."

"I know. I've screwed everything up, and now it's blowing up in my face." He rubbed his forehead. "Did you know Wilder knows my grandpa from his college days?"

"No." But that was great. That connection would make getting the man's money so much easier.

"Neither did I. Wilder said they roomed together for a couple years before serving in the same unit in 'Nam. Gramps saved his life there."

"That's fantastic," I said. "We don't need to pretend to be engaged. He'll invest with you because you're the grandson of his hero and friend."

"No." He grimaced. "It's more complicated than that. You're right that if he invests, he'll invest big. But my family and I haven't spoken since my divorce two years ago. If Wilder finds out, he won't give me money. He'll probably cheer on my ex." He growled. "He's invited my grandpa and parents to the cabin since they'll be on a cruise next week and will miss the engagement party. I want to back out, tell Wilder you and I are a joke, but that would doom EcoCore."

Ouch. Nothing like hearing where I stood in his eyes. "At least they're family. They love you, even if you haven't talked for a while."

"My parents don't love me. They believe the stupid media that I deserved prison." His nostrils flared. "Dad always said money and my temper would be my downfall. And he's always right, just ask him." His shoulders slumped.

I couldn't hold back my curiosity. "What really happened with your ex? Should I be worried about being fake-engaged to you?"

He started walking again. "I didn't beat her, if that's what you're asking. I don't know who did. Maybe her brother. They were thick as thieves. But I have no proof. All I know is I didn't break her arm or make her lose our baby." He glanced at me. "I'd never hurt you."

"Why didn't you defend yourself to the police? Why didn't you defend yourself to your parents, at least?"

"They didn't want the truth. They wanted confirmation of what they already believed. Angeline's a better actor, and the evidence was stacked against me. My innocence didn't matter."

"Your parents deserve the truth." My conscience pricked me, but I ignored it. This wasn't about me.

"Nothing I say or do will change Dad's mind. He's always been wrapped around Angeline's little finger."

I bumped his shoulder. "Maybe I'll wrap him around mine at the cabin. Change his loyalty."

He scoffed. "As charming as you are, you won't change his mind. It's set like concrete."

He thought I was charming? "Maybe I'll take a sledgehammer with me."

He smiled, and I told my heart to stop reading forever into it. Lincoln had a great smile. It didn't mean he liked me. He had money. Something I lacked. His kind fell for women like his ex who were beautiful, filthy rich, and had boob jobs.

"Thanks for being a good sport about this." He touched my arm, making me tingle all over.

I fisted my hands. He might think I was charming, but he wasn't charmed by me. He'd hardly noticed me last week when I'd been all glammed up. He certainly didn't see me now in my Cinderella rags.

"You're paying me well to be so."

His brow furrowed, and I wished to take my petty words back. The money and car were huge incentives to put up with his charade and the havoc he played on my heart...but I would've helped him even without them.

Call me a fool.

17

LINCOLN

hy was Gemma such a drama queen? Casey had called an hour ago to alert me that she had refused to go with him to the spa to get ready for our big debut tonight. I'd dropped everything to stop by the spa to pick up her gown and accessories, soothe Casey's ego with a tip, bribe the stylist to do an on-site appointment, and task Lionel with dropping by my house to pick up my tux and other necessities and meet me at Gemma's.

Thankfully, Lionel was parked outside her place when my limo arrived. I could always count on him.

I marched with Pico and Lionel toward her door, checking the time on my watch. Wilder would be pissed if we showed up late to our own engagement party. Not that we'd had much say in the matter.

Gemma opened the door and pouted, then smiled when she noticed Pico.

"Ah, *mia cara*," he said, hugging her.

I shoved the garment bag into her arms. "Get changed. Pico will do your hair." I glanced around the bedazzled apartment. "Where can I change?"

She pointed to an open door. "Tina already picked Altin up."

I took the tux and jewelry boxes from Lionel before sending him away. Gemma disappeared into her bedroom. I went into Altin's messy room. Good grief. Did she never pick up?

After dressing, I emerged and let Pico style my hair. Gemma cracked her door and waved for him.

"Can you zip me up?"

I glared at the guy.

He stuck out his hip. "Perks of being gay. I get to touch beautiful men... and women."

I paced across her living area, noticing Gemma's signature touch in the pompoms, fringed curtains, and gaudy artwork on the walls. Bedazzled posters made me smile.

There is no angry way to say bubbles.

When nothing goes right...go left.

Time is precious. Waste it wisely.

Speaking of time, I glanced at my watch and pounded on her door. "Hurry up. We're going to be late."

"Don't rush perfection," Pico said in his high voice.

The door opened, and I gulped. Gemma's beauty had shocked me the first time. She stunned me now.

"I can tell you like," Pico said.

I pulled out a wad of Franklin's to pay him. "Thanks for saving my butt."

"You have a nice one." He walked out the door.

Gemma laughed. "He's right."

We should not be talking about my butt. I opened the jeweler's box.

Gemma gaped at the large solitaire ring inside. "Are you kidding me?"

"This has to appear real."

"So it's fake."

"Absolutely not. This is the real deal." I grabbed the larger box and opened it. "So are these."

"Holy Shih Tzu." She touched the diamond necklace and earrings.

"Turn around."

She did, and I clasped the necklace around her neck. "Put these in." I handed her the earrings. "Quickly. We need to go."

She stepped up to a mirror.

"Why didn't you go with Casey?" She'd shot my afternoon to hell by not sticking to the plan. "You know how important tonight is."

"Casey's an asterisk. He wouldn't listen when I told him I didn't need hours to get ready." She bit her lip as she put in an earring.

"He knows how to make us look our best." I took her arm to lead her outside.

"You mean he understands what will make *you* look best. He's just a jerk to me."

"Well, you're a big girl. Deal with it next time."

The ride to the hotel chilled me. Gemma wasn't happy with me. That made us even.

The limo pulled up to the hotel, and I touched her hand. "Please try to act somewhat happy. If you keep scowling, Wilder will get suspicious." I didn't need a scandal on top of everything else.

"Don't worry. I'll smile and be pretty so you can win your precious investment."

Her snarky answer made me want to kick something. I couldn't say anything right around her. Of course, I cared about the money, but I didn't want her to be miserable to secure it. I'd hoped the new car and debt I'd paid off would've made her happy. Was I that terrible of a fake fiancé?

We walked arm in arm through the clapping crowd of guests Wilder had invited, and she did smile pretty. Gemma had an amazing smile.

Right before we reached the stairs, an urchin dropped a bag of jelly-beans. Everyone focused on him but I wasn't fooled. I spotted his *mom* on the other side of the rotunda, siphoning a wallet from a distracted patron.

"Stop that woman!" I pointed at the thief. "The kid's a distraction."

Hotel security quickly pinned the woman against a wall, stolen wallet in hand. I congratulated myself for thwarting her crime spree. But I'd lost Gemma in the melee. I caught sight of her on the other side of the rotunda. She'd worked her way up to the gypsy thief and was talking to her.

Cameras turned her direction. Damn! I hated the press. Had Wilder invited them, or had they smelled my blood with the looming court case?

I jogged over to intercept her.

"Is this necklace mine?" she asked, touching her neck.

Why would she ask that in front of all these reporters? Did she consider me a scrooge? "Of course."

She unclasped the expensive piece and handed it to the woman.

"What are you doing?" I said.

The gypsy slipped from the distracted guard's grip and took off. He gave chase, but it was hopeless.

I pulled Gemma's hand up to my arm, gritting my teeth. "Do you have any idea how much that cost?"

"Way too much probably, like most things you buy."

I pasted on a smile for the cameras. "You can't let people like that take advantage of you. They prey on kindness."

"If I gave it to her, she didn't prey on me. It was my choice, not the poor woman's."

"Poor woman." I scoffed as we entered the lobby. "She manipulated you." Gemma's soft-hearted do-gooding had ruined everything.

She narrowed her eyes. "I am never manipulated. She needed help."

"She was a professional con-artist. A thief."

"Maybe she has hungry children to feed."

"Or maybe she's a no-good gypsy."

She yanked her arm away from me. "Maybe you're a no-good rich snob. I need to use the restroom."

I kneaded my head as she marched away. The night was off to a fantastic start.

SAEMIRA

Age 13 – Fushë Krujë, Albania

DILEMMA: an undesirable choice with no good options.

⸙

*M*arble-sized pebbles filled Saemira's pockets. The first one she'd found near her bag at school, marked with an E, had meant Engjell was back after having been absent all week. The next pebble led into an alley. She retrieved it and jumped when her friend stepped out from behind a garbage container.

"What happened to you?" she asked. Bruises covered his entire face.

"Got in a fight with some kids." He stared at the ground.

"Liar. Your uncle beat you, didn't he?" When he said nothing, she stomped her foot. "You wouldn't steal for him, so he beat you." She'd worried that might happen.

"You talk too much."

"I hate him!" Saemira spat on the ground as Engjell had taught her.

He cracked a smile. "Uncle doesn't like you much either. Says you're a bad influence on me for teaching me the cursed language."

"English isn't cursed. Why does your uncle speak it if he thinks it's bad? He should be named Bengalo, not you."

Engjell kicked a can. "Westerners are evil. Your baba isn't because he left America. Uncle left Canada to return to his roots, and thank the gods he did, or I would've died as a baby."

That was the only good thing his uncle had done. "Westerners aren't evil. He's evil for beating you?"

"The gods cursed me, Gem." He touched his face. "You can't deny that. It's my turn to take care of Uncle, to repay my debt to him."

"But stealing?"

"How else?" He tapped his chest. "I'm Roma. A scarred and ugly one, at that. No one will hire me. Someday, when I have a fancy degree from your baba, maybe I'll get lucky. But right now, I must earn my keep."

"Let's tell Baba." He'd know what to do.

"No." He grabbed her arm. "He'd confront Duke and make things worse. Duke doesn't like outside interference."

She touched his bruised face softly, but he still winced. "I don't care what you say, I wish your uncle would burn in hell."

He chewed his puffy lip. "You don't understand how it is for us. You have your American baba to protect you. If it was just you and your mama, you'd see. You wouldn't have enough to eat. Duke's teaching me how to survive." He took the pebble from her hand. "You won't tell your baba, will you?"

She sighed. "No. But I don't want you to steal."

"You want me to get beaten?" He gestured to his face.

"No! Of course not. Maybe I can give you money and valuables from my house to give to Duke."

"I'm not taking from your family."

"You won't be. I'll give them to you."

He caressed her face, like how Mama did at night. "You've given me the world, Gem. I won't take any more."

Gemma

I DRIED my hands on an embroidered towel sitting in a basket, thinking about the confrontation with Lincoln and the poor woman outside. The woman who'd reminded me of Mama. Lincoln's fury had shocked me. He'd hated her for the color of her skin. Would he hate me, too, if he discovered who I really was?

"Gemma," someone whispered from the adjacent room.

I flinched, realizing I wasn't alone.

"In here." My friend gestured from a powder room.

"What are doing in here?" I joined him. "What if someone sees you?"

Angel closed the door. "A friend's watching outside. We have a minute."

I hugged him. It'd been ages since I'd seen him.

"My Gem." He caressed my back.

I pulled away. "I'm not your Gem. I'm engaged." I knew that news would crush him. Poor Angel had loved me for years.

He scowled. "Why are you pretending to be someone you're not?"

"You're one to talk, *Johnny Dicaprio*. We're both pretending, or have you forgotten?"

He touched my cheek. "Come with me, Gem. I can take care of you now."

I pushed his hand down. "Have you left Duke?" His head dropped, and I wilted. "Why do you let that no-good man run you?"

The muscles on his scarred arm flexed. "I'll leave him if you run away with me."

"I can't—"

He put a hand over my mouth. "The *gadjo* doesn't even know your real name. He doesn't love you, Saemira. Guys like him love money, that's all. I know the real you. I love you."

"That isn't enough."

His pained expression almost tempted me to admit the engagement was a farce, but Lincoln had warned me not to let anyone in on our deception. And as much as I cared for Angel, I didn't trust him not to tell his uncle. And that man must never know.

"Please, Gem." He tugged me closer.

I whipped my arm out of his grip. "You made your choice. I made mine." A lump formed in my throat. "I need to return to my fiancé." I hurried out and realized too late that I hadn't asked how he had found me. Was he stalking me? Was Duke? I shivered.

Lincoln stood near the ballroom entrance, Wilder beside him. The older gentleman greeted me with a smile as I linked arms with the man I presently despised.

We entered the ballroom, where Mr. Wilder introduced us to tons of important people. I forgot their names almost as fast as he said them. All I could think about was how I'd hurt my friend.

We ate a fancy meal I had no appetite for and made superficial small talk with people I had nothing in common with. Engjell was right. I didn't belong in this world.

For the finale, Mr. Wilder invited us onto the stage, where Lincoln fake-proposed to me again. I cupped my mouth and acted surprised as he slipped the gaudy rock he'd shown me earlier onto my finger. The crowd clapped below us as Lincoln pulled me close, his lips brushing my ear.

"Relax. This is just for the cameras." He cradled my face, and I couldn't breathe. Heavens. He better not let go in case I fainted. "Close your eyes and tip your head," he whispered.

Cameras flashed as I obeyed.

"Put your hands on my chest."

I did, and his lips grazed mine as they moved across my cheek and to my ear. His hand dropped from my cheek as he began to whisper the alphabet.

"A, B, C, D..." His other hand slipped behind my neck. "E, F G, H..."

His ticklish breath on my neck made my body react as if I'd gulped a can of carbonated fizz. It bubbled, popped, and zinged.

"...X, Y, Z." He kissed my cheek.

The audience cheered as Lincoln moved me down to the dance floor and wrapped his arms around me. I snuggled closer. Though we were acting, the moment on stage had seemed real. Being in his arms reinforced the false moment. I wanted to touch his face, squeeze the muscles under his tux, taste his lips.

I shook the stupid desires away. This was my boss. He was only playing nice to get Wilder's money. Still, I wouldn't mind a repeat of the ABCs in my ear, or a slow replay of his lips grazing mine.

His hand held mine, grip tender yet strong. His other hand moved up and down my back as we danced, and the bubbling fizz exploded throughout my body, making me full-on shiver. His thumb rubbed back and forth, and I thought I might melt into the dance floor.

He was just bored, hand moving by instinct, not actual desire. But I didn't want him to stop. I wanted his hands on me for eternity, though that was wicked. I should lift my head and make a glib remark. Tell him he was a jerk for how he'd judged the lady outside. But I kept pretending his thumb caressed me because it wanted to. I pretended our engagement was real and he adored me...though he had no idea who I really was.

"Eat your cereal," I said to Altin. Lincoln would be here any minute to pick us up. He'd insisted that since we were officially engaged, we needed to be seen together now. Picking me up for work and dropping off Altin at daycare would reinforce the false image of a loving couple.

I grabbed my mug of coffee but dropped it as I spotted a blue envelope on the floor beneath the mail slot in the door. The mug shattered.

"Mama oops!" Altin said.

Ignoring ceramic shards and coffee, I picked up the envelope and pulled out a typed letter. I staggered over to the nearest chair and started reading.

Engaged to the CEO. Nice work, Temptress. I always believed you would be of use to me someday. I'll expect three times our normal agreed upon amount within the next 24 hours.

OR you can choose an easier path, one that requires only an hour or two of your time, once a month. Be the respectable CEO's wife by day, and once a month, play the little whore for an hour. Be who you really are.

Make your choice—the hard road, where you never get ahead, or the easy path, which requires so little and allows you to care for your brother better. It'll also keep your fiancé from getting suspicious of where his money's going. Imagine the scandal if he discovered your criminal record. Foster care's hell for defective kids like your brother. Choose the easy path, Temptress. Choose freedom.
– D

Bile stung my throat as demons I'd thought I had banished screamed in my head: *You're evil! A whore!*

My fingers shook. This wouldn't be Duke's last demand. And the easier route wouldn't bring freedom.

Knocking made me jump to my feet and take several deep breaths.

"Mama oops?" Altin said again.

"Time to go." I picked him up and opened the door. "Here." I handed him to my boss. "Get him in his car seat. I have a spill to clean."

He left me to my task, and I soaked up coffee with several paper towels then hid the letter in a drawer next to the fridge, with the others. Tears pricked at my eyes, but I blinked them away. Somehow, I had to get cash by tomorrow. And make an escape plan.

Duke had found me.

I was no longer safe.

I situated myself next to Altin in the back of Lincoln's fancy SUV and began to play with the window controls. Up. Down. Up. Down. No sense in me being the only person to have a cruddy morning.

"You can't annoy me today," Lincoln said from the driver's seat. "I'm too happy. Read this." He tossed a paper back, folded to the second page. "They loved us. Said we were the fairy tale couple. Casey's getting a raise."

"Pig face didn't get me ready."

"Pig face," Altin repeated.

"He picked out the gown—which was gorgeous, by the way—and referred me to Pico. He's turned you into the new town darling."

"Oh, please." I was no one's darling.

"Did you have any idea we met one of the head reporters for the Tribune last night? That Gary fellow. And you wowed him. Whatever you said—or maybe it was your lowcut gown—he loved you."

"Pig face," I muttered. The man would never see me as lovable. And he shouldn't. Because with Duke on the prowl, I had to disappear. "Why do you hate gypsies?" I asked.

"I don't hate any group of people."

"Drop the PC act. You called that woman at the hotel a thieving gypsy."

"Well, thanks to you, she did steal twenty grand worth of diamonds."

"What?" I squeaked. He'd told me they were real, but my ignorance of the worth of diamonds now made me hyperventilate.

"You heard me. Thanks for being so generous with my money."

"I didn't know."

"You saw her steal that wallet while the child caused a distraction. Why would you give someone like that your necklace?"

I wouldn't have if I'd known its true value, though I wouldn't admit that. "People in desperate circumstances need the boldest of help. But you didn't answer my question. Why do you hate gypsies?"

"They're low-life criminals, all of them. Cops said they've been causing problems in the area for years." He focused on the road. "But forget them. We need to discuss your relationship with my publicist."

I grimaced. "I have no relationship with Pig-face."

"Casey can be blunt, but he's good at what he does. I've talked to him, and he's willing to forgive your stubbornness."

I folded my arms. "How noble of him."

"Now, please do the same with him, because you two are going shopping to prepare for the weekend with Wilder."

"What!" I made the window go up and down again. "There's nothing wrong with how I dress." I loved the wardrobe I'd put together over the years from various thrift shops.

"You must dress to impress, which means no pompoms or other dangling distractions."

"I think Mr. Wilder would appreciate my dangling distractions." He seemed to accept me for who I was.

"He won't."

Rude.

19

LINCOLN

*S*ilence prickled between Gemma and I as we took the elevator up to our floor. She was upset about having to go shopping with Casey, but it was necessary. We walked off together, heading past the sales cubicles.

Joe walked out of his office and whistled. "If it isn't our secret celebrity couple. When were you going to tell your best friend about your engagement?" He elbowed me. "Janey read about it in the paper."

Nosy press. "We only made things official Saturday night." I nudged Gemma to keep walking.

"Oh, no you don't." Joe blocked us. "You're not getting off that easy. You owe us a kiss for not telling us first, isn't that right, team?"

Gemma's eyes widened, but she covered her dismay with a tight smile as employees drifted out of cubicles.

"Kiss, kiss, kiss." Joe chanted. Others joined in, until dozens of employees chanted the words.

Joe was so dead.

Not wanting to raise red flags, I pulled Gemma close, hoping she wouldn't slap me. She didn't. It was like kissing a log.

Until it wasn't.

Something changed. Who knew what? She melted into me, wrapping her arms around me and pushing her fingers through my hair.

Whoa. I tightened my grip on her. I hadn't been with a woman since my divorce, and this felt incredible. A tiny voice told me to stop. This was Gemma. I'd promised to keep things professional between us. Yet, I liked her minty taste and couldn't get enough of her soft skin and pliable lips. Our audience's contagious enthusiasm added kindling to the fire between us.

When I did pull away, I averted my gaze from Gemma's red face and heaving chest. Joe patted my back as the others cheered.

I pulled Gemma into her office and scrambled to switch the glass to privacy mode. "I'm going to kill Joe."

She sat behind her desk and touched her lips.

I squeezed my eyes shut. "I apologize." What had I been thinking? "That won't happen again." The kiss had been necessary, but I'd gone far beyond what had been required to appease Joe.

Her eyelashes fluttered as if she were coming out of a trance. "Sorry I froze. I, uh..."

"Didn't see that coming?" *Welcome to the club.* I entered my office and stalked over to the punching bag. I didn't even pull on gloves before hitting the bag, pretending it was Joe's taunting face. How could I spend a whole weekend with Gemma? Wilder and my family would expect PDA, and jerk that I was, I wanted more lip action as well.

Punch-punch-punch.

"Lincoln?"

I whipped around to find Gemma standing in my office. I stepped away from the bag and took a deep breath. "I'm sorry," I said again. A broken record.

"Me, too. I should've put my hands around you faster."

"To strangle me?"

She smiled. "I just stood there like a zombie."

I walked over to my desk. "Trust me, you were no zombie." She was way too hot-blooded. "I won't touch you again." I picked up a folder. "If Joe gets bossy, I'll tell him to go to hell."

"Won't that seem suspicious?" She chewed her distracting lips. "How will we pull off that we're engaged if we never touch? Or kiss?"

She was right, but I wouldn't ask that of her. No more kissing, even if that's all I wanted to do.

"We'll discuss this later." I pointed to her office, dismissing her.

We had work to do.

SAEMIRA

Age 13 – Fushë Krujë, Albania

DESIRE: hoping for something, like attention from the opposite sex.

Saemira's heart beat faster than hummingbird wings when she spotted Esad waiting for her outside the school grounds.

"There you are," he said.

Her mouth turned to cotton as he took her hand. Esad was almost sixteen. The most popular boy at school. She couldn't believe he'd been paying her attention the last few days.

Not even a week ago, she'd been one of the girls he'd ignored. He'd liked the older girls with curves, like Ajola and Marsela. Baba had called him a bad apple when they were younger. But right now, with her hand in his, he appeared to be the most delicious apple in the orchard.

"I think you are the prettiest girl at school."

She smiled. "You're the most handsome boy in Fushë Krujë."

He wrapped an arm around her. "I bet you're the best kisser, too."

She shivered. A few weeks ago, she'd caught Marsela locking lips with him behind some bushes during lunch break. She definitely didn't know how to kiss like that.

"Will you teach me?"

His hand moved under her sweater, making her bare skin sizzle. "I'll teach you more than kissing."

What else was there to know?

She spied Engjell crouching behind a bush and turned toward Esad to keep him from seeing him.

"I'm a fast learner." Baba always said so.

"I like fast women." His fingers moved up her back, making her shiver again.

She imagined Marsela's pretty face when Esad told her he liked Saemira more than her. They would grow up and marry and he'd give her babies and love her as Baba loved Mama.

They reached the corner, and she hoped Engjell had left. Why did he insist on walking her from school to Baba's school each afternoon? They only fought and argued. He'd become so bossy.

Esad led her into the cemetery, where a few early-blooming wildflowers popped out among the gravestones. She'd have to return with her magnifying glass to study them.

He pushed her up against the mausoleum wall, making her gasp.

What was he doing?

His tongue shoved through her closed lips, activating her gagging reflex. Did Baba kiss Mama this way when their door was closed?

She winced as her head scraped against stone. Esad began tugging her skirt up her legs.

"Esad, no!" She tried to push his hands down, but he crushed her against the wall.

"You said you were a fast learner. Prove it. Put out for me."

She didn't know what that meant but didn't want to do it. He shoved his tongue deeper down her throat. She choked and tried again to push him off her.

"Stop fighting, whore!" He slapped her, making her yelp "You want this."

"No!" Whores made men do bad things with their bodies. She didn't want to be like that. "Stop. Please."

Esad shoved her to the ground. "You said you were a fast learner. Now learn!"

Someone jerked him back by the hair. "Don't touch her, you bastard!"

She scrambled to her feet and wiped her stinging cheek.

Engell stepped in front of her.

"What are you going to do, gypsy-monster?" Esad spat at his face.

Engjell punched him in the neck, making Esad fall. "Come on." He took her hand and pulled her after him.

They ran out of the cemetery and didn't stop until they reached the bottom of the hill, where she leaned over to pant.

"That boy is bad. Very bad." Engjell kicked up a dust cloud.

"Thank you." She swiped at a stray tear. "For saving me." She still couldn't believe what Esad had done.

He reached up to touch her tender cheek. "Are you okay? Did he hurt you?"

She blinked quickly and took a few deep breaths. "I'm okay." Now that she was far from Esad.

"Let's get you home to your mama." He took her hand. "We'll tell her dogs attacked and you fell down and hit your face."

Sweet Engjell. He was like Baba, wanting to take care of her. Only he was ugly and Baba was handsome. But she loved his ugliness. Deformed, burned boys didn't want to kiss girls and be bad with them. Engjell was safe. A true friend. Her protector.

She vowed to be a better friend to him from now on.

Gemma

HAD I honestly told Lincoln we needed to touch and kiss to pull off this ruse? My cheeks burned as I tried to concentrate on my work. I hadn't meant to imply that, even if it was all I could think about. Heavens! The man had imploded my worldview. Before kissing him, I'd never imagined I could enjoy the act. But I'd savored every magical second in his arms. I wanted to kiss him again, to test my hypothesis of whether the kiss could be topped? My prediction was it couldn't. But I'd love to be proved wrong.

Yet my suggestion that we have more physical contact had made Lincoln shut down and shut me out.

A short knock on the door made me look up as the sexy man I'd been stressing over entered my office. I wanted to hide under my desk, but I pulled my shoulders back and held my head high.

"I have an idea," my boss said. "Again, I'm sorry about what happened earlier. It won't happen again."

Ugh. "I get it, okay. I'm a terrible kisser. No need to keep apologizing. I haven't had a lot of experience, okay?" He didn't need to keep bringing it up.

He stared at me as if I'd lost my mind. Maybe I had. The man made me all sorts of crazy.

"You think you're a terrible kisser?"

"Of course I am. I saw the disgust on your face."

He blinked. "I wasn't disgusted." The infuriating man cleared his throat. "I keep apologizing because I promised this would be nothing more than a professional sleight of hand, and yet it's becoming messier by the minute."

"So, I wasn't a terrible kisser?" My whole body burned, but I had to know. Stupid competitive streak.

"Not that it matters since I'm your boss and you're my employee and we will never kiss again, but no, you, uh, were quite pleasing."

I smiled. "You were pleasing as well." Very much. "That's the only kiss I've ever liked. The others have been..." I stuck a finger down my throat.

He pursed his lips, which I now knew were tender, tasty, and wonderful. "You are the oddest woman I've ever met."

Ah. He would deflect with insults. "And you're the most boring man alive." He wasn't, but I had to say something.

"Perfect. Now, shall we get back to the reason I came in here?"

I waved my hand. "Please." And then leave.

"I've come up with some strategies to hint at intimacy without truly intimating."

I laughed. "You made up that word."

His eyes narrowed. "No, I'm certain *intimating* is a word."

I pulled my phone out to check. "Hmm. You're right, but I don't think you used it correctly."

He rolled his eyes. "Fine, I have three tactics to hint at intimacy without breaking the professional code between us."

"Much better." I refused to reveal how much his analytical scalpel cut me. "Enlighten me, o intimater."

He counted off on his fingers. "First, proximity. Last night at the engagement party, we appeared to the audience to be having an intimate moment, but my lips never touched you."

Not true. His lips had grazed mine. They'd also touched my cheek. And they'd definitely nuzzled my ear. Maybe he hadn't noticed, but I'd never forget how he'd set my lips, cheek, and ear on fire.

"Proximity gave the impression of blissful connection. We appeared to be having an intimate moment, but all I did was whisper the ABCs in your ear."

Which had been the sexiest thing ever. Goosebumps erupted on my arms just thinking about it.

"Is it too cold in here for you?"

Ugh. Dumb man. He was the only thing that was cold. "I'm fine. Proximity is genius."

"Why do I get the impression you're taunting me?"

I batted my eyelashes, making him growl.

"Two, whispering. When I whispered in your ear, it gave the illusion of sharing secrets. Even a fart joke whispered between us would give the illusion of passion."

"Check." I made a giant mark in the air. "I'll study up on fart jokes."

He shook his head. "Last, smiling and laughing, to give the impression we're smitten with each other. Couples think everything the other says is brilliant, when it's not." He raised an eyebrow. "Basically, don't scowl at me."

"But you're so scowl-worthy."

He laughed, making my heart ache. Why did everything this man do have to affect me?

"Got it. We could also share codes to our phones. That definitely hints at intimacy, like drinking from the same coffee mug."

"Absolutely not. My phone is off limits. So is my mug."

"You can have my code. 1 1 1 0."

He raised an eyebrow. "Please tell me you're joking. That's the worst code ever."

"Right? I wanted all ones, but the phone wouldn't allow it."

"No code sharing. I've already forgotten yours," he said with a smile. "Let's practice."

"Code sharing?" I wanted him to leave so I could hide my face in a funder file.

"No. The strategies. I don't want to get trapped in another compromising situation like this morning." He walked around my desk and leaned over me. Cool, minty breath made goosebumps prickle all over my neck and arms again. "We get close, like this." He dropped his voice, making me shiver. "We can combine tactics like whispering and proximity to strengthen the illusion."

I gulped to moisten my parched throat. "Okay."

"The breathy voice is a nice touch."

Ugh. Stupid jerk. "I don't see how this will help if Joe asks us to kiss again."

Shouldn't we practice kissing more?

THE CORNER BISTRO always unsettled me. I sat in a patio chair and closed my eyes. Lincoln and I would head to Park City soon, where I'd meet his parents. I'd already dropped Altin off at Miss Tina's.

Looking both ways to ensure I was alone, I pulled the envelope of cash out of my satchel and slipped it beneath the napkin dispenser, a ritual I'd performed every month for the past two years.

My mind rewound to that day I'd received my first paycheck from EcoCore. I'd been so thrilled because it'd matched what I'd made waitressing and cleaning offices and would put me about eight hundred dollars ahead since I wouldn't have to pay a sitter overtime any longer. I'd walked to my car, thinking of what I could buy to celebrate my luck. When I'd gone to shut my door, something had stopped it.

"Hello, Temptress."

I shuddered even now, thinking about the nightmare that'd started when I'd looked up to find Duke.

"You've had a run of luck, no?" He'd pointed to the check in my hands. *"Seems you should pay back the benefactor who set you up for success. It'd be a shame if I had to call in an anonymous tip about your kidnapped brother. Foster care can be awful for vulnerable kids like him."*

He'd demanded six hundred bucks for my silence, and when I'd told him I didn't have that kind of money, he'd shrugged.

"Not my problem. If you can't come up with cash, there are other ways to pay me." He'd put his hand on my leg and had inched upward, leaving no doubt as to what he'd meant.

I'd slapped his hand away. *"When hell freezes over."*

He'd dropped a card on my lap. *"That can be arranged. Leave the cash in an envelope at this address by the end of the week, under any napkin dispenser on the patio tables. I expect great things from you in the future, Temptress."*

The only great thing I'd done was make him rich. But Duke's last letter had proven what I'd believed all along—that he would never be satisfied until he owned me.

I must leave. But I needed money, and all my extra cash kept going to Duke. I stared up at the sky, pleading with God to show me a path.

Should I tell Lincoln the truth?

Could he help me?

My phone buzzed with a text from him, saying he was on his way. I sent him my coordinates so he wouldn't have to go all the way back home, then hurried inside the bistro to use a restroom. Anxiety had my stomach in a mess.

I locked myself in a dingy stall and took several deep breaths.

Lincoln couldn't know. He didn't like gypsies. If I told him who I really was, he might turn against me. I'd rather keep paying Duke than have that happen.

I washed my hands and headed down the hall when a sensation of being watched made me shiver. I ran to the exit and didn't stop until I reached the end of the block.

Baba had said to listen to my inner voice—my best defense against evil. I hadn't done that as a young girl and had paid a heavy price. But I listened now. And my inner voice said to get the hell out of there.

21

LINCOLN

*T*he drive up the canyon was quiet. The tense kind. Gemma didn't even play with the window controls. Was she still upset that I'd forced her to go shopping for new clothes with Casey yesterday? Or was it something else? She'd hardly said two words to me at work that morning, and she'd taken off without even a goodbye to take Altin to Miss Tina's. She'd been pacing up the block from the address she'd texted me when I'd found her.

What was up? Was she going through withdrawals? I'd have to keep a sharp eye on her this weekend.

The GPS announced we'd arrived at our destination. I pulled into a long driveway and parked. Wilder and my parents emerged from the cabin to greet us. I took my time pulling luggage out of the trunk, hoping Gemma wouldn't ruin everything.

"Oh, aren't you a doll." My mom pulled her into a hug. "I'm so sorry we missed your engagement party. We didn't get back from our cruise until this week."

"It's fine," Gemma said.

"Welcome." Wilder pulled her into another tight embrace.

"Wow," Gemma said. "You said a cabin. I expected a log hut in the woods, not this gorgeous mansion."

It was a dumb thing to say, but Gemma could do no wrong in Wilder's eyes, thank goodness. He laughed and ushered her into his home. I rolled my eyes and pulled suitcases behind me.

Buckle up.

A massive elk head and other animal trophies decorated the walls. Wilder had been an international hunter in his younger days. He introduced us to his wife, and Mom pulled us over to the couches.

"Tell us how you both met. You've been a naughty boy, avoiding your family for so long."

"Better he avoids us than beats us up," Dad muttered.

Luckily, Wilder was in the kitchen, showing Gramps his wine selection. "The charges were dropped," I said between clenched teeth.

"Only because you bought Angeline off with that massive divorce settlement."

This was why I avoided my family.

Gemma fidgeted next to me as Dad eyed her.

"How did you convince this young woman to ignore your past and link her fate to yours?"

"Lincoln's a good man," Gemma said, scowling at my father.

Gramps joined us, wrapping an arm around me. "How are you, my boy?"

I gave him a weak smile. "Great." Not.

Wilder gestured to us. "Lincoln and Gemma, why don't you tell us the details of your love story. I know I'm not the only one dying to hear how you met and fell in love."

I put an arm around Gemma, hoping she'd follow my lead. "There's not much to tell. Gemma worked for me in sales. Her stats drew my attention."

She giggled and ran a finger through my hair. "Only my stats, sweetie?"

My body responded to her touch like a hormonal teenage boy.

"Nothing else?" She smiled for our audience. "Like how I accessorize?"

What?

"I believe it was my Princess Leia ensemble that stole his heart. He hasn't stopped chasing me since I wore it."

I raised an eyebrow as she gave a dramatic sigh.

"A workplace romance, heaven forbid, where I fell for my boss." She turned to our audience. "He shocked me out of my shoes when he proposed over a Zoom meeting. It's one of those moments I'll never forget." She giggled and cuddled into me.

I pulled her against my body, liking it way more than I should.

Conversations started around us. I half-heartedly listened, focusing more on Gemma's flowery scent and the way she melded so perfectly into me.

"Gemma dear," Mom said, pulling Gemma away, "tell me more about yourself."

Gramps tugged me over to the large windows overlooking a pine-covered hill. "I read about that new laser technology for sensor detection," he said. "Pretty cool stuff."

I smiled, surprised that he'd kept informed about my company since I had avoided him the past couple years. Maybe Dad hadn't poisoned him against me.

"It's fascinating stuff." I went into more detail, and Gramps ate it all up. I'd definitely inherited my inquisitive nature and mind for mechanics from him.

Wilder uncorked a bottle of champagne and began pouring. I froze mid-sentence when Gemma accepted a glass from him.

What was she doing?

"I'll be right back." I left Gramps to run over and whip the glass out of Gemma's hands. Champagne spilled onto the wood floor, drawing everyone's attention.

"What's your problem?" Gemma sputtered and gave me a look that could kill.

"You should abstain from alcohol," I said under my breath.

"Absolutely not." She reached for the half-empty glass. "I need all the liquid confidence I can get."

I turned my body to block her. "One drink matters."

"What?"

I pulled her into the corner, keeping my voice low. "Didn't your son teach you anything?"

"What does Altin have to do with me drinking champagne?"

"You obviously have a drinking problem since you drank while you were pregnant."

She gaped at me as if I'd taken the last cookie before she had to go on a diet. She turned to Wilder. "Will you excuse Lincoln and I for a moment? He just informed me that he left my toothbrush at home."

Mrs. Wilder fluttered into action. "Oh, don't worry, dear. We have plenty of supplies here. I'll find you a new one."

"That's kind of you, but I was attached to my electric toothbrush and need to just...scream at my fiancé for a second. You don't have neighbors close enough to hear me, do you?" She charmed them again with her dazzling smile and preposterous words.

"Keep him on his toes." Wilder said with a chuckle. "Yell away, my dear."

Gemma dragged me outside and shut the door. "You think I'm an alcoholic?" She threw her hands in the air. "Of course, you do. Why am I surprised?"

"Don't play coy. You told the childcare director that Altin had FAS. He's disabled because you didn't stop drinking."

She screamed with her mouth closed. "You are so damned infuriating."

"Because I speak the truth?"

"No!" She stomped her foot. "Because you think you're so damned smart. But newsflash, Einstein! I'm not an alcoholic."

"But Altin."

"Is my brother, you fool! Not my son."

"But you said—"

She huffed. "That's just it. I never said a thing. You assumed he was my son because you always think the worst of me."

"But he calls you Mommy."

"Because he's a little boy who never knew his real mom. He calls Miss Tina Mommy, too. Will you accuse her of being an alcoholic also?"

I nudged a pinecone off the porch. "Why did you let me assume he was your son?"

She rolled her eyes. "Why have you let your parents assume you're capable of beating your ex?" She walked inside, slamming the door in my face.

I scratched my head. Whenever I thought I was getting close to figuring out my unconventional, quirky executive, she tossed me an open can of Coke and sprayed me with surprise.

Gemma wasn't a single mother.

She wasn't an alcoholic, either.

And she definitely wasn't happy with me.

Gramps tugged me outside as Mom and Mrs. Wilder cornered Gemma to talk about girl stuff. I'd feared she'd ruined everything when she'd marched outside, saying she needed to scream at me. What couple does that?

Yet Wilder and my family had taken her drama in stride. My parents already thought I was scum, so her words hadn't surprised them. They likely thought I deserved her wrath. And I did.

Why had I assumed the worst about her? Gemma had impressed me from day one when she'd marched into my office to seek the apology I'd owed her. Her confidence and charm. Her grace, even in her outlandish outfit. The fire in her eyes. Why had I looked for reasons to discount her?

I rubbed my aching head. Gemma's mom was the alcoholic. That's why she was taking care of her brother. Dammit. What kind of life had she lived?

Gramps looked out at the mountains. "Your girl's a mite upset at you."

"Yes, she is."

"You sure it's the toothbrush she's upset about? Or are there underlying issues in your relationship that need smoothing out?"

Oh, there were major issues in our relationship. "It was a very special toothbrush."

"Women are always particular about something."

"Was Gammie particular about anything?"

He smiled. "Shoes. They had to match her outfit. And she wouldn't abide secrets. Made me tell her everything about my first wife, your dad's mother."

I turned to gape at him. Had I heard him right? "Gammie's not my grandma?"

"Oh, she's your grandma, but not by blood." His brow furrowed. "I should've told you this long ago. Maybe it would've helped you understand your dad." He sighed. "The sins of the fathers visited upon the children."

I didn't speak. I couldn't. He'd just shattered my worldview.

"My first wife, Mary, abandoned me when your dad was three. After she left, I neglected Will. Oh, I fed him, sheltered him, but I wasn't there emotionally for him. He reminded me too much of his mother. I couldn't bear to look at him. Because of that, he was a lonely, sad little boy."

"I never knew," I said.

"Hazel always nagged me to tell you. But things were complicated between your father and I. Will didn't like the reminder of his mom any more than I did. We never talked of her. I see now I was wrong. Will never confronted his demons of being rejected. We should've grieved together instead of pretending the pain wasn't there. He was almost eight when Hazel rescued us both by marrying me. I didn't deserve her, but I thank God every day for sending her to me. Hazel couldn't have loved Will more than if she'd birthed him. And you and Cora were her greatest treasures when you came along. Gammie loved you beyond measure."

"I never doubted her love. Or yours."

"But you've doubted your dad's?"

I shrugged. "He's never loved me."

Gramps's eyes glistened in the golden light of the setting sun. "Oh, he loves you. He just has a hard time showing it. Being abandoned as a kid messed him up. Then he lost Cora. He's been cold and cruel since her death, a shield for his pain, I think. But I know he loves you. He wouldn't be here if he didn't. He's too proud and stubborn to be anywhere he doesn't wish to be."

"He loved Angeline." She'd wrapped him around her finger almost from the first.

Gramps put a hand on my shoulder. "You and Will are like me. Stubborn, driven, and prone to pity parties." I scowled, but Gramps just chuckled. "Like that."

I shook my head. He was right, even if I wished he wasn't.

"The only force more powerful than our negativity is a strong woman's grace and goodness. Your Gammie was that force for me. Your mom has tried to be that for your dad, but he hasn't let her. You can break his cycle of misery by doing whatever is necessary to keep Gemma happy." He winked. "Might be worth returning to the city to get her silly toothbrush."

"Getting the toothbrush won't solve anything." I didn't know what to do for her bruised ego.

Gramps squeezed my shoulder. "Well, before I mosey back inside, I will say this: a good woman makes all the difference. Angeline was a mistake. So was my first wife. But from first impressions, Gemma seems good to the core, like Gammie."

"She is one of a kind," I agreed. Unique, in the best of ways.

"Then sweet talk your way back into her good graces. And do it before she sleeps. A woman's wrath multiplies during the night."

"Good to know."

"What in the Helen Keller!" Gemma paced beside the bed as I shut our bedroom door.

I'd hoped to put aside our differences and talk things out. What I hadn't counted on was the one bed in the guest room. Or, more specifically, her reaction to it.

"Did you know about this?" she asked.

"I never thought about the sleeping arrangements."

She ran a hand across her face. "I thought I'd have my own room."

"Chill. I'll sleep on the couch." No way could we ask for separate rooms.

"But," she gestured to the bathroom, "there are no doors. It looks straight into the shower. A glass shower! And not SmartGlass. Nothing in this bathroom is smart. Even the toilet doesn't have a door for privacy." She shut her eyes. "Who wants to hear someone else pee?"

I laughed.

She huffed. "What's the point of having all this money if you don't put doors on the parts of your house where you need them most?" Her lips jutted out in a pout. "Do you have doors on your bathrooms?"

"I'm a huge proponent of doors."

She massaged her head. "Sorry. But sleeping with my boss is not what I signed up for."

I scoffed. "We're not sleeping together. I'll be on the couch."

"But in the same room."

"Gemma." I put my arms out to stop her pacing. When she glared at me, I let go. Touching her, even platonically, seemed unwise. "I said I'll sleep on the couch."

She frowned. "This is so awkward."

"Understatement."

She sighed. "Okay, fine. But we sleep in our clothes."

"Absolutely not. I sleep in the buff."

Her eyes widened, and I laughed.

"I'm kidding."

"Not funny." She climbed onto the bed.

I sank onto the couch and propped a foot onto the ottoman.

"Helen Keller," she muttered. "How did we get into this mess?"

"Why don't you use real swear words? Is it because of religion, like Joe?"

She snorted. "Ha. I can outswear you any day. My dad's second wife taught me a whole arsenal of words that'd make a soldier blush. But I've observed that a high percentage of the population here doesn't cuss. So I curbed my tongue to keep from offending anyone."

Huh. She was a better person than me. I enjoyed shocking members of Joe's church.

"What other swear-substitutions have you come up with?" Maybe if I kept her talking, she'd stop freaking out.

"Oh heavens. There's a ton. I use *freaking*, but have started using *Buckin'*, *Chuckin'* or *Luck* to be more original. It's only one letter off. For *dammit*, there's *rammit*. Or beaver dam. That doesn't seem too offensive."

I chuckled. Even she cracked a smile.

"Let's think of some new ones to use on my beaver dam mom and bucking dad."

She grinned. "How about your dad's a *basset turd*?"

"Not bad, but I can do better. Dad's a *mother ducker*."

She giggled. "He made me mad as *hail* when he said those awful things about you."

"That's just how he is." I stood and stripped off my shirt.

Gemma gasped. *"Dog gammit!"* She jumped to her feet, keeping her back to me. "What are you doing?"

"You don't expect me to sleep with a shirt, do you?"

"Yes! I don't want to know whether my boss has abs or not."

"All guys have abs." I kicked my shirt into the corner.

"Uh, no. All guys do not have abs like you." She ran into the bathroom and let out a slew of watered-down language. "Freaking son of a biscuit. Why in the *Helen Keller* would a mega-billionaire not pay for *bucking* doors?"

"Just use the facilities," I called. "I'll put in my headphones and listen to a book." She'd be gone a while if she was anything like my ex. Angeline had taken almost an hour to get through her nightly rituals.

But Gemma surprised me by returning a few minutes later.

I stood to take my turn in the bathroom. "You still pissed at me for assuming you were an alcoholic?"

She shrugged. "What do you think?"

"I'm truly sorry."

She wrinkled her cute nose. "Then I guess I'm sorry I told your mom and Mrs. Wilder you were a poo-poo head."

I snickered and headed into the door-less bathroom.

22

SAEMIRA

Age 13 – Fushë Krujë, Albania

ADORE: to love someone intensely.

*M*ama cuddled Saemira close as Engjell stretched out by the fan. They'd raced home after the encounter with Esad, out of breath and upset. Mama had brought them inside and made them hot tea. When she'd asked what had happened, Engjell had told her the stray dog story since he was a better liar than she was.

"Have I told you the story of the winged hero?" Mama asked.

"No." Saemira snuggled closer.

"There was an Albanian craftsman who took to drinking and gambling and lost all his money. He dreamed he should make wings. When he finished and screwed them into his shoulders, he flew to the emperor's castle.

"The emperor's son bought the wings for a thousand gold pieces. The prince attached the wings to his shoulders and flew far away, discovering a palace where a princess lived. Her father, a Roma king, had imprisoned her in a glass room at the top of a tower, not wanting her to ever leave him for a *gadjo*.

"The prince flew up to the glass cage to see the princess, and they fell in love. He returned to her each night, bringing gifts and telling her of the world outside the palace.

"The king discovered someone had been visiting his daughter, so he left

113

dough in her room. When the prince came next, the dough stuck to his shoes. Guards were sent out to check everyone's shoes. They found dried dough on the prince's shoes and bound him and brought him before the king.

"'I have been with your daughter,' he answered. 'I wish to marry her.' The king raged that a *gadjo* had dared infiltrate his kingdom to see his precious daughter. He sentenced them both to die by fire and thorns."

"Thorns?" Saemira said.

"Hush, Gem." Engjell threw a piece of corn at her.

"Yes." Mama caressed her hair. "The king's servants gathered every thorn in the kingdom. The Roma king planned to lower his daughter and the prince onto that fire and burn them, to keep his daughter pure."

"That's horrible," Saemira said.

"Yes. But the prince had hidden his wings under his cloak. He told his princess to creep close and hold onto his neck when he fell to his knees to say a last prayer. She did, and he opened his wings and flew into the sky before the flames could burn them. They flew to the emperor's kingdom, where they ruled with kindness and wisdom. And they lived..."

"Happily ever after," Engjell and Saemira said together.

Baba sat behind Mama, taking her hand. "That's a much better ending than the original story."

"What's the real ending?" Saemira asked.

"I know," Engjell said. "An auntie told me when I was younger. The prince and princess have a baby, and the princess's father comes and carries her high up a mountain to take her back to his kingdom. The prince's wings catch fire, and he can't fly up to save her. As he struggles to climb the mountain, a beggar comes along and fights him for the baby. They cut the kid in half so they each get a part."

Saemira punched his arm. "Gross. Are you sure your uncle didn't tell that story?"

Baba tousled Engjell's hair. "Better head home, son."

Saemira walked her friend to the door. "I'll have nightmares tonight, thanks to you. Mama's ending was much better than yours."

"Mamas make everything better." He frowned, and she knew he probably wished he'd grown up with a mama.

"Thanks for not telling my parents about what happened earlier," she whispered.

"Of course. It'll be our secret."

"I wish you could stay and not return to your uncle. Be my brother."

He touched her face, running a finger up her cheek and over her ear like Mama always did. "I don't want to be your brother, Gem."

"Why not? I'd be a good sister." Did he think her evil since she'd kissed Esad?

He laughed and stepped away. "Goodnight, Gem."

She frowned. "Goodnight, Engjell."

Gemma

Being smothered with affection by women felt weird. A good weird. Since Mama had died, I hadn't had much female companionship and I'd forgotten how much I craved it.

Mr. Wilder had taken the men golfing, so Mrs. Wilder and Mrs. McConnell, or Lucy, as she kept asking me to call her, decided to take me shopping. "To spend all their money," Lucy had said.

I wouldn't be spending a cent of Lincoln's money, though he'd pulled me aside before he'd left to slip me his credit card.

"Buy whatever catches your eye," he'd whispered, before pressing a kiss to my lips, a short, fiery one that'd shocked the Helen Keller out of me.

I still wondered why he'd done that. We hadn't had an audience.

"What about this one, dear?" Lucy handed me another dress.

The price tag made me choke, but I draped it over the other outfits in my arms.

"Lincoln will adore you in it." She squeezed my arm.

"I have a fitting room for you," Mrs. Wilder said. Ethel, I reminded myself, like ethyl alcohol.

I slipped into the dressing room and hung the clothes on a hook. They were expensive and beautiful, but none were me. Still, I tried them on to placate Lucy.

That's how we spent the next couple of hours—me trying on clothes my older companions thought Lincoln would adore and me not liking any of them. Another reminder why my one-sided feelings for him were doomed. The outfits weren't my style. They were for fancy, spoiled princesses like his ex. Not for poor Cinderellas without a caring fairy godmother to transform them.

Even if I did have a fairy godmother—which I kind of did at the moment, with Lucy and Ethel hovering over me—did I want to change to catch a man's eye?

I undressed, knowing the answer didn't matter. Even if I did want him, he'd never want me. And besides, I had to disappear.

We left another shop without buying anything. I felt bad for disappointing Lucy and Ethel but didn't want to owe Lincoln more than I already did.

"Let's try that shop over there." Lucy pointed across the street.

That *shop over there* screamed my name when I entered. *Saemira! We've been waiting for you.*

"Oh, my goldfish." I held my heart. "This is my store." The trendy Bohemian boutique was to die for.

It didn't take long to fill my arms with clothes. When I walked out of the dressing room, I held my head high, proudly displaying a beaded dress I'd fallen in love with. Lincoln had said I could buy whatever caught my eye. Well, this dress had grabbed and held on for dear life. Lincoln would never love me, but he'd buy me this dress. When we parted ways, I'd keep this token to remember him by.

"Wow," Ethel gushed. "You're right. It's perfect. You'll have to wear it for our farewell dinner Sunday night."

"My son won't be able to take his eyes off you," Lucy said. "Not that he can take his eyes off you already."

Her words weren't true. Lincoln had never seen me, and I wouldn't hold my breath that he'd notice me in this dress. But I was me again.

Take that, you shirking fairy godmother!

Lucy interlinked arms with me. "I can't tell you how happy I am that my son found you." She squeezed my arm. "I've wanted a new daughter for so long. Angeline, bless her heart, never liked me." Sorrow shadowed her eyes. "But that's in the past."

It was none of my business, but I had to ask. "You don't believe what that woman said about Lincoln, do you?"

She winced. "I never wanted to. He's my boy." She looked down at the ground. "But I saw Angeline. She came to ask my husband for help. The poor girl had a broken arm and bruises everywhere." She sniffled.

"He didn't do that."

"Then who did?"

"Who knows? But your son's innocent." The Lincoln I'd come to know was moody, but he would never lay a hand on a woman.

"Why hasn't he ever said something? He just disappeared after the divorce, wouldn't answer my calls, wouldn't come over. I went to his office, but his assistant said he was too busy to see me."

I frowned. "Men are idiots. But maybe this weekend will open doors between you two."

"Oh, I hope so." Lucy said. "I've missed him so much. I should've known he would never harm her. He's always been such a good boy."

"I assumed the worst about him, too, when I first read those headlines.

But as I've worked with him, I've come to know Lincoln could never have done what that skank claimed."

Lucy scowled. "I never liked that greedy, money-grubbing floozy."

I rested my hand on her shaky one. "Please don't tell Lincoln we talked about him. I just wanted you to know you raised a good man."

Lucy smiled. "You really are perfect for him, dear. I know you're not married yet, but I consider you my daughter already. You said you lost your mom. Could you maybe think of me as your adopted mom?"

A lump formed in my throat. "I'd love that." I'd missed belonging to someone and them belonging to me. "Can I call you Mom?"

She dabbed at her eyes. "That'd be wonderful, dear."

23

LINCOLN

---

*G*rrr. My shot went long. Dad scoffed and made another jab at my form before heading to the golf cart.

"I'll see you at the green." Wilder jumped in with him.

I shoved my nine iron back into my bag.

Gramps slapped my shoulder. "You're whooped, boy. Thinking about your girl instead of your game."

My lousy shots were due to the fact that I hadn't golfed in months. They had nothing to do with thinking about kissing Gemma before I'd left. Nothing to do with comparing her to my ex and finding her leagues above Angeline. Nothing to do with wanting this game to end, so I could see her again.

"Your Gemma's a sweetheart." Gramps frowned. "Sure wish you were getting married sooner so I could be there for the happy day."

"You'll be there." No way would I avoid him any longer.

"I don't think so. Doc found a brain tumor last week."

I waited for him to say, "Got ya!" He couldn't be serious. But there wasn't a trace of humor in his wrinkly face.

"It's terminal. He gave me two to four months."

A crater seemed to open up inside me. Gramps was in tip-top shape. Super-active. Always watching his diet. But the look on his face revealed he'd spoken the truth.

"Oh, Gramps." I hugged him. "I'm sorry." Why had I wasted the last two years running from my pain instead of turning to him?

He squeezed me. "Don't pity me, son. I'm ready to go. I've missed my

Hazel more than I can say." He pulled away and blinked. "My only regret is missing your wedding. But at least I got to meet your future bride, thanks to Alex. That's something."

That crater inside me caved in some more. "Does he know?"

He nodded. "But I haven't told your parents yet. I plan to tell your dad soon. I wanted you to know first."

We climbed into the cart and drove over to the green to join the others. Everyone took their turns putting, acting as if they hadn't a care in the world. But my world had fallen out from under me. Gramps had been the steadying influence in my life for as long as I could remember. When Dad had moved us to Utah, he'd followed. He'd come to all my baseball games and my debates that Dad had missed. He'd cheered me on through college and had encouraged me through the lean days of getting my company off the ground. He'd always believed in me, even when I hadn't believed in myself.

So why now, just when I was getting to a place where I could be close to him again, did he have to get cancer? I needed him. I'd need him big time when all this pretending with Gemma blew up in my face.

And it would.

I was in deep water. Not by my own choice. I hadn't meant to fall for my employee. But somewhere, I don't know how or when, my admiration had turned to affection. I dreaded the day we would break up and go our separate ways because I knew it would hurt. Bad.

WILDER AND GRAMPS ran into an old acquaintance and stayed outside the clubhouse as Dad and I glared at each other from opposite couches in the lobby.

"Gemma's an interesting character," he said.

"What's that supposed to mean?" My muscles flexed.

"She's a damn Latina, probably only after your money."

"Like Angeline?"

He scowled. "You're not ready to jump into marriage again. Your first one ended in disaster."

My hands clenched. "You know nothing about my relationship with Angeline."

"I know that poor girl deserved better. You shamed the family name by treating her so abominably."

To hell with his family honor. The hypocrite.

"Gemma's been pissed with you from the moment you arrived. That's not how normal relationships work."

"And you would know?" How many times had I found mom crying in the guest room as a teen? How many times had Dad left us for weeks, Mom not knowing where his selfish ass had gone, not knowing who he was with? He'd been a neglectful husband. An absent father. I didn't care what Gramps said about his issues, I hated him.

"If she doesn't toe the line, will you beat her, too?"

"I don't need this." I headed to the bar. Maybe a stiff drink would help. Maybe several.

I nursed a Scotch, mind spinning through the past, recalling when Joe had bailed me out of jail, how he'd let me hang out on his couch for a week before I'd gathered courage to drive across town to see my parents. The look on Dad's face when he'd opened the door had obliterated all hope I'd had of refuge or a listening ear.

"How dare you show your face here," he'd snarled. "Leave. And don't contact us again. If you call or try to see your mom, I'll call the cops and make sure to finish what Angeline didn't. I'll protect her from you."

I drowned the memory with more Scotch.

Wilder sidled up to me at the bar. "Lincoln."

I startled, my staring contest with my glass broken. "Hey, Alex. Can I buy you a drink?" I glanced behind us to see if Dad and Gramps would be joining us.

"I'll have a beer." Wilder frowned. "Your grandpa took your dad outside to talk." He sighed as the bartender set a beer in front of him. "He's going to tell him the news."

I tapped my glass. "Sucks, doesn't it?"

Wilder threw back a swig. "Sure does. Always thought I'd go long before Ed. He's always seemed invincible to me."

No kidding. I still couldn't wrap my head around the fact that Gramps could be gone in a couple months.

"He told me he wishes he could see you married."

That crater inside swallowed more of me. "I wish he had more time. I'd give him some of mine if I could."

Wilder threw back another gulp. "That's the thing. We do have more time. He's not dead yet. Ed's a good friend. I don't want him to have any regrets. Or you. I could put together a top-notch wedding in under a month. Give him his wish to see you and Gemma married."

I chugged down the rest of my Scotch.

"To sweeten the deal, I'll release the funding from my foundation to EcoCore as a wedding gift. One hundred million dollars."

"You..." I held up my empty glass to catch the bartender's attention. This was everything—and way more—that I'd worked so hard to secure. His money would save my company.

"You just need to move up the wedding date."

Hopes crashed into rocks of reality. No way could I ask Gemma to marry me. Pretending to be engaged had been bad enough.

"I...don't know what to say." *Where was my damn Scotch?*

"I hope you'll say yes."

"I..." The bartender set another drink in front of me. I lifted it with shaky hands. "Gemma might not be on board." Of course, she wouldn't be on board. "You know how girls are with weddings." Especially ones they'd never wanted in the first place. "She's planned this for years."

"She'll have her dream wedding. And your grandpa will be part of your happiness."

I gulped down more Scotch.

He slapped my shoulder. "Think on it. And don't worry about Gemma. She's too sweet to deny your grandpa's last wish."

Maybe. But I was a callous jerk who would have no problem doing so. Since it couldn't happen.

24

SAEMIRA

Age 13 – Fushë Krujë, Albania

PREJUDICE: an irrational attitude of hostility toward an individual/group that dehumanizes both victims and perpetrators.

❖

The sound of laughter made Saemira sulk on the steps of the schoolhouse. Since Engjell had punched Esad and saved her, Esad had tormented her at school, putting honey on her chair, snipping off a lock of her hair, and turning the other kids against her.

He played a game of stick ball with the other boys at the moment, so she was safe. He was still handsome to look at, but he was bad.

Or she was.

She turned an apple in her fingers, recalling how Engjell had wanted to kill Esad for what he'd done. But she'd welcomed Esad's attention, laughed at his jokes, leaned closer when he'd rubbed her leg during lunch. She'd wanted him to teach her how to kiss. Engjell thought Esad was bad. But Saemira feared she was worse.

A rock hit her. She rubbed her arm and looked up to find Esad and his friends surrounding her.

Dung beetle!

"Gypsy lover." He shoved her to her knees, and her half-eaten apple rolled into the dirt. "Saemira's mama is a *magjup* whore."

"She is not!" She straightened and dusted off her skirt.

"Is too. And you're no better." He grabbed his crotch. "I found Saemira and her gypsy lover naked behind the cemetery mausoleum."

"That's not true," she told her wide-eyed classmates. "I've never—"

Esad pushed her down again just as Mr. Shehu marched outside.

"What is going on here?" Teacher moved his portly frame into the middle of her circling classmates.

Thank the gods. Her hands were scraped, but Esad's accusations stung worse. Mama was Roma but they lived in town, not in the broken village. She wasn't like Engjell—poor, cast off, hated. She went to school and lived in a comfortable house. People didn't yell at her when she walked through the market. Her skin was lighter than even Esad's. She wasn't a gypsy. She was Albanian.

"Thieving gypsy." Esad spat at her feet.

"I didn't steal," she said again.

Esad faced Mr. Shehu. "She watched me put money in my bag this morning. Now it's missing. Check her pack. It's got to be there."

"I didn't steal your money." How could he tell these lies?

Mr. Shehu grabbed Esad and her by an ear and marched them inside. He stopped in the mudroom, where their bags hung. He let go of her stinging ear and pointed.

"Dump your belongings out."

Saemira obeyed, anxious to prove to him and her gawking classmates that she was honest and good. Mr. Shehu knew this. So did her classmates. Esad was the liar.

Everyone gasped when three five-hundred-lek notes fluttered to the ground with her sweater and pencil box.

"You see!" Esad said. "She's a thief like every other gypsy."

"That's not mine. I don't know how it got in there."

"You may return to recess, Esad." Mr. Shehu shooed the other students away. When they were gone, he pinched her ear and marched her into his office.

"I didn't steal." She whimpered. "Esad framed me."

"Silence, *magjup!*" Mr. Shehu pushed her into a chair and shut the door. "We have zero-tolerance for theft in my school. And for gypsies."

Gemma

THE SOUND of water running in the shower made it impossible for me to focus on my video chat with Altin. Lincoln was less than twenty feet away, naked, in a shower I could see into if I moved off the bed. I shouldn't imagine that, yet a naked Lincoln was all I could think about.

"Be good for Miss Tina, buddy," I said, waving at my brother on the screen. "Love you."

"Love you, Mommy."

I winced at that title. Moms provided a foundation of safety, belonging, and love. At least, my mama had for me. Altin's mom had been nuclear waste. I missed my mama and hated that I'd let sweet Lucy believe I could ever be part of her and her son's lives, no matter how much I wanted to be.

Lincoln walked out of the bathroom, bare-chested, only a towel around his neck.

"Put a shirt on, you animal." I concentrated on closing out the Messenger link on my phone, to keep from gawking.

He grabbed a shirt from his suitcase as I rolled off the bed to go brush my teeth.

"You're limping," he said.

"Yeah. My feet were casualties of shopping with your mom and Ethel."

He stood by the bed when I returned, holding a bottle of lotion. "Lay down."

"Excuse me?"

"I'll give you a foot rub."

"Uh, no." As much as I longed for him to touch me, I should resist.

"Come on. I used to give my sister massages when her muscles ached. She called me Super Fingers."

"Super Fingers?" I climbed onto the bed, feeling self-conscious in my tank top and shorts. Though I shouldn't. It wasn't as if he'd noticed me before. But I noticed him, even with a shirt covering his firm abs.

"Relax." He squirted lotion on my leg. "You'll want to run a marathon after I'm done."

"Ha. Run to the bathroom, more like it. You don't have to do this," I said as he propped my foot on his leg. "I just need to walk the stiffness out." But I didn't move. I moaned instead as his magical fingers worked their way up my calf. Holy llama, that felt good. "You do have super fingers. Tell me about your sister. Joe said she had muscular dystrophy."

"Yeah. Cora was the best. So full of life. So funny. So kind. As her disease progressed, her muscles ached more and more. Mom taught me how to give a decent massage to give her some relief."

"She was lucky to have you."

"Not as lucky as I was to have her."

Oh, be still my heart. He needed to stop being so sweet. "Was it hard to see her in pain?"

"Excruciating. I prayed all the time for God to give her pain to me so Cora could live a normal life." He lifted his eyes, and the agony there stole my breath away. "Cora didn't deserve the cruel lot life gave her."

I leaned against the headboard as his hands rubbed the balls of my feet. "My dad believed God lets bad things happen to help us grow and become more like Him."

He grimaced. "I don't believe in God, not after seeing my sister suffer."

I stared at the top of his head. "I get you. Dad believed a lot of hard things, like forgiving your enemies. I found that idea horrifying as a teen."

"And now you don't?" His eyes flashed with emotion.

"Now, I'm conflicted. I believe forgiveness can heal, but it's hard to practice."

He grunted and rubbed my ankle. "Have you forgiven me for roping you into this disaster, or is that too hard to do in real life?"

I smiled. "It's tough, but your foot rub might sway me."

"Good." He lifted my other foot and started to massage it. "Gramps dropped a bomb on me today," he said.

"Oh?" My words came out breathy. Embarrassingly so. I could hardly think from how good he made me feel.

"He has a brain tumor. Has two to four months left to live."

"Oh, Lincoln." I pulled my foot away and sat up, feeling guilty for my naughty thoughts. "I'm sorry."

"I'm okay." He pushed me gently back onto the pillow and brought my foot into his lap again. "He just wishes he could be at our wedding."

Ugh. I hated how our lies were affecting not only us, but his family now.

"Wilder wants to grant his last wish by throwing us a wedding in a few weeks." He scoffed. "Said he'll release funding for EcoCore as a wedding gift. A hundred million."

I started choking. "That's quite the gift."

"Yeah."

"I hate lying to them."

"Me, too. But what choice do we have?" He set the lotion aside. "How does that feel?"

"Amazing. Thank you."

"It's the least I can do for forcing you into this mess."

"You didn't force me." He lifted a brow, and I laughed. "It wasn't forcing so much as surprising me."

"Sorry."

"Don't be." I took his hand. "It's been kind of fun."

Again he lifted his brow. "Fun?"

"Interesting?"

"It has been interesting."

Our gazes locked, and the light-hearted moment became heavy and charged in a heartbeat. Or a thunderous round of heartbeats in my case. Maybe he moved. Or I did. Maybe both of us inched closer until we sat quite close on the bed, his lips hovering above mine. Our breaths mingled, his fresh and minty. Did I kiss him or did he kiss me? Who knows? But we kissed each other as I'd dreamed of doing non-stop since I'd experienced nirvana with him in the office, the moment he hadn't stopped apologizing for.

Crap! What if he apologized again? I should pull away, but I deepened the kiss instead, my body having a mind of its own. My feet had tingled from his tender massage. Now, my whole body tingled and burned as I lost sense of time and reality, my mind silencing the doubt that this would only lead to heartbreak. I shivered as he explored my neck and worked his way down my bare shoulders. Holy heaven above. This was much more intense and pleasurable than the first time.

How had I lived before kissing Lincoln?

He pulled back, and I cringed, waiting for him to regret kissing me. But he buried his head in my neck.

"I've wanted to hold and kiss you like that since the night of our engagement party when I whispered the ABCs in your ear."

My heart beat faster. "You have?"

He pressed kisses along my cheek. "Gemma, you're not just interesting, you're beyond tempting." He kissed me slower, with more purpose.

I caressed his five o'clock shadow. "What if we give Gramps what he wants?" I winced when his eyebrows shot up. "I mean, we could technically get married. For him. And for Mr. Wilder's money. That's what you want, right?" When he didn't speak, I added words I hated. "It'd just be business, like our engagement." I scooted away, chiding myself for reading more into his kiss. He'd said I tempted him, but probably like chocolate tempted a dieter, or beer tempted an alcoholic. Not in a good way. "We'll annul it once your grandpa dies." I covered my mouth. "Gosh! I'm sorry. That was insensitive. I hope he lives for years."

"He won't."

We stared at each other, and I couldn't guess whether he hated my guts or wanted to kiss me again. Both, maybe. His kisses hadn't meant anything. They'd just been a guy's reaction to a warm-blooded female in the same room.

"Would you truly go so far as to marry me?"

I squirmed beneath his gaze. "I like Gramps."

"He likes you, too." He walked over to the couch, putting distance between us. "This could work. We marry, give Gramps his wish, secure Wilder's money, and everyone's happy."

Except me, but I kept my mouth shut. Caring for and kissing Lincoln McConnell had to be the stupidest thing I'd ever gone and done.

"This could work."

"You already said that. The marriage would be in name only, right? No big deal."

"Yeah." He chewed those luscious lips I yearned to taste again. "Sorry for kissing you. I won't do it again." He watched me carefully. "Unless you want me to."

Was that a trick question? Of course, I wanted him to. But I wouldn't throw my self-respect at his feet again. He obviously didn't know what he wanted. And I refused to be a passing fling.

"I'm willing to marry you and annul our vows later," I said. "On one condition."

His eyes narrowed. "What's that?"

"You come clean about what happened with your ex."

Air whooshed slowly from his lungs, sinking my hopes. He wouldn't tell me. Why had I thought he would?

"The rumors going around the office are that you hide a dark side," I said. "They believe you beat your ex and killed your unborn child."

"Do you believe that?" He sounded angry.

"At first, I did. You gave her almost everything in the divorce. The news articles said you must've paid her well to buy her silence. But now, I know you're a good man. Grumpy at times, but you'd never hurt a woman."

He closed his eyes. "I did hurt her."

I gulped. What?

He sighed. "It was summer of 2020. I left the office late and got caught in a protest downtown that turned violent. Before I could back up and get away, my rear window got busted out by some crazies. I was stressed, not thinking straight by the time I made it home and found Angeline drunk out of her mind."

He stared at the floor, and horrible scenes filled my mind of him pounding on his wife as she screamed for mercy.

He continued. "I didn't mean to be an asshole. I was just so pissed that our child might be damaged from the alcohol she'd consumed. We hadn't gotten along for a while, so our arguing wasn't anything new. But when she said the baby wasn't mine. I..." He leaned over his knees. "I slapped her. Hard enough to leave a handprint on her face."

"So you did beat her?"

"No!" he cried, shaking his head. "I mean, I slapped her. But then I left for the nearest bar to cool off. I was furious at her but angrier at myself for losing control. There was no excuse for hitting her, even if she had betrayed me. After two drinks, I headed home to apologize. There were cops and an ambulance there. I freaked, worried that she'd hurt herself. She came out, bleeding and screaming for the police to keep me away from her. Two cops pushed me against my car and frisked me. I asked who had hurt her, but they told me I had the right to remain silent."

"She lied?"

His jaw clenched. "Lying was second nature to her. For our whole marriage, she accused me of everything you can imagine—not caring for her, lying, cheating, stealing, sabotaging EcoCore to keep her from profiting from it. I was so wrapped up in her constant drama that I couldn't see straight. Even as I was taken to jail, I doubted my innocence. She was a convincing gaslighter. I didn't think I'd done more than slap her, but her last words haunted me: 'He killed my baby!'"

"Oh, no."

He grimaced. "I spent that night and the next day in jail, wondering if our baby had made it, wondering if I'd battered my wife as she'd accused. I couldn't call my dad. I knew he'd take her side. I was too ashamed to call Gramps. I used my one phone call to ask Joe to bail me out. He held me together as Angeline continued to play with my mind to get everything in the divorce settlement."

"Why did you give her everything?"

"She threatened to press charges. Joe was furious at me for capitulating. It made me look guilty as hell and almost ruined EcoCore. But I just wanted her out of my life."

He stared off at nothing. "Joe and I worked our butts off to save EcoCore. The SmartGlass I'd postponed due to COVID took off last year. That's why Angeline's coming after me now. She received eight million in the divorce settlement, almost all my liquid assets. But SmartGlass put EcoCore's net worth at over eighty million, and stocks keep rising. That's why she's claiming it was her brainchild."

"What a ditch."

He pursed his lips. "Joe warned me she was no good. I wish I'd listened."

"It's easy to see what you want in the moment. But why haven't you been honest with your family? They deserve the truth."

"I just want to forget that period of my life and move on. Deep down, I feel I deserve what happened. I did slap my wife." His hands fisted. "I might not have beat her, but I wanted to. I wanted to punish her for cheating on me. I wanted to punish her for hurting our baby. That's why I ran away after I hit her."

His story made me sad. "You screwed up, but you're still a good man."

He stood and walked to the bathroom. "I don't feel like one anymore," he said so softly I almost didn't hear.

25

LINCOLN

*G*emma sighed in her sleep. I'd been awake for a while, watching her and waiting for her to do it again. Was she having erotic dreams, like me? I couldn't stop reliving that kiss last night. Although, I should. It'd been a bit of fun between us, that's all. A stress reliever we'd both needed. Gemma didn't like me that way. She kept making that clear by emphasizing how our marriage would be business only.

A knock made me bolt up on the couch.

"Lincoln, honey. Gemma. I have breakfast. Are you decent?"

"Just a sec, Mom." I kicked my blanket and pillow under the bed as Gemma sat up and rubbed her eyes. "Sorry," I whispered, climbing under the covers beside her. "Mom's always had a thing for breakfast in bed. You okay if I put my arm around you?"

She rolled her eyes as I draped an arm over her shoulders. "Come in, Lucy," she called, leaning into my bare chest.

Mom walked in with a tray. She'd probably been up for hours, baking, frying, and blending.

"You should sleep in, Mom. Enjoy your vacation." And not bother us.

"I want to spoil you while I can." She walked to Gemma's side. "Hopefully, when you're married, you can get this guy to visit his mom."

Only if Dad wasn't around.

Gemma leaned in more, and I couldn't breathe. I doubted she was conscious of what she was doing, but I was hyper-aware of every one of her curves, especially the ones releasing gentle friction against my upper body.

"I'll do my best, Mom."

I whipped my head around to see if Gemma had meant to call her that. She smiled at Mom, who seemed ready to cry with happiness.

"This all looks delicious," Gemma said. "Thanks for cooking for us." She picked up a fork and dug into her eggs.

Mom appeared pleased, so I dug in as well, though I hungered for other things, like Gemma's hot body. I was experiencing dry mouth, rapid heart-beat, and sizzling loin action by the time Mom bustled out of the room.

When the door clicked shut and we were alone, I shoved the tray onto Gemma's lap and jumped out of bed, keeping my back to her so she wouldn't see what she'd done to me.

"Sorry about that. Mom has the worst timing ever." I scurried into the bathroom, cursing the lack of doors. I hoped Gemma's sense of modesty kept her from peeking because I needed an icy shower. ASAP.

26

SAEMIRA

Age 14 – Fushë Krujë, Albania

PRETENSE: make-believe, professed rather than real intention.

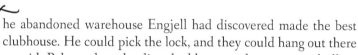

The abandoned warehouse Engjell had discovered made the best clubhouse. He could pick the lock, and they could hang out there after lessons with Baba and not be disturbed by stray dogs or street bullies. After being kicked out of Mr. Shehu's school, Saemira had become Baba's student, same as Engjell. She'd thought often of Esad's betrayal and had a new theory for what had happened as a child. Duke must've planted the amulet in her pocket all those years ago, just as Esad had planted his money in her backpack. Both were wicked to their cores.

"I have a surprise for you." Engjell handed her a gift, snapping her out of her head.

"What is it?" She tore the newsprint off the box.

"A late birthday present."

"Wow." She held a strand of green gems up to the light filtering through a broken window.

"Emeralds. Like your eyes. Not real ones. I can't afford those. But they're—"

"Beautiful." She turned her back to him. "Help me put it on."

His fingers clasped the chain as she studied the glittering jewels. "You didn't steal it, did you?"

132

"No. I did chores for your baba. That's why it's late. I didn't have all the money on your birthday."

"This is so nice. Thank you."

He chewed his puffy lips. "Did you hear that Sindi's been promised to Betim? They'll marry next year when Sindi turns fourteen and Betim is sixteen."

"Wow." She'd played with Sindi a few times.

"I'm as old as Betim. You're Sindi's age. That means we could marry now."

What? She took a step back from him. He'd teased about being her true love, but she hadn't thought he was serious. "You've never even kissed me. You can't know you want to marry me."

"I want to kiss you." His dancing eyes betrayed nerves as he closed the distance between them.

She shook her head. "You don't want to kiss me. I'm a whore."

"What?"

She touched the pretty necklace. "I make boys do bad things. Like Esad. I only meant to kiss him, but he wanted more. And at first, I did, too." She hung her head. "I'm not a good girl."

"Did you willingly spread your legs for Esad?"

"What?"

He rolled his eyes. "You don't even know what whores do."

"They do naughty things with men, with their bodies."

"What kind of naughty things?"

She shrugged. "Kissing. Touching."

He laughed. "You know nothing."

She put hands on her hips. "I do, too." Engjell always thought he knew more than her.

His face distorted with laughter. "Do you want to know what whores do?"

She nodded, and Engjell pulled her close and began whispering the specifics of whoredom.

"No," she gasped. "They really do that? For money? Why?"

"Men like it."

"Your mom?" She grimaced. "Did she do those things?"

"I guess."

She shuddered.

"You see? You aren't a whore."

"But I asked Esad to teach me how to kiss."

He laughed. "Men don't pay whores to kiss them. They pay for the other stuff, between their legs."

"Ew." That sounded nasty.

"I can teach you how to kiss since Esad failed."

"How do *you* know how?" She couldn't imagine girls lining up to kiss her scarred friend.

"TV."

"Oh." She didn't have one of those. Baba wanted her to learn with books.

"Let me kiss you."

She shuddered. Kissing Esad had been nasty. But Engjell was her friend. Maybe kissing him would be better.

"Okay. What do I do?"

"Close your eyes. I'll do the rest."

That sounded easy. She shut her eyes. "Ready." Maybe he'd hate it, too.

Engjell held her face and covered her mouth with his. She shuddered when he parted her closed lips with his slimy tongue, as Esad had. His breath reeked of garlic.

He pulled back. "The people in movies put their hands all over each other."

Maybe that would distract her from the rest.

She shut her eyes and let him kiss her again, wondering why people liked this. She gasped when his hands moved over the front of her blouse. She opened her eyes to find him smiling. He didn't pull his hands away.

"Move your tongue around in my mouth. Touch me, too."

She shivered. "Where?"

"Anywhere."

She closed her eyes again, wondering if she was abnormal. Most girls liked kissing. That's all they'd talked about at Mr. Shehu's school. Engjell moved his hands into her hair and pulled her hands around to his buttocks.

"Squeeze me."

She did, and he seemed to like it. She stepped back, hoping that'd been long enough.

"We need to get home." Kissing was gross.

Engjell took her hand and they crept out the back door. He relocked the building before walking her home. They didn't speak. Usually, she talked nonstop but kissing had changed things between them.

At her house, Engjell tugged her through the gate and into the backyard.

"Can I kiss you goodnight?"

She shrugged, wishing she didn't have to.

He pulled her close. She clenched her eyes and opened her mouth for him. His hands dropped to her buttocks, and the place between her legs reacted like fire as he rubbed against her.

"Saemira!"

She jerked away from Engjell as Baba spoke behind them.

"Engjell! What are you doing?"

Her friend's face turned red but he straightened his shoulders and met Baba's gaze. "I want to marry Saemira."

Baba grabbed her hand and pulled her to his side. "You will do no such thing. You will not even speak of it." The hardness in his voice shocked her. Baba liked Engjell. "Marrying at such a young age is foolish."

"But Sindi and Betim are promised to each other. They're younger than us."

"That's a terrible tradition which needs to change." Baba pointed. "Don't kiss or touch my daughter again. Promise me, Engjell."

Engjell frowned. "But Mr. Nikolla—"

"Promise me, or I'll forbid you from hanging around her."

Engjell looked sad when he turned to her.

"Make the promise," she said. "I don't want to marry you. You're like my brother."

His shoulders slumped. "Fine. I promise."

Baba still looked upset. "Saemira will not marry for many years. She'll get a higher education before she considers settling down and having babies. You should set your sights on an education as well. You have a bright mind. When you're grown and have a job, you can consider taking a wife. When you're a man, not a boy."

Engjell nodded.

"Go home," Baba said. "I'm not happy with you."

"Sorry, Mr. Nikolla."

"Show you're sorry by treating my daughter with respect. Don't take advantage of her innocence again."

Engjell left. Baba tugged Saemira to the bench by the back wall. "Come, *bijë*. It's time I told you a story."

Whew. She'd worried he might send her to bed without supper, but he must not be too upset if he wanted to tell her a story.

He wrapped an arm around her. "This story is your mama's. Did you know she was a child bride before I met her?"

"Really?"

"It's not something she likes to talk about. Her people promised her to a boy named Bajram at your age. He was sixteen. Mama was with child before her fifteenth birthday. She lost the child and four more babies. Each time she failed to carry a pregnancy, her husband beat her."

"He hit her?"

"He was a scared boy without a job. He had no idea how to care for a wife."

She clenched her hands. "I hate him."

"Hate does no good, *bijé*. Bajram wasn't bad. He was young. He'd never learned how to be a man. It didn't help that tensions were running high between ethnic Albanians and Serbs in Kosovo. Being Roma, they were despised by both sides. One night, they were driven out of their home by a mob of Serbs. Bajram was shot, trying to protect Mama from bad men."

"He tried to protect her?"

"In his own way, he loved Mama. How could he not? The men hurt your mama and left her for dead. When she regained consciousness, she fled across the border with other refugees."

"Poor Mama." She laid her head against his chest.

He caressed her hair. "I'd come here a few months earlier with the Red Cross to help the Roma and other refugees. That's how I met Mama. She carried water from the river, and I mistook her for an angel."

Saemira smiled. Mama had told her this part of their story.

He cupped her chin. "I'd never wish your mama's sufferings on any girl. Especially you, my precious daughter." He caressed her cheek. "What Engjell did today was wrong. He should not have kissed or touched you that way."

"I didn't like kissing him. It was gross." She frowned. "Is something wrong with me? I didn't like when Esad kissed me either."

Baba growled. "There's nothing wrong with you. Kissing is gross when done with the wrong person for the wrong reasons. But it's wondrous when done with someone you truly love."

"I didn't want to hurt Engjell's feelings."

"What about your own? Shouldn't Engjell have worried about your feelings, not just his?"

"But everyone bullies him."

"So, you let him bully you into a kiss?"

She frowned.

He squeezed her shoulders. "Your heart is yours to give to one special person. Don't pretend to love someone, even a friend. That's wrong. A lie."

Gemma

136

THE MORNING'S mortification curdled in my stomach as I sat at the breakfast nook. What in *dreqin* was wrong with me? Why had I thought Lincoln would welcome my advances after he'd rejected me soundly the night before? I'd practically thrown myself at him in bed this morning, curling into his bare chest when he'd climbed in next to me. He'd been utterly handsome, with his hair mussed from sleeping, the shadow of scruff on his jaw. But he hadn't hopped into bed because he'd wanted me. It'd been an act. For his mom.

"May I join you?"

I put a hand on my heart as Lincoln's sweet grandpa appeared. "Please do. Can I get you some coffee?" I needed more.

"That'd be wonderful, dear. I like mine black."

"Because you're already sweet."

He grinned. "My grandson's a lucky man."

I set a mug in front of him. "I keep telling him that, but I don't think he believes me."

"He does." Lincoln made me jump as he pulled up a stool beside me. "Hey, honey." He kissed my cheek and whispered near my ear. "I'm going to tell him we're moving up the date. You good with that?"

I nodded and let him take my hand.

"How'd you sleep, Gramps?"

"Not well, but that's not anyone's fault but my own. The book I'm reading is riveting."

Lincoln grabbed my coffee and took a sip.

I glared at him. "Do you need your own?"

"No. I'll share yours." He nuzzled my nose, bringing me up short. "Do you want to tell Gramps the good news, or should I, sweetheart?"

"Why don't you." My heart beat too hard to think of words to say.

"What good news?" Gramps asked.

"Gemma and I are moving up our wedding date."

His grandpa's eyes shimmered. "For real?"

I hugged the adorable man. It might kill me to marry Lincoln just to end it later, but I'd do it to give Gramps peace. I'd do it to secure Wilder's money for Lincoln.

"We want you to be there with us."

He swiped at his eyes. "That's wonderful, sweetheart." He put his hand on mine. "Are you sure though? I don't want you to change your plans just for me."

Lincoln put his hand on ours, making my heart race triple speed. "We're sure. I can't wait to tie the knot with this amazing woman."

If only his words were true.

His words weren't true because all Lincoln wanted to do was change me. You'd think he would give me the choice of wedding colors or flowers. Shoot, I would've been content just to pick out my freaking wedding gown. I had one on Pinterest that was gorgeous. And not too expensive. But Lincoln had taken even that decision away, telling me that condescending Casey would handle everything.

We chilled in our bedroom before dinner. Lincoln's publicist had sent me five dress choices, and I'd resorted to playing eenie-meenie-miney-mo to decide which I hated least.

"You should marry Casey, not me." I shoved my phone in a pocket.

"Just play along." Lincoln winked, making my insides do the tingly-squirmy dance. "Casey's doing us a huge favor getting everything ready last minute. Besides, it's not like a dress really matters."

That was easy for him to say. He'd look all debonair in his tux while I'd resemble Betsy the plow horse, pulling my long train behind me down the aisle. But he was right. I shouldn't care about my wedding since the groom didn't love me.

Lincoln sat on the edge of the bed. "You'll look beautiful in anything." He took my hand, tugging me toward him.

I lowered my gaze, feeling bashful at his words. Feeling guilty that I wanted to throw myself into his arms and kiss him until I ran out of air. Never had I believed I would like kissing, but I despised the space between us.

But I must resist.

"Stop thinking about the wedding." He squeezed my shoulder, sending swarms of butterflies throughout my body. "Tell me about your family. Is Altin's mom your mom?"

I longed to tell him the truth, but I couldn't let him charm me into giving up my secrets.

None of this was real.

"No, thank the gods. Altin's mom didn't care for anyone but herself."

"Where's your dad?"

"Dead."

He blinked. "I'm sorry. How long have you been on your own?"

"A couple of years. No big deal." Lies, lies, lies. He needed to stop getting personal. And I needed to pull away from him. But having his arm around me was heaven.

"Where did you live before you came here? You have a slight accent."

Crap, dung, and doo-doo. He was too observant? I pulled away to put necessary distance between us. No one had mentioned my accent before. Baba had worked hard to ensure I sounded American.

"I lived in the hood in Chicago for a while," I said, walking over to the closet to rummage through the awful clothes Casey had made me buy for this weekend. "The ghetto creeps out at times."

"You sound anything but ghetto. Where's your family originally from?"

"Chicago." Best to keep lies simple so I didn't get tangled up in them.

"No, I mean your roots?"

I froze, knowing he was trying to figure out my brown skin. I wasn't super dark like Engjell, but I wasn't European white either. Lincoln wasn't dumb. He knew I was an outsider. He was just trying to figure out how outside I was.

"My dad's people are Scottish," he said. "My mom's great-grandparents came from Norway."

Of course he would have a perfect Aryan bloodline.

He returned to my side and took my hand.

"Uh," I stammered, "my dad's from Canada. Mom's Indian." Close enough.

He ran his fingers through my hair. "It's a stunning mix."

Whew. He'd swallowed my lie. "So is the Scottish-Nordic mix."

He smiled, and my heart was lost when he leaned forward and pressed a sweet kiss to my lips. "I'd like to keep learning more about you, but we're going to be late for dinner."

Thank the gods for meal times. More questioning might make me lose my lunch. Or my secrets.

27

LINCOLN

*M*y head throbbed from a few too many drinks. That's what came of staying up after the women had gone to bed to play poker with the guys. I crept into the room, not wanting to wake Gemma. But the lights were on and I spotted her pacing out on the balcony. I smiled. Maybe I could learn more about her now. Or kiss her. I'd wanted to kiss her earlier, but had resisted. She wasn't attracted to me. But in my inebriated state, I didn't care.

I joined her on the balcony. "What's wrong?" I wrapped my arms around her, pulling her close since the mountain air was chilly. I wasn't quite drunk but was buzzed enough to be turned on by her fruity scent.

"Casey just texted that the dress I chose won't be ready in time. He's ordered that chucking Cinderella dress."

"You'll look stunning in it." I nibbled her earlobe.

"But I hated that one most." She pushed me away.

"Hey, your dress doesn't matter to me."

"It matters to me. Shouldn't I like my own wedding dress, even if none of this is real?"

Ouch. I rubbed my arms. "What kind of dress would you choose?"

She smiled, and the hope in her eyes made me understand why she drew others to trust her, to give their money to EcoCore, to kiss her when they had no business doing so.

"I saved a dress on Pinterest. Want to see?" She pulled out her phone.

"Sure. But inside." I was getting chilled.

She followed me inside, and we sat beside each other on the couch. I longed to pull her close and kiss her but knew I wasn't in the right frame of mind.

Her thigh rubbed against my leg. "This is my dream dress." She handed me the phone.

I gazed at the model in the picture, having no trouble visualizing Gemma in the Cleopatra-style gown. I leaned closer.

"You'd look sexy in that."

She shoved me. "You're drunk, aren't you?"

What the hell was I doing? She was my employee. But my body didn't care. I pulled her closer and words slipped off my tongue.

"Maybe. But I'm not blind. You're the most beautiful woman alive. And I want you."

Shut up, shut up!

She scooted closer. "You won't remember any of this in the morning, will you?"

"Maybe."

"What was the name of your Jeep in high school?"

I wasn't that drunk. I closed the distance between us, and she met me halfway, brushing her hands through my hair. I pushed my hands up her tank, caressing the silky skin of her back, wondering if I dared explore her front. We connected like the last two pieces of a complex puzzle. Perfection. She sighed, and I rolled her onto her back.

Gemma was beyond hot. I'd wanted her almost from day one, wild braids and all. Each day spent with her, especially in close quarters, was exquisite torture.

I straddled her, turned on like a nuclear reactor. I wanted her. Needed her. We kept kissing and touching, temperatures rising. So much potential pleasure within my grasp, our bodies in meltdown. She didn't like me, but she wouldn't stop me.

But I stopped myself as I seemed to awaken from a trance. A small part of my brain still worked, and it scolded the hell out of me. I slipped off her, realizing my head was throbbing. I could ignore that pain for the pleasure she promised. But I couldn't ignore my conscience.

"I'm going to puke." I stumbled to my feet, sickened by what I'd been ready to do. What I still wanted to do. The more we kept playing pretend, the more real my feelings were becoming. Not good.

I escaped into the bathroom, wishing there was a freaking door on the toilet area. I fell to my knees and hung my head over the rim, hating myself for leading her on. She was an innocent, going by her genuine reactions.

The lights turned off in the bedroom. Thank God. I couldn't face her. How could we pull off this ruse and seek an annulment, pretending nothing had happened between us? Because that was the greatest farce of all. Something had changed between Gemma and me. If we stayed together and played this out to the end, something more would happen. And one or both of us would be hurt. Likely me, since she didn't seem invested.

I stayed in the bathroom until I was certain she'd fallen asleep. When I stretched out on the couch in the darkness, something hard jabbed my thigh.

Gemma's phone.

I entered her ridiculous password, and Pinterest popped up, her dream dress displayed. The Egyptian-style gown seemed more costume than wedding attire. Yet I could picture Gemma in it easily. And it wasn't an unpleasant picture.

I sent a screenshot to my phone before turning hers off and curling up on the couch with my pillow. Too bad there wasn't time to give Gemma her dream dress.

She'd look amazing in it.

SAEMIRA

Age 14 – Fushë Krujë, Albania

AUTHENTIC: true to one's character.

The work was done. Saemira and Engjell had cleaned the school from opposite ends since Baba still wouldn't allow them to spend time together. Her friend had taken Baba's anger hard. So had she. Not having anyone to hang around with on her off-time was boring.

She peeked inside Baba's office and blinked when she saw Engjell there.

"Come in, Saemira." Baba waved for her to enter.

Not daring to sit by her friend, she threw him an apologetic look as she sat two chairs away.

Baba folded his arms. "I'm tired of being upset with Engjell for taking advantage of you."

He hadn't taken advantage of her. Engjell had been polite, asking permission to kiss her. But not wanting Baba to think she was bad, she remained silent.

"You two may resume your friendship, on one condition." He stared hard at Engjell, who squirmed.

"Anything, Mr. Nikolla."

Baba pushed his glasses up his nose. "Be authentic with each other."

"I can be authentic," Engjell said.

"Me, too," Saemira said, though she couldn't remember the exact meaning of the word. She'd look it up later.

Baba turned to her. "Being authentic means being honest and telling Engjell how you felt about him kissing you."

She froze. *No. Not that.*

His stern gaze softened. "Saemira, you do yourself and Engjell no kindness by being dishonest. Silence is another form of lying."

She chewed her lip and faced her friend. "I..." She turned beseeching eyes on Baba, but he gestured for her to continue. "I didn't like kissing you." Her friend slouched, and she added, "But I love you."

Baba growled.

"You said to be authentic, and I do love him."

Engjell's expression brightened.

"As a friend, not a boyfriend," she clarified.

He pouted, but Baba had said to be authentic. That seemed to mean being honest.

"You're like my brother. I hated kissing Esad, too, and he has no scars. This isn't about your looks." She tapped her lips. "There must be something wrong with me. Maybe I'm bad at kissing. But I'm glad we did it, or we'd never know how we felt, right?"

"Since we're being authentic, I'm glad we kissed, too, for I will remember our kisses all my life. You are not bad at kissing, Gem."

She grinned, grateful to know she wasn't deficient in some way.

Baba cleared his throat. "No more talk about kissing. As I said, I want you both to be authentic. You now know my daughter didn't enjoy kissing. Promise to be her friend without pushing for physical affection."

Engjell hung his head. "I promise."

"Honor her. Be her protector and brother."

Engjell winced. "I will never be her brother."

"Then her protector and friend."

"I will always be those."

"Very well." Baba brushed his hands together. "You may resume your friendship."

Engjell and Saemira smiled at each other. Then she pulled out her black light.

"Race you to the clubhouse."

Gemma

LINCOLN ENTERED THE BEDROOM, and my equilibrium flew out the window. Why did he always make me crazy? Wilder had taken the men out to the shooting range while my two *moms* had taken me to the spa. Lincoln looked as if he could've used the spa as well. He was sunburnt and appeared exhausted.

He threw himself onto the couch.

"Was shooting that bad?"

"I hate guns," he said. "They're loud, have a bruising kick, and shoot my self-esteem to hell. Kind of like my father."

"Sorry."

"Meh," he said. "It is what it is."

He needed cheering up. I hurried into the bathroom and returned with my hair pulled into a towel-turban.

He squinted. "You doing a face mask or something?"

"No." I knelt on the plush carpet and took his hand. "I'm Madame Saemira," I said in a dramatic voice. "I'm going to read your future." I caressed his hand, trying to ignore how my body pulsed with desire and fear. I'd just told him my real name. "I see that you're at odds with the spirits."

He tried to pull his hand away. "Stop being ridiculous."

I rubbed the lines of his palm. "I see you've conquered an army today."

He snorted.

"And you have hayfever, no?"

He tried to pull his hand away again. I stroked his palm, and he stopped resisting.

"You're upset with your father, no?"

"How did you deduce that, Einstein?"

My lips twitched. "Madame Saemira, not Einstein. You are like your father, yes?"

He yanked his hand from mine, throwing me off balance. "I'm nothing like that man." He stalked over to the mini-bar and poured himself a drink. "Stop acting like a damned gypsy."

Ouch. That hadn't gone well. "What do you have against gypsies, besides a few misdemeanors? You can't judge a whole race by a few."

He tossed back a gulp. "They're not a race, they're criminals. Like pirates. Just because movies and books have romanticized them, doesn't make them noble. They're a—"

"What?" I stood. "What are they, Mr. Judgy-pants?"

He tossed back another shot, escaping into alcohol because the subject had turned uncomfortable. He was good at that.

"Your attitude's appalling," I said. "This is how racism thrives, because of good people like you who put another group down because of preconceived notions when you understand nothing about them."

"I'm not racist."

"You called all gypsies worthless criminals. What if I had gypsy blood? Would you call the cops? Have me arrested?"

"You're not a gypsy."

"What if I was? Would you have even hired me if I had Romani blood?"

His brow furrowed.

I threw my hands in the air. "You don't even know what Romani is, do you? FYI, it's a race of people. The Roma were dispersed from Northern India between the sixth and eleventh centuries and are scattered worldwide. Some call them gypsies or travelers. Pirate is another word for gangster. Pirates *can* be from any race or nationality. Gypsies *are* a race. They have a culture, a language, traditions, feelings. I'm offended on their behalf that you demean them without understanding who they even are."

Lincoln wasn't alone in his ignorance. I'd faced outright persecution in Albania because of who my mama was. Angel had faced daily bullying because of who his mama wasn't. I'd come to America, believing this to be a melting pot where everyone got along. But I'd been quickly cured of that false notion. Racism existed here in subtle, more dangerous attitudes most people weren't even aware of. Almost everyone thought they were better than someone else because of wealth, political views, culture, race, religion, sexual orientation, gender, or the music they enjoyed.

"Gypsies are criminals," he argued. "I understand who they are. So do the police!"

"You can't judge them all by their worst elements. Sure, maybe some are hardened criminals. But what if others were driven to crime by desperation? What if some are trapped by economics or blackmail?"

Lincoln tossed back another shot.

"That's it," I said. "Get drunk like last night." I turned my back to him. "You probably don't remember anything that happened. And you'll forget this conversation by morning. Alcohol's a great way to escape your conscience, isn't it?"

"I wasn't drunk last night."

I turned to read his expression, but it was icy.

"I remember everything."

I looked away.

"I'm not the only one who judges others. What about you—judging me for being rich. For being the CEO. That's prejudice, too."

I didn't have to listen to him.

"Do you have any idea how many people hate me because of my

money? They assume I think I'm superior, so they justify stealing from me or destroying my reputation. They think I'm lazy and had success handed to me, and so they work to strip away everything I've struggled so hard to achieve. Nobody knows how many years I lived in a crummy apartment with Joe, eking out an existence as I poured every piece of my soul into EcoCore."

We sized each other up. Admittedly, he'd given me a new perspective to consider, one that made me feel small. He was right. I had judged him. And I hadn't even realized it.

"I apologize for what I said about gypsies. About Romani. Obviously, I should do some research about them. But maybe you should look inward. You and me, we come from different backgrounds, but does that make me better than you because I'm rich? Or you better than me because you're not?" He took a step closer. "I get the impression you assume things about me which aren't true."

"Like what?" I shivered as his hands caressed my arms.

"That I could never care for a woman like you unless I was drunk."

"I...uh..." The uncanny way he seemed to read my mind made me squirm.

He raised a brow. "Let me make myself clear. I want to kiss you all the time. Drunk or sober, it doesn't matter."

Helen Keller. His body pressed into my space, and I stared at the carpet.

"What do you want from me, Gemma?" Goosebumps erupted clear down to my fingertips as he rubbed me. "You give off so many conflicting signals. Sometimes, I feel as if you want me, but the next, you're pushing me away."

"W-what about you?" Stupid traitorous voice. "You kiss me like that but then talk about how this is an act and our future marriage will be annulled?"

He scowled. "*You* kept emphasizing the annulment. Not me."

"Liar. You look at me with adoration one second, then want Casey to change who I am the next. Do you have any idea how small that man makes me feel? I've tried to be a good employee and do your bidding, but you and Casey see me as a gutter rat who's invaded the pristine kitchen. You say I'm biased against you because you're rich. But you're biased against me because I'm poor. Admit it! You don't think I'm good enough for you. You think I'm a gutter rat. An alcoholic!" I turned my back to him as I choked on emotion.

"What a mess." He stretched out on the couch and pulled a blanket over himself. "I don't feel like talking anymore. I need some sleep."

My world tipped precariously at his dismissal. I'd bared my heart, and he'd tossed it aside. I'd hoped he would pull me close and say I was good enough. That he wanted me. I'd hoped for courage to tell him the same. But not having a clue about where I stood made that scene impossible. Actually, watching him turn his back to me sent a clear signal about where I stood.

Lincoln McConnell would never love me. Tomorrow, I might grab his attention when I wore the dress I'd bought with his mom the other day—well, the dress he'd bought—but I'd never win his heart.

29

LINCOLN

My heart beat out of my chest as Gemma entered the room. Late, but spectacularly so. Talk about making an entrance. Mr. Wilder had insisted on holding a formal dinner to bid us adieu. And Gemma had just brought light to a dark room.

Her dress couldn't be of Casey's choosing. He would've turned his nose up at it. Gemma was right. I'd tried to make her into something she wasn't. And suddenly, I hated myself for that. Gemma was magnificent, not because she'd conformed to the silent rules of high society, but because she'd shattered them to become a masterpiece.

"Ah, my dear Gemma," Wilder said. "You look breathtaking."

"Isn't she lovely, son?" Mom said beside me.

I pulled Gemma's seat out for her. "You do look stunning."

She frowned, and I read her doubt. I'd have to fix that. Honestly, I had tons of things to fix between us. But not here, with an audience. When we returned to Salt Lake, we'd talk.

"I love the dress," I said, once we both were sitting.

"Thanks. You bought it for me."

"I have good taste."

Focusing on the amazing dinner became impossible. All I wanted was to be alone with Gemma. We'd gone horseback riding earlier, but Mom and Wilder's wife had monopolized Gemma's attention.

I wanted this weekend over so we could finish our talk from last night, the one that'd stunned me with possibilities. Could Gemma harbor real feelings for me, as I did for her? I hated that she'd linked me to Casey, saying we'd made her feel small and insignificant. Casey, maybe. He was an arrogant ass. But I respected her.

After dessert, everyone insisted on hugging as we made our way outside. I hugged Gramps.

"I'll see you at the wedding, my boy."

"Yes, you will."

I threw Gemma's suitcase into the trunk and relaxed as we drove away. Neither of us spoke. But we would soon.

A half-mile down the road, at a bend in the road, I ran over something that caused several loud explosions that brought us to a halting stop.

"What in the jello was that?" Gemma said.

I hopped out to see that all four tires had been shredded by a puncture strip. "Damn it." What in the hell was that doing out here? There'd been no warning sign.

"Put your hands up."

I spun around to find two masked men with guns. They must've been hiding in the brush on the side of the road.

Gemma screamed.

I spun around to see two other men pulling her from the car. "No!" I took off to help her but something hard hit my head. I slumped to the asphalt, watching helplessly as Gemma was carried, kicking and screaming, to a van.

Must get up.

I rolled onto my hands and knees. "Gemma," I said, right before the hard thing hit my head again.

QUICKSAND OF INJUSTICE

"A fall from such a height is rarely straight downwards."

— *THE HUNCHBACK OF NOTRE DAME* BY VICTOR
HUGO

30

LINCOLN

My head throbbed. Had I drunk too much? I went to turn but couldn't move my arms or legs. I opened my eyes, but the hammer in my head made me groan and close them again. I needed a bathroom. And what was in my mouth?

Water dripped nearby. Where was I?

Then it hit me like an ax to the head. Actually, something *had* hit me on the head before I could rescue Gemma. I tried to flail my arms, kick my legs, thrash my head, scream, but I was fully restrained. My eyes adjusted to the darkness, and I noticed zip ties binding my ankles and wrists to a chair. Cloth had been wedged into my mouth.

Oh, God! Where was Gemma? Was she okay?

I heard footsteps, then a voice.

"Is he awake?" Shadows hid my captor's face.

"Yes," another voice answered, making me flinch. I hadn't been aware of anyone else in the darkness with me.

"Leave us."

The one disappeared. The other grabbed my hair. I choked as the cloth was ripped from my mouth.

"Welcome to my mansion, *gadjo*." The shadowed man spat in my face. "It's not as nice as your friend's posh cabin, but it's more secure, no?" He laughed, making my skin crawl.

"What have you done with my sister?" I hoped that title would protect Gemma.

"You mean your tempting fiancée?" He held my head at an agonizing angle.

I gritted my teeth, wondering who he was, how he knew so much. "I demand to see her."

"You're in no position to make demands." His fist slammed into my gut. Again. And again. And again.

When I gained consciousness, I knew from the agony in every part of my body that I was a prisoner. The zip ties had been cut, freeing my feet and hands. But I couldn't move because of the pain.

"You know your place now, Mr. McConnell?"

I couldn't see my captor, but I hated him. Hated his superiority, his smugness.

"Where's...my...fiancée?"

"I'm glad you asked."

A computer screen lit up, revealing the outline of my captor's masked face. A live feed appeared, showing Gemma tied to a chair, still wearing that alluring off-the-shoulder dress she'd had on at dinner. She was blindfolded and gagged, and a masked man stood behind her, holding a knife to her neck.

Seeing her in that vulnerable position made me regret wasting the time we'd had together. Why hadn't I confessed my feelings as soon as I'd recognized them? I'd guessed near the end that she might have felt the same. Would I ever get the chance to find out now? Would we survive?

"Let her go. Keep me, but don't hurt her. Please. She has nothing to give you."

"She could give me much." His finger moved over the screen, stopping on her chest. "Yes," he licked his lips, "I could get much pleasure from your temptress."

"Don't touch her!" I shouted.

A fist slammed into my stomach. "Remember your place, Mr. McConnell. You will make no demands of me. Are we agreed?" When I scowled, he slugged my cheek. "Are we agreed?"

"Yes. Please, don't hurt her."

"She's a beauty, yes? My men would have much fun with her."

Oh, God! Facing death and seeing the woman I loved threatened made me reconsider a Higher Being's existence. I wanted Joe and Mom and every other believer to be right about a living, loving God who could rescue sinners. Who could rescue Gemma! If He saved her, I'd give my life to Him. Literally.

"Please," I begged, both to my captor and to the God I hoped lived.

"If you want your fiancée back untouched, it'll cost you."

"Name your price. But swear you won't touch her. Please," I added when his brow lifted.

"Three million cryptocurrency for her release. We know you invested in Bitcoin in 2017. This should be simple."

Damn Angeline. Her lawyer's machinations had probably put my assets out as open-source information.

"If you want her untouched though, I'll need three million more. Two million for your freedom."

He was unhinged. That was everything Angeline had encouraged me to invest. That nest egg had been all I'd had left after the divorce.

But it was only money. If it could free Gemma, I'd gladly give it all up.

"How do I know she's alive? This could be a recording."

He hit a button. "Unmute and ungag her."

Gemma's captor pulled the knife from her throat and moved in front of the screen. She whimpered as he pulled the gag out of her mouth, much more gently than my captor had taken mine out, thankfully.

"Gemma!" I shouted.

"Lincoln!"

I closed my eyes. Praise God! She lived. "I'll get you out of this!"

My captor punched me. "Mute," he said.

I watched helplessly as Gemma's lips kept moving and her face contorted before her captor gagged her again. My captor brought up another screen, and Gemma disappeared from view.

"Complete the transaction."

"Free Gemma."

Even in the shadows, I saw his face grow splotchy. "Don't make demands of me." He grabbed hold of my hair with one hand, and slugged me with the other. "Transfer the money."

I coughed, wanting to retch. "Not until I see Gemma."

He flipped out a blade, but I knew he wouldn't kill me. He needed my money.

31

SAEMIRA

Age 14 – Fushë Krujë, Albania

TERROR: paralyzing fear you never want to speak of or think about
again.

$\mathscr{E}$ngjell gave Saemira a playful shove. "I should get you home," he
said.

Sometimes his motivation to please Baba made him lame. "The sun's
not even down yet. Let's play another game of Hansel and Gretel." They
were too old to still play the game, but she wanted to see if the rocks she'd
painted with the new solution would glow under the black light.

"I don't know."

She shoved the black light into his hand. "Stay here. Count to three
hundred." She took off to hide before he could protest.

"Don't go far!" he yelled.

He couldn't tell her what to do. Saemira dropped rocks sporadically on
the way to the warehouse. She couldn't pick locks so she slipped into the
back lot, thinking to challenge his finding skills by hiding in one of the
empty cargo containers littering the area. But she'd only leave a rock by the
container she hid in. It was kind of cheating, but Engjell was a good tracker.
He'd find her. Eventually.

She giggled and ran past several rusty containers, zigzagging toward the
middle. A squeak made her stop and look around.

Had that been a rat?

She shuddered. Engjell had chased many of those away. She dropped a rock and moved forward, but a strong hand covered her mouth, and someone kicked her pebble away.

She tried to get traction as the person dragged her backward, but whoever had her was strong. Her heart raced as she was pulled into a pitch-black container and shoved to the ground.

"Ah, my little thief."

Her legs warmed with urine as Engjell's uncle spoke.

"You're not so high and mighty now, are you, Temptress?" His hand pulled her skirt up, and he touched her urine-soaked panties. "The scent of fear." He put his fingers to her nose, and she wanted to die of shame.

"Gem!" Engjell called from a distance. Not close enough to help, even if she could call out, which she couldn't. "Where are you? Come out. I need to get you home."

"If you make a sound, I'll kill him." Something hard and cold touched her cheek. "I'll slit his throat. Nobody will miss the ugly devil boy. I'll kill your baba, too. And I'll make a whore of your mama."

He lifted his hand from her mouth, and she choked back sobs.

"Gem!" Engjell called again, closer, but yet so far.

"Should we let him find us," he hissed, "so I can cut him up?"

"N-n-no," she stammered.

"You're a wicked little whore. A thief, stealing my mind like you have."

Engjell called her again, sounding farther away. That was good. She didn't want her friend to die.

The monster growled. "It's time you repaid me, Temptress."

Gemma

LINCOLN WAS ALIVE!

It seemed as if hours had passed since the masked men had kidnapped me. I'd been terrified that they had killed Lincoln and left him on the side of the road. The men had driven forever with me tied up in the back, before pulling me out and leading me down a steep walkway. I hadn't gone back up. We must be below ground, in a basement or tunnel.

But who had kidnapped me?

After Duke had terrorized me as a child, I'd had nightmares for years. But this kidnapper seemed somewhat decent. He hadn't assaulted or groped me. He'd made me lose control of my bladder a few minutes ago when he'd pressed a knife to my throat. That's when I'd heard Lincoln scream my name from a computer monitor.

What would they do to him? Would they hold us for ransom? If so, I'd never be freed since I had no money. Duke had made sure of that. But Lincoln had plenty, something he'd claimed made people see and treat him differently.

I hoped our kidnappers would treat him differently now. That they would let him go. I only wished I could tell him that his stupid portfolio meant nothing to me. I cared only for him.

My kidnapper untied the blindfold and let it fall to my lap. I looked up and inhaled sharply.

"Angel?"

He leaned in and pecked my lips. "Sorry to scare you, but it worked. Your rich *gadjo's* transferring millions to Duke as we speak. Cryptocurrency. It's untraceable. We can live like kings and queens, you and I. You don't have to marry a man you don't love and who definitely doesn't love you back."

I dropped to the floor to dry heave. Angel? My best friend. My savior. The boy who'd sacrificed everything for me and Altin. He had kidnapped me?

He pulled hair back from my face. "You all right?"

"How could you do this?" I whispered.

He rubbed my back. "I saved you."

"No." I scrambled back from him. "You've doomed us all."

His puffy lips twisted. "Duke said your fiancé beat his first wife, made her lose a baby. I won't let you live with a man like that."

"Oh, Angel." I rocked back and forth. "Duke lies. Remember the night you found me in the cargo container?" I trembled at the memory.

He winced. "I'll never forget. That's why I won't let you be hurt again."

I choked on tears. "Duke hurt me that night. He said he'd kill you and Baba if I ever revealed the truth."

My friend's eyes widened. "No. You're wrong."

I buried my head in my hands as the sobs I'd restrained for years finally broke free.

32

ANGEL

Age 17 - Fushë Krujë, Albania

*N*o crying! Engjell swallowed against a massive lump in his throat. Sour. Bitter. But Saemira's swollen eyes made him act brave.

The past month had been rough on her. And him. Not that the five months before had been easy. When he'd found her in the second-to-last cargo container, skirt up around her waist, soiled panties lying a few feet away, he'd dressed her and rushed her home. Mr. Nikolla had taken her to the hospital and had called the *policia,* but the perpetrator hadn't been found.

He hadn't blamed Mr. Nikolla for being furious with him. He'd hated himself for what had happened to Saemira. But too soon, Mr. Nikolla had forgiven him, saying none of what had happened had been his fault.

He was wrong.

When Saemira hadn't come out when he'd called for her, he'd thought she was being stubborn. Instead of looking for her, he'd sulked in the warehouse, waiting her out. Only after the sun had set had he worried that something might be wrong. Too late, he'd searched every cargo container with the blacklight until he'd found her.

For months afterward, she'd wanted nothing to do with him. A just punishment. But then she'd sent a letter through her baba, apologizing for being a bad friend and asking for time to get her head right. His poor, sweet friend had been worried about him, when he'd deserved hell's flames.

That's why he loved her.

Six weeks ago, she'd agreed to see him. Her mama had sat between them while she'd told a story of her people.

It'd been enough.

Though he'd missed studying with Gem and going on adventures with her, he'd understood her suffering. Mr. Nikolla had confided that she acted skittish even with him. Time would ease her fears. Until then, he'd urged him to be patient.

He would've been patient for as long as needed, but Saemira's mama had gone into early labor and died in childbirth, along with another premature son. Their deaths had thrown Mr. Nikolla and Saemira into deep mourning.

"Thanks for coming." Saemira's soft voice snapped him back to the present. She faced him, unsmiling, but still beautiful. Her Mama's amulet hung on the silver chain around her slender neck.

He pulled her into a hug but let go when she stiffened. Since the assault, she'd let nobody touch her.

"I don't want to go," she said.

"I don't want you to either."

If Saemira had been devastated by her mama's death, her baba had been destroyed. He'd turned over management of the school to his second, Mr. Sokoli. He hadn't told stories or played his sharkia. He'd hardly even talked to his daughter, which revealed the depth of his pain, for Saemira was his life. But losing his wife seemed to have killed part of him. He'd decided to return to America with his daughter.

"You will write me, won't you?" Gem asked.

"For sure." Engjell gave her a shaky smile.

"I'll send letters in care of Mr. Sokoli at the school."

He wished he could hold her, but he was helpless to heal her wounds.

She pulled something from the bag her mama had sewn for her. "I want you to keep this." She handed him her black light. "Find me someday when you come to America. Give it back to me."

Fat chance of that happening. He had not a *lek* to his name. And Duke wouldn't share.

"I'll treat it as my most priceless gem." The lump in his throat grew. Saemira was his treasure. But she was leaving. Would he ever see her again?

She stepped forward to give him a stiff embrace, and he knew the gesture had cost all her courage. He buried his head into her neck and inhaled her sweet scent. If Mr. Nikolla had been himself, he would've shooed him away and said they'd held each other long enough. But he just watched from the car, glassy-eyed and numb, like the zombie dead.

"Goodbye, Engjell." Saemira walked around the car to climb into the passenger seat beside her baba.

The lump in his throat threatened to burst and send a wave of tears out his nose and eyes as he watched them pull away.

He thought of Saemira's book of English words she'd learned over the years. *Lost* would be his word today. Never again would he see Saemira's smiling face or hear her bubbling laughter. Never would Mr. Nikolla expand his mind with learning, making him see possibilities he'd never imagined. Never again would Saemira's mama tell him stories and fill him with the warmth of her acceptance.

Never. That's what *lost* felt like. A whole string of nevers folded out on the horizon.

A hand slapped his shoulder, making him flinch.

"They're gone, no?" Uncle spat on the ground. "Good riddance. That *gadjo* and his half-breed temptress were pulling you down."

Engjell blinked fast and swallowed. Uncle had no tolerance for weakness.

"Trying to make you into something you're not, Engjell," he said in a high voice, mocking Saemira. "Bah! You're no angel. You're Bengalo. Look at you." He shoved him to his knees. "Ugly freak. Bastard son of a diseased whore. They educated you, but you were a joke to them." He nudged him with his boot. "I won't give you false hopes and then leave. I'll teach you how to take what you deserve from this cruel world and run from it."

Saemira's tears and revelation gutted me. This wasn't how this should've gone down. She was supposed to be grateful for my intervention. I'd saved her from the monster in fancy clothes.

She should love me!

Duke couldn't be the rapist. It'd been dark. She'd been scared and young. No way could she have known who hurt her that night. She would've told me. Told her baba. Uncle couldn't have been the one who'd changed my fun-loving friend into the cowering mute she'd been before leaving Albania.

"Bengalo." Uncle spoke into my earpiece. "Bring the temptress to make the *gadjo* cooperate."

Blood turned to ice in my veins as I realized Uncle could indeed have hurt her all those years ago. He still hurt people. Especially women. And girls.

"Gem." I pulled her to her feet. "Come with me. We'll run away, far from Duke and the *gadjo* who's confused you." I could get her to safety.

"No." She yanked out of my grip. "I need to help Lincoln. Please, if you love me at all, help me free him."

I couldn't do that. Dammit. Who was I trying to fool? Duke had a plan. I had no power to foil it, nor did I dare. Besides, Uncle hadn't lied about her *gadjo*. He'd shown me an old paper that showed what Saemira's fiancé had done to his last wife.

"We must go." I gripped her wrist and yanked her out the door. "Stay quiet and do as I say." Uncle had summoned us. If she wouldn't run away with me, we must go along with Duke's plan.

Gemma would be safe. Duke wouldn't touch her. Maybe he'd hurt her in the past, but she was under my protection now.

I'd given my soul to purchase her safety.

33

SAEMIRA

Age 16 – Detroit, Michigan

UNFAITHFUL: breaking vows; untrustworthy.

*L*oud music from the apartment next door made the couch vibrate. Saemira turned on the TV to block out the neighbors' noise through the thin walls. She missed the calming sounds of her home in Albania. The wind rattling the shutters. The hiss of the heater. The sweet tune of Baba's sharkia at night. She clutched Mama's amulet, missing her most. This apartment in Detroit that Baba had rented had no soul.

"Baby girl."

She flinched. Baba rarely spoke, not since Mama had died. She wondered if he still blamed her for her death.

He sat beside her but didn't speak. She didn't mind. Just sitting near him soothed her rattled heart. She longed to have him hold her, caress her hair as he had when she'd been younger, tell her everything would be okay.

Baba shuddered, and she realized he was crying.

"What is it, Baba?"

He sniffed. "I'm getting married tomorrow."

Her whole body chilled. They'd been here over a year and he'd never even gone out with a woman. How could he be marrying one? And why would he want to? Nobody could replace Mama. No one should.

"Her name's Rosie. I know this is a surprise." His face puckered. "I still can't believe it, either."

Her stomach began to churn. "Do you love her?"

He pushed his glasses up his nose. "No. I met her at a bar a few months ago. I got drunk, ended up at her place for a few hours." He pursed his lips. "She's pregnant, Saemira. I have to do the right thing."

She pushed him away, unable to imagine anything worse than Baba lying with a woman he didn't love and putting a baby in her. "How could you?" She fled to her bedroom and locked the door.

He knocked. "Saemira, I'm sorry. But this could be good for you. Rosie has a house. We'll get out of this crummy apartment. You won't be alone after school. You'll have another woman in the house with you. A brother or sister, too, in a few months.

"Go away!" She didn't want to hear how good this could be. He'd done a wicked act with this Rosie. Been unfaithful to Mama. To her!

Gathering clothes from her closet, ones that hugged her body, she carried them to her third-story window and threw them out into the night. Boys always whistled and called her hot, saying they wanted to do nasty things with her. She must hide her body. Bury the evil the gods had cursed her with.

She wouldn't be like the whore Rosie who'd tempted her baba to be evil with her.

Gemma

Tears leaked from my eyes as Engjell pulled me through a dark tunnel. How could he have forsaken the values Baba had taught him? How could he have chosen his horrid uncle over me?

"Where are we?" I asked.

"Do not talk, Gem. Please."

I leaned back to keep him from pulling me any farther and yanked my hand out of his. "I hate you."

"I hate myself." He clenched my wrist and forced me forward, making me stumble.

"Why are you doing this?"

A light up ahead made my heart pound. I squeaked as we drew closer and I spotted Lincoln on the ground, gasping for air. I shoved out of Engjell's grip to run to Lincoln.

"Are you all right?" I gathered him in my arms, and Lincoln wrapped me up in a full body hug.

I sighed. Duke still held us hostage, but at least we were together.

"I love you," he whispered.

"Hush." He must be delusional from his abuse.

Duke laughed. "What a sweet reunion." He pulled Lincoln up by his hair, making him grit his teeth.

"Leave him alone!" I tried to claw Duke's face, but Angel restrained me.

"Be calm, Gem," Angel whispered near my ear. "Trust me."

"Let me go!" He'd betrayed me. I tried to escape his grip.

"She's here, as you asked." Duke shoved Lincoln in front of a computer. "Now make the transfer."

Lincoln typed something as Duke watched over his shoulder.

Duke thumped his head. "All of it, or she dies." He marched over and grabbed me by my hair. I screamed as he dragged me across the cement floor and brought a knife to my throat.

"Do it!"

"Let her go," Lincoln said. "So help me God, you won't get another cent unless she goes free. You can keep me, but she goes free."

Duke's blade pricked my neck. "You are in no position to make demands."

"Neither are you." Fury transformed Lincoln's face. "When I see proof that she's safely away, I'll transfer the rest. Not a second before. And I'm taking off a mil for nicking her neck, you bastard."

"That's not how it works!" Duke's hand grazed my mouth, and I chomped down on his finger. He screamed and threw me to the ground.

My head hit hard, and pain engulfed me. I tried to focus, but my vision blurred and I felt as if I might puke.

"You promised nobody would get hurt," Engjell shouted, dropping down beside me. His arms wrapped around me, but they didn't bring comfort.

"Get out of the way, boy." Duke clenched my upper arms, lifting me up into a spinning world.

Angel shrieked. "No! You promised not to hurt her!"

I didn't see what happened next. Duke let go, and I slumped to the ground and vomited onto the cement. Duke screamed somewhere above me.

"Gemma." Lincoln touched my head. "Are you all right, love?"

"Get her out of here," Engjell said, urgency in his voice. "We don't have much time before he comes to. Go left out the door and run. Don't stop."

He handed something to Lincoln. "Call the police as soon as you have bars. Now get the hell out of here. I'll try to lure Duke's men the other way."

Lincoln helped me to my feet. My stomach heaved like the sea in a hurricane, so I held onto him like a life preserver.

I wanted to thank my friend for whatever he had done. He must've knocked out Duke somehow, but Engjell took off, and Lincoln practically dragged me the other direction through the dizzying darkness.

34

LINCOLN

---

*T*he bandage around Gemma's head made me furious as my driver pulled away from the hospital.

"You all right?" I asked.

We'd escaped what had turned out to be a system of storm drains on the outskirts of town. Gemma had been woozy from her head injury. I'd barely dragged her out of there, not feeling so well myself. My security team had met us near the end of the tunnel and had taken us to the hospital. Gemma had a concussion. No surprise there. I had two broken ribs and bruises everywhere. The police had questioned us, leaving me with more questions.

"I'm fine," she said.

"Can you see all right?" Her vision had been blurry and she'd puked several more times as I'd half-carried her away from our captors.

"Better," she said. "What about you? You seem shook up."

Understatement. "Those gypsies knew too much." She frowned. "Sorry," I said. "I mean kidnappers. They must've been stalking me to know we were at Wilder's cabin."

The color drained from her face, and I chided myself. I should be comforting her, not stirring up more fear.

"I'm sure we're safe now. It's just unsettling."

She stared out the window.

I leaned back in my seat, trying to forget what had happened. To me. To her. We were lucky to be alive. We wouldn't be if the younger thug hadn't gained a conscience at the last second and attacked his leader with a metal rod.

Gemma's window moved up and down, and I relaxed. If she was messing with the controls, she must not be too freaked out.

The city sped past. For some reason, the gypsies—kidnappers—had targeted me. Gemma had been sucked in by association. Now that they understood how vulnerable she made me, would they try to kidnap her again?

"Where are we going?" Gemma asked. "This isn't the way to my place."

"My house. I want you and Altin near me. For your safety."

She looked down at her hands.

Not many hours ago, I'd proclaimed my love for her when we'd been reunited, but she hadn't returned the sentiment. She'd told me to hush. Had I scared her? Or did she not feel the same?

A streetlamp revealed her glistening eyes. I undid my seatbelt and scooted over to wrap my arm around her. Right now, I wouldn't worry about that. She'd been through an ordeal and needed comfort.

"Hey, it's okay." I tucked her head into my shoulder, though my ribs hurt. "Please, stay. I'll be worried sick if you don't."

She swiped her eyes. "I'm so sorry."

"For what?"

"For the money you lost. I'll get it back somehow, work extra hours to—"

I put a finger to her mouth. "I don't care about the money." I pressed my lips to hers, soft and quick since my upper lip had been cut by an assailant's ring. "You're all that matters."

We stayed like that, holding each other, until the driver pulled into my rounded driveway.

I unwrapped my arms from Gemma and stepped out to give her a hand. The two of us hobbled to the front door, where my housekeeper met us.

"Are you hungry?" I asked. It was almost sunrise, but we hadn't eaten or slept all night.

"Starved."

Mrs. Tan brought out muffins and milk.

"Is Altin here?" Gemma asked.

"No, I asked Miss Tina to keep him until tomorrow. I figured you would need to rest. But don't worry, they've been taken to a secure location."

She pushed her nibbled-on muffin aside. "I should get some sleep. My head's killing me."

"The nurse said I should check on you hourly, with your concussion."

"Please, don't. I want to sleep long and hard."

Did she think she could? I'd be reliving nightmares.

I showed her to the guest room. "I hope you don't mind," I said. "I had

Lionel grab the extra key to your place and bring over clothes and nightwear for you and Altin, when he joins us. They're in the closet."

She yawned. "How do you always think of everything?"

"I hire good people to do the thinking." I fidgeted, wondering where we stood. Was our engagement and upcoming marriage still business? I wanted it to be more. I cared for her. Heavens, I loved her. But she looked exhausted. That would have to be a discussion for another day. "I'll leave you."

"Thanks for everything," she said.

"Of course. I'm glad you're alive." She'd never know just how much.

35

SAEMIRA

Age 17 – Detroit, Michigan

FORGIVENESS: stopping anger against an enemy, which frees us from them.

Shouting downstairs woke the baby, and Altin started to cry. Saemira rolled over in bed to pat his back as her stepmother kept screaming.

"I'm not moving to freaking Alberta!" Rosie shouted, except she used the real f-word Baba had forbidden his daughter to use. Or even think. Didn't matter that she heard it hundreds of times a day from his new wife, the evil temptress who'd made not only his life miserable, but hers as well.

She patted three-month old Altin. "Your mama's a piece of work. Doesn't know the difference between Alberta and Albania." The only good thing about Rosie was Altin, or Floyd, as Rosie had named her baby brother. Saemira liked Altin better and called him that to piss Rosie off.

America hadn't turned out to be the land of opportunity Baba had made it out to be when he'd told her and Engjell stories about his homeland. His savings had been tied up in the school in Albania. When they'd left, they'd come with only the belongings in their suitcases and a few thousand dollars Baba had remaining to his name. They'd scraped by in the crummy ghetto in Detroit until Baba had gotten Rosie pregnant.

Now, Saemira had a stepmom who hated her, and they lived in her mouse- and cockroach-ridden house on the other side of town. Her new school had been worse than the old one. After some psycho girl had tried to kick her trash the third week of school, Baba had pulled her out and enrolled her in an online school.

She heard his calm voice, followed by Rosie's high-pitched screaming. Saemira put her hands over Altin's tiny ears when Rosie started calling Baba horrible names.

"Don't listen, sweet boy. Baba's a good man, even if he was seduced by your evil mama."

He cooed and batted her face.

"Love you too, buddy."

When Rosie stopped screaming and a door slammed, Saemira crept downstairs to make a bottle.

Baba sat on the couch in the dark, staring at the wall. "Hey, baby girl. Is Altin awake?" He liked her name for the baby better than Rosie's.

"Yep. Rosie woke him up."

"Sorry. She was drunk."

"What's new?" She walked upstairs with the bottle.

He followed. "Mind if I sit with you while you feed him?"

She clutched Mama's amulet, praying to the gods that Baba wouldn't find her beautiful, as he must've found Rosie. After she'd dumped her clothes, he'd taken her to a thrift store to replace them when he'd noticed her wearing the same outfit day in and day out. She'd bought baggy clothes to hide her figure, never wanting to tempt Baba or any other man.

Baba was quiet as Altin drank. They sat on the bed, shoulders touching. Maybe she was wicked for not moving, but she longed for connection. Baba usually spent nights with Rosie, trying to make her happy, something she'd come to realize was utterly impossible.

Altin fell asleep, but Baba didn't leave. "Thanks for being a good sister to Altin." He stroked her long hair as she pulled the blanket over her baby brother.

"I love him."

"Me, too."

"But I hate Rosie's guts." She squirmed, expecting him to chide her. But he just sighed.

"I don't like her much either." He patted Altin's back. "But we must make the best of this for Altin's sake." He squeezed her hand. "Thanks for being a good daughter."

Saemira festered with the horrible secret she'd kept hidden for so long. "I'm not good. I'm evil."

"Impossible, princess."

"I am. Duke said so. Engjell's uncle."

He stiffened. "Is he...who hurt you?"

Shame burned tears out of her. She nodded, and he pulled her into his arms.

"Don't touch me." She scrambled off the bed. "He said I tempt men to do evil things." She swiped at her eyes. "Even you. I'm a whore. The devil made me."

Baba's eyes glistened as he held out a hand. "Those are lies, Saemira."

She looked at his hand, wishing she could believe him.

"The God of Heaven made you. He made you good—beautiful, too. Duke lied when he blamed you for his evil. All of us are responsible for our own choices, *bijé*."

She stared at his outstretched hand, but the horror of that time with Duke locked her arms in place at her sides.

"I did an evil thing with Duke." She still woke up gasping from the shame, the helplessness, the terror of that night.

"No. He forced himself upon you. He raped you and took away your choice."

"I didn't fight him." A good girl would've. "Engjell said whores spread their legs willingly, and I spread mine for Duke." She looked away, unable to meet her baba's intense gaze.

He didn't withdraw his hand. He still reached out, palm up. "Answer me this, *bijé*. Did you want to obey, or were you scared?"

She brushed at the stinging skin below her eyes. "Scared." Her body convulsed.

"He terrorized you, Saemira. You're *not* to blame. You were a victim. He can never make you evil."

"But Rosie made you be evil with her."

He closed his eyes but didn't drop his hand. "I chose to get drunk. Rosie's not responsible for that. The world would have you believe that women are to blame for men's bad choices, but that's a lie. Men are accountable for their own behavior. Regardless of what a woman wears or how she presents herself, a man always has a choice. I chose grief instead of love. It was a terrible mistake. I hope you'll forgive me someday."

She lifted her hand, taking courage from the hope that brightened his eyes. It'd been ages since she'd seen light in his face. Her fingers touched his, and he wrapped his big hand around hers and pulled her into his arms.

She curled into him, wondering why she'd avoided him for so long. He was her anchor. Her strength. She cried as she hadn't done for over two long years, a flood of emotions breaking free. Anger, that she hadn't listened to Engjell and gone home that night with him. Fear, that Duke would find her again. Shame, for her lost innocence. Fury, at the horrid images still in her head. Sadness, for the relationships she'd damaged.

Baba didn't shush her. He just held her and healed her. In his arms, her heart became full again, not empty.

"I'm sorry for being a bad daughter," she said between sniffles.

"You've never been bad. You're a brilliant light and hold my whole heart."

They sat back on the bed, hands clasped.

"Do I hold your heart more than Rosie?"

He grimaced. "I don't love Rosie. She makes it hard to do so. But I don't hate her either. She's my wife. And your stepmother."

She made a face. "She doesn't like me."

"She doesn't like me either," he said, and they both laughed. He cupped her chin. "We need God's help to forgive her."

"I don't want to forgive her. She's mean."

He squeezed her hand. "God requires more than what makes us comfortable."

That's why his God was more powerful than Mama's gods. But Mama's stone gods were easier to please, only requiring drips of water, or at most, a dab of blood for a potent blessing.

"Are you sure I'm not a whore?" she asked. "Duke did bad things to me."

He traced a heart on the back of her hand. "What he did was immensely evil. But you are pure and innocent in God's eyes. And mine. Boys and men will notice you. You are a pretty girl, turning into a beautiful woman. That's how God wants it to be. We glorify Him when we shine, not when we hide ourselves." He pulled at her baggy sweatshirt. "That's what you've been doing, isn't it?"

She chewed her lips. "Sorry."

"You have nothing to be sorry about, bijé. Nothing. Remember: Duke has no power to write your story. You and God are the only authors."

She rested her head on his lap, letting him stroke her hair.

"Why didn't you tell me this before?" he asked. "Right after it happened so the police could've locked him away."

She shuddered. "He said he'd kill you and Engjell if I told."

Baba's hand stopped in her hair and he trembled. "No wonder you've been so scared."

A lump formed in her throat. She still feared there'd be a price to pay for breaking her silence. "I worry for Engjell."

"I always worry for him. His uncle took off and left him last year."

"He did?"

"Engjell's better off without him. He's a bright boy. And I have good news. That's what upset Rosie earlier."

Whatever upset Rosie was probably a good thing.

"I've been working to sponsor Engjell to come here for college, especially now that he's on his own. His application was approved. He'll be here for winter semester at University of Illinois at Chicago."

Saemira sat up and grinned "That's wonderful."

"He'll do good things." He wrapped an arm around her. "Sorry for what that man did to you, for how he hurt you physically, but also for how he twisted your mind with lies to make you fear. He's an evil man, but you must forgive him."

She shook her head.

"Forgiveness is for you, not him. What he did was despicable. Inexcusable. Forgiving doesn't mean his actions are acceptable. But when we hate or fear those who've wronged us, we stay chained to them. Forgiveness is the only thing powerful enough to set us free."

That didn't make sense.

"When we give judgment to God, He lets us move on and be happy again. You deserve all the happiness life has to offer. When we don't forgive, we take the role of judge upon ourselves, a heavy burden. Too heavy for any mortal." Baba lifted Mama's amulet. "Forgiveness freed your mama, you know?"

"How?"

"A group of soldiers raped her in Kosovo."

She'd known that. Mama had confided to her that experience after her own assault.

"She'd healed physically by the time I met her in the refugee camp, but she hadn't healed in here." He pointed to his head. "Or here." He touched his heart. "She feared everyone, even me."

She understood that fear. After Duke's assault, she'd been fearful of everyone as well.

"Over the next year, I taught her about Jesus Christ and forgiveness. She called Him Sky God because when she put His teachings to work and forgave her enemies, fear disappeared and she felt she could fly." He smiled. "She was free to love me as I already loved her."

"What if I'm not as strong or good as you and Mama?"

He kissed her hair. "You're stronger and better than both of us. It won't be easy, but I promise forgiveness will free you of that man and his lies." He let the amulet drop. "After I lost your mama, I hated God for taking her and another child from me. But look at what hate did. I withheld the love you needed. I left Albania to escape memories of her and ended up in the bed of a woman I despised. So much pain could've been avoided if I'd given my sorrow to God, instead of holding onto it tight."

"Have you forgiven God now?"

"Yes. It's taken a while. But I'm happier, even if Rosie still screams at me. God has freed me from the bitterness in my soul." He rested his head against hers. "Will you forgive me for ruining everything?"

Saemira snuggled closer. "Nothing is ruined as long as I have you. And yes, I forgive you."

Gemma

THE CEILING FAN spun above me in Lincoln's guest room. My brain spun faster, sifting through the last twenty-four hours and connecting dangerous dots.

Duke had been tracking me. Maybe since the day I'd set foot in this valley.

Had Angel known?

When Lincoln had asked the police how the kidnappers had known to set their trap in Park City, the answer had hit me like a brick to the head.

My phone.

Ugh. It was so simple. Why hadn't I considered the possibility that he'd put a tracking app on my phone? Engjell had given me the phone when we'd first arrived in Salt Lake, along with forged documents. When I'd asked where he'd gotten everything, he'd said they'd come from his friends at the university.

But it had been Duke.

In the back of Lincoln's SUV on the drive home from the hospital, I'd played with the window controls, and when Lincoln had looked away, I'd tossed the cursed phone out onto the freeway.

Duke wouldn't find me now. Lincoln's home would be a safe haven.

But for how long?

The kidnapping had proven I was a threat to anyone close to me. Lincoln had lost millions. He could've lost his life if Angel hadn't freed us. As much as I loved him, there was no hope for us. He'd said he loved me when we'd been reunited, but I wouldn't hold him to what he'd said under duress.

I must earn back his lost money, even if it meant calling every foundation and venture capitalist out there. But returning to work meant Duke might track me again. If that happened, what would stop him from setting another trap for Lincoln—or heaven forbid, Altin?

The fan kept turning like my busy brain. Running away with Altin, as I'd always planned, was out of the question now. I couldn't subject my brother to life on the streets, and that's where I'd be. Going through with this wedding would secure a good life for my brother. My final act of love before I disappeared from his life. Maybe I could leave Lincoln a note, telling him who I really was and why he must protect Altin. He was a good man. Surely he wouldn't abandon my brother.

The door opened, and I pulled the covers up to my nose.

"Sorry. It's just me," Lincoln whispered. "It's been an hour. I'm here to check in. How are you?"

"Still breathing."

"How's your head?"

"Still pounding."

He fidgeted, and I noticed he held a blanket. "Mind if I borrow a pillow and sleep on the floor? Then I won't have to walk as far to check on you in another hour."

"You don't have to check on me." Though I loved that he cared enough to do so.

"The nurse said I should."

I threw him an extra pillow. "Don't snore."

He spread out the blanket and winced as he knelt. Poor guy seemed to be in a lot of pain.

"I feel bad making you sleep on the floor in your own house."

"This carpet's the best money can buy."

Shocker.

I took comfort in having him a few feet away and must've fallen into a deep sleep. When I awoke, I touched my bandaged head. It didn't throb as much as it had.

"Hey, sleepyhead."

I yelped as Lincoln sat up on the floor beneath me. Oh, right. He'd come in to check on me and then stayed.

"What time is it?"

"Almost midnight. You hungry?"

"Crap! I slept the whole day? I need to get Altin."

"Shh." He put a finger to my mouth. "He's here. I had Tina bring him back at dinner time."

My brain seemed too groggy to think.

"Feel any better?"

"Yes. But I feel lazy for sleeping the whole day. I've never done that before."

"You've never been kidnapped and brutalized either."

I wished that was true.

Two days had passed at Lincoln's place. We hadn't done much except sleep and rest. My head still ached, but less than before. Lincoln was sore and walked like an old man. Poor guy.

"Wink!" Altin cried, breaking away from Tina to run to him.

Lincoln held out his hands to catch my brother before he tackled his healing ribs. "Have you had fun with Miss Tina?"

"Teenie fun," Altin said.

Tina fidgeted. She was an excellent teacher and caregiver but was super shy around Lincoln. I don't think he realized how intimidating he came across to most people.

"Are you sure you're okay with me leaving, Mr. McConnell?"

"Totally. I appreciate the time you spent with him the last couple of days. You need a break."

"Thank you." She took her leave.

Lincoln glanced over at me. "Want to get out of the house?"

"I do have a buttload of work to do."

"Not work." He shook his head "I'm sure your boss doesn't want you going in right now. He wants you to recover. Have some fun. You deserve that."

I didn't deserve anything for upending his life. "I'll stay and play with Altin."

"That's the problem. There are no toys here. What do you say to a trip to a toy store?"

"No. I don't want you to—"

"Gemma." Lincoln put his hand to my mouth, making my lips tingle. "Altin and I want to visit the toy store."

His finger against my lips took my breath away. Talk about heaven. I shouldn't enjoy his touch so much.

My brother's eyes lit up. "Toys?"

Lincoln held out a hand. "Care to join us?"

"I guess."

The afternoon sped by in a blur of fun. Lincoln turned into a total goofball inside the toy store, playing with every toy on display and making Altin laugh hysterically.

Lincoln beeped and pushed Altin's car into my leg. "Oh, no!" he said. "Mommy monster made us wreck."

Altin parroted him. "Oh no! Mommy monstow weck."

"I don't know how I feel about being called mommy monster."

"Very loved." Lincoln pecked my cheek, and I tingled from that brief contact.

He gestured to a salesclerk. "I'll be right back."

"Altin doesn't need much," I reminded him.

My brother obsessed about the straightness of his car line as I watched Lincoln and the pretty salesclerk chat. She laughed, and I could tell he'd already charmed her.

He returned with only one bag, and we hopped in his fancy SUV—the Jag couldn't fit Altin's car seat—and he gave my tired brother a lollipop and a super-soft teddy bear I'd oohed and aahed over. Altin stuck the unwrapped sucker in his mouth and cuddled the bear.

I looked out the window.

"You okay?" he asked.

"Yep. I'm great. Thanks for making Altin happy."

"Have I made you happy?" He reached for my hand.

I squeezed his fingers. "Yes." But he needed to stop. Lincoln was a man I could totally fall for. Who was I kidding? I'd already fallen for him. Big time. But he didn't have any idea about my past.

And he never would.

36

LINCOLN

Gemma entered the family room, wearing a loose pair of teal, maroon, and cream pants. A purple tank clashed on top.

"Nice parachute pants," I said.

"Harem pants. And they're fabulous."

I grinned. Her quirky outfits had bothered me initially, but I'd come to appreciate her uniqueness. She was definitely fabulous.

"Tell me about this." I lifted the bluish-green stone that hung on the necklace she always wore, alone or with other jewelry.

"It was my mama's. She wore it for protection. My bah—Dad gave it to her. Said the stone symbolized forgiveness."

"It's beautiful." Though it didn't match her outfit.

"Thanks."

"Did he go to bed easily?" I asked about her brother.

"Yes. You wore him out at the store."

"He's a good kid."

Her expression softened. "Altin's the best. I worry about him." She chewed her lip. "What if I'd died in the attack? Who would've cared for him?"

I covered her hand, wanting to reassure her. "Nothing happened."

"But it could have. And I've made no arrangements for him."

"If it makes you feel better, I'll have my attorney write up a will. Do you have any other family? Aunts? Uncles?"

"No. It's just me and him."

"I'll see to his care if anything happens to you—which it won't. If something happens to both of us, heaven forbid, maybe Joe and Janey could be his guardians."

"Would you really do that?"

"Consider it done. I'll text my attorney tonight."

"Thanks."

I pulled her close. She melted in my arms and seemed open to my lips exploring her cheek. But when I reached her neck, she tensed.

"There's something else I wanted to discuss. But first, promise to always care for Altin, no matter how you feel about me."

"Of course. I care for you, Gemma." Blast it all, I loved her. But she didn't seem ready for me to say that again. "What do you need?"

"Do you promise?"

"Yes, I'll care for Altin. I already care for him."

She smiled. "He likes you."

"Do you like me?" There. I'd asked. Sweat trickled down my spine as I waited for her answer.

The doorbell rang, making me curse as she pulled away.

"I'll get it," she said, since Mrs. Tan had already left for the night.

I followed her downstairs and groaned as she opened the door to reveal my family on the doorstep.

Mom pulled Gemma into an embrace. "Oh, you poor dear. How are you?" She caressed her bandaged head.

"I'm fine," Gemma said. "Tomorrow they'll take the bandaging off."

"Lincoln!" Mom caught me up in her arms next. "I've been worried sick about you." She kissed my cheek. "Why didn't you call to let me know you were home? I went to the hospital and they told me they'd already released you."

"Sorry." I was a grown man and didn't need to check in with my mom. "We've been trying to recover." She went to hug me again, but I stepped back. "No more touching, per my aching ribs."

"Oh, you poor dear."

I looked at Gemma and rolled my eyes.

"Let us in, boy," Dad said. "We want the whole story."

"Read the Tribune. They covered the incident in detail this morning."

"I've read the damned Tribune. Now tell me the truth. Was it a play for money? I told you money was the root of all evil."

"Ah, let him be." Gramps pushed past him, patting my shoulder. "Glad you're both okay. I was worried sick about you when your car was found abandoned in the middle of the road."

Mom took Gemma by the arm and guided her into the formal sitting area. I frowned. My family had the worst timing ever.

Gemma hadn't answered my question.

37

ANGEL

Age 19 - Fushë Krujë, Albania

*T*he sound of a whistle made Engjell tense. "You there, gypsy!" He turned to see a *policia* pointing a baton at him. "Why are you hanging around this part of town? Move on."

He scampered off before the man could hit him, circling back to the abandoned warehouse—his home since Uncle had split. Zinzan had invited him to stay with his family, but their house was cramped and downwind of the incinerator. Besides, Engjell was a man and could fend for himself.

He peeked out a broken window, wondering if the *policia* had left. He needed to see Mr. Sokoli before he left for the day. When Mr. Nikolla had left Albania, he'd arranged with Mr. Sokoli to continue teaching Engjell at school. But Mr. Sokoli hadn't followed through. He hated the Roma Mr. Nikolla had accepted.

Engjell pulled out Gem's black light and shone it into the corner, where he'd piled shredded tires and an old blanket for a bed. A few of Saemira's glowing rocks formed a circle around it.

Would he ever see her again?

Would she forget about him now that she lived in the promised land?

He turned off the light and crept out of the building, staying to the shadows. The hope and excitement he'd once felt when entering Mr. Nikolla's training school was gone now.

The pretty new secretary in the front yelped when he entered. "Mr. Sokoli," she yelled.

"It's all right," Engjell said, speaking clearly in Albanian as Mr. Nikolla had taught him. "I'm here to see if I have mail for Engjell Romani."

"Mr. Sokoli," she called again, backing into the hallway.

He took a seat to appear less threatening. The last thing he needed was for her to call the *policia*.

Mr. Sokoli appeared and scowled. "Why are you here, *magjup*." He shooed him. "Leave."

"Do I have mail from America? From Mr. Nikolla?"

The man shuffled through papers and handed him a letter. Engjell snatched the envelope before he could change his mind.

"Do not return."

Gladly. Engjell hurried out and made his way back to the warehouse. Inside, he held the black light over Gem's letter. Her cursive words turned neon in the darkness.

Engjell (or Angel, your name in English),

First, can you read this with the black light? I experimented with several ink solutions. This yielded the best results: a highlighter (pulled apart, of course, because...science, duh), hot water, and laundry detergent. I won't bore you with the details, but someday when you visit, I'll show you my lab. [Insert evil genius laughter]

But seriously, how are you? I'm freaking fantastic. Not. I hate Baba's new wife. Remember when I taught you those bad English words when we first met? Rosie is all of them. Add the super crude words Baba won't allow me to even say in my head. Yet Rosie uses them constantly.

Baba's teaching at a high school up the street, did I tell you? He doesn't like it near as much as when he taught in Albania. He says the kids here have no motivation. I wish we'd never left.

But enough about me. What are you doing? What are you learning? Don't get smarter than me or I'll make you eat Rosie's cooking. Blech! Anyway, I miss you and will write you more later. Baba wants to write a note before I send this. Don't forget me.

Saemira

PS. This is Taavi. Good news. The sponsorship went through. The University of Illinois in Chicago has awarded you a full scholarship to attend in January. Congratulations. I'll send a list of documents to

*procure, in care of Mrs. Hoxha, our next-door neighbor. I've received
conflicting reports about Mr. Sokoli and do not trust him. Mrs.
Hoxha will expect you. She's a good lady, but stern. Don't be afraid.
She said she remembers your face.*

How could anyone forget his face? Most strangers called him monster.
Kind ones called him gypsy.

But whatever. He was going to America!

Hope filled him as he imagined the opportunities that would soon be
his. People didn't care who you were in America as long as you were willing
to work hard. No one would care about the color of his skin or that his
mama didn't want him. Best of all, Saemira was there.

Maybe she would love him when he became a smart university man.

BLOOD GUSHED from my mouth and nose, but Uncle kept kicking. I'd
known when I'd knocked him out to help Saemira and her *gadjo* escape that
there would be consequences. I'd hidden for a week, but Uncle's men had
found me.

"Traitor!" Duke's boot connected with my ribs. "You're no different
from your whore mama, willing to sell yourself for nothing."

I curled up to protect my ribs, trying to distract myself from the pain by
picturing Saemira's emerald eyes and how they crinkled when she laughed.
I hoped she was safe.

Uncle stepped on my hand and brought the burning butt of a cigarette
down onto my skin. I gritted my teeth to keep from screaming.

"You think the temptress loves you?" He pulled the cigarette away but
stamped my wrist next. "You are nothing to her, Bengalo."

I'd never hated him. Even when he'd beaten me as a boy, I'd taken his
abuse without a word. I'd done everything he'd asked—stolen for him,
played lookout, rubbed him when he'd needed pleasure, carried water from
the river for baths, and gathered information by spying on his enemies.
Deep down, I'd believed he loved me since he'd saved me. But Saemira was
right. Maybe he'd saved me as a baby. But Uncle had cared for nobody but
himself since. He'd violated my friend. He'd wanted to kill her and her
gadjo.

Now, he would kill me.

"When you helped her escape, did she thank you? Did she give you a
parting kiss goodbye? No." He pounded the cigarette into my arm, making
me groan. "She only worried about the rich *gadjo,* her ticket to decadence."

I clenched my fists, preparing for the next burn. Uncle was long-winded and often mixed words with pain.

"I'll make her pay."

"Leave her alone. She's nothing." If I acted like I didn't care, maybe he'd forget her.

"She's everything, don't you see?" Uncle sneered. "No. She has blinded you."

The cigarette seared into my neck, making me shriek.

"No worries. I'll burn her evil out of you."

38

SAEMIRA

Age 17 - Chicago, Illinois

RESILIENT: capable of recovering from or adjusting to misfortune or change.

*T*he University of Chicago campus was an explosion of smart people. Engjell and Saemira weaved their way through the cerebral chaos toward a burger stand in the commons area. Baba was meeting with the sponsor coordinator, so they had some time to themselves. Saemira was giddy that her friend had made it to the United States. It'd been three years since she'd last seen him.

"Have you tried a burger? Or American pizza?"

He laughed. "I just got here. I haven't tried any food. What do you suggest?"

"Which word do you like better? Hamburger or pizza?"

"Hamburger."

She giggled. "You say it funny. We'll have to work on your accent."

"Hamburger," he said again.

"You're hopeless."

They bought their meals and found a table.

"So, you're doing school online?" he asked.

"Yep. Some girl wanted to beat me up for thinking I was better than her, which I didn't. Well, I did after she started acting all uppity. But before that, I didn't notice her. She thought I was Muslim, which seemed a sin in her eyes. I couldn't have pleased her if I'd wanted, and I don't want to please people like that. But the good thing is, I'll graduate at the end of the month. I'm almost done with my online courses." She pointed to his meal. "You like the burger?"

He grunted. "It's good."

"I'm good. Burgers are fantastic. Use your words right."

He grinned. "I've missed you, Gem."

"Of course, you have."

A group of boys at a nearby table snickered and pointed at her friend.

"So, what have I missed at home?" she said to distract him.

He ducked his head. "They probably wonder why you're eating with a freak like me."

She set her burger down. "I'll tell them." She stood. "Hey, you."

Their expressions changed when she called to them. Baba had been right. Guys did notice her, but their attention didn't make her bad.

"This is my friend, so stop laughing at him. It reflects more on you than him. Engjell's a genius, come all the way here from Albania. You'll probably wish you could work for him someday when he has his own company. Anyone who can count him as a friend is lucky."

She turned her back to the jerky guys.

Engjell nudged her. "Thank you."

"It probably won't make a difference."

"Makes one to me."

She took his hand. "You really are a cool guy. I'm definitely lucky."

"It's good to see your fire again. I worried about you when you left."

She stared at her burger, losing her appetite as ugly memories surfaced. "We're fine. Baba messed up by marrying Rosie, but we're resilient. Things will get better." She elbowed him. "They already are, with you here."

"Yeah, but we'll be five hours apart."

"Better than an ocean and a continent," she said.

He grinned. "You're right."

Of course she was right.

Gemma

THE SUN HADN'T EVEN RISEN, but I couldn't sleep. Lincoln couldn't either, apparently, because he'd beaten me to the coffee.

"Good morning, beautiful."

I frowned. "There's nobody to act for right now."

"Thank God." He lifted the pot. "Coffee?"

"Please."

"How's your head?" he asked.

"Meh. It's fine. What about your ribs?"

He set a mug in front of me. "Okay, if I don't move."

Poor guy. "Sorry."

"What for? You didn't kick me." We finished our coffee in silence, then he motioned me to follow him. "I want to show you something."

I followed him upstairs and froze in a doorway.

He looked back at me. "Think he'll like it?"

I couldn't answer. The room had been transformed into a child's paradise, with every toy we'd played with in the shop two days ago. The floor was covered by a rug with roads and a city on it, for cars. A shelf held baskets with puzzles, blocks, and books. A rocking giraffe sat in the corner, a kid-sized car parked beside it. A pile of Mega-Blocks Lincoln had helped Altin build with were scattered about on another rug. Stuffed animals were piled in the corner with several beanbags.

Something blocked my throat. Embarrassing emotion, probably.

"The clerk gave me the name of an artist who paints murals. Maybe you can give him some ideas of what Altin would enjoy on the walls."

I stumbled over to a rocking chair and buried my head in my hands.

"Are you okay? Did I do something wrong?"

"No." Baba had encouraged me to kill my enemies with kindness. I'd never understood what good that could do. Until now. Lincoln's sweet gesture crushed me.

For the last few months, I'd judged him to be better than me because of his money. But that had nothing to do with anything. He was better simply because he chose to be a better person. Yes, he had flaws, such as his tendency to profile others based on the color of their skin. But I'd profiled him for different reasons. Yet when I'd pointed out his flaws, he'd apologized. When he'd pointed out mine, I'd hated him for it.

"What's the matter?" He tipped my chin.

I swallowed. "This is the kindest thing anyone's ever done for me."

"Technically, it's for your brother." He winked. "But if you want to play in here, I won't judge."

I hugged him. "Thank you. Seriously. Altin's going to love this."

His arms wrapped around me and his lips pressed against my ear. "You never answered me last night," he said, voice husky. "About whether you liked me or not."

"Mama! Mama!" Altin cried from the other room.

I stepped back, feeling an immediate famine of warmth. Lincoln's slumping shoulders revealed disappointment. I couldn't have that. I reached up to kiss him on the lips. Short, but firm.

"I more than like you." Then, coward that I was, I ran from the room.

THE DOORBELL RANG. Lincoln growled and sat up from where he'd been building a tower with my brother. "Better not be my family. Don't they understand they can wear out their welcome?"

I took his spot next to Altin. "Be nice."

He winked and left the room.

Altin and I added another level to his creation. The three of us had passed a wonderful morning exploring the playroom. Altin had been in heaven. Lincoln had given him a childhood, the kind I'd never been capable of granting him. My heart would break when I had to leave my little brother, but there was no one better I could leave him with than Lincoln.

"Look who the cat dragged in," Lincoln said as two rambunctious boys raced in and overtook the room like Thing One and Thing Two from *The Cat in the Hat*.

Joe appeared behind them. "Gemma, how's my second favorite girl?"

A cute blond woman followed. She must be his wife, the number one girl.

I hugged Joe and was caught off guard when his wife embraced me as well.

"Hi. I'm Janey. Joe has told me all about you. We wanted to check in and see how you both were doing."

"She brought a casserole," Lincoln said. "A total Mormon thing to do."

"Don't pretend you're not excited," Joe said.

"I'm ecstatic," Lincoln said. "I love Janey's cooking."

Joe's twins were a force of nature. I was used to my sweet, orderly brother, but the twins quickly emptied puzzles, blocks and other toys from the neat and tidy shelves Lincoln had worked on setting up all night.

Joe caught me staring. "The monsters are Smyth and Sutter. Don't worry. Janey and I will clean up their mess before we leave."

"Hey monsters!" Lincoln called.

Smyth and Sutter perked up and each clobbered one of his legs, beating their tiny fists against him.

"I got ya, Uncle Link," one said.

"Give me a horsie ride," the other hollered.

I looked at Joe. "He has two broken ribs."

He shooed his sons away. "Uncle Sausage Link's hurt. Ride him another time."

The boys took off to cause more destruction as Lincoln joined Altin, who stood frozen in front of his building. "Smyth. Sutter." He waved. "Come here and meet Altin."

They ran over, the one eyeing Altin's building with a devious glint.

"Don't think about it, Sutter," Lincoln said. "You won't get a treat if you do."

The boy pouted, but he didn't break Altin's building. Thank goodness.

"Say hi to Altin."

I watched in awe as Joe's boys transformed into tiny gentlemen and said hello to my brother. Lincoln turned to Altin. "Can you say hi to Smyth and Sutter?"

Altin did a fair job repeating their names. Lincoln enticed the boys to work on Altin's building and another tower next to it.

Joe grinned. "My boys love Uncle Link. They have eight other real uncles between Janey's family and mine, yet he's their favorite."

"Because the goofball plays with them," Janey said.

I'd witnessed that silly side of him and loved it. Maybe too much. As I'd watched him with my brother, I'd imagined living out my life with him. Our own little family. Happy. Hopeful. Safe.

But I mustn't be greedy. It was enough that Altin would have that life. He wouldn't if I stuck around.

Joe joined the boys on the floor while Janey and I sat on beanbags in the corner and visited. Two hours passed like a snap of my fingers. After Joe and Janey cleaned up after their boys and Lincoln found treats for the twins, we walked them outside.

Janey hugged me. "It's like I've known you forever. Thanks for letting us hang out with you this afternoon. I know my boys can be overwhelming."

"I love them. Don't be a stranger," I said. "You're always welcome here."

She grinned. "Throw the casserole in the oven about forty-five minutes before you want to eat."

"Thanks."

Their rowdy, cute little family drove away, and Lincoln lifted Altin into his arms.

"He needs a nap." I held my arms out to take him.

"I need one, too." Lincoln carried Altin upstairs. "Can I join you guys?"

"I guess. Or you could nap with him, and I could go into work." I needed to start mapping out new investors to call.

Lincoln tapped my nose. "Stop thinking about work. You and I are on forced leave." He stepped closer. "Let me join your group nap."

Those words sounded sort of naughty coming out of his mouth. My heart beat double-time as I stretched out beside Altin, turning my back to Lincoln. He crawled onto the bed and I was ultra-aware of him. His scent. His muscled body. The rhythm of his breathing. I went through my routine with Altin, changing the Albanian song I usually sang to just humming. Speaking of humming, my body soared to life as Lincoln caressed my arms.

So much for sleeping.

"Tell me the name of your Jeep," I said softly, after my brother had conked out.

Lincoln's rumbling chuckle made me want to purr. "You're never going to let that go, are you?"

"No. So you might as well fess up."

He kept caressing my arms. "You'll laugh at me." His minty breath against my ear made goosebumps erupt along my neck.

"I won't. I promise."

"Doesn't matter. I'm not telling you." His tantalizing cologne made me long for more.

But it would be wrong to complicate our relationship. With secrets or with more intimacy. I didn't deserve to know the name of his dumb Jeep. And I certainly didn't need to turn around so I could kiss him.

Nope.

Today had been perfect. Whatever was happening between us right now would come to an end, but for now, I savored his tender touches to remember when I left this all behind.

39

LINCOLN

*W*ilder and his wife sat across from Gemma and me in my living room. They'd come bearing gifts and goodwill, something I'd honestly tired of over the last few days.

"Your story in the paper caught the eye of the general manager of the St. Regis in Park City." Wilder grinned. "He's offered up his facilities next weekend for your wedding."

I watched Gemma for a reaction. Ever since the attack, an underlying tension simmered below the surface. I knew she cared for me, but she hadn't brought up the L word. And I hadn't dared bring up the topic again. How did she feel about moving up the wedding date?

"That's wonderful." I took her hand.

"Your grandfather will be thrilled," Wilder said.

But would Gemma?

We made idle chitchat until the Wilders left. Tina had put Altin to bed. So, ready or not, Gemma and I needed to discuss this new development.

"Want to go outside under the stars?" I said.

"Sure." It wasn't a super enthusiastic response, but I grabbed a blanket and led her into the backyard.

A slight breeze from the canyon made me shiver. I shook the blanket out and sat with her. Neither of us spoke. We just looked up through the pines at the stars, waiting for the other to start things rolling.

"So," I said, "how are you feeling about the wedding plans?"

"Good," she said. "I want EcoCore to get Mr. Wilder's money."

I reached for her hand. "I don't care about the money. This was a game at first, but everything's changed." I waited for her to look at me. I needed her to look at me. "I love you, Gemma. I don't know if you feel the same, but I can't keep dancing around the truth. I need to know if you feel anything for me, or if I'm way out of line."

She didn't look overjoyed by my confession. Quite the opposite. "I care for you, Lincoln, more than I've ever cared about any other man."

Not love. And she'd led in with a positive, meaning a huge BUT of negative would follow.

"But we're polar opposites. You're rich and successful. I'm a ghetto brat. We both went through a traumatic experience, and your feelings transformed overnight. They're not real. I mean, you don't even trust me with the name of your Jeep. And I get that. Your feelings for me will fade with time." She withdrew her hand.

"That's not true. My feelings are real. You want to know the name of my Jeep? It was Princess Genevieve." My whole body warmed in embarrassment. "It was Cora's favorite Barbie movie, The Twelve Dancing Princesses. Cora called me Derek, the royal cobbler Genevieve is in love with. And she was Lacey, Genevieve's younger sister. I called my Jeep Gen for short."

Gemma blinked but didn't laugh, for which I was grateful. This was something only Joe and Cora had known about, something I'd gone along with only for the sake of my sister.

"Look, I'm grateful for all you've done for Altin and me. I will marry you next weekend to make your grandpa happy and to secure Wilder's funding. But we need to be careful and not do anything either of us will regret later. Face it. You're going to want to annul this marriage when you realize what you imagined was love only stemmed from stress and fear."

"Gemma, that's not true." I'd told her about Gen, for heaven's sake.

She stood. "Let's just keep this business only, as we originally agreed." She grimaced. "I need to get to bed. My head's killing me."

She left me there—alone and cold. And humiliated.

She was wrong. I'd fallen for her long before the attack. That'd sped up my admission of the truth, sure. But my devotion was real. It wouldn't change.

I loved Gemma Stone, damn it all.

But how could I convince her of that when she'd already made up her mind about me?

40

SAEMIRA

Age 17 - Detroit, Michigan

CALAMITOUS: disastrous; marked by great loss and suffering.

lass broke downstairs as Saemira shoved clothes into her suitcase. Nine-month-old Altin fussed on the bed. She walked over to pat his belly. "Don't be scared, bro. You won't have to put up with the witch after tonight. Baba has a place for us in north town. We're moving out of this hell hole."

Rosie kept screeching at Baba. Saemira didn't understand why he'd given her so many chances. They should've moved out months ago. Rosie was unfit to be a mother. Unfit to be a human being.

She zipped her luggage and set the cases by the door. Baba would get them when he was ready. He'd told her to stay in the room with Altin until he gave the all-clear. Rosie was an ugly drunk.

A sharp explosion sounded downstairs, making her eardrums ring.

She turned to the door, unable to breathe. What was that? Had the gods come to punish her after all?

Saemira shoved pillows around her baby brother and raced downstairs to see if everything was all right. She froze on the bottom step when she saw Rosie standing over Baba with a gun. He was sprawled on the kitchen floor, chest bleeding.

Had she shot him?

She wanted to scream at Rosie to get away from him, but she couldn't move. She just watched, until adrenaline, shock, or anger yielded a pathetic whimper.

Rosie flinched and turned the gun on her.

Would she shoot her, too? The evil woman hated her.

"Stop looking at me like that, you filthy gypsy!" Rosie threw the gun down and ran to the door.

When the screen slammed, Saemira stumbled over to her dad. "Baba!"

His eyes slowly focused on her. "It's okay...baby...girl." He closed his eyes. "Call...9-1-1."

She did as he asked, telling an operator through her tears that her baba had been shot by Rosie, who had run away. The operator told her to stay on the line but Altin's screams from upstairs made her frantic. What if he rolled off the bed?

Saemira took the phone to Baba. "Help's coming." She caressed his forehead, but he didn't move. Didn't speak. His eyes were open, staring up at the ceiling. "Baba?" she put her head to his heart. No heartbeat. No up or down movement of his chest. "Baba!" she cried.

The baby's frantic screaming pierced through her hazy shock, and she dropped Baba's phone. Tears blinded her as she felt her way up to her bedroom to pick her brother up. She patted his back and shushed him as she dialed Engjell's number.

"Hey, Sammy," he said, teasing her with a new nickname. "What's—"

"Shut up and listen," she choked out. "Baba's been shot. He's dead." She swiped her eyes and shushed her brother again. He was as upset as she was. "Rosie murdered him." She wiped snot from her face, trying to erase Baba's blank stare from her mind, the blood on his chest. "Rosie ran, but her gun's downstairs. What should I do?"

"Calm down, Saemira."

"What if the police take us away? I can't lose my brother."

"I won't let you lose him."

The lump in her throat burst. "You're my only friend," she sobbed. Nobody in America liked her. She was different. She wasn't white. Now, she was an orphan.

"And you're mine. I won't leave you."

"What if they put us in foster care?" She'd read a book about that.

"I'll get you out."

"How?"

The door burst open downstairs and she heard shouting. "Police! Get down on the ground with your hands above your head!"

"Get down, Gem," Engjell said, having overheard.

She set Altin on the bed in the middle of the pillows and curled up on the floor.

"Hang up and put your phone in your pocket. Don't lose it," her friend said, sounding panicked.

She slipped the phone in her pocket and put her hands above her head. Altin screeched above her on the bed.

Please, God, don't let him roll off.

Heavy footsteps stomped upstairs as she sobbed into the carpet.

For the second time that night, she waited to be shot.

Gemma

HIGH-END, snobby store shopping didn't appeal to me as much as thrift store treasure hunts. But Lucy had insisted that retail therapy would help me. So, I'd humored her. She understood my preferences now and had found several Bohemian shops for me to peruse.

"Could you drop me off at EcoCore?" I asked, after the required therapy had ended. "I have a few phone calls to make for Lincoln, but the files are at the office." In truth, I needed time alone without him breathing down my neck. I'd hurt him by being honest, but distance and boundaries were needed. I couldn't let him love me. That would endanger him.

"No problem, dear. I'll wait for you in the lobby."

"You're sweet, but I'll have Lincoln pick me up later."

"Are you up to working? How's your head?"

"It feels great. I've been dying to return to a normal routine, but Lincoln's been a mother hen."

It took more convincing, but Lucy eventually dropped me off at the office.

I switched the glass to privacy and pulled out several files. Leaning back in my chair, I propped my feet up to admire the new pumps Lucy had persuaded me to buy. I'd have to carve a cool pattern into the bottom to bring the soles to life.

For the next hour, I leafed through pages of research half-heartedly as I obsessed about Lincoln. By the gods, he'd told me the name of his Jeep. And had blushed like crazy in the process. It had been utterly adorable, and had taken all my willpower and more not to kiss him senseless right there on that blanket, under the stars. I had ached to reciprocate and tell him my real name, my real problems and fears. But if this all ended in annulment—and it would—I needed to stay silent. I didn't have a lot of confidence that the police would find Duke. So, the less Lincoln knew about me, the better.

Still, I was so tired of living a lie.

The door burst open, and I flinched as Lincoln marched in, appearing madder than a nest of hornets at a piñata party. He slammed the door.

"Is Altin okay?" I asked.

He scowled. "I've been calling and texting you for over an hour. Why haven't you answered your phone?"

"I, uh..."

"Dammit, Gemma, you scared the shit out of me. I called Mom, and she said she dropped you off here over an hour ago. I've called and left messages, and nothing!"

"I, uh..."

He stalked around my desk, yanking me out of my chair. I cringed, but he pulled me into his arms and cradled my head. "Sorry." He let out a long breath. "I didn't mean to yell. I've just been scared out of my mind."

"I didn't mean to worry you. I lost my phone in the attack." More lies. The dang things fed off each other. "I wasn't purposely ignoring you."

He brushed his lips over my forehead. "Why didn't you tell me? I'll get you another one ASAP."

"No, you don't need—"

"You'll be my wife in a week, which means you will have the best phone money can buy, with a tracker. I don't ever want to worry about where you are again." He buried his head in my neck. "I feared the kidnappers had found you again."

I shuddered. "I'm fine. And please, no tracker." I didn't want to have to ditch my phone when I ran someday.

He frowned. "Didn't I tell you not to come into work? You're recovering from major trauma. Besides," he looped his fingers through my belt loops, tugging me closer, "you have an 'in' with the boss. Rumors say he really likes you."

His lips found mine with an intensity that stunned me. Holy heavens, I loved kissing him. Fire spread through every cell in my body as I dug my fingers into his hair and kissed him back. Lincoln tasted of cinnamon, kindness, and passion, and I was starved for all of it.

He picked me up and set me on the desk, and my legs wrapped around him. Who knows how long we kissed, or why we did. I'd told him we should keep things professional. So what was I freaking doing?

I pushed him away, though I wanted to pull him closer. "We can't do this." Although kissing him was all I wanted to do. "We need to stay friends only. Kissing only when required." This couldn't last. Duke would make certain of that.

"To me, kissing is always required." He cradled my face, still breathing heavy.

I steeled myself against his charm and pushed his hands off me. "This isn't real." Even if I wanted it to be.

The desire to sob almost paralyzed me, but I managed to grab my satchel and head out the door.

41

LINCOLN

emma didn't speak on the drive home. I'd crossed the line she'd firmly drawn between us, but I wouldn't apologize. The way she'd kissed me back had told me all I needed to know. Gemma might push me away and say she wanted only friendship, but that was a lie. She was scared and didn't trust that my feelings were real.

I would prove her wrong.

She avoided eye contact as she climbed out of the Jag, not waiting for me to open her door. I blocked her before she could escape inside. She wasn't getting off the hook that easy.

"I know you liked that kiss as much as I did."

She blushed and looked down. I took advantage of that to pull her in by the waist.

"Lincoln," she said, "don't do this."

"Don't make you uncomfortable so you have to admit the truth?" I rubbed her moist lips she'd just licked.

She winced.

"Why don't you trust me?" I asked.

"Trust has nothing to do with it. You're a good man. I just don't want to hurt you."

"As if you could ever do that."

"You don't know me at all," she said.

"I want to. I want to know everything there is to know about you. When did your parents die? How long have you been on your own? What are the names of your cars. They definitely can't be as embarrassing as mine." I caressed her cheek. "Where's your favorite place to be kissed?"

I grinned as her cheeks turned crimson.

"We can't kiss again, Lincoln." Tears filled her eyes, and the smile slid from my face.

"I'm sorry. I didn't mean to upset you. We'll take things slow. We don't have to go through with the wedding if it's stressing you out." Which obviously it was. "Gramps will be okay."

"No. We're going through with it. EcoCore needs the money. And I don't want to disappoint Gramps. I just don't want to complicate everything with physical affection."

I stroked her cheek, and Gemma melted into me. But then she jerked away.

"Trust me, this is for your own good." She slipped inside to find her brother.

I trusted her. But keeping distance between us wasn't good for me at all. Why couldn't she see that?

42

SAEMIRA

Age 17 · Farmington Hills, Michigan

FUGITIVE: a person who flees or escapes; a wanderer.

*D*ust filled the long dirt path to where Saemira now lived. She'd sworn to never live apart from her brother, but within a week of Baba's death, the authorities had taken Altin away, saying he'd be given to a family that could care for him. She'd been given to another. The Barbers. Kent and Kay treated her as an enlisted soldier, and her life boiled down to a monotonous routine of chores and more chores.

There were five other foster kids with her. She was the oldest at seventeen and shared a room with a white girl named Terri, who smoked. Two other girls, Molly and Desiree, shared another room. Two boys shared a room downstairs—a nine-year-old Hispanic kid named Jose and eleven-year-old Rich. They were quiet and kept to themselves. They all did. Kent and Kay gave extra chores if you opened your mouth.

Saemira watched the dust trail grow, hope rising as she tried to identify the driver. The authorities had confiscated her phone early on. Foster kids didn't get any rights or belongings, at least not any that came with a monthly bill.

The gray car took the corner by the clump of willows fast. She jumped off her bed and ran downstairs. Just in case.

Kay stood on the porch, hands on her bony hips. Saemira tensed behind her as a battered car screeched to a stop.

"Come on," Engjell called out the window. He wore a beanie over his head and a neckerchief over the bottom of his face, but she still recognized him.

Kay cursed as Saemira shoved past her. "Stop!" she hollered.

Saemira jumped into the rear seat and shut the door as Engjell turned the car around and headed back the way he'd come. Faster than hell.

"I hope you know what you're doing," she said, climbing over the seat. "Kay's likely calling the cops." Her heart beat triple speed, making her wonder if she was having a heart attack. If so, at least she was with someone who loved her. She hit Engjell's arm and laughed. "Took you long enough."

"Excuse me for not understanding how things are done in America." His strong accent made her smile. "It took time to figure out where they'd taken you and Altin."

Hearing her brother's name made her deflate. "Did you find him?"

He placed a hand on hers. "He's down south in a town called Plymouth." He pointed to her feet. "Get the map. Tell me where to go."

A little later, they found the house where Altin supposedly lived. Her stomach churned at the thought of breaking the law. But families shouldn't be torn apart.

Luck was with them. A teen girl swung a baby out on a swing in an unfenced yard.

"Is that him?" Engjell asked as he parked across the street.

"One way to find out." Saemira strolled into the neighbor's yard, hopping the three-foot fence halfway back. Bushes hid her as she peeked out at a blond girl who held her giggling brother.

She jumped out, making the girl scream. "Give me my brother."

The girl tightened her grip on Altin. "He's not yours."

Saemira pounced, pulling at the white girl's hair as she wrestled Altin from her arms. Once she had her brother, she stomped on the girl's arm and took off.

Engjell peeled out when she climbed inside, leaving Plymouth in their dust as they drove to who knows where. Saemira didn't care. She had her brother. That's all that mattered. She sang to Altin and kept kissing his cute cheeks. He'd grown in the weeks they'd been apart.

Engjell stopped outside another town. "The *policia* will be looking for this car. I bought this one for cash." He pointed at a white car, way more beat up than the stolen one.

She hugged him. They were fugitives, but smart ones.

They switched cars and drove for several more hours before Engjell pulled over in a wooded area to sleep.

"It might be a week before the university calls the authorities about me missing. I went to classes until the end so I'd have internet to find where you guys were being held."

Altin had fallen asleep. Saemira climbed over the seat to talk with her friend. "You were brilliant. Thanks for rescuing us. You're my knight in shining armor."

He reached for her hand. "I'll always take care of you." He pulled something from the glove box.

"My black light." She caressed the old gift they'd played with as children. "You still have it?"

"You said to return it when I came here someday."

She touched the light. Things were different now than when they'd lived in Albania. She was scared and hungry, thrilled and lost. She didn't know how she'd take care of Altin or keep the police from finding them, but she couldn't ask for a better companion on this wild ride.

She hugged Engjell, grateful not to be alone any longer.

Gemma

STROKING my baby brother's head, I kissed him goodnight and turned to check the mirror. The orange and yellow blouse with flared sleeves was gorgeous. I rubbed Mama's amulet.

"Please tell me what to do," I whispered.

For the last five days, I'd managed to avoid or only have minimal contact with Lincoln. I'd still seen him. We lived in the same house, for peanut butter's sake. But I'd kept Altin close or I'd locked myself in my room to study *Popular Mechanics*. I'd jumped at chances to hang out with his mom. But my head, heart, and body were in an all-out war. My head said to hold steady. Keep the friends-only line firmly in place between us. My body wanted to attack Lincoln, kiss him long and hard to eradicate that stupid boundary. My heart tried to compromise, knowing there was danger in caring for him, but recognizing it was already too late. Maybe his feelings were true. Maybe we could make this work.

But not unless I came clean.

Lincoln needed to know the truth, even if he hated me for it.

I left my room and bumped into him at the top of the staircase. "Oh, hey," I said.

"Hey, gorgeous. Is this new?" He tugged at my sleeve.

"Your mom made me buy it."

He grinned. "You're the only girl I know who's *made* to buy anything."

"It was expensive."

He pulled me closer, making my legs go all limp-noodle. "Stop stressing about money. I promise that even if Angeline wins the lawsuit, I have enough to live on. We'll be okay."

I didn't worry about that. Buying expensive clothes just made me feel guilty since he'd lost millions to Duke because of me. I knew I could buy them for a fraction of the cost at a thrift shop.

"I need to tell you something," I said. No more hiding the truth.

"Same, but let's go outside." He led me out the French doors and into the backyard.

I paused on the patio. What in the world?

Hundreds, maybe thousands, of twinkle lights covered the entire backyard.

"Holy heavens," I said. "It's beautiful."

"Like you." He tugged me to the back corner where a trickling waterfall fell into rocks.

"Who put up all these lights? And why?"

"I've helped the ground crew put them up for the last three days while you've been hiding from me."

I blushed. Why had I thought he wouldn't notice my avoidance tactics?

"And this is why." He knelt on the grass and pulled out a black jeweler's box.

I covered my mouth as he opened the lid to reveal the most stunning ring I'd ever seen. A tear-drop bluish-purple stone that matched Mama's amulet was set in a gold-filigreed band.

"Gemma Ann Stone, the last time I asked you to marry me, it was a joke. I needed your help to save face and not lose Wilder's support."

I wrinkled my nose, hating the reminder of the dangerous game we played.

He pulled the diamond monstrosity off my finger. "But today, I'm asking for real." He slid the gorgeous new gemstone onto my finger. "This is Tanzanite. The jeweler said it's a thousand times rarer than diamonds. There's only an estimated thirty-year supply left in the world. It's unique and one of a kind, like you." He squeezed my hand. "I don't care about Wilder's money or fulfilling Gramp's last wish. I only care about you. Will you marry me and be my wife, in every sense of the word? I absolutely do not want an annulment. I love you."

I pulled my hand away, tears pricking my eyes, guilt pricking my heart. "I'm not worthy. Seriously. You own your own company. I barely graduated from high school."

He put a finger to my lips. "You own my heart, Gemma. You're precious and wonderful, and I cannot bear to live life without you."

"But Altin?"

"I'll adopt him. I love him, too. Please accept my heart. It's all yours. Marry me."

"Are you serious?" If he adopted Altin, my brother would be safe. Did I dare tell him the truth now? What if he hated me...and Altin, too? Maybe I should wait until my brother was legally his before spilling my secrets. If he hated me then, I would disappear from his life. But my brother would have a dad to care for him.

"Completely. Didn't confessing my Jeep's silly name prove that to you?" He pressed a kiss to the back of my hand. "I want to share my mind and heart with you. Build our dreams together. I want to name our cars together. Have babies together. I want to grow old with you by my side, watching our babies' babies grow up as we argue about the weather."

I laughed, caught up in his vision. It was everything I wanted, my girlish fantasies of true love put into words.

He pulled me close and kissed me hard. I buried my head in his neck, breathing in his spicy cologne, wanting him to kiss me again.

"Please say yes."

What else could I say? His sweet words and kisses still had me floating above the clouds. "Yes," I said, pulling him closer. "How about we tie the knot tomorrow?" As planned.

Lincoln chuckled and worked his wonderful magic on me again, kissing me deeply and reverently with all his heart. And for that moment, I gave him my heart as well, wishing I could give it to him forever.

43

LINCOLN

$\mathcal{M}$y heart rejoiced as I savored Gemma's mouth, her lips, the velvety soft skin on her cheeks. She'd said yes! This wasn't a game any longer.

I buried my head in her luscious neck, feeling grateful for this amazing woman who'd transformed my life. After Angeline, I'd kept my distance from women, fearing I'd be manipulated by one again. I'd fought against my attraction to Gemma but had come to realize she was nothing like my ex. Angeline had been a master at telling me what I'd wanted to hear, even while carrying on an affair with her current husband behind my back for over a year. But Gemma—dear, sweet, wonderful Gemma—was genuine. She didn't lie or give me half-truths. She told it as it was, and I loved her for that.

I caressed her hair, before pulling away and clasping hands. "You've made me the happiest man alive." Something I had believed impossible only a few short months ago. I gave her a firm kiss on the lips and tugged her toward the house. "Come. There's something else I want to show you."

We walked beneath the canopy of lights, and I led her inside and up the stairs, wondering what her reaction would be to my surprise. Would she like it?

She bit her lips as we entered my master suite. I'd never brought her here before, not wanting to push boundaries we hadn't yet mapped out. But she would be my wife in less than sixteen hours. The boundaries seemed firmly in place.

"You have doors," she said, glancing into my bathroom.

I laughed. "Absolutely. If someone has money, they should put doors everywhere."

She giggled.

I pulled her over to my bed and gestured to the large silver gift. "Open it."

"It's so beautiful. I hate to unwrap it."

"What's inside is more beautiful." At least, I hoped she thought so.

She gave me an impish smile, before carefully unwrapping the box. When she lifted the lid, she put a hand to her heart. "Whoa. Is this…?"

"Your wedding dress."

She turned to stare at me, then lifted the gown out. "I thought Casey dropped off my dress yesterday."

"That was the one you hated. I'm hoping you love this one."

A sigh escaped her as I led her into the bathroom so she could hold the dress up to the mirror.

"How?" She ran a hand down the Egyptian-style gown.

"I sent a screen shot from your phone to a tailor I know. He'll be here in the morning to make adjustments since he guessed at your dimensions by using another dress of yours."

She caressed the bedazzled neckline. "Are you okay with this? I know—"

"I'm boring?"

"No." She smirked. "I only called you that to annoy you. I actually find you appallingly sexy in a suit. And naming your Jeep Princess Genevieve made you ten times sexier."

I laughed. Her excitement was contagious. She'd never cared about the gown Casey had chosen, and for good reason. That'd been made for a socialite wannabe like Angeline.

"Seriously, though." Worry lines formed between her eyes. "This thumbs its nose at convention." She caressed the gown and hesitantly set it on the counter. "I'll wear the other one. I know how much your image means to you."

"Absolutely not." I shuddered. Gemma's unparalleled beauty came from confidence in her uniqueness. And this dress was distinctive. I'd scoffed at first, thinking it more costume than gown. But Gemma would shine in it tomorrow. I didn't want her to be anyone but who she really was. I placed the dress back in her hands. "I went to a ton of trouble to have this made for you." I reached for the beaded headpiece I'd hung by the shower. "Let's see this on you." I placed the tiara on her head.

"By the gods," she murmured, seeming almost as stunned as I was at her reflection.

"You are definitely a goddess." I winked. "Do you like it?"

"It's spectacular. Even better than the one on my Pinterest board." She held the gown up to her body.

"You are indeed spectacular."

Gemma wrapped her arms around me, kissing me hard. I reciprocated, smashing the gown between us.

GEMMA SHONE like the sun on our wedding day as she exited from the back of the St. Regis hotel and began the march up the aisle to meet me. Gramps escorted her, and they smiled at each other as they slowly stepped to the wedding march.

Joe and Janey and their two whirlwinds grinned up at me from the first row of guests. Bless Joe for having the foresight to stop me months ago from making the biggest mistake of my life by firing Gemma. The Wilders sat next to them. Bless him also for pushing us into an engagement. My parents sat at the end. Mom beamed up at me with unmasked delight. I had to admit, it was nice having her back in my life. Dad scowled. No surprise. I had wanted to uninvite him, but Gemma had said it would hurt Mom. She was probably right. Joe's parents and a couple of his sisters sat behind them. Other guests took up the other seats.

But I only had eyes for Gemma.

Gramps stopped in front of me, sending me a conspiratorial wink as he lifted Gemma's hand from his arm and placed it on mine.

"You two have made this old man truly happy." He kissed Gemma's cheek and left to take his seat beside Wilder.

Gemma looked up at me with so much love in her eyes that I wanted to bag the ceremony, steal my bride, and skip straight to the honeymoon.

"I like this look on you," she said, playing with the top button of my shirt.

"Are the Tevas too much?"

She'd insisted last night that I should loosen up for our wedding. Think comfort, not stiff tradition. I'd wondered all night how to fulfill her wish. I'd decided to wear the tux but lose the bowtie and unbutton the top two buttons of my shirt. I'd also worn Tevas instead of my Italian dress shoes.

"Absolutely not. Now we can enjoy ourselves."

I'd felt ridiculous at first, especially when I'd caught furtive glances from arriving guests. But with Gemma pleased, I didn't care about anyone else's opinions.

The ceremony began, and the clergyman said the oft-repeated words: "Do you take this woman to be your lawfully wedded wife?"

I grinned and said, "I do."

He asked if she would take me to be her lawfully wedded husband, and Gemma's expression nearly made me melt into the grass as she said, "I do."

We kissed, and I couldn't quench my thirst for her. We were married. For real. Gemma loved me. I loved her. We would spend the rest of our lives together, have little whirlwinds to match Joe's and Janey's, and grow in our love, instead of growing apart as Angeline and I had done.

I'd gotten it right this time.

Gemma pulled away to laugh, then yanked me back to kiss me longer, deeper. I vowed right then and there that I should always give my wife what she wanted.

44

ANGEL

Age 20 - Tulsa, Oklahoma

*S*aemira and Altin had fallen asleep in the rear seat. Engjell pulled over somewhere outside of Oklahoma, Tulsa to nap. Fourteen hours separated them from Michigan, though it'd taken three weeks to get there, zigzagging across county lines to find places to hide each night.

The first week, he'd had enough money for food and gas, having had weeks to stash it away as he'd searched for Saemira and her brother. But his cash was almost gone. He'd resorted to *shopping,* as Duke had taught him. Uncle hadn't made life easy, but he appreciated his hard lessons now.

Saemira hadn't been built for a life on the streets though. He knew hunger. She and Altin didn't. On top of physical privations, she still grieved for her baba. The first day after he'd rescued them, she'd been energetic and eager, like the young friend of his childhood. But she'd soon become sullen and withdrawn, reminding him of the traumatized girl she'd been when she'd left Albania.

He stared into the darkness. What was he to do? Saemira had her honor. Her ethics. She hated when he stole food, unable to wrap her mind around the fact that it was necessary. America was the land of opportunity, but not to a runaway deformed immigrant on a student visa.

He slipped out of the car to be alone, walking up the dirt road a ways. Crickets chirped from the cornfields as his mind churned options. What should he do? Where should he go? He'd exhausted almost all his resources. He had ninety-seven dollars left for gas. It was impossible to steal that. But once that cash ran out, they'd have to ditch the car or figure a way to get more money.

Uncle had always bragged about his connections in Canada. That was above America. Uncle had lived there as a child and still had relatives there. That's where he'd said he was going when he left Albania.

Could Duke help him now? If nothing else, maybe he could give him ideas where to go.

Engjell glared at his phone, remembering Uncle's pounding fists and ugly words. But he was a man now, not a naughty boy. Uncle was family. What was the worst he could do? Say no and hang up?

He shivered as he punched in Uncle's number by memory. Hopefully, the number still worked. Uncle picked up on the third ring.

"Who's this?"

"Eng—Bengalo." Uncle had beaten him the first time he'd asked to be called Engjell. He'd never asked again.

"Why are you calling, boy?"

"I'm in America, outside Oklahoma, Tulsa." Population 403,733. He'd looked that up on Google while Saemira slept. But Uncle would mock him if he tried to sound smart.

"Ah, I'm in America, too."

He was?

"I'm running operations in Utah for my cousin. You looking for a job? You were always skilled at picking pockets. And your English is decent."

Engjell blinked. This was a blessing from the gods. "Yes. Thank you. I'm not alone. You remember Taavi Nikolla and his daughter, Saemira?"

"The temptress?"

He scowled. "Her baba got murdered. Saemira and her baby brother were put in foster care. I helped them escape. We're on the run from the *policia*."

Uncle chuckled. "You've always been trouble, Bengalo."

Causing trouble had never been his intention. "Saemira can't know, though. She doesn't approve of stealing."

"Didn't you steal her from foster care?" Uncle asked.

"That's different."

"Is it? Seems your temptress has a double standard. Stealing is okay, as long as it benefits her, no?"

"It's not that." Uncle would never understand. Neither would Saemira. They both viewed the world in black and white. Duke saw black, Saemira white.

"Whatever, boy. Get yourself here, and I'll put you to work. I have a place you can stay with your temptress and her bastard."

He gritted his teeth but didn't correct him.

"You'll need documents. Send me pictures of you and your temptress."

Uncle must be doing well if he could secure papers. "Can I pick our new names?"

"Get your pretty little sidekick to Salt Lake City, and you can do whatever you want. I'm proud of you, boy."

Engjell stood taller. Uncle had never praised him before.

After Uncle hung up, Engjell Googled Salt Lake City. A large metropolitan valley ringed by two mountain ranges with a city population of 200,000. County population about a million. The mountains reminded him of Albania, but the city's elevation almost doubled Albania's at 1319 meters, or 4,330 feet above sea level. Americans had a weird measurement system. The area also had the largest saltwater lake in the Western Hemisphere. Best of all, Salt Lake City was approximately eighteen hours away.

He yawned and headed back to the car to sleep before the sun rose. Tomorrow would be a long driving day.

UNCLE SHOVED me to the ground. After beating me, his men had manhandled me into a trunk and driven me into the mountains. Nero and Slam had led me into the trees, a hoodie over my head to hide my bruised, deformed face. There, they'd set up a post to watch Saemira's wedding below on the grounds of a ritzy hotel.

Duke handed me a pair of binoculars. "Watch, Bengalo."

I watched through the lenses as Saemira smiled up at the *gadjo* I'd warned her about. My heart shattered as I watched the girl I'd loved for years pledge herself to a monster. The *gadjo* took her in his arms and kissed her long and deep.

Uncle chuckled. "Think the temptress wishes the *gadjo* was you, boy? Scarred? Monstrously ugly? Evil-eyed?"

I ignored him to watch Saemira pull away. She appeared happier than I'd ever seen her. And beyond beautiful. She pulled the man back for a second kiss, longer than the first.

I hated him. He hadn't been her friend for years, protecting her from bullies and playing games with her after school. He hadn't sacrificed an education to save her and her brother from foster care. He hadn't struggled to keep her alive on the streets. He hadn't held and comforted her each night as she'd grieved for her parents.

No. This man had been handed life on a silver platter. He was soft, spoiled, useless. And he hid a vicious temper.

He was dressed casually. Shirt unbuttoned at the top. Suit pants rolled up to his calves. Sandals. Didn't people dress up for weddings? His lack of respect for Saemira infuriated me. So did his possessive arm around her as they greeted guests. A sign of ownership he didn't deserve. Yet Saemira kept stopping to kiss him after they talked to each person.

How had he blinded her?

Or had she been drawn to his money? She'd never be hungry with him.

Uncle chuckled. "The *gadjo's* getting horny. Wants the party over so he can ravish his new bride, no?" He yanked the binoculars away.

I stared straight ahead, unwilling to give him the satisfaction of a response.

He shoved me. "Your temptress betrayed you, but we'll have the last laugh, boy."

SAEMIRA

Age 17 - Denver, Colorado

BOND: a uniting element in chemistry, families, friendships, and marriages.

The house was sketchy, a new English word Saemira had picked up, which meant questionable.

"This guy's cool," Engjell said. "Said we can stay the night while he fixes our tire. You can use the shower."

That did sound nice. She hadn't been clean since escaping Kent and Kay's almost a month ago. "What does he want?" Being homeless had taught her that no one gave them anything without wanting something in return.

"I'll buy some of their cheeba, and we'll be cool."

What was cheeba? "We don't have much money left. We need to save it for gas."

Engjell winked. "We have more cash now, thanks to my new friend."

She frowned. Had he swiped a wallet and replaced it a little lighter? She hugged her brother. "I hate when you steal."

"Tomorrow, I'll never steal again. My university friends have a place and a job for me. We'll live normal."

Normal sounded nice. "Can the guy fix our tire now so we can get back on the road?" She didn't want to stay here longer than necessary, even for a shower. "I'll switch off with you so we can drive through the night."

"You've never driven at night," he said. "Besides, I want to be clean and presentable when we reach Utah, Salt Lake. And beggars can't be picky."

She cuddled her brother. "Stop saying the state before the city. People will know you're not American. Just say the city."

"Salt Lake." He pulled her toward the door.

Hours later, way after midnight, Saemira lay awake on a thin blanket in the sketchy house, cradling her brother. They were clean, but a shower didn't wash off the stain of drugs, and lots of people were doing those.

Thankfully, a tattooed woman had taken her and Altin into a room upstairs and had spent hours doing her hair into dozens of braids. Cheater dreadlocks, she'd called them. They might last a few months if she was careful, not years like dreads.

When she'd returned to the main part of the house, Engjell had been in a corner with his new friends, smoking something and acting weird. The tattooed woman had given Saemira a blanket. She'd curled up with Altin in a corner to sleep. But every person, every sound, every smell made her cringe.

Her stomach growled as she stroked her brother's soft head. Had she made a terrible mistake taking Altin away from his foster family? The blond girl had seemed nice. Saemira might've liked her in a different setting. And Altin would never have been hungry with them.

Engjell weaved his way over, humming too loud.

"Shush, idiot. You'll wake Altin."

"Sorry." He snuggled up behind her. "You smell pretty."

"Go to sleep."

He put an arm over her. She let him because he was warm and the house was cold. He stroked her skin.

"I love you," he mumbled.

"Shut up." She'd yell at him in the morning, when they were far from this place. He probably wouldn't remember anything she said tonight anyway. His mind was gone. And maybe that was a mercy. Engjell had been stressed with the burden of taking care of them.

He deserved one night to forget and be free.

Gemma

RED ROSE petals lay scattered across the white carpet leading up the stairs to Lincoln's master suite. My husband—ah! I loved the sound of that!—carried me in his arms up to his bedroom.

The day had been perfect. The cool mountain breeze. The touching ceremony that'd bound us together. The scrumptious food. The stolen kisses. And Lincoln's smiles. Getting him to let loose a little—taking off his bowtie, wearing sandals, and losing the suit jacket—had given him permission to be himself, not the uptight businessman he pretended to be. The Lincoln I'd married had been fun and addicting, a man I could love forever.

Maybe he wouldn't hate me when I revealed the truth. He seemed sincere in his feelings.

The scent of roses made me sigh as he laid me on the comforter. He grabbed a rose from a vase beside the bed and traced the velvety petals down my nose and lips.

My body hummed. "Today was perfect," I whispered.

His gaze made my insides smolder. "Thanks for marrying me." He pulled me close, taking my breath away as he began peeling off my gown. Inch by inch, his lips caressed my bare skin, making me shiver.

"I don't know how to do this," I admitted. I wasn't a virgin, yet I had no experience with consensual sex. Mama had promised that the man I married someday wouldn't be cruel, and the act would not be painful or ugly. I prayed she was right.

Lincoln moved his tantalizing lips down my shoulder, eliciting all sorts of yearning. "I'll teach you."

And he did.

Mama had been right. Intimacy with someone you loved was beautiful. Wondrous. Lincoln made me feel adored, worshiped, and I soon gained enough confidence to reciprocate. We paid devout attention to each other, and I experienced a rainbow of emotions: joy, as he tickled me, panting pleasure as he touched me, tears of happiness as he whispered his love. I'd understood from watching Baba and Mama together that they'd had a deep and powerful bond. Now, I was connected with Lincoln in the same way, body and soul.

I didn't want to leave him. Surely, he wouldn't hate me for who I really was.

He pulled me against his strong body, and I closed my eyes and listened to his heartbeat. I was now more than Saemira Elira Nikolla. Lincoln had transformed me. I was his, no longer my own. And he was mine.

We were each other's.

"I love you, Gemma."

I winced, wishing he knew my true name.

But not tonight. Not when everything was so perfect.

"I love you more." He'd never know just how much. I hardly understood myself.

46

ANGEL

Age 20 - Midvale, Utah

*T*he cross-country trip had taken a toll on Gem. She'd lost weight, probably because she kept giving her portion of food to Altin. She'd been upset with him for getting high in Colorado but playing along with those punks had yielded great rewards. A fixed tire. And three hundred bucks, after paying for the cheeba. The losers had been none the wiser as they'd left.

He slipped his phone in his pocket and returned to the car. Saemira played with Altin, trying to teach him Pat-a-Cake.

"Was that your friends on the phone?" she asked.

"Yes. Everything's set. Soon we won't be homeless."

"Thank the gods," she said.

Thank Uncle. His generosity had saved them. He hadn't expected it and wouldn't tell her just yet. Maybe never. Saemira didn't like Uncle. He had reservations about working for him as well. But this was America. The future was bright. Saemira and Altin were his family now. He was Altin's baba and Saemira's husband. He provided for her, lived with her. Someday, when she didn't miss her baba so much, he'd make babies with her. They'd have her pretty green eyes.

His loins filled with heat as he recalled last night. The euphoria of getting high had been incredible. For a while, as he'd cuddled beside Gem, he'd felt powerful. Desirable. He'd pressed himself against her in the dark, and she hadn't pushed him away.

In time, she would be his.

They arrived at the apartment complex Uncle had directed him to, and his mouth fell open. There were trees, bushes, even grass. It seemed like heaven compared to his village in Albania. Uncle must be doing well.

Saemira gathered Altin in her arms, and Engjell led them up the stairs, grabbing the key from beneath a potted plant by the door of 124. Everything was as Uncle had said it would be.

They entered, and he stood taller as Saemira walked around the kitchen. The place had come furnished. A table and chairs. Couches. None of it broken. It seemed like a palace. Their documents were on the bed in a manila envelope.

He handed Saemira a new driver's license and birth certificate. "You are now Gemma Stone. My Gem."

She shoved him and laughed. "Don't be a weirdo."

"I'm Johnny Dicaprio."

She snorted. "That's the dumbest name ever."

"Is not." The name combined his favorite actors.

"You might as well be named pizza, it's so cheesy." She turned on the TV for Altin. "I'll call you the English form of your name. Angel. You look like an Angel."

He scoffed, knowing he had the face of a monster.

"I'm not joking." She patted the couch, and he joined her, pulling Altin onto his lap. "You'll always be my Angel because you rescued us."

He squeezed her delicate hand, finding her sexy with all her braids. The wild hairstyle made her appear older, not as innocent, which was good. Looking tough would protect her, keep her safe from men who preyed on the naïve.

"I will always take care of you."

She pulled her hand away and studied her driver's license. "Gemma. That's going to take some getting used to."

"Not much. I already call you Gem." That's why he'd picked it.

She stuck out her hand. "Hi, I'm Gemma Stone."

He shook her hand. "Johnny Dicaprio. But you can call me Angel."

"Angel. That's a cool name."

"Ay-lel," Altin said.

She smiled. "Altin likes your name." She looked at her ID again. "Your friends are amazing, giving us this apartment and IDs."

"They got me a job, too. I'll head out first thing in the morning." He puffed out his chest, proud that he'd done right by her. This apartment was amazing. And the papers looked legit. He owed Uncle big time. This was more than he deserved. "You'll have to stay here while I'm gone. But there's food in the fridge. I can buy more with the money I get from my job."

"What will you do?"

"Construction work." He would be constructing a new life for them here in this strange, beautiful city. That's all she needed to know.

She accepted his lie with ease. "Cool. Let's eat that food in the fridge."

THE GADJO'S mansion appeared magnificent in the moonlight. Maybe I could forgive Saemira for marrying her *gadjo*. I'd done my best to provide for her and Altin, but we'd always lived on the edge. I'd given her food to eat and a tiny apartment and had imagined I'd given her the world. Seeing the luxury she'd married into, I realized I hadn't given her near what she deserved.

Still, her new husband hid a dark side.

Uncle's thugs manhandled me through prickly trees that ripped at my skin. The high-end neighborhood was quiet as we crept along the perimeter wall.

"The *gadjo*'s keeping the temptress warm tonight, no?"

Uncle hadn't stopped taunting me since the wedding earlier. It was bad enough that I'd lost the woman I loved and was lost without her. Why did he keep throwing acid onto my wounds?

Nero pushed me to a hole in the wall. He'd likely dug it days ago. Uncle had probably scoped out this property for weeks. They dragged me feet first through the hole, and I ate dirt and pine needles.

Nero and Slam forced me toward the mansion.

"Time to redeem yourself, Bengalo," Uncle said. "I've given you everything. The temptress has only taken from you. Now she destroys your dreams by sleeping with another, betraying her noble heritage and tossing you aside like garbage. Time to destroy her dreams."

Nero and Slam picked up canisters stashed behind bushes and began dumping liquid around the foundation. I tensed when I smelled gasoline.

Uncle held a lighter in one hand, a gun in the other. "Prove yourself. Set the flame to this damning infatuation. Burn the devil girl out of your life."

Was he crazy? I swiped the lighter from his hand and threw it over the wall. I'd never harm Gem.

Something hard hit my head. I wobbled on my feet, ground spinning.

"I regret the time and resources I've wasted on you, boy. You've been nothing but a disappointment." Uncle brought the butt of his pistol down against my skull a second time.

SAEMIRA

Age 18 - Midvale, Utah

DECEIVE: to trick to accept as true what is false.

———✦———

*W*hat had she eaten? Saemira opened the car door just in time to empty the contents of her stomach onto the asphalt. Ugh. She'd tried to work through her sickness, but her manager had finally sent her home. Hopefully, he wouldn't fire her.

Angel would be glad if she lost her job. He hadn't wanted her to get one in the first place, insisting that he could provide for them. But they'd barely been getting by. Baba had taught her to save for hard times.

She hobbled to their apartment, adding up how much longer she'd need to save to get a bigger place. For the past six months, she'd shared one bed with Angel and Altin, which made things super awkward. She cared for her friend, but he wanted more. He hadn't said so or pushed her at all, but she'd noticed how he watched her. And she hadn't forgotten how he'd touched and kissed her when he'd been high in Colorado.

No way would she be his lover. Anyone's lover. The mere thought of sex made her want to puke again.

She unlocked the apartment door but froze. If her bladder hadn't been empty, she might've wet herself.

The demon from her nightmares sat at the kitchen table across from Angel, her eighteen-month-old brother on his lap.

Duke's filthy gaze raked her up and down. "Ah, Temptress."

She wanted to run but couldn't leave her brother.

"You're home early," Angel said, not meeting her gaze.

"I'm sick." She walked to the bathroom and shut the door. Hell and damnation. Her whole body shook.

Ah, Temptress. Those words resurrected every nightmare she'd worked so hard to bury. How was Duke here? In America? In her kitchen?

Angel must have deceived her. No university friends had given him any of this. It had been his uncle.

She slid to the ground, head throbbing, stomach churning. Duke would hurt her baby brother if she didn't return. She splashed her face with freezing water and shuddered as she walked out the door.

"I'll take my brother." She reached for him.

Duke stood and stepped back. "He likes his Uncle Duke, no?" He put a hand around Altin's neck and tickled him. "Such a fragile child. So vulnerable."

A scream filled her throat. "Give him to me."

"It's all right, Gem. Altin's fine. Go rest." Engjell tried to pull her from the room, but she shoved him.

"I want Altin."

Duke handed him to Angel. "Change the boy. He stinks. I'll see you tomorrow."

Angel glanced between Duke and her, but Duke snapped at him.

"Go!"

Angel hurried into their bedroom with her brother. Thank the gods.

Bile rose up her throat as Duke dragged her to the door. In the stairwell, he traced the chain of Mama's amulet down her chest.

"Don't touch me!" She pushed his hand away.

He shoved her against the brick wall. "Careful, Temptress. Don't cross me, or I'll snip your precious Angel's wings and cast him down to hell where he belongs." He ripped Mama's amulet off her neck, making her yelp. "And your brother..." He let the amulet dangle in front of her. "...I'll cut into pieces and drop him into the river, then frame you for the grisly murder."

Vomit stung her throat.

He pinched her chin. "Now be a good little girl and don't misbehave." He headed down the stairs.

Saemira touched her stinging neck and hurried inside and locked the door.

"Why are you acting so weird?" Angel said, making her jump.

She wanted to fall to the ground and weep. The safety she'd felt in America had been snuffed out in a heartbeat.

"He took Mama's amulet." She couldn't inhale enough air.

Angel took her hand. "Don't worry. I'll get it back for you."

"No! It's too late." She yanked her hand away. "How could you deceive me, telling me your university friends helped us when it was your uncle?"

He lowered his head. "We'd be homeless without him. You don't have any idea how bad things can get."

"You're working for him?"

He nodded.

"What does he have you do?"

"Just stuff," he said, sounding defensive. "It pays the rent and buys food for you and Altin."

Food that kept her captive. She pushed past him and went to get her brother. She returned with her pillow and blanket.

"What are you doing?"

"Take the bed. Altin and I will sleep on the couch."

"We didn't have any other options. Okay? Why are you so upset?"

She'd take foster care or homelessness over being under Duke's thumb. "Stay away from me." She glared until he hung his head and walked into the bedroom.

She slammed the door shut between them, then set Altin on the couch and turned on the TV. Her brother watched *Sesame Street* as she stared at the ceiling, knowing she had to leave.

The sooner, the better.

Gemma

FIRE! I bolted up in bed as smoke alarms shattered the stillness. I coughed and looked around, wondering where I was. This wasn't mine and Altin's room.

Memories returned of last night's wedded bliss. I blinked. Altin was with Miss Tina since Lincoln had booked tickets to Aruba for early this morning. I patted the bed but found my husband's spot empty.

"Lincoln?" I coughed as I pulled a robe around me. "Lincoln!" I ran down the hall but had to bend over to cough again. "Lincoln!" I raced down the stairs.

Had he evacuated without me?

"Lincoln!" I staggered through the smoke-filled living room but stopped in the hallway. A heat wave blasted me from the direction of the fitness room. "Lincoln!" I shouted.

Please, let him have gone outside.

I stumbled toward the front door, feeling lightheaded. Outside, I breathed in fresh air and raced across the yard. An orange glow from the back of the house made my heart pound.

Please, God. Don't let him still be inside.

I sprinted to the side gate. "Lincoln!" I yelled as flames shot up into the sky from the corner of the house.

Where was he?

I cut in toward the patio, away from the flames, peeking in every window and screaming Lincoln's name. I tried a door but it was locked. My lungs burned but I kept screaming.

"Lincoln!"

I had to find him.

48

ANGEL

Age 20 - Midvale, Utah

Gemma had dinner on the table when Engjell walked through the door. A first. He dropped his bag and took a seat.

"What's the occasion?"

She set a pan of burek on a hot pad. "We're celebrating."

"What? Christmas?" It was only a week away.

"Eat and I'll tell you." She placed Altin in his booster chair and cut his food into tiny pieces.

Engjell spooned a piece of meat into his mouth. "Delicious." He licked his lips. "As good as your mama's."

She rolled her eyes. "Eat with your mouth closed, you animal."

He shoveled more food in, buoyed by her good mood and good food. She'd been surly ever since seeing Duke a couple weeks ago.

She set a notebook in front of him. "I've been saving for a new place. One Duke doesn't know about."

He froze.

"Places are cheaper in West Valley. I found one with two bedrooms that can fit us better. With first and last month's deposit, this is how much I need." She pointed to a number. "I have that, plus a grand more. You can get a job that doesn't include selling your soul to the devil. My manager said he'd hire you."

"Gemma, we can't leave." She didn't understand what he'd promised to set them up here. If he turned his back on Uncle, he'd make him pay. He might make her pay. "If this is about your mama's amulet, I'll get it back. Give me time. I haven't figured out where he's hidden it."

"This isn't about the amulet. I just refuse to be beholden to your uncle any longer."

"He's family."

"What about me and Altin? You're my brother, Engjell." She used his Albanian name when upset.

"I don't think of you as my sister." He loved her as a man loves a woman.

"He beat you, called you vile names, let you go hungry. You owe him nothing."

"I owe him my life!"

She scowled. "He's stolen your life."

"You don't know him." Uncle used brute strength and hard knocks to teach him, but he cared. How could she not see that after everything he'd done for them?

"Thank the gods. I do not want to know such a man." She folded her arms. "Will you come with us or not?"

"You can't leave, Gemma." He took her hands across the table. "Uncle has promised a big payoff soon. We'll have more than enough to meet our needs."

She whipped her hands out of his. "I won't be tied to that evil man." She began to clear the table.

Too late. She was already tied to him, whether she liked it or not. But he could protect her.

She washed dishes and crawled onto the bed to read to Altin as he watched TV. When Altin fell asleep, she joined him on the couch.

"Here." She handed him her black light.

"Do you want to play games?" he teased.

"No. I'm tired of games. I'm giving this to you to help you find your way back to me someday. When you're done with Duke. Altin and I will leave in the morning."

"Gemma."

"I put down first month's rent and deposit already."

"You can't leave me."

"I don't want to."

"Fine. I'll come with you." He'd explain to Uncle, spin her motives to be near her job or something.

"No. Don't come anywhere near me until you've cut ties to that man. For good."

"Gemma, he's family."

"Good night, Angel. Please sleep on the couch. I want one last night of comfort before I leave." She shut the bedroom door. And locked it.

I GROANED as I gained consciousness. My head throbbed and I smelled smoke.

Fire! I scrambled to my feet, swaying as I watched flames engulf the corner of the beautiful mansion. The one Gemma was inside!

I stumbled through foul-smelling smoke to a window and used a metal patio chair to smash through the glass. Smoke poured out as I climbed through, cutting my hands and knees. I dropped to the ground.

"Saemira!" I crawled past couches, bumped into a table, and knocked off a lamp. My hands and knees throbbed. "Saemira!" I turned into a hallway and stumbled over something.

No, someone.

I patted the person. A man. Gemma's rich *gadjo*. Seeing his hairy chest through his robe made me livid. He'd touched my girl. Slept with her!

Heat from nearby flames scorched my skin. I kept my face to the ground. No one could fault me for leaving him. He might be dead already. A corpse could never harm Gemma. She'd be a widow. We could be together.

I scooted backward but paused when I heard someone scream from outside.

"Lincoln!"

I closed my eyes and cursed. Gemma didn't know what was good for her. Hearing her scream this man's name made me know I couldn't leave him to die, even if he deserved that fate.

Hefting the *gadjo* by the feet, I dragged him around the corner, staying as low as possible. Maybe he was dead. I was dizzy and hadn't been inside near as long as he had. The man groaned and mumbled something that sounded very much like "Gemma" as I dragged him to a door.

"Lincoln!" Saemira screamed again from outside.

I unlocked the door and opened it. Fresh air gave me a burst of adrenaline to pull the *gadjo* out, before collapsing onto the cobblestone patio at his side. I wheezed and drew in clean, cool air.

"Lincoln!" Saemira ran to us, but stopped when she noticed me. "Angel?"

SAEMIRA

Age 18 - West Valley City, Utah

UNYIELDING: inflexible; uncompromising.

❖

*T*he sun was weak in the sky, temperature a few degrees above freezing. Saemira tilted her head to bask in the beauty of being outside, even in an alley behind Denny's with two trash receptacles as her companions and a cinder block wall for entertainment.

She prayed to God to watch over Altin while they were apart. The crummy dive she'd secured was scarier than Engjell's one-bedroom apartment in Midvale. But this was hers. Duke had no part of it.

"I hoped to find you out here."

She yelped and turned to find Angel standing near a dumpster. "You scared me."

"Sorry."

She threw herself into his arms. Heavens be thanked. She'd worried constantly about him since they'd parted two months ago.

He spun her around. "I've missed you."

"I've missed you, too." She adored Altin, but he didn't fill her hours with sharp conversation or teasing. She'd had to take him in twice to the emergency room for seizures. So scary. With her brother, she had to be an adult. With Angel, she could be herself.

He kissed her cheek.

She grinned. "I have to clock back in but my shift ends in three hours.

Then I'll take you to see Altin. It's a studio apartment. When you didn't come with us, I downgraded to save money. But I'll make a bed for you on the floor."

Angel placed a finger against her mouth. "You talk too much and work too hard." He frowned. "You look terrible."

She worked long hours at the restaurant and for a janitorial service in the mornings. She averaged about five hours of sleep on a good night. With Altin's medical issues, she'd gotten less lately.

"Come back with me, Gemma. You don't have to work like a dog. I can take care of you."

Her excitement fizzled as she realized he hadn't left Duke.

"I'm making good money." He pulled out a wad of green bills. "You don't have to live in the slum."

She felt faint. "I need to get back to work."

He grabbed her arm. "I can give you a better life than this."

She caressed his scarred face, wishing she could tell him the truth. "I won't be linked to your uncle."

His eyes narrowed. "Stop being so unyielding."

She smiled. His uncle hadn't ruined him completely. Angel still used English words for specific purposes.

"Uncle's changed. He helped us. Helped you. We would've both been locked up in jail or deported if not for him." He pulled her mama's necklace from his pocket.

Saemira inhaled sharply. As much as she'd acted unaffected, she'd grieved the loss of this amulet. It was the one thing tying her to Mama. And Baba, since he'd given it to her.

"You stole it from him?"

"No. Duke had a bag of loot to pay us. I grabbed this before anyone else could take it."

She cradled the amulet to her heart. "Thank you."

"Come with me."

"Not until you make the right choice." A lump formed in her throat as she waited for his answer. When he frowned, she pushed him away. "Don't find me again until you're done with Duke."

"Gemma."

She slipped inside and shut the door, clutching Mama's precious stone to her heart.

Gemma

228

GOOSEBUMPS PRICKLED up and down my arms when I saw Angel. Not even two weeks ago, he'd held a knife to my throat to force Lincoln to transfer millions to his evil uncle. Had he started this fire, and now played hero out of guilt?

"Why are you here?" I asked.

Angel coughed. Lincoln groaned, and I turned from my former friend to help my new husband.

"Lincoln?" I rolled him onto his side as a hacking cough seemed to rip his poor lungs apart. But he lived! I kissed my husband's eyes, his cheeks, his lips. "Are you okay?"

He tried to sit up. "I'll..." cough cough "...be fine."

I looked up to find Angel watching me with a stricken expression.

"Are you hurt?"

Sirens sounded. Lincoln leaned over to retch. When he looked up, I could tell the instant he registered Angel's presence. He tensed, and then burst into adrenaline-fueled action, tackling my skinny friend to the ground.

"Bastard!" He pummeled Angel with his fists.

"No!" I tried to pull him away.

Someone pulled me away instead. Two policemen manhandled my husband and Angel apart, and the scene blurred through tears as Lincoln collapsed and started choking.

A paramedic began taking my vitals but I pushed him away. "I'm fine. Where's my husband?" In the melee, he'd disappeared.

"The paramedics took him to the ambulance, ma'am. He needed oxygen."

"What about the other guy?" I couldn't say my friend. I didn't know if Angel was friend or foe. But he'd saved Lincoln.

"Ma'am, calm down."

"Take me to my husband," I said. "Please."

He led me around to the front of the house, where all sorts of emergency vehicles were gathered, their red and white lights making me dizzy. My stomach churned as I looked for my husband. When I spotted him inside an ambulance, a mask over his face, I ran to him.

Another paramedic helped me into the back of the vehicle. Lincoln reached for my hand, and I hid my face in his chest. He'd almost died! He would have if Angel hadn't pulled him out of the burning house.

He caressed my hair. "It's all right, love. They caught the bastard who did this. One of the kidnappers. I'll press charges and see that he rots in prison."

"No." They had the wrong man. Angel had defied Duke by helping us escape. His uncle must've exacted revenge by framing him for the fire.

229

Angel never would've sanctioned burning Lincoln's house down, knowing I was inside.

A police officer approached. "My men are taping off the area for an investigation. You and the missus can go in with Officer Mendoza real quick, to dress and pack up some essentials to see you through the week."

We both donned oxygen masks and followed the officer inside. Only a couple of rooms on the south side had been burned, but smoke had filtered through the entire house.

My eyes stung. This was my fault. First, the ransom money. Now, the loss of his beautiful home. He'd almost lost his life as well. I bent over, sick with the realization that Duke would never leave me alone.

I had to leave and pray Lincoln would honor his promise to care for my brother. I couldn't wait around for something else to happen.

Lincoln wrapped an arm around me. "It's okay, Gemma." His voice sounded raspy. "We're safe now."

He and Altin would never be safe as long as Duke hunted me.

The officer led us to Lincoln's bedroom—our wedding suite not too many hours ago. He stood outside the door as we entered and walked into the closet. Lincoln gently sat me on an ottoman and took my face in his hands.

"You're going to be all right, love."

I swiped at my eyes. If I loved him—and heaven knew I did!—I must leave him.

"I'm fine. I'm just glad you're okay. I love you." That was dangerous to say, but I wanted him to know the truth.

"I love you too, sweetheart." He yanked off his robe, and I gawked. He grinned. "You're not embarrassed by my nudity, are you, Mrs. McConnell?" He coughed and grabbed a pair of boxers.

"I just don't want Officer Mendoza to walk in and get an eyeful."

He chuckled, which eased the pain in my heart. He'd be okay. His lungs would heal. His heart would, too. Lincoln was resilient.

I slipped into my own clothes, knowing I had one more wrong to right.

"There's been a mistake." I sat on the ottoman, not feeling steady on my feet. "That boy didn't start the fire. He pulled you out of the house. I saw him."

"After he almost killed me. And you! They found gas canisters by the side of the house. It was arson."

"No. He's innocent. Engjell fell in with the wrong crowd and has done bad things, but he isn't a bad person." Neither was I, I almost added. "Please don't press charges. We need to help him."

Lincoln gaped at me. "What did you say?"

"He's innocent."

"No. You said his name."

I cringed.

Lincoln grabbed my shoulders. "How do you know his name?"

"He's my friend," I sobbed, the dam of control I'd barely shored up breaking completely. "We grew up in Albania together."

His fingers dug painfully into my skin. "You lied to me?"

I winced, and he let go and stepped back, blocking my only escape route.

"I-I didn't w-want to. I wanted to tell you the truth, but I was afraid you'd hate me. Hate Altin." Oh, God of heaven! What would happen to my brother? "You'll take care of him, won't you? You said you loved him."

"You're one of them?" he spat.

I looked at the ground, unable to bear his disdainful look. I'd seen it in Esad's face when he'd thrown rocks at me. I'd seen it in Mr. Shehu's expression when he'd informed me he had zero-tolerance for theft and gypsies, as if they were the same. I'd seen it in Duke's shadowed face that night he violated me.

"Tell me everything."

I sniffled. "My real name is Saemira Elira Nikolla. I'm half-Roma, or gypsy." Why I chose to reveal that fact when there were many other details to share I'd never know. Maybe the smoke had affected me.

Lincoln staggered back another step.

"Please," I said, knowing by his icy glare that I'd lost his heart forever, if I'd ever really held it. "Give Angel a second chance."

And me, I wanted to beg.

ROCK OF DIGNITY

"Oh, love! That is to be two, and yet one."

— *THE HUNCHBACK OF NOTRE DAME* BY VICTOR HUGO

50

LINCOLN

*E*very muscle in my body spasmed. She'd lied to me! This woman— this stranger!—had manipulated me even more than Angeline had. She'd deceived me, making a mockery of sacred marital vows.

"Mr. McConnell," I heard the officer call from outside the room. "We should probably get going. Are you and the missus almost done?"

I scowled at Gemma, or whoever the hell she was. Her face was blotchy from tears. The woman was a good actress, I'd give her that.

"Just another minute," I said, grabbing a suitcase.

Gemma crept toward the door.

I lunged and gripped her forearm. "You're not going anywhere."

"Just let me go," she cried. "You'll be safer if I'm gone."

I'd be safer when she was in prison, where her gypsy gang belonged. But I wouldn't turn her over to the cops just yet. I needed answers. God as my witness, she would pay for her lies and go down on my terms, not the cops'. They could have her once I knew the full extent of her part in all of this.

I yanked her behind me, and with my other hand, pulled clothes from her side and mine into the suitcase. Keeping a firm grip on her arm, I gathered essentials and zipped the luggage.

"Keep your mouth shut," I said. "We're going to march out of here and leave. If the cops question you, give them the basics. None of what you just told me. Understand?"

She nodded, and I had to avert my gaze from her pitiful expression. Even knowing her crimes, I felt myself softening at her distress.

But it wasn't real. Or if it was, it was because she was desperate to escape now that I'd found her out.

She wouldn't get that chance.

For the next hour, I performed the greatest act of my life. Academy-Award worthy. Officer Mendez escorted us out of the smoky ruins of my home, and the paramedics insisted on checking us again. I kept a sharp eye on my wife, not letting her get more than a few feet away as we both received more oxygen. I answered questions for the police. The cops left Saemira alone, judging her to be too distraught to be of any help. She probably did this type of acting every day.

One hoodwinked paramedic kept her in the ambulance after releasing me, worried that her vitals weren't normal.

Superb acting indeed.

Keeping an eye on her, I called Lionel and my security chief to work out details for when we left here. When we were finally allowed to drive away, Gemma spoke.

"I'm sorry, Lincoln. I wanted to—"

"Silence!" I growled. She was a master liar, manipulating me into marrying her, getting me to give her my heart. Somehow, I must get it back. The first step was not to let her get back inside my head.

She cringed, making me feel bad. But no! That was her game, to confuse me so I couldn't see through her lies. I wouldn't feel bad now that I knew who she was—a deceitful, criminal mastermind. A gypsy.

Ha. She'd probably had a good laugh that day she'd lectured me about the difference between gypsies and pirates.

But I'd been right. They were one and the same.

The clock showed that Gemma and I would've been lifting off right now from the airport to fly to Aruba for our honeymoon. Instead, I sat alone in my office, wanting to punch something. I'd left my wife—if that traitorous woman could even be called that since she'd lied about everything—under watch in the rental I'd let her live in for the last couple months. Lionel had booked a wing of rooms at a hotel for me to stay in until my house was restored. I'd sent Miss Tina there with Altin. I needed to figure out what to do about the kid. Was he even related to Gemma? He wasn't a gypsy, going by his skin tone.

I tipped a bottle of Scotch to my lips. It had taken intense self-control not to hand Gemma over to the cops. When we'd arrived at my rental, my security chief had been waiting. Gemma had freaked out when I'd asked two of Brown's men to escort her inside.

She'd turned to me, tears in her eyes, and lied one more time. *"I understand why you're angry, Lincoln. But I do love you. I didn't lie about that."*

I took another swig of Scotch and glared at the police reports in front of me. She wouldn't know truth if it hit her in the face. The proof of her treachery rested on my desk. The crimes at EcoCore had begun a week after she'd started working on the janitorial staff in 2020. Mostly petty crimes. These reports hadn't come to my attention until I'd asked security to bring me all incident reports from the last two years. When Gemma had moved onto Joe's team six months ago, the incidents and frequency had ramped up.

What was her part in it all?

Before leaving, I'd warned Brown and his men to be on guard. My wife would play the innocent and try to twist their loyalty. They were not to listen to or give heed to anything she said. I'd also tasked Brown with searching the place for any evidence of foul play.

I clenched my aching fingers. Gemma had worked her way into my life so smoothly, I hadn't even guessed that I'd played right into her nefarious plans. I'd given her my heart. My trust. I'd been ready to give her everything.

I pounded the desk, seeing the kidnapping with new eyes. She hadn't been a victim, but a player. She'd known we would be in Park City and had given her comrades the details to know where to stage a kidnapping.

Disturbed by this realization, I called Brown again. She was more dangerous than I'd considered. Maybe she was the damned ringleader. She was definitely smart enough.

"Yes, Mr. McConnell."

"Assign two more men to Gemma Stone's place. Secure the perimeter and don't let anyone near the place."

"Is there something I should know, sir? Is your wife in danger?"

I grimaced, not liking the reference to her new title. "She's a flight risk. Suffice it to say I need her contained until I do more investigating. Make sure no one tries to break her out. She's not to leave the house for any reason. Evidence has come to light that..." I paused, hating to admit how manipulated I'd been. Once again, I'd trusted and fallen for the wrong woman. "She may be working with the gypsies that've been giving us trouble."

I tossed back the rest of my drink, feeling like the most gullible man on the planet.

51

SAEMIRA

---

*S*omeone knocked, but I didn't lift my head from my knees. Why bother? I couldn't leave or go anywhere. Lincoln had made me a prisoner in my own house. Well, his house, technically, which made it worse.

Speak of the devil. He cracked the door and called in. "Are you decent?"

I didn't answer. What did he care? He could see me stark naked and it wouldn't be as humiliating as his judgment had been. In his eyes, I might as well be a serial killer.

The rustle of cloth and a daunting pressure inside my head alerted me that he stood nearby. Too close. I looked up at my husband.

His eyes narrowed. "Get changed. And then you will eat. No more of this forced fasting to prove some moot point."

"Go away." I had no appetite. Honestly, I'd tried to eat when my guards had fed me. But the little I'd forced down had come up later. The thought of food still made my stomach churn. Or maybe it was the knowledge that my husband hated me so much and trusted me so little as to believe I needed four jailers.

"I will not go away until you eat." He lifted a plate.

The smell of lamb from Shish Kabab didn't thrill me because the look on his face revealed no sweetness behind the gesture.

"I'm not hungry." A lie. But my body wouldn't let me eat.

"Bring it in here," he said to someone outside. Two of my jailers—who'd been pretty decent guys, as far as jailers went—carried a folding table in and set it up next to my bed. Lincoln set the styrofoam container down as two other jailers carried in chairs.

Lincoln pointed to one. "Sit."

I obeyed, not because I was compliant, but because I felt dizzy. He sat across from me and pushed the container in front of me.

"Now eat."

I nibbled on a spoonful of Basmati rice, avoiding his hostile gaze. The one positive of having four jailers was that Duke couldn't touch me. But I also couldn't run. And I had to get out of here. What if Duke tried to hurt or kidnap Altin or Lincoln while I was locked up?

"Where's Altin?" I asked.

"Somewhere you'll never find him."

His coldness sliced through me like a machete, especially cruel after what we'd shared on our wedding night.

Stupid tears welled up in my eyes. "You promised you'd care for him if anything happened to me."

Lincoln scowled.

"You promised you wouldn't hand him over to the state."

"I made those promises to a woman who turned out to be a figment of my imagination. They hold no merit."

I dropped my fork and put a hand to my mouth. *Please, God! Don't let my brother be hurt by my actions.*

"He's fine," he snapped. "Pick up your fork and keep eating." He looked away. "He's with Miss Tina, somewhere safe."

My throat burned as I tried to swallow food.

"Why does it matter who has him?" he snapped. "Even the worst foster home would be better than what you've subjected him to."

His words hit me like acid to the face. "You've always assumed the worst about me."

"You haven't given me a reason not to."

My fingers squeezed the fork. That was cruel. And unfair. I'd been a damned good employee, going along with his farce of an engagement and marrying him. When my feelings had become real, I'd even given him my heart, for all the good it'd done me.

"What bothers you most? The fact that I'm a criminal or a gypsy? Or are they the same to you?"

He banged the table. "Don't try to manipulate me. You knew the guy who tried to burn my house down, with me in it."

"Yes. I know him. You don't. His name is Angel, and he was your literal angel that night."

"He—"

"You were *not* conscious," I yelled, standing up and looking down on him. "I was." My chest heaved with emotions. "I woke up frantic when the smoke alarms went off. You were gone. I ran through the house, screaming your name, trying to find you."

I held onto the table as a wave of dizziness swept over me. "I ran outside, past flames, thinking you were still inside, thinking you were dying or already dead. I kept screaming your name, trying to find a way back inside. Then Engjell was there, pulling you out of the back door. He was the last person I expected to see. Honestly, I never wanted to see him again after the kidnapping. But I'm glad he was there for whatever reason because you would've died otherwise. And though you hate me, I'm grateful you still live. But you want to punish your savior."

"He stole millions from me." He hissed. "How much was your cut of that?"

I sank into my seat, focusing on the window that let muted sunlight into the room. Of course, he'd jumped to the worst conclusion. There were many legitimate reasons to be angry with me. I'd been dishonest. I'd married him under a false alias. But he vilified me, liking his fictional fantasies better than truth.

He growled and stalked over to the door.

"You told me once that your nasty divorce helped you distinguish between friend and foe," I said.

He stood rigidly beside the door as my stomach, head, and everything else pounded like an unbalanced washing machine.

"Thanks for helping me see which one you are."

He opened the door. "Get dressed. And *please* finish your meal."

I perked up at the hint of pleading in his voice.

He stared at the door, not me. "Mr. Wilder heard of the fire and has invited us to stay with him and his wife until my house can be restored. It might be a couple months."

I dared not breathe. "You want to stay married?" I'd expected him to annul our vows and hand me over to the police.

He frowned. "In name only. There's nothing real between us. But I don't want Gramps to know what you've done. That would hurt him."

My hopes that he still cared even a little died as he walked out and shut the door.

52

LINCOLN

*B*rown, my security chief, motioned me over to where he stood near a desk in the kitchen. He held a bundle of blue papers. "You asked me to search for evidence of your wife's duplicity."

Yes! I rubbed my hands together. "What did you find?" This could be the proof I needed to cut Gemma out of my mind and heart forever. Maybe evidence to press charges against her.

"Blackmail notes, it appears."

I knew she was a con-artist.

"They don't say her name or the sender's. But they're enlightening, especially the last one. They're not dated, but seem to be in chronological order, going by the increasing amounts demanded."

I slipped the bundled stack of papers into my briefcase. "I'll look these over when I get to the office."

I glanced back at Gemma's door. Or Saemira's. Dammit. I didn't even know the name of my own wife. Never in my life, even in the midst of Angeline's drama, had I felt so conflicted. Her last words haunted me. Maybe she was guilty, and I had every reason to be angry with her. But what if I didn't? I'd pledged to love her through good and bad. Yet when the first gnarly wave had hit, I'd abandoned ship, after locking her up in the brig. It had felt like the right thing to do, until I'd seen her just now. The bags under her eyes and her obvious physical weakness bothered me more than I cared to admit. When Brown had informed me that she'd hardly eaten in the past three days, I'd determined to force-feed her.

I grimaced. Had she seriously searched for me that night? Terrified on my behalf? Was there a chance she hadn't played me? That she honestly cared?

My head throbbed with questions. But if she cared about me, why had she lied for all these months? Only a guilty person kept secrets.

I wanted to barge back into her room and take her in my arms. Hold her. Kiss her, just to see how she'd respond. But I wouldn't be fooled again.

I needed to figure out the truth.

Heaven help me, I loved her still, but I'd loved Angeline once, too. Heart and soul. And she had almost destroyed me. I wouldn't give that power to a woman again unless I was absolutely certain of her. And right now, I was so uncertain about Gemma or Saemira that it wasn't funny.

I focused back on Brown. "Make sure she eats. And be kind."

My chief sputtered. "I assure you, my men and I have been completely professional."

"I know. Just...she's..."

"Your wife," he said.

I clenched my teeth.

"Don't worry, Mr. McConnell. I'll treat her as I would my own daughter."

That made me feel somewhat better. "Thanks." I left before I lost my good sense and barged back into my wife's room.

THE COUNTY LOCKUP made me queasy. I hated being here with these types of people. But things weren't adding up about my wife, if she could be called that. I had no idea how the law worked. Since she'd married me under an alias, was our marriage even valid?

I waited behind plexiglass for the prisoner to be brought in. His forged papers identified him as Johnny Dicaprio, but he'd disclosed his real name of Engjell Romani. An illegal immigrant from Albania, brought here on a student visa by Saemira's own father. He'd disappeared from Chicago around the same time Saemira had been kidnapped from her foster home.

The guy entered the room. Kid, really. Did he even shave yet? He sat in a chair on the other side of the plexiglass and scowled.

I cringed at his deformed and scarred face.

"What do you want?" he said in a thick accent.

"The truth about you and Saemira."

"I don't have to tell you anything."

"Why did you save me?" Or had he?

His lips jutted out. "Because I love Gemma, and she loves you."

243

"Yeah, right. *Saemira* played me to get millions by pretending to be kidnapped. It was a brilliant plan, I'll give you that."

His eyes moved about, not focusing on me. On anything. "Fool. Gemma had no part of that. If you don't know that, you don't deserve her."

Was he covering for her?

"Who's D?"

His brow furrowed.

"Someone's been blackmailing her." Not her blackmailing others, as I'd assumed. "I found notes in her apartment, signed by D. Her blackmailer called her Temptress."

The boy's eyes bulged. "He's been blackmailing her?"

"Who is he?" I asked again. "He threatened her with jail and losing her brother. What did she do?"

He scraped a scarred hand over his face. "Saemira did nothing. It's me. She told me to leave Uncle, and I didn't. Duke's his name." He grimaced. "He promised he'd leave her alone. He promised."

"Is he the man you hit to help us escape that night?" I shuddered at the memory of my time in captivity.

He nodded. "Duke promised if I did what he said, he wouldn't touch her. I've worked for years to keep her safe, and now"—his expression contorted—"you're telling me he's been threatening her all along?"

"The last note suggested she work a night a month for him, with her body." Blood boiled beneath my skin at the vile suggestion.

The boy bolted to his feet, making the guard reach for his baton. "Do you have her somewhere safe? Is someone watching her?" He noticed the guard and quickly sank back into his chair. "If Duke's sending notes like that, he's ready to bring her into his web."

The guard watched him as the kid pressed his face closer to the glass. "Is Saemira safe?"

Hell. What had I done?

"I have six men with her," I said, ashamed that they guarded her as a prisoner, not a victim.

The boy closed his eyes.

"Did you set the fire?" I asked, though I already guessed the answer. My wife had told me the truth.

"I'd never harm Saemira. Duke forced me to come. Wanted me to light the gasoline to redeem myself. But I didn't." He chewed his puffy lips. "He must've knocked me out. When I came to, your house was burning. I busted a window to find Gemma but found you instead."

My God. What a mess! I'd accused my wife of criminal intent when she'd only been trying to keep her head afloat in a sea of madness.

"Why did Duke target Saemira? The crimes started happening at my company right after she started working there. Was Duke responsible?"

He nodded. "Intimidation. He scares you, threatens to frame you for certain crimes, threatens family members." He rubbed his chin. "I didn't learn this until the kidnapping, when I was alone with her. She told me Duke raped her as a teen. I knew about the assault, but I didn't know it was him." His nostrils flared. "I swear, if I'd known, I never would've called him for help when we were on the run."

"Wait. Why were you on the run?" His explanations just unearthed more questions. "I read your file. You walked away from a full university scholarship. Why?"

"Saemira called and asked for my help after her baba was shot."

"Her dad?"

He nodded.

"He was shot?" What in the hell had my poor wife been through?

"His second wife shot him. Saemira said she was really messed up. Anyway, she called, terrified that she and Altin would be separated. She begged me to help."

"And you did."

"It took a while, but yes. We spent three weeks on the road, sleeping under the stars or in the car. I didn't know where else to turn when money ran out. She was hungry. Altin, too. I could've lived on the streets, but she deserved better. Duke agreed to help. For a price."

Hell. This kid wasn't my enemy. He was only desperate. His vile uncle had taken advantage of him. And Saemira.

"When she figured out Duke was helping us, she split. Said she wouldn't be tied to such a man. I didn't know he'd raped her. I thought I was protecting her by working for him. He said she'd be safe as long as I did what he said."

"Don't trust the promises of evil men."

The kid looked pained. I knew the feeling.

"Help me take him down," I said. "I'll drop all charges and let you go free." Maybe I could make this right.

"I tried to be a hero and just screwed everything up. Duke's right. Society hates me for the blood in my veins and these scars on my face. Nothing I do will change that."

"Your uncle hurt Saemira. He hurt you. Cooperate with the police. Let's bring him to justice."

He stared at his lap.

"Two minutes," the guard said behind him.

"Help me protect Saemira," I pleaded.

Hope drained away as a minute ticked by without a response. Was the kid angry? Scared? We had no chance of finding Duke without him. If he chose the coward's way out, I'd still drop all charges. He was innocent of the crime I'd accused him of.

I started to stand, but he spoke.

"I'll help you. But first, tell me this: I know you beat your first wife. Duke showed me pictures from the newspaper. What's to stop you from hurting Saemira? I'm not helping you just so you can hurt her worse than Duke."

I let out a long breath. "That's a fair question. I did strike my first wife. She was drunk, pregnant, and taunted me that the baby wasn't mine. I slapped her and left. When I returned, she was battered, as the papers showed. But I didn't do that. I regret slapping her. It was wrong, I know. But I didn't beat her and cause her to miscarry. I don't know who did. But I swear on my life, I didn't beat my ex. And I'd never lay a hand on Saemira. I love her with all my heart." I stared at my hands. "I've screwed up, accusing her of being in league with Duke. I hope she forgives me. But whether she does or not, Duke needs to be locked away so he can never hurt her again."

The boy rolled his eyes. "You're an idiot for believing Saemira could be bad."

"I know."

"But she really does seem to love you. I've never seen her so happy as that day you two married. So I'll help."

"Time," the guard said, walking over to take hold of the boy.

"Thank you," I said. Thank God! We'd fix things for my wife. Somehow, we'd keep her safe from the monster who'd threatened her for so long.

53

SAEMIRA

---

*K*nocking made me open my eyes, but I had no energy to raise my head.

"Gemma?"

I buried my face in a pillow, unable to face Lincoln again.

The edge of the bed dipped down beside me. "Gemma?" He caressed my hair. Why was he doing that? He hated me. "I'm so sorry, love." His voice sounded hoarse still from the fire. The fire that could've killed him.

He gently rolled me over and groaned. "What have I done to you?" Tears filled his eyes. Did it hurt to speak? Had his throat been damaged by the smoke?

He lifted me into his arms, jarring me out of my dreamlike stupor.

"What...are you doing?"

"They said you vomited up everything you ate again. I'm taking you to the hospital."

I closed my eyes, head hurting too much to protest. My stomach churned, though there was nothing in it. And my throat burned.

"You don't need to—"

"Shh." He pressed a kiss to my forehead. "Just rest, love. I'm a fool, but I'm starting to see straight. Let me take care of you."

I must be dreaming. If Lincoln was really here, he wouldn't be talking so sweet and being so gentle. He'd be glaring at me, telling me I deserved to be in jail.

Dream-Lincoln kissed me on the lips. "Forgive me, Gemma. I deserve to burn in hell for what I did to you, what I believed about you."

I snuggled into his chest. Dream-Lincoln even smelled real.

"Can you drive us?" Dream-Lincoln said. "She's not in good shape."

Why did he want me to drive? And how rude to talk about my body like that. I was in decent shape.

"Yes, Mr. McConnell. I've already called ahead to Uni. They're expecting her."

Who was that? I tried to open my eyes, but sunlight blinded me.

Doors shut. An engine started. My mind filled in every detail, but all I cared about was cuddling as close as possible into Dream-Lincoln's warmth, breathing in his spicy cologne, savoring his loving arms while I could.

He kissed my forehead. "Hold on, Gemma. You'll have help soon."

I had all I wanted already.

LINCOLN SAT BESIDE THE BED, asleep in a chair. I'd been watching him for a few minutes, trying to get my bearings. I seemed to be in a hospital, hooked up to tubes. I felt normal. No broken bones or painful areas that might have been operated on that I could tell. I was weak. And super tired. But why was I here? What had happened?

Lincoln opened his eyes and sat up straight when he saw me watching him. "You're awake."

"Why am I in a hospital?" Or was I?

"You were dehydrated. I brought you here after my security chief called, worried that you couldn't keep anything down."

Hazy memories teased my mind. "I'm sorry." It hurt to swallow.

His brown eyes glistened. Or was I imagining things? Lincoln bent over, brushing his cheek against mine.

"No. I'm sorry, love. I really screwed up, accusing you of belonging to those gypsies." He winced. "I mean gang."

"No. You're right. I am a gypsy. My mama was a full-blooded Roma."

"And I'm sorry I ever thought less of you for that." He kissed my forehead. "I'm sorry I believed for even a second that you could've been behind your own kidnapping."

A tear trickled down my cheek. His accusations had hurt. Still did. I doubted I'd ever fully trust him again. But he'd been right. I was a thief. I'd stolen my brother from foster care, taking a life of ease from him. I'd stolen food with Angel when we'd lived on the streets. I hadn't done the actual swiping, but I'd eaten Angel's stolen goods and had been glad for them. I'd stolen a new name and had deceived everyone I knew into believing I was a decent person.

"Gemma—I mean Saemira." He caressed my face. "Please forgive me."

"Stop wallowing in guilt." I gulped, wishing my throat didn't hurt so bad. "I get it. You're better off without me. I've put you in danger. Just leave."

"I'm never leaving you again."

"Why? Our marriage isn't real since I married you under a false name. We'll keep acting for the Wilders while we stay with them so he doesn't sue us for fraud or something. But then we'll end this joke, as you wish."

"I don't wish that."

"Yes, you do."

He sat on the edge of my bed, crowding me. "No. I wish for my wife to recover her health so I can take her in my arms without worrying that I'll break her. I wish to kiss you, every inch of you. I wish to make love to you and spend the rest of my life proving that I adore you. I wish to erase all the doubts you harbor right now because of my stupidity and arrogance. I wish to do penance for my days of doubting you by giving you foot rubs, roses, trips to your favorite destinations—whatever your heart desires. I wish to sit with my attorney to work out what needs to be done to get your true name back, to reclaim the dignity of your roots. I wish to hold you late into the night and listen to childhood stories of your parents, of your friendship with Angel, my savior. I wish to see you as the mother of my children and to grow old with you, to never spend a day apart from you again, because the last four days without you have been an agonizing hell."

Did he really mean all those things? I gulped, realizing it didn't matter. With Duke on the loose, I still posed a threat to anyone close to me.

I couldn't let Lincoln love me because when I recovered my strength, I must leave. For his safety. For Altin's. For everyone's.

54

LINCOLN

*W*ilder's sprawling city estate came into view, and I thanked God that my wife was beside me again. After almost two days in the hospital, she'd been released into my care. I had hoped my declaration of love would sway her. But the damage I'd caused was too great. A simple apology and declaration wouldn't cut it. I'd known they might not.

I opened her door and took her hand. She didn't withdraw from my touch, but she held herself aloof. The bubbly, sparkly Gemma was gone. Maybe that had been a mask she'd worn. Maybe Saemira was a quiet, more sullen character. If so, I would love her just as much as I'd loved the vivacious Gemma Stone.

I led her to the wing the Wilder's had graciously given us to use for the next couple months. Opening the door to our suite, I gestured for Gemma to enter. I stayed at the door to watch her reaction.

"Mommy!" Altin jumped off the bed where Miss Tina had been sitting with him.

Gemma, or Saemira—it was hard to think of her by her new name—picked him up and started bawling.

"Mommy sad?" her brother said.

She pecked his cheek. "No, silly. I'm super happy." She caught my gaze and mouthed *Thank you*.

I nodded, hoping this would ease her pain. I felt terrible for the stress and anxiety my petty rage had caused her.

She kept hugging Altin until he squirmed out of her grip. She let him go, but only for a second before she caught him up again and kissed his cute face a few more times.

"Stop kissing me," he said with a laugh.

"Silly boy," I said. "I'd never say that."

"You did say that," she snapped. "By locking me in that house."

Ouch. I glanced at Tina, who looked like she wanted to be anywhere but here with us. "You may leave for the night," I told her.

Once she left the room, I turned to Gemma. "I was confused. I'm sorry. But why didn't you tell me who you were before the wedding? I would've understood."

"Would you?" she asked.

Probably not. No matter when she would've told me, I would've felt betrayed. Angeline had made a habit out of lying, but I had believed that Gemma was forthright and honest. To know she hadn't been for all the months I'd known her bothered me.

I picked up Altin and nuzzled his cheek. Right now, I needed to drop this line of arguing. It wouldn't help matters between us. "Want to show Gemma another surprise?" I asked her brother.

She scowled. Honestly, her scowls gave me hope. They showed my wife's spunk, which I preferred over that docile, lethargic creature who'd scared me to death in the hospital.

I held out my hand. "Come on. I promise you'll like it."

She rolled her eyes and ignored my hand. We walked into the hall, Altin squirming in my arms. I opened the second door from the end, and my wife started crying again as Angel took her up in his arms.

"Angel!" She ran her hands through his hair, making me frown.

He peeked over her shoulder and stepped back when he saw me.

Saemira turned and glared at me. "Leave us."

I opened my mouth to argue but slumped and walked out without closing the door. She was right. I had no right to witness their reunion when I'd been the arrogant fool who had torn them apart.

55

SAEMIRA

*P*art of me felt bad for being so cold to Lincoln. But the only thing that mattered was keeping him safe. And to do that, I must put distance between us.

"Oh, Angel, you're free." I hugged my friend again.

"Yeah." He cupped my face. "I'm so glad you're safe. Can you ever forgive me for what happened? I feel terrible."

"You're forgiven."

He brushed my cheeks. "Your husband," he gulped, "said Duke's been blackmailing you. Why didn't you tell me? I would've taken you and Altin far away if I'd known."

"He said he'd kill you and take Altin away. I didn't dare say anything. I wanted to protect you both."

He pecked my cheek. "And I wanted to protect you. That's the only reason I kept working for him."

"This is all my fault. You would've graduated from college if I hadn't begged for your help. I should've stayed in foster care. Altin, too. The Barber's didn't care for me, but they didn't harm me either. And I think the people who had Altin truly loved him."

"Shhh." He caressed my head. "You talk too much. I don't regret my time with you. I only regret getting involved with Duke. I'll never forgive myself for that."

"You'd better, or I'll beat you up," I said.

He laughed. "Ah, Gemma. How I love you."

Lincoln cleared his throat behind us. He still held my brother and must've slipped back in while we'd been talking.

Angel flinched and released me.

Lincoln pulled me to his side. "Don't touch my wife again."

"Y-yes, sir," Angel stammered.

I shoved Lincoln and walked back to my friend. "Don't get all jealous. Angel and I are just friends. We have been since I was seven. He's like a brother to me." Angel pouted, making me huff. "Don't give me that look. You are my big brother. I love you, but not like I love my husband."

Lincoln's eyebrows shot up. "You love me?"

I held out my hands for my brother. "I never stopped loving you, rammit. But I don't know if I've forgiven you. I'm still incredibly angry."

He handed Altin over and gave me a curt nod. "As you should be." He touched my arm. "So you know, even when I had you under guard and thought you had betrayed me, I never stopped loving you either. It took every speck of willpower I possessed not to take you in my arms and kiss you when I visited you that day before I went to see Angel in jail."

I buried my head in my brother's shoulder.

Lincoln wrapped his arms around us both. "I'll regret my actions these past few days for the rest of my life. I truly am sorry, Gemma." He winced. "I mean Saemira—lamb-it."

I giggled, and he grinned.

"I'm still here," Angel muttered behind us. "And she's used to either name, so don't sweat it. I called her Gem for years."

Lincoln pulled back. "Which name do you prefer me to call you, love?"

My body warmed at his endearment. "Saemira." I rubbed his prickly jaw. "Baba said it meant *so good*. He said I embodied all that was good to him and Mama." And I wanted so badly to be good again.

"Saemira." He pulled me closer. "You definitely embody all that is good to me." He nuzzled my cheek as Altin giggled between us. "So good."

A lump formed in my throat as I pulled back to look at him. "I love you," I said. *I forgive you* was implied.

He smiled—that dazzling Lincoln smile that made me feel as if everything was right with the world. "I love you, too. And I'm going to prove that for the rest of your life."

I smiled, but my heart ached, knowing I couldn't stick around long enough for him to prove anything.

"There's one more surprise." Lincoln pulled me toward the stairs.

"What else can there be?" Altin and Angel were all I needed. My heart was full and happy for the moment.

"You'll see."

We made our way downstairs, where I heard a voice that made my heart jump with joy.

"Gramps!" I said, as he and Alex came into view.

"Gemma!" Gramps's smile lit up the kitchen. Only a few days had passed since he'd walked me down the aisle, but it felt like years.

Lincoln took Altin from me so I could hug the sweet man.

"It's so good to see you," I said. Lincoln took Altin over to some toys Mrs. Wilder had brought in for him.

"He's moving in," Alex said, putting a hand on his friend's shoulder. "This place is big enough, and I thought the more the merrier."

I hugged Gramps again, getting choked up. I'd known him for such a short time, but I already adored him and knew his death would leave a hole in my heart.

"Now, now," Gramps said, tipping my chin, "what's that sad face for?" He tugged me away from the others and gestured for me to get comfortable on the couch. "What's troubling you, my dear?"

I blinked to get control of my emotions. "It's nothing."

"It's everything. Tell me. I'll keep your secret safe."

Sadly, he knew none of my secrets. Wilder and Gramps still needed to be told, but I worried about their reactions. Lincoln had been utterly shocked at my revelation. I didn't want to cause these old men—especially Gramps with his brain tumor—physical distress. I'd have to discuss this with Lincoln. Maybe we wouldn't tell them anything. Did it matter who they thought I was? I was still the same person, whether they called me Gemma or Saemira.

"It's just when I think about losing you, I want to cry. I'm sick of losing everybody I love. My mom. My dad. You soon. What if I lose Lincoln, too?" Which I would when I left him. "It will break my heart."

"Ah, sweet Gemma. Love always comes with risk. When I lost my Hazel, I didn't want to go on. But one day, I woke up and realized I hadn't really lost her. Sure, she wasn't there with me, but she was here." He touched his heart. "And here." He touched his head. "She lives on in the way my grandson looks at the world through that curious lens of learning, in the way he gestures to people. I see my Hazel in the matching shoes other ladies wear, in perfumes I smell, in a certain lilt to words. When I leave this life, remember how much I love you and know that I prayed you into my grandson's life to rescue his battered heart." He patted my hand and gave

254

me a tender look. "Death isn't the end, sweetheart. Even if you don't buy into an afterlife, the memories of our loved ones are always with us. In that way, we're all immortal."

"You're wise, like my baba."

"Ah, he lives on in me." He smiled. "Don't worry about losing Lincoln. That boy is yours completely. I've never seen him so happy. Savor each day you have together."

I blinked back tears, wanting to heed his advice and savor each moment with Lincoln as if it was our last.

Because soon, it would be.

56

LINCOLN

atching my wife brush her teeth and get ready for bed was sweet torture. I longed to take her in my arms and pick up where we'd left off on our wedding night, before I'd jumped to the absolute worst conclusion about her and ruined everything. But I could tell by the way she avoided my eyes in the mirror that my desire wouldn't be sated tonight. I'd lost too much ground and would have to carefully build back trust.

I followed her into the bedroom and tugged my shirt off. "Do you want me on the floor?" I asked.

She chewed her tempting lips and looked at the bed, then me, then the bed again. "I don't know."

"I know I've lost my right to..." I trailed off.

"Sex?" she finished for me.

I nodded, my traitorous body gearing up for action, even as I told it that nothing was happening. "I promise not to push you. I know I have to—"

She threw herself into my arms, surprising me. "I'm so sorry I didn't tell you the truth about who I really was. I wanted to. I should've done it before the ceremony. But I was so scared you would hate me, that you'd reject Altin, and I wanted him to be cared for if I had to disappear."

I nuzzled her soft neck, hating the thought of the terror she'd lived with for so long. "I'm sorry I proved your fears right. I'm a stupid fool. Please forgive me."

Her tears wet my cheeks, and I leaned back to wipe them away.

"Gramps told me to savor each day with you," she said. "But I'm still so scared. With Duke free, I fear you'll always be in danger because of me. I couldn't bear it if something happened to you."

Her words hit me like ice water in the heat of summer. "You were going to leave me that night, weren't you?" Her downcast eyes told me I was right. "You weren't running from the police, you were running from me. You tried to slip out of the closet." I raised her chin. "You're still planning to run, aren't you?"

Her chin jutted out defiantly. "If that's what it takes to keep you and my brother safe, then yes." Her lips quivered. "You still don't know everything. I kidnapped Altin from his foster family. I'm not a good person."

"Saemira." I cradled her face in my hands. "You are all that is good. And if you think that leaving me would ensure my safety, think again. I'd find you, no matter the danger involved." I kissed her nose. "What you did with your brother was a misguided move stemming from youth and love. You had no other motive. I'm sorry I thought you ever could. You're not a criminal. You're Altin's hero. And mine."

"But Duke's still a threat."

"Yes. But we'll face him together. You married me for better or for worse, not for better and for splitting up to keep me safe."

Her brows furrowed. "Are we even truly married since I was dishonest?"

I kissed her worry lines. "I married Gemma Stone legally. But we'll talk to my attorney about whether I need to marry Saemira Nikolla. Honestly, I wouldn't mind marrying you again. The first time was a lot of fun." I waggled my brows.

She snuggled into me. "It was fun, wasn't it?"

I closed my eyes, savoring her delicate body in my arms.

"Lincoln?" I heard the hesitancy in her voice.

I raised my head to gaze at my beautiful wife. "Yes?" Would she tell me to get another room? I knew I deserved worse.

"Gemma wants to make love to her husband."

"Really." I wanted to scoop her into my arms and run to our bed. But I exercised restraint. "You don't have to do that. What does Saemira want? We can take things slow, until you're both certain. I know—"

Her lips crashed into mine. "Oh, shut up and love me, you fool."

I swept her up into my arms, not needing to be told twice.

SAEMIRA

*L*incoln scooped me into his arms, and it felt like coming home. We'd only spent part of a night together as newlyweds, and even then, I'd held myself back, believing I would have to leave him.

But he'd set my heart at ease on that matter. I couldn't leave him now. He wouldn't let me. He loved me. Accepted me. He would suffer with me, if it came to that.

"I don't want us to ever end," he said, slipping the nightshirt off my shoulder. "You hold my heart, love. Don't ever think of running away with it."

I explored the muscles on his chest, and he pulled me into a tidal wave of desire that I couldn't have escaped no matter how hard I tried. Lincoln took me to heaven and back, a seamless union that made me see stars. Our wedding night had been bliss, but tonight, there was an intensity and purpose to his touches and kisses that awakened a dormant and wonderful hunger inside me. Our loving involved searching, exploring, and more importantly, forgiving and healing.

I drifted off to sleep in his arms and awakened when the morning sun filtered through the large window. He stroked my belly, making my body hum.

"Was last night real?" I murmured.

"It was to me." He kissed me.

I snuggled into his warm body. "What are we going to tell Gramps and Alex?"

"Let's not worry about that for now. I'll have my attorney look into your case, figure out how to get guardianship of Altin. Wipe your slate clean if there's anything messy on it. He'll look into whether we need to redo our wedding vows, too. Once we know those details, we'll proceed."

He started kissing my neck, and I got lost in his love once again. But doubts niggled at the back of my mind. If we were still keeping secrets, that meant our union wasn't as all-the-way real as I wished.

Would it ever be?

OFFICER TAYNE SHOWED up two days later, throwing a monkey wrench into our happiness. I'd let myself forget about real life as I'd savored time with my husband, brother, best friend, Gramps, and the Wilders. Lucy had dropped in to spoil me, and Ethel had introduced us to her craft room. She'd invited me to use the room and supplies as much as I'd wanted. It wasn't a science lab, but it was something to dither my time away on when Lincoln was busy with work duties.

Seeing Officer Tayne brought me crashing back to painful reality. Lincoln tried to shield me from the detective, leading him and Angel into the study and starting to shut the door, but I refused to be left out.

"Hey, don't forget about me."

"Or me." Gramps joined us.

Lincoln stepped out and took hold of my arm. "You don't need to be present, love. It'll just stir up bad memories."

True. But if he and Angel could hear what the detective had to say, so could I. "I was there, too. I need to know what's being done to find Duke."

"I'll give you a run-down later."

"Oh, let her in, son," Gramps said.

Lincoln frowned, but it was two against one.

"Thanks," I whispered to Gramps as we followed my disgruntled husband into the room.

"Don't mention it."

"Mrs. McConnell." Officer Tayne walked over to shake my hand. "Thanks for joining us. I was hoping to talk to you."

I gave Lincoln a little smirk, and he rolled his eyes.

"Have you had any luck finding the men who started the fire?" I asked.

"No, ma'am. Not yet. There were no prints or clues to tie any of them to the crime scene."

"But Angel could identify them." I glanced at my friend. "His testimony would stand up in court, wouldn't it?"

"If we can apprehend the culprits, then yes, his testimony will be crucial."

We took our seats, and Angel chewed his lips as Tayne began to interrogate him. I listened in horror as he revealed all he knew about Duke's organization.

To summarize: Duke's Canadian cousin ran an organized crime syndicate that had cells from Canada to central America. Duke had been given control of the Salt Lake cell, a smaller, but more specialized group that worked in sex trafficking and drug distribution.

My stomach churned as Angel unveiled gory details of girls as young as eight and women into their fifties being stolen off the streets or lured into Duke's evil web by social groomers—handsome men who enticed victims to send them revealing photos to be used later to threaten or blackmail them into submission. Like the letter to me, Duke would promise they'd only work a few hours a month for his silence. But after the victims met for the horrid exchange, Duke would wield even more power over them. Once-a-month sessions became twice a month, then weekly, until victims were either killed by abusive clients or took their own lives to escape the guilt, horror, and pain of their ruined existence.

Poor Angel had worked in various capacities in this vile environment for years. To protect me!

"Is there a chance Duke could be set free," I asked, "even after standing trial?"

"There's always a possibility," Officer Tayne said.

That wasn't what I wanted to hear. "Have you checked out that cafe where I left my blackmail money?"

Officer Tayne nodded. "We've had a plain-clothes officer watching it for the last several weeks. So far, nothing suspicious."

"Son of a ditch," I muttered.

Lincoln smiled.

"What if I reached out to Duke—with a note or something, saying I'm willing to make a deal with him?"

"Absolutely not!" Both Lincoln and Angel stood and scowled at me.

"But I could draw him out for the police."

"I said no!" Lincoln growled. "I won't risk your life."

"But Duke has to be stopped. Besides, I wouldn't be in real danger, right?" I looked to Officer Tayne for backup.

"Not technically. My men could put a wire and tracker on you so that—"

"My wife will not be part of this," Lincoln snapped.

Angel nodded vigorously. "He's right, Gem. It's too dangerous. Duke would take out his revenge if he ever got his hands on you."

I squeezed Mama's amulet. "Isn't it more dangerous to sit here and wait for him to catch us by surprise again? Next time, someone could die. At least, if I go—"

"You aren't going," Lincoln said again.

I smoothed the protective amulet, then looked closer at the stone. "Could Duke have tampered with this?" I asked Angel. "He tracked me with my phone to Park City. I got rid of it by throwing it out the window on the freeway, but he still found me at Lincoln's."

"You threw your phone out the window?" Lincoln said.

I ignored him and watched Angel's face. "This is the only other item I have that might link me to him."

Angel shook his head. "He didn't care about the necklace. He put it out in the bin of things to grab for payment."

"Don't you find that suspicious?" The others were all watching me now. I twisted my necklace. "He cut my neck pulling this off me. Did you ever ask him about it?"

"Of course." Angel glanced around the room then back at me. "You tried not to act upset, but this was your last link to your mama. I knew how important it was to you."

I let the stone dangle on its chain. "So, Duke knew. And he just happened to *allow* you to take it as payment?"

"You're overthinking this, Gem. You always do."

I pulled the necklace off and walked over to Officer Tayne. "He put a tracker in this. I'm sure of it."

"Is that true?" Lincoln put a comforting hand on my back as the detective held my stone up to the light.

"I can't tell. The stone's too cloudy. But I can have the lab check it out."

"Do it," Lincoln said. "Get that thing away from my wife."

I put my hands on my hips. "That stone's not going anywhere without me. My mama gave it to me." I focused on Officer Tayne. "Can I go to the lab with you?"

"Of course. That might be best if your theory's right and Duke is tracking you with it."

"I'm going with her," Lincoln said, his arm moving around my waist.

I pushed his arm off me. "Stop treating me like a little girl."

"He's treating you as a good husband should," Gramps said. "I'll come with you guys."

I sighed, knowing I couldn't argue with him.

"You're all welcome to come," Officer Tayne said. "But it might be a wait. The lab's not known for their efficiency."

"That's fine," I said. "I need to know. If he's tracking me, we can lure him out of hiding. I could—"

"You'll do nothing," Lincoln said.

"Your wife has a point, Mr. McConnell," Officer Tayne said. "There is no one better to lure Duke out than her."

My husband gave the detective a scathing look. "My wife is not to be used as your bait to draw out the monster. If you risk her life in any way, I will sue you and your precinct for everything they own. Do you understand?"

The poor detective paled. "Completely."

"Then this discussion is over."

I stared again at my amulet, knowing that no matter what Lincoln wished, this wasn't over.

Not by a long shot.

58

LINCOLN

$\mathcal{M}$y wife had holed up in the craft room since the detective's visit. The meeting had left her out of sorts. Me, too. I couldn't stand to look at her amulet now, knowing it might be tampered with. But we would know in the morning, when we took it to the police station.

I slipped into the craft room without knocking. Saemira appeared like a Roma queen, sitting before a table, a beaded barrette in her hair, wearing an orange and purple top that brought out her golden skin tones.

I cleared my throat, and she looked up from her project.

"Hey, sexy," she said.

"Hey, beautiful." I lifted a gift bag.

"What'd you bring me?"

"It's for both of us." I set the bag down and studied the half-done pants in her lap. "Those pockets are too angled and loose. Things will fall out of them."

She held up the muted-gray material, twisting it back and forth. "Have I told you I love you today?"

I leaned down to kiss her. "Several times, but I wouldn't mind hearing it again."

"I love you, my missing Link."

I groaned. "Joe's infected you."

"You didn't think that was clever?"

I slipped my hand up her blouse. "So clever I want to lock the door." I tugged her blouse up.

She giggled and pushed my hands down. "Behave."

"Look in the bag," I said.

She pulled tissue out and lifted two matching T-shirts with a picture of us from our wedding day, goofy grins on our faces. "Oh," she breathed out, "I love these."

"I love us, too. Maybe we can model them for each other tonight. With nothing else on."

She smirked. "What kind of girl do you think I am, Mr. M?"

"My girl." I gave her another quick peck, then sobered. "Are you ready for tomorrow?"

"Yes. I need to know."

We both needed to know if her amulet posed a threat.

"You're not going to offer yourself up as the sacrificial lamb again, are you?"

Her shoulders sagged. "I want to. Duke's been an anchor holding me down since I was a child. I'll never feel safe until he's caught. Let me work with the police. You heard Officer Tayne. He thinks I'm the best chance to trap him."

"I don't care if you're the only chance to trap him. I won't put you in harm's way. When I married you, both times!"—I smiled as I thought of the quick ceremony at the courthouse downtown yesterday afternoon, with just Joe and Janey standing in as witnesses—"I vowed to honor, cherish, and protect you. That doesn't mean letting you risk your life needlessly."

She concentrated on her pants and changed the subject. "You don't appreciate my wonky pockets?"

"They're crooked." I hated when things weren't precise.

She waved a dismissive hand. "I think they're perfect. A work of art."

I tugged her into my arms. "You're a work of art. A masterpiece."

Saemira, Gramps, Angel, and I sat around a table in a conference room at the precinct. My wife's amulet sat on the table in front of Officer Tayne, along with a lab report.

"A microchip is embedded in the bottom of the stone." He held up what appeared to be an X-ray. "You can see the laser cuts here. It was inserted and pieced back together. The lab tech said it was an amateur job but the stone's cloudy texture hides it well. It's only detectable with jeweler's glasses."

"Can you get the chip out without destroying the stone?" I asked. "It has sentimental value to my wife."

"No," Saemira said. "Leave it in. Let's use it to trap Duke."

I scowled at my wife. "We've already discussed this. I cannot in good conscience let you be involved. You're not trained. You could be hurt."

Gramps patted her hand. "I agree with Lincoln, sweetheart."

Tayne pursed his lips. "I understand your reservations, so I've come up with an alternate plan. We'll have a female officer dress up as you and lure Duke out where we can catch him."

"Excellent idea." Any plan that didn't involve my wife was a winner.

"That won't work," Saemira argued. "Duke's men will know right away the decoy isn't me."

Tayne frowned. "You're still our best option."

"Leave my wife out of this." How many times did I have to tell him?

"Can you insert another tracker in the stone?" Saemira asked.

Tayne smiled. "I like the way you think."

What was she thinking? I wasn't following their train of thought.

He dropped the amulet back in the plastic bag. "Let me take this back to the lab. Get yourself a drink from the vending machine in the hall while you wait."

I turned to Saemira after the detective left us. "I don't want to take that cursed amulet home if Duke can track you with it."

"I'm not leaving here without it." She folded her arms.

Gramps put a hand on both our shoulders. "Trust your wife, son. She's got a good head on her shoulders."

I agreed. But I wanted to keep that head on her shoulders.

59

SAEMIRA

---

*T*he small knife dug into the bottom of my new sandals as I carved a geometric design to work out my frustration. Lincoln needed to chill out. He wasn't willing to listen to any plan to bring Duke down that involved me, even in minimal roles. He didn't even like me wearing Mama's amulet now.

But Tayne knew better. I did, too. In my heart, I knew I was the only one who could get Duke to show his face.

It wasn't that I was necessarily brave. I didn't want to be anywhere near the monster. But by luring him out and getting him to let down his guard, the police would have a better shot at catching the bastard and putting him behind bars where he belonged.

I finished cutting the last curlicue and slipped the shoe onto my foot. Time for step two. I placed my shoe into a pan of glow-in-the-dark solution I'd mixed earlier, then stepped onto the concrete and walked around the room.

I pulled out a bin of rice that'd been drying for the past week. I'd soaked it in the same solution. I ran my hands through the dry kernels, then walked around the room and dropped rice near the walls. After I concluded this experiment, I'd sweep up the mess so as not to attract mice, although mice might not like the tainted rice. That would be an experiment for another day.

With the prep work done, I texted Angel to meet me in the craft room.

He appeared less than a minute later. "Hey, Gem. What's up?"

I handed him my black light. "I'm turning off the lights. See if you can find the trail." I flipped the switch, and the windowless room became quite dark.

Angel turned the black light on and shone it against the floor. "Ah-hah. Here's your footprint. Nice design."

"Thanks."

"Here's another. And what's this?" He shone the light against the wall, illuminating a line of kernels. "Rice?"

"Yea!" I switched on the light. "I didn't know if the rice would glow or not."

"You have quite the mess to clean up," he said.

"All in the name of science."

He snickered. "You're still the same girl who got more excited about a science experiment than a toy." He handed me the black light, but I shook my head.

"Keep it."

He didn't realize what a breakthrough this was. My husband might be against me drawing Duke out into the open, but I refused to sit back and do nothing.

Baba had always said to prepare for any eventuality.

60

LINCOLN

*G*ramps seemed contemplative tonight. Seven weeks had passed since the doctor's diagnosis. Besides needing a couple long naps during the day, he seemed fine. I'd caught him wincing a time or two when he thought he was alone, so I knew his days were numbered.

That's why I sat with him every opportunity I could. "How are you doing, Gramps?"

I always asked, hoping he would be honest and tell me if he was in pain. Hoping he would ask for help if he needed.

"Wonderful, my boy. Wonderful." He gave me the same answer he'd given for the past twenty years. "Sit by me a moment. I'd like to talk."

I got comfortable on the sofa.

"Where's your sweet wife? Is she still putting her brother to bed?"

I nodded. "Altin is on one tonight." The trip up the canyon this afternoon had overstimulated him.

"Probably all that ice cream."

I smiled. "Probably."

"Oh, it definitely was the ice cream," Saemira said, bending over the couch to kiss my cheek, before joining me on the couch. "Try spoiling him with broccoli or salad tomorrow."

I clasped her hand. "Was he awful?"

"My brother is never awful. He's determined."

Gramps chuckled. "You two do my old heart good." He reached over to touch a box on the coffee table. "I have something for you both."

"You didn't need to get us anything," Saemira said. "Your wedding gift was way more than enough."

I smiled. My wife really was a treasure, so content with life and unaffected by the trappings of wealth. She didn't care about what car she drove or the labels on her clothes. She just wanted to be herself and seemed to thrive on finding discounts and deals to accomplish that.

"This has a more personal connection." He tapped the box. "Go ahead. Open it."

"Why don't you do the honors," I told my wife.

She lifted the lid and sighed. I leaned over to see two jeweler's boxes.

"I want you both to carry around a part of me when I'm gone," Gramps set the bigger box in my hands and handed Saemira the smaller one.

Mine held a slick-looking watch.

"It's engraved on the back," Gramps said.

I turned it over to read the inscription. *Never forget that I believe in you. Gramps*

"Thanks, Gramps."

Saemira unveiled a beautiful silver ring. *"I am with you always,"* she read the inscription inside the band. "Oh, Gramps." She moved over to hug him. "This is beautiful. Thank you so much."

"I love you, sweetheart. Don't ever forget that."

"I love you, too."

"You both have made my last days happy and fulfilling. I hope you'll wear these to remember me now and when I'm gone."

Saemira slipped the ring onto her pinky finger. "I won't ever take it off."

I clasped the watch around my wrist. "Me, neither."

Gramps hugged us both. "That means the world to me."

He meant the world to us.

SAEMIRA

This was the moment of truth. And ugly clothing. I stood beside my desk, wearing a stuffy business suit and wondering how women tolerated squeezing into these straight jackets.

Officer Tayne had called to run through a plan he needed our help with. I was all for helping, though I hadn't liked Lincoln's role once I'd listened to all the details. He would escort the lady officer impersonating me out of town, hoping to draw an ambush from Duke's men. Tayne and his team would intercept. I'd been willing to put myself at risk but hated that Lincoln would now be in the most danger.

My husband kissed me hard on the lips. "Go straight home. Don't go anywhere else."

"Don't worry," I said, my stomach churning with nerves. "Everything will be fine. You just stay safe."

"You, too. I love you." He walked out the door with my doppelganger, who didn't really look like me. She only dressed as me. Hopefully, that would be enough to fool Duke's men.

When we'd arrived, I'd switched clothes with the female officer and shimmied into this monkey suit. For my part, I was to wait fifteen minutes to ensure Duke's minions had left the vicinity before heading to an unmarked car in the parking garage and driving home.

Not very exciting.

As soon as my husband and the officer left, I hurried into the restroom to switch out of the horrid suit. I'd brought my wonky pocket pants that Lincoln had made fun of. I took the bag of rice from my fake briefcase and filled my loose pockets. Next, I took out my water bottle with the glow solution and loosened the lid so it barely clung on. Maybe I was being overly paranoid, but better vigilant than victim.

With my pockets full of glow rice and my bottle of glow solution at the ready, I checked the clock just as my phone rang. I didn't recognize the number but answered in case it was one of the officers checking in with me.

"Hello?"

"We have your husband and will kill him if you don't do exactly as I say," a deep voice said.

I froze. They had Lincoln?

"W-where is he?" I asked, a tremor to my voice.

"Just follow directions, and no one will get hurt. Leave through the front doors so we can make sure you're not followed. Walk toward the cafe. You know the way."

"Don't hurt him," I said, but the person hung up.

I leaned over my desk and shuddered. *Keep it together. You won't be able to help him if you're freaking out. Oh God!* I pleaded, *Keep my husband safe.*

Joe's door was closed as I walked toward the elevator. Thank the gods. I didn't want anyone I loved to see me and try to follow me out. I had to keep my husband safe.

My skin prickled as I exited the front doors of EcoCore and walked down the stairs. I gripped my water bottle and took courage from the rice in my pockets slapping against my leg. It didn't fall out as Lincoln had predicted. I'd experimented with angles until I'd gotten it just right, where only a slight nudge would send kernels out.

You've got this, girl, I told myself as I headed toward the cafe. I had prepared for any eventuality. Things would work out. They had to! I reached up to touch Mama's amulet, but it wasn't there.

Ugh. Officer Snyder had it. I knew I shouldn't have parted with it.

Something sharp and cool settled against my back. I flinched as a huge man wrapped an arm around me.

"Don't scream or I'll slice ya," he said in a gruff voice.

I couldn't have screamed if I'd wanted to. Every muscle in my body had frozen up. *Don't let fear control you.* My brain would help me if I remained calm and composed. It wouldn't if I let emotions run rampant.

"Where's my husband?" I asked and felt proud that my voice didn't waver.

"Shut up and keep walking. You'll see soon enough."

A car door opened up ahead. Another man stepped out, glancing around like he was guilty. I stumbled and let my water bottle spill solution onto the wheel.

My captor cursed and clenched my arm painfully as he pulled me up. I made sure to step into the syrupy solution before the other guy dragged me into the back of the car.

The car took off, and one of the men squeezed my face. "She's a beauty."

I slapped his hand, making the other man laugh.

"Patience, Ringer. Boss said he'd let us have some fun with her once we bring her in."

"She's *in* the car," Ringer said, running his hand down the front of my blouse.

I spat in his face, making him curse as the other man guffawed.

"Serves you right, you greedy git. I told you to be patient."

Ringer glared at me. "I want to have fun with her right now, before the others." He pulled me hard against his mouth, choking me with his nasty tongue. I tried to fight, but he had me pinned too tight.

The other guy knocked his friend's head with a gun. Thank the gods! I sucked in clean air, wanting to vomit.

"Leave her alone. I don't want a knife in my side because you pissed the boss off."

Please, Angel, I prayed, hoping he'd seen what had happened. He'd told me before Lincoln and I had left that he would park down the street to make sure no one followed me home.

Remember Hansel and Gretel. Find my trail.

62

ANGEL

*G*ramps leaned forward in his seat as my heart pounded. Did Saemira have a death wish? Why had she come out the front doors in broad daylight instead of going to the parking garage as Officer Tayne had told her to?

"We have to follow them," Gramps said, breathless as we watched Ringer and Slade force her into a car.

"Answer!" I yelled at my phone, but Officer Tayne's phone had gone to voicemail.

"Lincoln," Gramps said next to me, and I realized he must've called his grandson. "They have Saemira. They're taking off with her in a white Honda Accord."

"Tell him to meet us at the cafe on Fourth," I said, slamming my phone down so I could turn the car around and follow.

He repeated my words to Lincoln as I focused on driving. They had to have taken her to the cafe. It was the closest location from here. I parked a block away, not wanting to alert them to the fact that they'd been followed.

Gramps told Lincoln where we'd parked and to hurry his butt up. I grabbed Saemira's black light from the bag next to me. I'd carried it with me ever since she'd insisted I keep it, knowing she must have had a reason.

Had she known this would happen? Had the foolish girl planned all along to go it alone?

I opened the door. "Stay here and wait for Lincoln. I'm going to check the perimeter for guards. Keep trying Tayne. Let him know what's happened."

"Will do." Gramps looked angry, not scared. "Go find our girl."

I would find her, or die trying.

63
LINCOLN

*A*ngel was just walking away from his car as I pulled up. "Wait for me," I said, running over to Gramps. "Get out of here. It's too dangerous for you to stick around."

Officer Snyder and I hadn't gotten very far up Red Butte Canyon road before we'd been shot at by another vehicle. Snyder had been hit in the shoulder, and the other car had sped away as I'd pulled over to help the wounded officer. Tayne's men had shown up within minutes. Frantic to see my wife and make sure she was okay, I'd left the scene after assuring them that I'd check in with Tayne. Gramps had called right after that, and I'd sped like a maniac back to the city, hoping I wasn't too late.

"Take my car and go home." I handed him the keys. "Call 9-1-1 if Tayne won't answer."

Gramps took hold of my wrist, pressing against the watch he'd given me. "Be careful, son."

"I will." But I'd do whatever it took to get my wife back, even if it involved taking risks.

Angel frowned as I caught up to him "Hunch over. You stand out with your confident stride. Try to blend in. Be invisible."

I did as he ordered, and we slipped into a back alley.

Angel pointed. "Their car's here. And I found Saemira's footprints with the black light by the back door. No one's guarding it, cocky bastards."

The door was locked. I pulled out my phone to call for help, but Angel batted my arm. "Silence your phone. It will only hinder us from here on out."

I obeyed and looked up to see Angel jimmying something in the lock. The knob turned in his hand, and he pushed it open, peeking inside before motioning me to follow.

We crept inside and he waved me up the hall. "Keep a lookout," he whispered, before shining his flashlight over the floor and walls.

I stood there, trying to decide what I'd do if someone caught us in the dark hallway. Would I rush them? Act lost? We were in a back storage area where non-employees shouldn't be. I doubted anyone would believe I'd lost my way.

"Ah ha," the kid said softly. "She left us a trail." He pointed the beam against a door, where a geometric pattern footprint glowed in the dark. "She must've kicked it."

Again, the door was locked.

My stomach churned at how much time had passed.

Angel had the door open within seconds. Thank God he knew what to do.

I texted Gramps to tell him we were inside and had left the second door from the back unlocked for the police when they arrived.

Please, let him get a hold of Tayne.

We made our way down a cobwebbed stairwell that made me itch. "Have you been here before?" I whispered.

"No. But I'm guessing this is the *diner* Duke referred to. Tunnels connect it to other hideouts."

I followed his black light into the void, skin still itching. The basement had three tunnels leading out of it. Thankfully, my brilliant wife had left us another trail to know which one to take.

"There you are." Angel picked up a glowing piece of rice.

"You don't seem surprised."

"Gem and I always left trails for each other as kids. She was experimenting with making rice glow last week. She showed me her experiment so I was looking for rice. Let's hope the rats don't eat her trail away."

At the mention of rats, I shuddered, but continued into the darkness. Nothing would stop me from finding my wife.

64

SAEMIRA

My captors hadn't bound my hands. Though I'd practiced for that scenario with my crazy pocket pants. Releasing bits of rice was easier with my hands free. Hopefully, Angel would pick up my trail and lead the police to this den of vipers. If he didn't, I'd be worse off than dead.

My captors weren't gentle. The one called Ringer couldn't keep his paws off me, and the grumpy one with the gun liked to yank me faster than I could walk in the dark.

A light up ahead made me squint. Boxes cast eerie shadows on the floor and walls as we entered what appeared to be a warehouse. Windows up high gave me some hope that I wasn't lost forever into a dark and sinister maze.

Duke and four others greeted us with catcalls and whistles.

"Ah, Temptress." Duke motioned to my captor. "Bring her to me. We're all hungry for fresh meat, yes?"

The men cackled.

My captor manhandled me to stand before his evil boss, leaving my arm bruised. Duke waved him away.

"You tried to trick me, but I turned the table on you and the police. The cop wearing your clothes was shot. So was your husband. They're both dead."

I sagged to my knees. "No."

"Yes. You're a widow now. Maybe a rich one, yes? I'll let you live, Temptress. You might be my cash cow. But first, you owe me and my men some pleasure for all the trouble you've caused."

"Go to hell." I spat on his boots.

His fist came out of nowhere, knocking me to the cold concrete. Blood filled my mouth.

"Watch your mouth, Temptress." He clapped. "We have an initiate who needs breaking in. Who's ready to help tenderize this fresh, delicate, scared piece of meat?" He nudged me with his boot as his minions cheered.

God, I cried, knowing He was the only one who could help me now, *give me wings to fly away.*

65

LINCOLN

Gramps's watch showed we'd been wandering these tunnels for twenty minutes. Would my wife be alive by the time we found her?

"Do you think she'll be okay?" I asked my brooding partner. I needed him to tell me Duke wouldn't touch her. That he wouldn't violate her or kill her. But Angel had said in jail that his uncle had raped Saemira as a child. He would definitely hurt her again if we didn't find her.

What if we were already too late?

"I don't know," Angel said.

"She'll be okay," I said.

"She'll be okay," Angel repeated, but I could tell neither of us felt reassured.

Please, God, let us find her in time. I hadn't stopped praying since I'd gotten Gramps's call that my wife had been taken.

Angel turned off his light. I felt my way toward where I'd seen him last.

"What is it?" I whispered.

"Light up ahead. See the glow?"

I squinted but couldn't see anything.

"No light from here on out. Try not to bump into something and give us away."

Minutes ticked by as we maneuvered into a warehouse with boxes and crates stacked around the walls. A group of men stood in the center of the room, cheering and howling. They circled something, or someone, and didn't notice us creep inside and hide behind the boxes.

Please, don't let the thing they're circling be my wife.

"Who wants to go next?" the leader yelled. He had a large hoop earring in one ear and a cruel face. Angel's uncle.

The circle opened slightly, and every muscle in my body spasmed as I caught a glimpse of Saemira on the ground, blood smeared around her mouth and nose.

"Let me at her," said a sinewy man.

"No, me!" another said, beating his chest. "A real man."

The leader motioned to the burly guy. "You have a minute."

The thug pumped his fist in the air and raced up to Saemira. He yanked her to her feet and tried to kiss her. She spat in his face.

I willed her to hang on until we could help her.

He growled and ripped her blouse down the middle, sending buttons flying and making her wince. Thankfully, she had a tanktop underneath. I moved forward to protect her, but Angel yanked me down.

"There's too many," he said under his breath. "Stay here. I'll distract them." He shimmied behind another pile of boxes.

The thug held onto a flailing Gemma, smashing his face into hers, then rearing back.

"She bit me!" he roared.

The leader laughed and motioned to the smaller man. "Maybe you can do better." Duke stared at his watch as the others chanted like fiends from hell.

The sinewy guy chased my wife around the circle and tackled her to the ground. My eyes stung as I watched the monster grope her.

Where are you, Angel?

My hands fisted as I prepared to run to her rescue. I couldn't sit here and watch my wife get ravaged.

"Time," the leader said.

The smaller man cursed. Saemira had a wild look in her eyes as she faced the next guy who came at her. She was a goddess surrounded by devils, refusing to break.

But I was ready to shatter.

66

ANGEL

hree, two, one. I took a deep breath and stepped out from my hiding spot, stumbling toward the group of former coworkers.

"Hey," I said, acting drunk. I recognized Slade, Tito, Boxer, and Ringer. I didn't know the other two. "You started the party without me."

Duke pushed out of the circle, a murderous expression on his face. "Should've guessed you'd come for your whore. Just like your pathetic mother, trying to save a lost cause."

I froze, and he laughed.

"Didn't know your mama tried to save you, did you? She owed me money and couldn't pay. I took you down to the river to teach her a lesson about priorities. She begged for your life, willing to give me anything in trade. So, I took the whore right there as you squealed in the mud, like the pig you are."

The others hooted. Saemira tried to pound her fist into Slade's manhood, but she missed, and he wrestled her to the ground.

Hold on, Gem. I didn't know what to do besides keep Duke talking. There were seven of them, and only Lincoln and me. We couldn't win this fight. But by the gods, maybe I could kill Duke for raping my mama. For raping my friend.

"I drowned her to the sound of your squealing." Duke smiled as words choked in my throat. "I should've drowned you, too, but I hoped you might grow up to be of use to me." He pulled out his gun and cocked it. "I was wrong."

"You-you killed her?" I shuddered, realizing everything he'd told me my entire life had been lies. He wasn't my uncle. He was my mama's murderer. My mama had been good. She'd tried to save me. She'd loved me.

"Yes, Bengalo. And now, I'm going to kill you, as I should've back then." He raised the gun.

"No!" Saemira screamed from where Slade had her pinned to the ground.

Duke laughed. "After I kill you, I'll have my way with your Temptress. Again. And again. And again. Until she doesn't please me. Then I'll kill her, too."

Saemira cried and fought to escape. I wished I could hold her one last time, tell her I was sorry for failing her.

The lever of the gun clicked.

This was it. Duke would win, as he always had. The gun discharged, but something heavy hurtled into me, knocking me to the ground and crushing the breath out of me.

Chaos erupted as men grunted and yelled. Duke shouted. Saemira screamed again.

I lifted my head to see who was on top of me. My eyes bulged when I saw Lincoln. He'd pushed me to the ground. Saved me.

And he was bleeding!

By the gods, he'd taken Duke's bullet, the one meant for me.

67

SAEMIRA

———— ✦ ————

*J*abbing back with my elbow, I connected with my captor's sensitive region and heard a groan. I rolled over, ready to fight all seven men to get to my husband, who wasn't dead as Duke had told me. My husband who'd just been shot and might still die.

That couldn't happen.

I scrambled to my feet and sprinted toward Lincoln, but Duke grabbed me before I could reach him.

"Don't be rash, Temptress." He brought the muzzle of the gun to my temple.

I watched helplessly as my husband kept bleeding.

"Leave her alone!" Engjell rolled out from under Lincoln's body and climbed to his feet. "Fight me." He hit his chest. "Best man gets to keep her."

The others prowled around, preparing to take him from behind.

Duke waved them away. "Step back. Bengalo's mine. And the girl."

He held me in a hold Engjell had taught me how to break as a child. If I relaxed my arms and stepped back into him, I'd be able to free myself. But the gun made me hesitate. He could shoot me. Or my friend. I glanced over at my bleeding husband.

Angel's hand shot forward, releasing rice. Duke raised both hands to protect his face, and I kicked back with my foot to connect with his crotch. He crumpled to the ground with a shriek. Angel launched himself on top of

Duke, bringing his hands behind his back. I stepped on Duke's face, crushing his cheek into the ground as I retrieved the gun.

"Nice work," Angel said to me.

"You weren't too shabby either."

I aimed the gun at the other devils. "Who wants to make my day? I might not have bullets to kill you all, but I'll send several of you to hell." Where they belonged. "My daddy taught me how to shoot."

We were dead. Outnumbered. My husband bleeding out. I kept Duke's gun raised, but all I could think about was Lincoln. Would he die before I could get to him, as Baba had all those years ago? I waved the gun in front of me, making several of the men step back.

"Put the gun down, girlie," one of them said.

I aimed low and shot at him. Baba hadn't taught me to handle a gun, but Ken Barber, my foster dad, had.

My aim wasn't too far off. I'd been aiming for the man's nether regions but hit the middle of his leg. He fell to the floor, holding his leg.

"Rush her, you fools!" Duke yelled.

Angel slammed Duke's head into the cement, but not before three men heeded his words and rushed me. I fired another shot and missed. One of the men tackled me to the ground, and the gun flew from my hand, sliding across the floor toward Lincoln.

The man crushed air out of me, and I knew we were goners. Though these men deserved to die, I hadn't been able to kill when the moment had come. I hadn't been able to shoot at their black hearts. Baba's voice had whispered to leave judgment in God's hands. And I had.

But they wouldn't be as merciful.

68

LINCOLN

*M*y wife was manhandled to her feet, and I wanted to scream. She was bleeding from her mouth and had scratches on her hands and bloody holes in the knees of her pants. She looked as if she'd run through a battlefield.

And I could do nothing to help her.

I wanted to hold her before I died, tell her I loved her. Blood seeped from my wound as I helplessly witnessed my wife's humiliating last moments.

Why, God! I cried. *Why do you take everyone I love? Take me instead. Let her escape.*

"Drop your weapons, you sick bastards."

My eyes widened. Though it caused immeasurable pain, I turned my head to see what couldn't possibly be.

Gramps moved out from behind a stack of boxes, holding a gun with both hands, looking like a soldier, not a dying man.

"The police are on their way," he said in a commanding voice. "Let the girl go and get up against the wall if you want to live."

The man nearest Saemira grabbed her in a chokehold, pulling a knife from his pocket and holding it against her neck.

"I'll kill her!" he screamed, using her as a human shield as he moved backward.

Saemira, my brave, courageous wife, slipped her foot behind his leg, then brought her hands straight up, catching him off guard. He tripped over her foot when he tried to turn, and she pounded his groin, doubling him over.

I reached for the gun she'd dropped, and aimed the weapon at two of Duke's minions moving to intercept her. "Saemira!" I called. "Get behind me."

She hurried over, taking vigil beside me as I collapsed. She retrieved the gun and stroked my head.

"Face the wall," Gramps ordered the thugs.

Two of them tried to rush him. Gramps dropped one with a well-placed shot in the knee. The other guy dropped from a shot fired from another direction.

"Mr. Wilder?" Saemira said next to my ear.

"Put your hands in the air," Alex said, before calling the criminals words only a soldier would speak. They deserved each epithet he flung at them.

"We need a medic," Gramps said.

"Already ahead of you, old boy," Alex answered.

I pulled my wife close. For the moment, we were safe. Alex and Gramps had all seven men against the wall, guns trained on them. Right then, it wasn't difficult to picture them both out in the jungles of Nam, hunting the Viet Cong together.

My wife pulled away. I opened my eyes to see Tayne and another officer tugging her away from me. Hallelujah. They'd arrived.

"It's about freaking time," Saemira snapped at the detective.

"The paramedics are just behind me," he said, lifting my shirt and rolling me onto my side. "Looks like the bullet went right through. That's good." He applied pressure, making me suck in air and hiss.

"It hurts...like...Helen...Keller," I said through clenched teeth.

Saemira returned to my side, kissing my cheek, and stripping off her ripped blouse. "Use this to stop the bleeding," she said, handing it to Tayne.

"You're bleeding, too," he said, before wadding the cloth up and pressed it against my wound.

Was my wife wounded? Had the man with the knife cut her?

"I'm fine." Saemira whispered in my ear. "You're not allowed to die on me, do you hear? If you do, I will personally kill you myself."

I winced as Tayne kept applying pressure.

Saemira squeezed my fingers. "You officially have hero status, so no more heroics." She swiped at her eyes.

"Love...you," I said, beyond grateful that the bad guys couldn't hurt her any more.

"Shhh. Tell me later, with lots of kisses."

I closed my eyes, head swimming with pain. But my wife was safe. That was all that mattered.

My body ached. My stomach burned. But my eyes feasted as I opened them. "Aren't you the...most lovely sight. Ever." I found it difficult to speak, like my mouth was lined with cotton.

Saemira sat beside me, stroking my arm. "You look like caca-doodoo."

I smiled...or tried to. My lips were dry and cracked. She didn't look much better, honestly. She had an awful-looking black eye, a nasty cut on her swollen lips, and a bandaged arm.

But she was alive!

"Now that I know you're going to live, thank you for saving Angel." She pressed a kiss to my cheek. "If you'd died, I never would've forgiven you."

"How did Gramps find us?" I must've lost consciousness because I couldn't remember anything after my wife had taken her shirt off to staunch my bleeding.

"He's Superman." She lifted my watch from the table. "The sly old soldier tracked us with this. And my ring. He said he felt nervous after the talk with Officer Tayne. Gramps and Alex came up with a plan to track us in case something went wrong, which it totally did."

Good old Gramps. He'd always been there for me, saving me literally and figuratively throughout my life. "I love you," I said.

Saemira blinked and looked away. "I have so much to atone for."

What did she mean?

"I've ruined everything. Cost you millions. Cost you your house. Almost cost you your life."

"Shh." I put a finger to her battered lips. "Angel's right. You talk...too much."

A knock kept me from assuring her that none of those things mattered.

Alex Wilder entered with flowers. As if I needed any more of those. My room already looked and smelled like a damned floral shop.

"Alex." Saemira wrapped the old soldier in a hug. "My brave protector. Thank you for coming." She took the flowers. "These are beautiful."

"Ed is resting at home. He's dizzy and told me to tell you to hurry up and get better so he can see you."

I still couldn't wrap my head around the fact that two old men had saved us. If it hadn't been for Gramps's timing, one—or all of us—would've died. "Thanks...for saving us," I said.

He growled. "It's galling what you two have endured."

Saemira's eyes glistened with tears, and I understood what I had to do. Wilder's visit was fortuitous.

"Honestly, Alex, it's galling...what I've done to you."

He gave me a weird look. "What do you mean?"

"I have a...confession."

Saemira's eyes widened. She seemed to grasp immediately what I intended to say. She pushed between Wilder and me, blocking him from view.

"My husband's loopy right now from the meds."

"I'm lucid. Let me get this off my chest."

"Maybe you should come another time." She tried to tug Alex toward the door.

"No. He needs to know the truth." She wouldn't stop me. "Saemira and I...weren't engaged." A weight seemed to release my chest from the burden I'd carried for months. "When Scaglione got overly friendly with her at our first meeting, I lied and said she was my fiancée to get him to bug off."

"He's delusional," Saemira said. "Don't listen to him."

"Go on," Alex said, looking at me.

Saemira slumped, knowing she'd lost.

I licked my stinging lips. "It's my fault. Saemira wanted to tell you but I persuaded her to go along with the ruse. For the money."

"He's making himself sound worse than he is," she said.

"No, I did wrong. To both of you. I bullied Saemira into playing a part." I reached for her hand. "Our marriage is real now. I love her. But I'll understand if you want your money back. I manipulated you in the beginning. And her."

Saemira buried her head in her hands. I wanted her to look up, to see that I loved her.

But she was too distraught.

SAEMIRA

*L*incoln squeezed my hand, but tears leaked out in a fissure of pain. Why was he doing this? Ruining everything we'd worked so hard to secure? This was a terrible time to come clean. We'd told Gramps and Alex about my real name and why I'd hidden behind an alias. But the rest of it—the fake engagement, the fake marriage in the beginning —hadn't mattered since we loved each other now.

Alex was a hard-nosed solider, as proved by his and Grandpa's rescue mission. He wouldn't look kindly on being manipulated, even if everything had turned out right in the end.

"Step outside with me, my dear," Alex said.

Maybe I could do damage control. Clear Lincoln's name and take all the blame.

He gestured to a bench in the hallway, and I sat. He sank down next to me and patted my hand.

"Do you love Lincoln?"

I swiped at my stinging eyes. "With all my heart. But he deserves better than me. I fooled him into caring for me."

His white brows raised. "Your husband hasn't been fooled, my dear. You only have to search his eyes to see the truth. The man is completely smitten by you. But what's this about him lying about your engagement?"

"It was my fault. I feel horrible for deceiving you since you've been nothing but good to us. But I thought it'd be the best way to get you to invest in EcoCore."

Alex watched me intently. "Tell me exactly what you two did."

How could I spin Lincoln in a good light? He'd suffered too much already because of me. I didn't want him to be hurt any more.

"Lincoln was trying to save me from your CFO. He obviously doesn't think quickly on his feet because he's not a practiced liar, so he told Scaglione we were engaged. He never expected Scaglione to tell you. I played along and forced Lincoln to go along with it longer than he wanted. You mustn't blame him. He's an honorable man."

Alex patted my hand. "You really love him, don't you?"

I hugged my body. "He's my world."

"That makes me happy to hear. I worried about Lincoln at first, wondering if he'd do the right thing by you. It took his mind more time to catch up to his heart than yours did. But even that first night we met, I had no problem believing his lie could become the truth."

What?

He winked. "My dear, you didn't really think I bought his lie that night, did you?"

My mouth fell open.

He chuckled. "Lincoln really is a terrible liar. Scaglione bought it because he was blinded by guilt. The man's married."

I gasped. "That snake."

"Yes. But he's a snake who's genius with finance. Still, I wish you could've seen Lincoln's face when Scaglione took you out on the dance floor. I thought he would burst a blood vessel."

"All I remember is feeling invisible that night."

Alex laughed. "Oh, my dear, believe me, you were not invisible to a soul there. Lincoln couldn't keep his eyes off of you. I watched you two interact and could sense your attraction, yet you both tried so hard to act unaffected. It was comical. When Lincoln abruptly left the table, I knew he was finally ready to stake his claim. Scaglione returned and asked if I'd known you two were engaged. I decided to play along to see how you'd react."

"You wily fox. When will I learn not to underestimate you? Here we thought we were pulling one over on you, and you pulled one over on us."

His eyes crinkled. "It worked out for the best, did it not?"

I hugged him.

He patted my back. "You truly are a gem, and your husband recognizes that now. I dare say he made his confession for you, not me. He seemed to want you to understand he didn't care about losing my money, which you haven't. He cares about you." He kissed my head and stood. "I'll leave you two to talk things out. But before I go, I have one more secret to share."

I didn't want any more secrets. I wanted my life to be an open book from now on.

"I hired a private investigator to dig a little deeper into Lincoln's ex-wife after she came to me with some 'evidence' against your husband."

I grimaced. What had that vile woman given him?

"The 'evidence' was garbage, but my PI stumbled upon quite a load of smelly dirt when he sniffed around some more. Let's just say that Lincoln need not be concerned about that woman gaining control of EcoCore. Ever. No court on earth will award her a dime when I leak her scandal to the district attorney's office. And I have documents from an abortion clinic that prove Lincoln didn't cause her *miscarriage*. She had the baby aborted an hour before she called the cops and claimed those aggravated battery charges."

"Seriously?" What had he found? And would it really keep the she-snake from undermining all of Lincoln's hard work?

"Quite serious, my dear."

I laughed, feeling beyond relieved. This would make my husband so happy. "How can I ever thank you enough for everything you've done? Lincoln truly is the best of men. Thank you for clearing his name. I hope his luck turns, and he can be rid of that woman forever."

"He will be, dear. Trust me." He shooed me. "Now, get back in there and let your husband finish what he was trying to tell you before I stole you away."

70

LINCOLN

The door opened, and Saemira stepped inside, looking relieved and happy. Maybe Alex hadn't chewed her out.

I motioned her to my bed. "What did he say?"

She grinned. "The sneaky old man knew the truth all along. We weren't playing him as much as he was playing us."

"Thank God for the trickster."

"Yes," she agreed.

"I really don't care about the money," I said, intertwining my fingers with hers. "If he'd taken it all away, I'd still be the happiest man on earth as long as I had you."

She sniffled. "Your meds are making you talk like a crazy man."

"I am crazy for you." I brought her hand to my mouth, kissing her soft skin.

"You deserve so much better than me."

"Not true. I'm the one who doesn't deserve someone as amazing and wonderful as you. But love has nothing to do with what we deserve. I'm better with you in my life, Saemira. End of discussion. I hope you feel better with me."

"I do." She kissed me softly on the lips. "I feel like me again."

I ran a hand through her hair. That's exactly how I felt, too. I was me again, better with her by my side. I vowed to work the rest of my life to try to be the man she needed me to be. To show her how much she meant to me.

I caressed her face. "I'd given up hope I would ever be happy again, but you giggled and made me see you."

She snorted. "You didn't want to see me."

"Not at first. But now, you are all I can see." I pulled her down for another kiss. "Marrying you is absolutely the best thing I've ever done. Nothing else compares. Nothing else ever will."

"Hush," she said, lips touching mine. "You talk too much." She deepened the kiss, and though my lips still stung, I didn't stop her.

GRAMPS MOVED his knight and chuckled when I frowned. "Still thinking about your girl, not your game, I see."

I moved a pawn, knowing my rook was a goner. "Can you blame me?" Saemira and the others had gone to bed over an hour ago. Gramps and I tended to get overly competitive when we played chess, which we had done every night since I'd been released from the hospital.

"Don't blame you at all," he said. "Saemira's a treasure."

I studied the board.

"How's your wound?" he asked.

I'd gotten the all-clear from my doctor two days ago to resume normal activities. "Mostly healed," I said. Was he trying to distract me from a move I was missing?

"You're not overdoing it, are you?"

"I'm fine. I wouldn't call chess strenuous."

"I'm just worried about the emotional turmoil I'm putting you under," he said with a mischievous wink.

I chuckled. "What about you? Are you overdoing it?" I kept studying the board. Gramps claimed his pain wasn't bad, but he'd missed several dinners the past week, instead opting to stay in his room.

"Nothing I can't handle."

The tumor obviously wasn't affecting his intellect. I'd lost four of the last five games. I moved another pawn toward his bishop, hoping to draw him out onto the board.

Through the next few moves, we chitchatted about Angeline's upcoming legal battle. He knew more than me since Alex kept him apprised of each new development. Three weeks ago, the story had been leaked to the press that my ex was having an affair with the mayor's assistant and siphoning tax dollars from the city budget. The press was having a heyday with the juicy political scandal. Angeline might end up in prison if a jury found her guilty.

"How's it going with Altin's guardianship?" Gramps asked, moving his queen toward my knight.

"Court's moving slow. Poor Saemira's dying." The State of Michigan seemed in no hurry to make a decision. My wife was usually optimistic, but on the matter of her brother, she couldn't believe that the state would be merciful and grant her guardianship. She kept waiting for something bad to happen.

"She'll get custody," Gramps said. "Tell her not to stress. It's not good for her health. If cancer has taught me anything, it's not to worry so much."

I soaked in his wisdom. "Got any more advice?"

He pursed his lips. "Be grateful for each new day. Treat it like it's your last. You'll never regret doing that."

I moved my knight away from his queen, and he swiftly moved a pawn on the other side of the board. I swore when I realized he'd cornered my second rook.

He winked. "Love more. Judge less. Make connections with others."

"I'd like to connect with that damned queen of yours," I muttered.

He chuckled. So did I. Though I would surely lose again, I savored our time together. Each night, he sprinkled wisdom in with his brutal chess moves.

We began discussing my pet projects at EcoCore. He loved the EcoWalker most. I had a love-hate relationship with it since we'd had several setbacks.

"You know, son," he said, when I had only two more pawns left on the board. "EcoCore is definitely an achievement to be proud of. Your inventions have changed lives for the better. But don't forget at the end of the day that it doesn't matter what your stock is worth if you've neglected your family. When you're my age, you won't care a damn about your company. But you will care about Saemira. You'll care lots about your children and their children. Make them your top priority now so they're still there when you're older."

Gramps put me out of my misery and called the game.

I hugged him. "Thank you."

"For whipping your butt?"

"No. I'll kick your trash tomorrow, just you wait. Thank you for always putting me first. You've always been there for me, and I've never really thanked you or told you how much that meant to me. You never stopped believing in me, even in the face of evidence against me."

"You're a good kid, Lincoln. Now pass the love on to your wife and future children to repay me." He squeezed my shoulder.

"I'll do my best. At least, better than my chess game," I teased.

71

SAEMIRA

---

*T*he turkey looked divine—a beautiful, smoky golden-brown. I couldn't help but squeal and do a little victory dance. Lucy laughed when I pulled her into my celebration.

"We did it!" My first Thanksgiving meal for the books.

"You did it," Lucy said, hugging me.

"You know that's not true, Mom." She loved when I called her that, so I tried to sprinkle the title in a few times when we were together.

She grinned. "Our guests will love it."

"They'd better." I untied my apron and set it on the counter. We'd spent almost five hours slaving away in the kitchen. If anyone complained— or rather, if William, AKA Dad or Jerkface, as I often called him under my breath, complained—I'd toss him out on his backside.

My gaze traveled across the expanse of the delicious-smelling kitchen. The renovation of Lincoln's house had taken longer than planned, but that had worked out best for Gramps, since we didn't want to move him by the end when he was declining. We'd moved in two weeks after his funeral in September.

Gramps had been gone for over two months now. I still missed him every day. Lincoln really missed him. Gramps had been more of a father to him than his own had been. For that reason, he struggled with bitterness that his dad was alive while Gramps wasn't. I didn't blame him. William was a killjoy who seemed to wear foggy spectacles that gave him a gloomy view of the world and everyone in it. Especially family. He'd learned to hold his tongue around me because I had no qualms about calling him out and demanding apologies. Lincoln had almost come to blows with him about some of his mean remarks. Made me love him more. Not that I wanted my husband and father-in-law to fight, but I didn't mind that Lincoln was willing to defend my honor.

We'd been married for six months. Lincoln was a doting husband, a fantastic father to Altin, and a caring son—at least, as much as he was allowed to be. Lucy ate up every crumb of kindness he threw at her, and I'd encouraged him to give her meals of the affection she craved since she got nothing from her deadbeat husband.

Lincoln stepped into the room, my brother on his back. "How's it going in here, my angels?"

Lucy giggled, slurping up his cheese.

"We're almost ready, my missing Link," I said.

He winked at me. "I'll gather everyone." He disappeared again.

Lucy and I put a few last touches on our spread, and Lincoln soon had all our guests situated at the table. He was in charge of the next part since I'd never participated in an American Thanksgiving before. Baba had splurged on a turkey dinner at a buffet once, before he'd met Rosie. That was the limit of my experience.

I looked around the table at family and friends. Lincoln's parents, Angel and Altin, and the Wilders. Eight of us. The table looked like *Downton Abbey*, with the fancy china and silverware and crystal goblets Lucy had insisted we use from our wedding. I felt like Cinderella again, except surrounded by people who loved me—excluding my wicked dad-in-law, who wasn't really wicked as much he was irritable, racist, and moody.

Lincoln tapped his goblet with a knife. "Thank you all for coming to Saemira's and my first Thanksgiving together. We hope to have many more of these in the future."

"Hear, hear," I said, tapping my glass. Why should he get to have all the fun?

Lucy gave me an adoring smile, and I wanted to run around the table to hug her. Though William was a challenge, I adored my new mom. Lucy was the best, a fairy godmother of sorts. She would totally dress me up in a fancy ball gown if I asked, but thankfully, she knew my tastes better now and didn't push for that.

"Before we say grace and start loading our plates," Lincoln said, draping an arm over my shoulders, "I thought we'd go around the table and say what we're thankful for."

William scowled, but stayed quiet. I was grateful for that.

"I'll start," Lincoln said. "I'm grateful for the time I had this year with Gramps."

His father's scowl became more sour, if that was possible. Now I wanted to walk around the table to smack him. Couldn't he ever be happy? I inhaled deeply, remembering Baba's admonition to forgive. To search for divinity in everyone, even grumps like William.

"He told Saemira once that no one we love truly dies if we let them live on in our hearts. Those we love help us even when they're not with us. During some of the toughest times in my life, I would think about what he might do if he were in my shoes, and his example would guide me. He helped me be more patient, more persistent, more determined. Since losing him, I hear him telling me to treasure my wife more, spend more time with Altin, do something kind for a stranger. Gramps still lives." He touched his heart. "I'm so thankful for that."

I put my hand on his knee under the table, my heart full to bursting. I still sometimes wondered if I would wake up to find this had all been a sweet dream and be back in my ghetto apartment, desperate to make ends meet and not be sucked into Duke's evil web.

But Lincoln was real.

And he loved me.

He leaned over to kiss my cheek. "I'm also grateful for my wife and for the two meddling old men who brought us together." He grinned at Alex and lifted his glass of bubbly. "Thank you from the bottom of my heart."

"My pleasure." Alex raised his glass. "May you have many more happy years together."

"I plan on it." Lincoln kissed my cheek again. "How about you go next?" he said to Alex.

He nodded. "I'm grateful for life's little ironies." Lincoln and I chuckled. "And I'm grateful for my good friend, Ed, who saved me in so many ways."

"Hear, hear," Lincoln said, raising his glass.

I was too teary-eyed to say anything.

Ethel was grateful for new and old friends alike.

Angel was thankful for our graciousness in letting him live with us—which wasn't really graciousness as much as greediness on my part. I hadn't wanted him to be on his own. Duke and some of his minions had been locked up, but there were others who might take out revenge on him. Besides, our massive house had plenty of room for guests.

"I'm also grateful for the chance to go to school again," Angel said.

Obnoxious tears filled my eyes. Geesh. What was wrong with me? Had I cut up too many onions earlier?

Lincoln squeezed my shoulder. I patted his knee, loving him for caring not just about me, but about Altin and Angel, too. Altin adored him. And Angel was coming to idolize him as well. Lincoln had worked out a deal with the University of Utah for Angel to start school in January. He'd also taken my friend to an eye doctor, who'd thought his eye issues might be caused by poor nutrition and head trauma in his youth. Living with us and eating a better diet had helped some. He'd also put on muscle and didn't look like a wraith anymore. And Lincoln had an attorney helping Angel with the naturalization process to become a citizen.

Lincoln's dad went next. "I'm thankful Thanksgiving is only once a year."

Jerk. I could tell by Lucy's sagging shoulders that she had hoped he might be grateful for her. He should be. His wife was a saint.

Lucy focused on my brother, who absolutely adored her. "I'm grateful for my son, daughter, and grandson." She rubbed Altin's cute head.

"Gwam, candy?" My brother was such a mooch.

"No, sweet boy," she said. "We're going to eat dinner." She dabbed at her eyes. "You each have made my life heaven. Thank you."

I blew her a kiss. "Thanks for all you do for us." Now it was my turn. I looked around at all my people and felt a lump grow in my throat. Dang onions. "I'm grateful for all of you. Angel, my best friend since I was a bratty girl of seven who threw rocks at him because I thought he could steal my soul."

He grinned as I swiped more tears away.

"I'm grateful for Wily Wilder and Sneaky Gramps for their part in helping Lincoln see that he couldn't live without me."

"Hear, hear," Lincoln said, banging his glass like a goof.

"I'm thankful for Ethel and her graciousness in letting us crash at her home for months while we waited for the repairs on this place to be done. I hope when I grow up, I'm half as classy as you are."

"You've already surpassed me, my dear," she said.

"You're a brilliant liar," I said, making everyone laugh. "And I'm thankful Altin's mine now so no one can take him away from me again." I blew a kiss to him as a few tears escaped.

Seriously? Was I getting sick? I never cried.

"I'm thankful for my new Mom." I smiled at Lucy, and she wiped at her own tears. "Thanks for loving and accepting me."

You're welcome, she mouthed.

"I'm grateful to William for hooking up with Lucy—though she deserved way better—and creating the baby who grew up to become my husband."

Lincoln scoffed into his hand. He lived for these moments when I threw some cheek at his dad. I made sure not to do it often, just enough to keep the man off balance.

"I love you," I said to my husband, loud enough for everyone to hear.

"I love you more," he said, that sexy grin forming on his way-too-handsome face.

"Stop making goo-goo eyes at each other and let's say the damned grace," William grumped.

I laughed because, seriously, that was irreverently funny.

I snuggled against my husband's bare chest, basking in the bliss of finally being alone with him. The day had gone off without a hitch, even with William being around. The food had turned out divine, especially the pumpkin cheesecake. Lincoln had eaten two slices. The games had been fun. The visiting had been lively. Everyone had enjoyed the day, even William, though he would never admit that.

"How did I get so lucky to marry you?" I said.

"I'm the lucky one." He traced a finger down my neck.

I squished his cheeks between my hands. "Seriously. I love you more than I did this morning. How is that possible?" I ran my hands through his hair.

"Who knows? But I won't complain." He rolled me over onto the fluffy pillows and started kissing me.

I never tired of his kisses, but my head was spinning with thoughts. I pushed his head back so I could look into his eyes.

Should I tell him now? What if he wasn't excited by my announcement?

Drawing in all my courage, I pulled his hand down to my flat belly.

No more secrets.

"I'm...uh, guessing you're going to be a daddy later next year."

His eyes widened as he stared at his hand on my belly. "Truly?"

What did that mean? Was he truly happy? Truly Horrified? Maybe I should've done something to prevent pregnancy, but I hadn't thought about the consequences of a blissful marital relationship until too late.

Oh, please, let him be pleased! I already loved the little one inside me with all my heart.

"I haven't gone to a doctor yet to confirm, but I've been nauseous for about six weeks." I'd kept track on my phone. "And my period hasn't started. I looked it up and—"

Lincoln silenced me with a kiss, the type which meant business. I kissed him back since I was a hard-working girl.

Did this mean he was happy?

He pulled away but kept rubbing my stomach. "This is amazing! I'm so happy I could burst." He kissed me again, shutting up my anxious self-talk. "How about we find you an OB/GYN first thing in the morning and make an appointment? I'm coming with you."

"You will?" Thank the gods. Taking Altin to the emergency room at the beginning of the year had freaked me out. "Thank you. I've been scared to go alone. I don't know what questions to ask, and I don't want the doctor to think I'm unfit to be a mom."

"Heavens, love." Lincoln pressed a caressing hand to my belly and silenced me with another kiss. My favorite way to be silenced. When he came up for air, he grinned. "You'll be a fantastic mom. You've worried over nothing. And no way will I let you go alone. What kind of Neanderthal husband do you think I am? This is our baby. We'll do this together."

I buried my head in his shoulder, unable to stop my runaway emotions from flowing out in messy sobs. "Sorry." I sniffled. "I don't understand why I'm so weepy. I'm not a crier."

He rubbed my stomach. "Pregnancy hormones can do that, they say."

"Really? I'm not having a mental breakdown?"

He laughed. "You're normal, love. Well—not really."

I huffed.

He kissed my nose. "You're breathtaking and beautifully unique. There's nothing normal about you."

I soaked in his praise, appreciating his compliments even if they were way over the top and untrue.

"I hope I have a normal pregnancy."

"It'll be great." He smiled at my stomach. "I can't wait to be a dad." His minty breath made my spine tingle.

"You'll be the best, like my baba."

"I hope so." He stroked my arms. "All I've ever wanted was to have a family of my own. And now I do." He teased my lips. "Thanks for making me the happiest man alive."

It was the least I could do since he'd made me so incredibly happy.

EPILOGUE

Lincoln

*A*dorable coos melted my heart as I leaned over the crib to pick up my eight-month-old daughter.

"Is Daddy's princess awake?" I nuzzled her soft cheek, making her giggle as I stretched her out on the changing table.

"Dadadadada," she said, reaching for my face.

I lifted her panda shirt and blew on her tummy, making her giggle more. Never had I imagined I could love someone so quickly and so thoroughly as I loved this tiny gem of a girl who looked so much like her mother. From the second I'd held my sweet Bella, she'd stolen my heart. I knew I'd never get it back.

That was okay.

The doorbell rang downstairs. I grabbed a new diaper and got my arsenal of wipes ready, then undid the old diaper to see what misery awaited me. I wrinkled my nose.

"We need to start potty-training you, Princess," I muttered.

Bella batted her arms and cooed.

"You think you can bat your eyes and charm your way out of this?" I said, using about eight wipes to clean up the nastiness.

She fake-laughed, something she'd been doing often lately. Cutest thing ever.

I secured the new diaper and snapped her britches closed, then scooped her up in my arms. "You're right. You can." I zoomed her around the room like an airplane to make her giggle more. I never tired of her happy sounds.

"Let's go see Pompa and Gram." I headed for the stairs. My parents had jumped at the chance to watch Bella and Altin while I took Saemira out to a fancy dinner and show for Valentine's Day. I wasn't the only one besotted with my daughter. Mom adored her and Altin. And surprisingly, Dad had a soft spot for his granddaughter. Even more shocking was how much Bella seemed to love the old grump, always wanting Pompa to hold her when he was around.

I kissed her lotioned cheek as I joined my family in the living room. Altin tugged at my mom's pants, begging for candy.

Saemira reached for our daughter. "You're going to spoil her rotten, Daddy."

I let my daughter go to her mama. "I'm definitely going to spoil her. How can I not? She's my princess. But she's not rotten. She's perfect."

"True." Dad reached for Bella, and she almost leaped from Saemira's arms to get to him.

"Pompa," Bella said, and giggled as my dad started kissing her chubby cheeks.

I turned away from the disgusting display of undeserved love my daughter heaped on him. "Are you ready to go?" I asked my wife.

Saemira nodded. "Just call if you need anything. Angel's up in his room studying. He knows where everything is if you need help."

"We know the routine," Mom said.

Saemira gave a few last kisses to Bella and Altin before letting me tug her into the garage.

I opened the door of the Jag. She paused before getting in, catching my face in her hands and pulling me close for a sizzling kiss.

"You're not going to get fed if you keep that behavior up, Mrs. M." I winked.

"Is that a threat?" she said.

"It's a promise, baby." I hurried to my side and climbed in next to her. "Have I told you yet how sexy you look tonight?" I started the car.

"Not yet."

"You're beyond sexy, my beautiful, amazing, incredible, breathtaking wife."

She took my hand as I backed out. "It's been a good year, hasn't it?"

"The best. Definitely worth celebrating."

Duke and some of his gang had gone to prison. Angel had undergone extensive facial reconstruction. He still couldn't hear out of his restored right ear, but the improvement in his appearance had buoyed his self-esteem. His eye issues had improved as well. They weren't quite normal, but they were much less distracting than before.

"Your dad's come a long way, don't you think?"

I grimaced, not wanting to ruin our night by talking about my father. "I guess."

She gave me an impish smile. "You guess? Haven't you noticed how much happier your mom is lately?"

I scowled. "Buying her a few bouquets of roses doesn't make up for years of neglect and cheating."

"Now, who's being grumpy?" Saemira said.

"I just don't want to talk about him."

"I think he's changing. He hasn't said anything rude to you for months."

I rolled my eyes. "Because he knows I can keep Bella from him."

She looked thoughtful. "He hasn't been a jerk to me either. I can't remember the last time I had to demand an apology."

"He knows I'll bust his jaw if he screws up again." Like he had in the early days of our marriage when he'd made jabs about her ethnicity. I'd shoved him against the wall and told him in no uncertain terms that he was banned from my house until he could treat my wife with respect. I'd let Mom still come and have dinner with us or hang out with Saemira, but Dad had stayed clear until about six weeks after Bella's birth. Then he'd promised to be civil if he could see his granddaughter.

He'd kept his mouth shut since. But that didn't mean he'd changed his colors as my sweet wife seemed to hope.

"How's that project for Statics coming along?" I asked, to change the subject.

Saemira leaned over the gear shift to kiss my cheek. "It's so fun. Angel and I finished the required labs two days ago. Now, we've been experimenting with concepts in the next chapter." She kissed me again. "Thanks for the lab. It's seriously the best gift ever."

I'd had the contractors build a basement science lab in the renovation of our house to surprise my wife. Several of my development techs had helped with the specs. Saemira had thanked me almost every day since I'd unveiled the room to her.

Best money ever spent.

Angel was in his sophomore year in mechanical engineering and was working through the naturalization process. Saemira had started last fall in the same major. She was still a freshman. But they'd worked out several classes to take together this semester. Both of them were geniuses, which was shocking considering their dysfunctional lives during their formative years. I wished I could've known Saemira's father, Taavi. He must've been one hell of a teacher to inspire such brilliance in his daughter and her friend.

"What are you thinking about?" Saemira caressed my clean-shaven chin.

"About how brilliant you are. And how much I love you."

She patted my face. "I can live with that."

I grinned. My wife was seriously the light I'd searched for all my life. She reminded me in many ways of my little sister Cora—her goodness, her zest for life, her genuine love for others. Altin could be a challenge, but I loved him as well and couldn't imagine life without him. And Bella, my precious princess—I loved her beyond words. My family was everything to me.

At the steakhouse, I helped my wife out and handed my keys to a valet. I paused for a moment to admire Saemira. The Bohemian style she pulled off so well had definitely grown on me. I'd become adept at picking out other women in crowds who sported the style as well. But nobody came close to doing it with quite as much flair and elegance as Saemira. She was in a class all her own.

And she was mine.

AUTHOR NOTE

Thanks for reading *Of Stone and Sky*. If you enjoyed Saemira's and Lincoln's story, please leave a review on Amazon or another site. Reviews help out a ton, and bonus—no one grades you.

Roma throughout the world are looked down upon and labeled as gypsies or thieves. They often have higher unemployment rates and subpar housing. In some places, they are refused medical care and educational opportunities. Some stereotypes are founded in truth. But the danger of stereotypes is that they keep people in boxes or become self-fulfilling prophesies. They make you think you know someone when you don't.

Zinzan, a minor character in the book, is based off a man my son knows (name changed for privacy). He can fix anything, from broken door handles to automobile engines. Yet even with those valuable skills, he's had difficulty finding steady employment due to his heritage. When he arrived in Montenegro, he received permission from the city to build on a plot of land outside of town. Later, the city built a dump there. Now, smoke from burning trash is the new air Zinzan's family breathes; trash their new vista.

I recently got to meet Zinzan when my son Skyped him. I didn't speak Montenegrin, Romani, or German, and he couldn't speak English. We did little more than smile at each other as my son translated between us. But his smile has stayed with me. Zinzan was completely happy, and goodness radiated from him. I want to be more like him: happier with less, kinder to more, grateful for all God has blessed me with.

Racism in any form belittles and demeans. It divides and blinds us to the hearts of others. The best way I've found to get rid of prejudice is to listen to those who are different than me. Learn from their stories. When you learn more about someone, you can't help but start to love them.

JUSTICE FOR ALL

I've included some quotes by Martin Luther King Jr. His autobiography was life changing when I listened to the Audible version. I highly recommend that version, as it has live speeches. My book lightly touched on racism, but I hope you will learn more and always stand for justice for all, even for those you don't agree with (maybe especially for them).

"I have a dream that my four little children will one day live in a nation where they will not be judged by the color of their skin but by the content of their characters..."

— **MARTIN LUTHER KING, JR.,** *I HAVE A DREAM*
SPEECH, 28 AUG 1963

"Shallow understanding from people of good will is more frustrating than absolute misunderstanding from people of ill will. Lukewarm acceptance is much more bewildering than outright rejection."

— **MARTIN LUTHER KING, JR.,** LETTER FROM
BIRMINGHAM JAIL, 16 APR 1963

"Actually, we who engage in nonviolent direct action are not the creators of tension. We merely bring to the surface the hidden tension that is already alive...Like a boil that can never be cured so long as it is covered up but must be opened with all its ugliness to the natural medicines of air and light, injustice must be exposed, with all the tension this exposure creates, to the light of human conscience and the air of national opinion before it can be cured."

— **IBID, KING**

"We will have to repent in this generation not merely for the hateful words and actions of the bad people but for the appalling silence of the good people. Human progress never rolls in on wheels of inevitability; it comes through the tireless efforts of men willing to be co workers with God, and without this hard work, time itself becomes an ally of the forces of social stagnation. We must use time creatively, in the knowledge that the time is always ripe to do right....Now is the time to lift our national policy from the quicksand of racial injustice to the solid rock of human dignity."

— **IBID, KING**

"Was not Jesus an extremist for love: 'Love your enemies, bless them that curse you, do good to them that hate you, and pray for them which despitefully use you, and persecute you.' ...So the question is not whether we will be extremists, but what kind of extremists we will be. Will we be extremists for hate or for love? Will we be extremists for the preservation of injustice or for the extension of justice? In that dramatic scene on Calvary's hill three men were crucified. We must never forget that all three were crucified for the same crime—the crime of extremism. Two were extremists for immorality, and thus fell below their environment. The other, Jesus Christ, was an extremist for love, truth, and goodness, and thereby rose above his environment. Perhaps the South, the nation and the world are in dire need of creative extremists."

— **IBID, KING**

BOOK GROUP QUESTIONS

1. What misbelief was planted inside Saemira's mind as a little girl on her first trip to the Roma village? How did this influence her decisions and actions later in life? How can you challenge your worldview to ensure you don't hold on to misbeliefs that could make you stagnate?

2. Saemira's baba asks her to do an experiment regarding dignity. In the process, she befriends Engjell. What prejudices does she still hold against him even after they become friends? Do you judge those closest to you at times? How can this hurt your relationships?

3. Saemira's baba teaches her the following principles about forgiveness and choices. What do you think of these?

- We are all responsible for our own choices. We are not to blame for the bad choices of others that affect us negatively. But we do have the choice to forgive and move on.
- God requires more from us than what makes us comfortable.
- Forgiving someone doesn't mean what they did was right or acceptable. It means you break the chains binding you to the person who hurt you. You give judgment to God, who allows you to move on and be happy again.
- When you don't forgive, you take the role of judge upon yourself, a burden too heavy for any mortal.

4. Gypsies (*magjup*) are a stereotype in this story. What other stereotypes did you notice? What factors lead to people stereotyping others? How

can you overcome the tendency to stereotype? What are the benefits of seeing people as they really are (not how you believe they are)?

5. The theme of prejudice is woven throughout this story. There is the obvious example of treating someone differently because of the color of their skin, but there are other ways we judge others. This feeling of superiority (whether due to religion, sexual preference, weaknesses, economic status, career choice, family status, political party, etc) is ALWAYS a sign that our hearts aren't right before God and our fellowmen (and women). How can you keep your heart right before God?

6. Saemira believes she isn't as good as Lincoln and others who are *white*. She doesn't seem to be aware of this misbelief, but it creeps out in the way she sees groups and experiences. You see it in how she compares the shade of her skin to others in her mind. How can misbeliefs about your own perceived shortcomings hold you back? How can misbeliefs that others may be judging you (even if true) lead you to become prejudice against them (becoming what you hated, so to say)?

7. Gramps tells Saemira to savor each day as if it's her last. He says she'll never regret doing that. How would your day be different if you took this advice to heart tomorrow? What things would you do differently? What activities would you leave out?

8. At the end, Saemira is hopeful that Lincoln's dad is changing for the better. Lincoln isn't so sure, due to the scars he carries from his dad's neglect and verbal beatings. How can past history taint hope for future change? How can you turn hope into a catalyst for positive change?

9. What one thing will you do (or not do) to be more merciful in your judgment of others? What one thing will you do to stand for justice for ALL?

ACKNOWLEDGMENTS

Thanks to my awesome cover artist, Susie, for her beautiful work. A huge basket of gratitude goes to my amazing editors, Jenny Proctor and Emily Poole, for keeping me from releasing garbage into the world. It's terrifying to hand over my manuscript because I know they will never say, "Wow! This is awesome." I hand it over anyway, with confidence that they will find weak spots, holes, and glaring errors, and respond with graceful honesty. Thanks to my son-in-law Matthew, my son Curtis, and my daughter Jessica for sharing their stories about the Roma people they met in Albania, Montenegro, and Georgia. And thank YOU for taking a chance on this book by reading it.

ABOUT THE AUTHOR

Charissa Stastny is an avid reader, happy writer, wasp-hater, flower-lover, and food connoisseur (especially sushi and chocolate, but not together). She was born and raised in Las Vegas, Nevada, but has never pulled a handle of a slot machine and can't shuffle cards to save her life (thank goodness for auto-shufflers). She lived in beautiful Idaho for ten years (yea for potatoes!), but currently lives in central Utah (yea for fry sauce!). She's the author of nine books and 'imagine-eer' of many more. To learn more, visit: www.CharissaStastny.com.

Made in the USA
Las Vegas, NV
11 May 2021